The Kingdom of the Good People

The Book of Sorcha

by

Melissa Helm

TELEMACHUS PRESS

This book is a work of fiction. Names, characters, places and incidents are either the product of the author's imagination or are used fictitiously. Any resemblance to actual persons, living or dead, or to actual events or locales is entirely coincidental.

THE KINGDOM OF THE GOOD PEOPLE

The publisher does not have any control over and does not assume any responsibility for author or third-party websites or their content.

Cover designed by Telemachus Press, LLC

Cover art:
Copyright © iStock/2220921/Soubrette
Copyright © iStock/3364321/woogies1
Copyright © iStock/18866246/sankai

Published by Telemachus Press, LLC
http://www.telemachuspress.com

Visit the author website:
http://www.thekingdomofthegoodpeople.com

ISBN: 978-1-941536-17-9 (eBook)
ISBN: 978-1-941536-72-8 (Paperback)

Version 2014.11.14

Printed in the United States of America

10 9 8 7 6 5 4 3 2 1

Dedication

This book is for my sisters, who suffered through the first painfully rough drafts and yet still found the love to encourage me to carry on. Thank you for your stamina and ability to convince me that you would like this book even if I weren't your little sister.

Acknowledgment

Thank you Cheley and Tres for standing over me until I overcame my insecurities and hit the "send" button. You were fearless when I was not.

The Kingdom of the Good People

The Book of Sorcha

With the chaos-governed universe as their playground,
the undulating parallel waves
taunted and teased each other with near-misses
dancing their seemingly flawless dance of give-and-take
yearning and reproach
until
in a measureless moment
in non-existent time,
they touched.
From this fortuitous caress
worlds were born.

PROLOGUE

IF FOLKLORE WAS gold, if secrets were encrusted with jewels, if history was counted in coin, then the coffers of Ireland would overflow and spill forth into time eternal.

Ireland is a country inseparable from its history and loved by a people whose present is sewn to their past with abiding threads woven of fate and destiny. In the golden age of Eire's "Once upon a time ..." before the Viking raiders, before the Anglo-Normans, before Saint Patrick and Christianity, various tribes laid claim to the Emerald Isle. Among them were the Fir Bolgs, the Tuatha de Danann and the Milesians. Of all the ancient inhabitants of Ireland, perhaps the settlers to make the most enduring impression were the Tuatha de Danann, not only for their place in Ireland's history, but for their place in Ireland's present.

The Tuatha de Danann were a peaceful race, a clan that legend held were born of a goddess. Majestic and skilled, they lived a life filled with peaceful pursuits until others came to challenge their rights to the land. In their first and second calls to war, the Tuathans emerged triumphant on the battlefield. It was not until they were called upon a third time to defend their homeland, that they encountered a people far more mighty and knowing in the ways of war than they. It was this first taste of defeat that changed the children of the goddess Danu forever.

After their overthrow in the great Battle with the Milesians, the Tuatha de Danann were sentenced by the sons of Milesius to a life of exile underground. It was there, under the faerie mounds found scattered across the length and breadth of Ireland, beneath the very hills and fields where they once hunted red deer and wild fowl, that Danu's children were forced by Fate to begin anew.

And begin anew they did.

No longer known as the Tuatha de Danann, they were referred to as "the Sidhe," "wee folk," "the good people," or "faeries."

They called themselves "myth."

The myth endured, living peacefully in their secret world until the events following the tragic loss of their king revealed to them the threads sewing their past to their present.

This is the story of the "good people."

This is a *real* faerie tale.

CHAPTER 1

THE LAST OF the retreating daylight clung to the walls of the crowded room as if desperately reluctant to leave its occupants—leaving them in the dark with their dying king. As the light lost its tenuous grip and began its defeated slide down the walls and across the earthen floor, thousands of dust and dirt particles danced and collided in the receding rays.

Some said that he would be more than a 1,000 cycles old by the next new moon. No one challenged this measure, as even some of the eldest members of their society had known no other leader. The High Myth was the one that led their clan here, to E'lore, after the crossing. At the time of the exodus, their numbers were so dangerously diminished that most assumed their extinction was imminent. The badly defeated and war-weary clan had come to this place exhausted and broken. They had neither the energy for survival nor hope to flourish, but flourish they had. And since that time, they had known a multitude of cycles of peace and prosperity, and they cherished their ways and heritage as only those who have very nearly lost themselves do.

King Bhara lay peacefully on a nest of soft, brindled moleskins, his head supported by a mound of whortleberry blossoms, their feathery and aromatic petals releasing sleep-inducing wisps of scent that spiraled and swirled around the king. His garments were no different—no more or less grand—than those of the gathered members of his clan. He was king by deed and by heart, and no need to outwardly distinguish himself had ever been necessary. His face, so childlike for one his age, still bore the scars given him in the last great war—The War of the Exile. This brutal war with the Milesians had not only cost them their former king, but their homeland as well. It was only by the mettle of their soldiers and the cunning of their sorceress that the myth had been able to escape the otherwise certain promise of annihilation. Of course, the clansmen were not called myth then—they had a different name then.

Bhara suddenly gasped for air as if he had held his breath for too long underwater. Startling the dozens of onlookers as this was the only move-ment he had made since he had been brought to the Ulster Mound five days before, they all jumped in unison. Carefully resuming their places closer to the crossing bed that held their prostrate leader, they waited anx-iously hoping for another sign of life, which came almost immediately. No sooner had the watchers regrouped around their king than the High Myth's eyes suddenly opened and focused upon the bewildered face of the young-est and meekest of his gathered clansmen, as hers was the face directly in his line of sight.

In a tone and inflection as calm as if discussing the day's weather, the ancient myth said, "There is one ... not from among us, a brave, strong ... human, a finder ... a champion living among the nambors of Doog. This outlander must be found and brought here. This is our path ... this will decide our survival. The clan ..." Bhara's focus seemed to drift as he watched the vision in his head play to its conclusion. After a pause and without drawing another breath, he added, "the Fomorian come."

Una, who had been the one to discover Bhara in his declining state and had alerted the others, had not left his king's side. As his self-appointed aide, he busied himself with attending to Bhara's needs. Una raised the king's head with his left hand, and offered him a sip of tea with his quiver-ing right. The king brushed the tea away and instead motioned Una to come closer. Una lowered his left ear to his ruler's mouth, and while Bhara's lips moved slowly and feebly, Una listened intently and nodded his head as a sign of his understanding. After only a few moments, Bhara's lips stopped moving and an unprepared Una hesitantly turned to look at his regent's now soulless eyes. As he gently returned Bhara's head to rest again on the mound of whortleberry blossoms, Una lovingly brushed his king's eyes closed as warm tears began their journey down the aide's cheeks. Every head in the assembly was cast downward in grief as the High Myth passed. Leaving his physical self behind, the spirit of the aged warrior-king crossed to the next plane of awareness.

And the clan mourned.

Three of the gathered mourners had huddled quietly together toward the back of the crowded room. After the king's passing, they conversed briefly. One of the three broke from the triad and walked slowly and solemnly to the death bed. He placed a comforting arm around the grieving aide's trembling shoulder, bowed his head and was seen speaking to him. Una nodded his head and spoke in return. When he finished, the myth from the group of three gave him a gentle squeeze on his shoulder and left his fellow clansman to his grief. Once rejoined with the other two, the three myth spoke briefly before turning collectively and walking single-file from the chamber. They each, in turn, cast a reverent gaze upon their beloved leader silently promising to pay their respects later, privately, before taking their apparently urgent leave. Once outside the dwelling, the three were able to speak in less hushed tones.

Banth was the first to emerge from the mound. He had assumed that the day was older than it was judging from the darkness in the inadequately windowed Ulster Mound. He was pleased to see the sun's position in the sky and grateful for the gift of the warmth it offered. As he squinted and blinked to adjust his eyes to the relatively brighter lighting, he gave his arms a stretch and fluttered his wings, lifting himself off the ground for a few paces before landing gently with a sigh. Yarn and Meeks followed, choosing to keep their feet on the ground, but blinking and rubbing their eyes, as well. They stood together in silence, eyes cast downward and hearts heavy with the burden of sorrow, each temporarily lost in his own private thoughts. As if in telepathic sync, they simultaneously raised their heads with a shake and cleared their throats of ascending sadness. They each needed their wits about them now, more than ever; they knew that they did not have the luxury of giving in to their grief—not now.

"Well then, what did Una say, Banth?" Meeks, who had resumed massaging his eyes, had unfurled his wings for a stretch as he spoke to his fellow myth.

"It seems that Bhara described the nambor that he spoke of to Una."

"Well, at least we know what it looks like," Meeks countered.

"Not exactly. Bhara spoke of this nambor's 'bravery, strength and determination,'" Banth answered.

Meeks smirked at the response. "A 'brave' nambor, he said? Our king always had a soft spot for humans, did he not? So, what do you mean by 'not exactly'?"

"I mean he did not get to the physical description before he …" Banth stopped, unable to finish his sentence. Yarn placed a consoling hand on his friend's shoulder.

"Did he happen to say *where* exactly we would find it?" Meeks asked, proceeding with the business at hand.

"No, no. I'm afraid no mention of that either," Banth answered without averting his gaze from the ground.

The three stood in quiet reflection before Yarn chose to break the silence. "He said Fomorian, did he? Did you hear that right?" Yarn asked his fellow myth.

"'Tis what Una heard." Banth responded.

"Fomorian? Is that possible? I mean, could they still be …?" Yarn felt uncomfortable speaking of life, given that his lifelong friend and king had just lost his.

"I cannot imagine how, but I suppose that anything is possible, even that," Meeks speculated.

Collecting his wayward thoughts, Yarn returned to the original topic.

"First things first, I think," he said with a heavy sigh. Placing his hands on his hips, he continued, "Even though we have no idea where this nambor is yet, we can still proceed with preparations to fulfill Bhara's divination. I do not believe that we can afford the extravagance of procrastination. We must decide who is to go."

Meeks continued to stare at the ground, but Banth looked up at his friend and advisor. "Well, 'tis better to be prepared. Better to be doing something than nothing, I suppose," he responded.

Meeks was now shaking his head. "I'm sorry, but how do you propose that we find a nambor that we would not recognize even if we knew where to look for it?"

"How do you want to go about this?" Yarn, choosing to ignore Meek's question, asked both of his companions.

Before Banth could answer or Meeks could protest, the doors to the Ulster Mound creaked open and the mourners began their slow procession out.

"Come, these are discussions best had in privacy," Banth suggested.

Without having to voice their accord, the three turned and headed toward the village center and the director's office.

***

In the distance, just over a mossy knoll freckled with Shannon blossoms, an unseen explosion of light flashed in the glen beyond a pasture of grazing quagga. The noiseless burst emanated from a ball of pure white light with tendrils of illumination waving out in all directions from its center. It hung low to the ground amongst the standing stones, centered between a pair of ancient gooseberry trees. Once the billions of luminous sparks from the initial explosion fell to the ground, the orb displayed ribbons of brilliant aquamarine and turquoise blue, which radiated out from the nucleus and dissipated through its alabaster tendrils. There it hovered between the pair of primordial trees, hovering and growing.

CHAPTER 2

THE *BAILE* OF Aislinn was the core of the myth's realm. As the most densely populated area in the kingdom, it naturally evolved into the center of administration, fellowship, and trade for all of E'lore. The village itself carpeted the sloping north bank of Lake Sheelin. In a half-moon pattern, it sprawled from the lake's shore to the crest of a knoll where the lush hillside was met by the dense forest. The western-most boundary of the town was determined by this impenetrable wood, its wayward underbrush encroaching upon the smooth, moss-covered landscape of the village.

To the east, Aislinn's limit was defined by a towering mist fall. Clouds of fog, always present due to the moist climate of E'lore, rolled across the pastures and meadows and through the forests and groves to meet at the crest of the fall. Drawn by an imperceptible, inherent force, the hazy wisps spawned and spiraled their way from all corners of the faerie's realm to the pinnacle of the fall. There they joined in a velvety, white whirlpool before plummeting down the narrow chasm, which ended deep within the lake below. The vapor that formed over the lake's waters also made the pilgrimage toward the rapid's summit.

As the clouds formed on the loch made their ascent, they were met by the plunging mists of the land. The consequence of the encounter was the formation of a rainbow—the resplendent and piercing colors of which were not known to any other world. Droplets of dew fragmented from the rainbow and fell like rain, disappearing into the mist that blanketed the lake below. It was in this cascade and these relentless rainbows that the mist myth dwelled.

It was the wood myth of Aislinn who provided for the entire community. When they first arrived in E'lore, it was the strongest among them who hunted the abundant game, gathered the berries, edible herbs and wild mushrooms of the surrounding forests. These bounties were brought to the marketplace in the center of Aislinn where all were welcome to share. As the exiled Tuatha recovered and their numbers grew, the duties of provision and methods of procurement became more efficient and specialized. Although the practice of exchanging currency for goods was gaining popularity in their realm at the time of the War of the Exile, this custom found no foothold in E'lore. They lived as a clan and for the clan. Soon, most myth possessed many skills, and all were expert in at least one. In no time, Aislinn counted among its colonists: potters, bakers, hunters, carpenters, tailors and tanners.

It was to this marketplace that all in E'lore would come and help themselves to the wares or skills provided by their clansmen. Those with weaving skills made scarves and cloaks, leggings and hats, and brought them to the *ola's* cottage for anyone in need of a warm, soft scarf or cap. There were harvesters of the forest's root vegetables and abundant and various fungi, which they gathered and deposited at the *pratha's* cottage in great woven baskets heaped to overflowing. Row after row of filleted meats lay on a cold slab of stone under the roof of the *fia's* croft. On occasions when the trapping and hunting had been especially successful, the excess meats were thrashed into small bits and stuffed into casings, which were then hung from the rafters of the croft like edible banners signifying the clan's bounty. Those gifted with light hands spent their time in the *aran's* cottage where the vented smoke from the ovens wafted through the village, as the bakers filled basket after basket with sweet smelling heather cakes, puddings, *brisgein* breads, tea *bracks* and scones. Platters, plates, crocks and cups made their dizzying circuit from wheel to kiln as the potters made simple clay vessels and tea pots for the dinner tables. No member of the myth clan went without or wanted for anything.

It had not been long after their coming to this new world that the Tuatha de Danann discovered that they were not its only inhabitants. Small, strangely clothed creatures made themselves known to them not long after their arrival. These beings were odd in their nature and habits, so much so that the myth saw them as a curiosity rather than a threat. They dressed elaborately in woven tunics of brilliant green, and upon their wee heads were bright crimson hats—netted broadly at the rim before spiraling with exaggerated height to a meandering, pointed tip. On their odd little feet they wore coverings of tanned animal hide. The cured skin was sewn in such a way that it conformed to the very shape of the stunted creatures' feet. On top of the foot garb was a large, squarely forged metal buckle, whether for function or fashion the myth were not sure, but it only served to increase their fascination with these articles of clothing and enhance their desire to have them for themselves. The exiled Tuathans were so intrigued that they seized upon the natives' obvious trepidation over their arrival and struck a bargain with them. The odd little creatures were told that they would not be harmed in exchange for providing the myth with footwear of their own. The anxious, shod creatures—having no idea that the newcomers had no intent of enforcing their side of the bargain—agreed. The previously sole citizens of E'lore had convinced themselves that these towering strangers had come to steal their gold, so upon the realization that this was not the case, they obligated the newcomers to their bargain immediately, before they realized that the shoemakers had something far more valuable to barter with than shoes. The wee, odd creatures gave their promise to supply the myth with as many shoes as they wished for as long as they wished. Convinced that they had duped the over-sized outsiders, they tripped and tumbled their way back into the woods, drunk with self-satisfaction. As the amused myth watched their shenanigans, they struck upon a name for their new neighbors, and from that moment forward, the little creatures were known in the old language as *leipreachans*. Of course, it was not long before the leprechauns realized that the outsiders had no use for their pelf and that their deal had been made in vain. It was because of this age-old bargain in which the shoemakers had given their irrevocable word, that nestled among the various shacks and stalls of the Aislinn marketplace could be found a *cordswainer's* cottage. Cursing with every cut, and groaning with every stitch, the reluctant shoemakers labored over their lasts until the very minimum of their obligation was fulfilled and they could abandon their production in favor of more entertaining pursuits. They would then disappear into the woods leaving tools strewn about and orders unfinished to pursue some mischief and merriment, until their misguided promise obligated them to return. And return they would, with each day-break, to pick up where they had left off the day before, cutting and stitching and fashioning slippers and shoes of all styles, save the very type that they, themselves, wore, all the while lamenting both their promise and the futility of their existence. The myth, long accustomed to the leprechauns relentless complaining, simply ignored them and brushed by the stall without so much as a glance of acknowledgment. As a less than passive tribute to their discontent, the leprechauns refused to make any two shoes the same—one shoe was made at a time—never in pairs. Much to their dismay, this practice only served to increase the myth's desire to don their labors, and the shoemakers orders increased exponentially. The adjacent cobbler's cottage was even more boisterous in wailing and complaints of "Who told you to wear these outside?" and "I dunna care that these are your favorites," whenever their half-hearted labors fell in need of repair. Truth be told, the leprechauns' efforts to be of more trouble than help indeed gained the desired results, but the myth had no intention of releasing them from their archaic obligation.

The buildings that comprised the marketplace formed a semi-circle around the only structure whose purpose was not connected to trade. Unlike the cottages built for the marketplace, this structure had not been built by the myth, but had existed long before they arrived. It was the remains of an enormous and long deceased hawthorn tree, sacred in the land from where they had come. At the time of their arrival, it had been designated as the center of sovereignty for their new kingdom. It was from this core that all decisions relating to the governing of the land were made, which, given the peaceful and industrious nature of its inhabitants were few and far between. More importantly to the myth of E'lore, it housed the ancient talismans.

The four treasured talismans that made it safely to E'lore at the time of the exile were the *slea'*, the *cloch*, the *citeal* and the *claiomh*, and they resided in a specially altered cache in the main chamber of the director's office. The *slea'*, or spear, ensured that the clan would always be single-minded in purpose. The *cloch* was a ceremonial stone that held within its impenetrable core the true heart of its people; upon this rock, kings had been crowned and laws had been forged. The *citeal*—cauldron in the old language—insured that the clan never knew hunger or want. The hearths would always be lit and the clan always fed. The fourth symbol in the chamber was the sword. It was this talisman that some myth felt had abandoned them. The sword insured the clan's victory against their enemy and safeguarded their land and kinsmen, yet they had not been given victory over the Milesians. The Tuatha lost many of their clan and their precious Eire.

It was the fifth talismanic treasure that the myth regarded as the crown jewel of their clan's emblems. This missing talisman was unique and profoundly personal as it contained the ancient dogma of their clan, their ancestry, and their divine heritage. As cherished as this information was to them, the talisman also contained a knowledge that had been whispered of, but never fully understood by the myth and certainly never committed to testimony anywhere else. It held the lore and laws of their physical world, but more importantly, the laws of other worlds as well, worlds studied and interpreted by Sorcha, the Tuathan's powerful sorceress, whose talents and wisdom had made magic manifest and enchantments tangible.

The fifth talisman was a book.

It was Sorcha who had discovered E'lore. When it became clear that the Tuatha de Danann were no match for the invading Milesians, it was she who led them to the entrance of their new world. She entrusted her priests with the task of carrying the four talismans through the breach so they would not fall into the hands of the enemy. The book was the last of the emblems conveyed to the portal and it was carried by Sorcha herself. But it was while the sorceress was passing the fifth talisman to the priest standing in the open gateway that she was seized by a Milesian soldier. It was the last that was ever seen of the supreme sorceress—or her book.

Once the elders of the exiled clan had recovered from their wounds and adapted to their new world, they set upon the task of recording the history of the clan and committed to parchment as many of the old laws and customs of their former society as they were able to. It was these recalled decrees on hastily prepared parchments, which were used to lay the ground work for their precepts in Aislinn. These scrolls of mottled vellum were also housed in the main chamber of the hollowed hawthorn tree.

Presiding over this center of the town's little exercised government was the Director of Aislinn, Banth Bellweather. He had been appointed director by King Bhara. Immediately after their exile, survival was the only priority. With time, as the clan went from strength to strength, they naturally began to integrate the guidelines and parameters that define and lend structure to all societies. Bhara created this position to instill his clan with a sense of organization and community, two traits he felt were vital to encourage his kinsmen to undertake the daunting task of rebuilding their lives in this new and strange domain. Banth had grown into the role of Bhara's aide. At first, this post involved the most meager of tasks, but Banth proved a dauntless assistant and at the tender age of ten and seven cycles, Bhara gave Banth the responsibilities of administrator for the *baile* of Aislinn.

Though the hawthorn stump was large, its walls were thick, which made for rather cramped quarters inside. Several alcoves had been carved out of the petrified base of the ancient tree. There was a small office where Banth carried out the affairs of his post, if and when affairs did indeed present themselves, an even smaller antechamber into which was built a fireplace, as well as a cupboard and table to hold the necessities for tea making, and the cache, where the talismans were kept. After his appointment, a few small, cramped private quarters had been added for Banth's personal use. It was in the small office that the three myth that had left the Ulster Mound before the others had come to discuss the issues advanced by their king in his deathbed prophecy.

As the trio rounded the last turn on the path leading to the entryway of the great tree, they spoke to each other in anxious tones.

"E'lore is without a king. We have that to deal with, as well," Meeks proposed to his colleagues.

"'Tis true, but perhaps we should secure E'lore's safety first. No point in having a king if there is no kingdom to rule," Yarn rebutted.

"Are you sure *this* is the way to go about it, Yarn?" Banth asked with apprehension.

The director, who was struggling with the thick rope-pull used to open the door, did not wait for Yarn's reply, but continued breathlessly. "'Tis a monumental undertaking. Surely we do not want to entrust this to someone based on the luck of the draw."

"I have to agree with Banth," Meeks interjected as he grasped a piece of the pull and helped his friend with the heavy portal.

"This requires much more than sending the least lucky of the eligibles," Meeks uttered between grunts and groans.

The thick door finally yielded to Banth's and Meek's efforts, and as soon as it had been opened enough to pass through, Yarn strode in, leaving his panting companions outside.

Banth smiled at Meeks, who in turn simply rolled his eyes and shook his head before following Yarn into the cool darkness of the office.

"Perhaps we should consult the parchments. Maybe they can guide us on how to proceed," Meeks said as he opened the shutters, allowing the soft glow of late afternoon into the sacred tree's interior.

"Now then," Yarn said as he took a seat and motioned to Banth to do the same. "Let us hear everything—*everything* that Bhara said before he passed. Leave nothing out now."

Instead of answering straight away, Banth suggested, "Put some tea on will you, Meeks? I will be right back."

With a shrug, Meeks excused himself and strode over to the hearth. Banth had left his office abruptly when he received word that Bhara was near the end, and had left the fire to fend for itself. Meeks stoked the ebbing flames and set the still brimming kettle of water over the growing blaze. Reaching into the exposed cupboard overhead, he pulled down a mole-hide bag cinched at the top with straw. After pouring some of its contents into a spouted clay pot, Meeks retied the hide pouch and returned it to its place on the cupboard shelf. Turning to a side table, he picked up three cups made of a finer substance than that of the clay pot. They had been fashioned from the crushed bones of various species of animals with which the myth shared their world. The skeletal remains of long deceased quagga, moles, and nekton were infused with the ash of cremated bones salvaged from the *fia's* croft in a process brought with them to E'lore. The artisans who had created the cups were highly skilled, and with an inherent sense of irony, had hand-painted the vessels with portraits of the animals who had lent their very bones for the making of the fragile gossamer vessels.

Blowing into the cups to expel any dust, Meeks set them softly onto a tray of carved cullen wood before rejoining Yarn in Banth's office.

"The kettle was cold," he said, answering Yarn's questioning look at Meek's empty hands.

Meeks and Yarn were the unofficial "officials" of Aislinn. So in tune were the inhabitants of Aislinn with the needs of their village, so focused was their collective desire to see the clan prosper, that under Bhara's rule, the necessity for an organized government had become obsolete. Still, occasionally circumstances would arise, which required experienced and level-headed counsel, and it was in this capacity that Yarn and Meeks came to be counted on by Banth. No sooner had Yarn nodded his head in understanding, than Banth returned to the room with arms overflowing with rolls of yellowed vellum. Using his chin as a counterweight, he did his best to control them. The director managed to carry the pile of papers over to the large stone table in the center of the office before Yarn or Meeks could come to his aid. There, he allowed the parchments to tumble from his arms. Between the three of them, they were able to corral the papers and kept them from spilling onto the earthen floor below.

The water in the tea kettle made its readiness known by boiling out of the spout and tumbling onto the fiery logs below. The hissing of the droplets of water as they turned to steam summoned Meeks back to the pantry to finish preparing the tea. He poured the scalding water into the clay pot, causing its dried contents to turn from pale sage to deep black-green and sent wisps of earthy-sweet scent into the faerie's face. He put the kettle to rest on the stone hearth, and after covering the teapot with its lid he placed it carefully on the wooden tray with the cups. As he grasped the platter's handles, a patch of ruddy cloth caught his eye. The bit of fabric was caught under the lid to a large urn next to the hearth. Meeks gave a cursory look over his shoulder before gingerly grasping the urn lid and lifting it from its base. There, unsuccessfully hidden inside the pot was a pink parcel, which any myth in Aislinn would recognize instantly as coming from the *arran's* cottage. Meeks smiled to himself as he pictured his friend Banth hastily stuffing the package into the vessel. The director's fondness for sweets was no secret in the village, and Meeks knew that his friend enjoyed his treats the most when they were eaten in private, in front of the fire and with no one around with whom he would have to share. Meeks rescued the bundle from the urn, placed it on the tray with the tea, and brought the whole lot into the office. There, Banth and Yarn had each taken a seat on opposite sides of the stone table and were contemplating the heap of aged vellum scrolls before them. Meeks set the tray down on the only bit of table not buried under parchment, and while avoiding eye contact with Banth, took the last remaining seat for himself.

As he reached for some tea, Banth caught sight of the pink parcel lounging on the tray next to the crock of ferntickle sap. He tried to give Meeks a scowl, but Meeks was busy ignoring him.

Without further bidding, Banth relayed to his companions their king's final words, in their entirety, as told to him by Una. Meeks and Yarn said nothing during Banth's briefing, and continued to say nothing after he was done. For some time, the three sat quietly thinking and drinking, until finally, Meeks broke the silence.

"So what are we looking for?" he asked, surveying the mound of parchments as he returned his empty cup to the tray.

"Some precedent for our current situation—a clue as to how to proceed," Banth answered, still sipping his now tepid tea.

"Proceed with which, dealing with the king's passing or finding an alternate solution for choosing a fulfiller to the prophecy?" Yarn asked of Banth, as the elder myth reached for a heather cake.

Without moving his gaze from the papers, he answered, "Both my friend, both."

CHAPTER 3

THE LATE AFTERNOON in Aislinn was achingly beautiful. The market, long since done with the day's business, was bereft of activity. The stalls and sheds had been broomed and tidied and any surplus goods were left out for those who might find themselves wanting a loaf of bread or a loin of meat for a late supper. Now that the din of the busy market had subsided, the roar of the mist falls was once again the alpha sound. The crashing together of the land and water mists seemed so loud that one wondered how even the most boisterous of markets could ever drown them out. No matter, as afternoon succumbed to twilight and the converging mists sent their radiant, iridescent droplets skyward and the atmosphere traded its soft vanilla hue for a velvety pale plum, no village or town in any dimension could rival the beauty of Aislinn of E'lore. It was this soft purple sunset that bathed Banth's office as those inside continued in their quest to resolve the events of the day.

A gentle, low knock on the heavy door was a welcome break in the room's anxious silence. Yarn raised his hand to Banth as a signal that *he* would answer. Banth gave no reply other than resuming his seat. Meeks, who had assumed a post next to the door, stood beside the older myth and lent his shoulder to the task of opening the massive portal. There, to no one's surprise, stood a young, wide-eyed female. The youngest myth in Aislinn, Yarn had sent her on the task of collecting as many shed quagga whiskers as she could find in the nearby pasture. She had gathered the thick black whiskers from amongst the mosses and blossoms of the pasture floor, and now presented the bundle of *weeze* with unbridled excitement to the oldest myth in the realm. Yarn thanked her with a heather cake taken from the tea tray, which she gladly exchanged for the parcel of dirty whiskers. Yarn smiled and nodded to the wee girl, who smiled in return and with a giggle, bit into her cake before fluttering off in the direction of her family's cottage.

With Meek's help, the unwieldy door was again closed and the dismayed silence returned to dominate the dwelling. Banth, Meeks, and Yarn were no longer alone in the chamber. The director had summoned to his office the four most able-bodied males of the clan—the same four young myth who assembled four times a cycle and made the trek to Doog's dimension to gather four-petals. Four-petals did not grow in E'lore, but were essential to daily life, a tradition that harkened back to before the exodus. Unlike those routine gathering expeditions, where nambors were painstakingly avoided, this mission's purpose was to intentionally seek out, and make contact with, a human.

Banth had hoped that one from the gathered would volunteer, but when none had, it was not lost on him as to why. All had homes, loving families and friends in this idyllic world. All were very much aware that this would not be like their excursions to gather four-petals. All knew that this trip to Doog could potentially be their last. Therefore, when none stepped forward and no other options could be found in the parchments, it was agreed upon that they would use the timeworn system of chance. Hence, the need for the *weeze;* it was to be decided by a drawing. Yarn took position at one end of the lineup of young eligibles while Banth and Meeks sat quietly at the stone table allowing their tea to go cold. The room was silent until Yarn asked, "Are we ready, kinsmen?" Three in the line nodded in the affirmative, while the fourth made no movement and continued to stare directly ahead without emotion.

Banth looked to Yarn, who nodded at the director before stepping up to the first of the young myth and presenting him with his fistful of five whiskers, one of which was shorter in length than the others. So as not to give anyone an advantage over another, the exposed sheaths had been arranged so as to appear of equal length.

The first myth eyed the bundle for some time and seemed to choose his whisker carefully and with method. He pulled his choice from the elder's grip. Relief washed away the worry on his face as he surmised that he had chosen wisely and that his was sure to be one of the four longest. The second myth's eyes never left Yarn's as he reached for and chose his whisker without hesitation. He returned his hand to his side without looking at his choice. Neither he nor Yarn knew yet of his fate. The third myth's system was much like that of the first. Not having as many whiskers to choose from, he took less time, but he chose with careful consideration, and when he pulled a whisker from the remaining three, he, too, determined that it was of the longest length and seemed reassured as he let out a long-held breath and let his shoulders relax.

Yarn had allowed his gaze to fall to the earthen floor of Banth's office as he approached the last of the four chosen as able to seek out the nambor of the prophecy. As he turned to stand face-to-face with the young myth, Yarn forced his gaze upward until he looked him in the eye. With that, the fourth myth, for the first time since arriving, broke his locked stare at the empty wall ahead of him and exchanged it for looking directly into the eyes of the older myth. He then looked down at the last two remaining *weeze* and grasped one between his fingers. Yarn placed his free hand on the fourth myth's shoulder as the last contestant slowly drew out his choice. The elder myth could not conceal his dread as he looked down at the whisker in the young myth's grasp. Myth one through three were now staring intently at the fourth's hand, eager to learn of their collective fates. When the last myth held his whisker up for all to examine, relief overtook the first and third myth in the lineup, and they embraced and congratulated one another with indiscreet abandon. The second drawer, who chose quickly without looking at his *weeze*, marched straight up to the fourth myth, grabbed his right hand in his, and offered a hearty congratulations as well as his assistance in any matter in which the chosen one might find himself in need.

"Thank … you … Pethbol, I … I … thank you," was all that the stunned myth holding the short whisker could sputter out.

It was the loud, exaggerated clearing of Banth's throat that ended the rejoicing of the two relieved myth. Revelry turned to remorse as embarrassment over their selfish and thoughtless behavior cascaded over them. They turned in unison toward their elected clansman. As they proceeded past Banth, Meeks and then Yarn, each remorseful myth gave an apologetic bow. They then gave their elected comrade an embrace and words of encouragement before joining Pethbol and taking their leave of the chamber. Meeks escorted the visibly weary Yarn from the office, giving Banth a subtle nod as a bid goodnight. He closed the heavy door by himself, leaving the director and the chosen one alone in the great hollowed trunk of the ancient hawthorn tree.

CHAPTER 4

"I DO NOT want to go!"

"You drew the short *weeze*, you must go! Do not tamper with the augury, Tobas—'tis your duty now," Banth chastised the chosen myth.

"But this is ridiculous! Besides, nobody believes that the Fomorian still exist!"

"And why would they not?" Banth asked. "The fact that *we* exist is proof that they may have survived, as well."

"I suppose, but surely you do not believe that a nambor is the answer to our problem," the overwrought young myth replied with a heavy sigh.

"'Tis not for me to know, Tobas, but what I do know is that you are going to do your part to fulfill the prophecy. You must find this nambor."

"Nambors!" Tobas said with disdain. "They are clumsy, smelly, earthbound … They cannot even find their way out of their own dimension! And you want me to bring one of them back here! I can see it now. Give this … *thing* one day. I promise you … *one day* … Everything we have will be in ruins and everyone will blame me because I shall be the one who brought it here!"

Tobas, exhausted from his frenzy, slid down the wall and brought his bottom to rest on the soft ground.

"Can you not pick someone else?"

"No! Besides, 'tis the Fomorian that are the threat here. The nambor, evidently, is for protection."

"Wait 'til Sarla hears about this. *She* will be thrilled. A living, breathing nambor in our house! She will want to keep the thing, no doubt. What have I done to deserve this?" he moaned as he gripped his shaking head in his hands.

"'Tis no time for selfishness, Tobas. Bhara has seen our future. You were close enough to the crossing bed to hear him yourself, the Fomorian are coming! How can you speak so narrowly of inconvenience at this time? We are speaking of the survival of our clan. All *you* think of is yourself!"

Tobas stood himself up and brushed off his bum. "I cannot believe this," he muttered to himself. As he walked past the administrator's desk, Tobas did his best to stare holes through the diminutive director, but Banth Bellwether did not divert his eyes from the stacks of parchment work in front of him. The developments of the day had left the director with several administrative loose ends to tie up, and the sooner he finished, the sooner he could settle in for the evening with a hot cup of tea and a sweet. Banth did not look up or even offer to see the young myth out, as he had no desire to be distracted any longer by Tobas's grief. He pretended to write and scrutinize the papers before him until he heard the entry door open and then close with a heavy thud.

Banth lowered his quill and lifted his gaze, allowing it to fix upon the display of the four talismans on the wall opposite him. He removed his woven cap and ran his fingers over his head before bringing his hands to a stop under his jaw, his elbows resting on the desk. He drew in and let out a weighted breath as he stared at the empty space between the sword and the cauldron, where the book was meant to reside. He had become rather accustomed to staring at the empty space. Somehow, it had become a source of comfort, and the book did not have to be there for him to see it. He remembered watching Sorcha as she inscribed the book's pages. He cloaked himself in the thick, emerald Eire grass and watched the beautiful sorceress as she documented her knowledge and observations of their world. Being a sorceress, he knew that she was also filling the pages with magical spells and incantations, but he was not as interested in the contents of the book as he was in the author herself. It was because of her and his desire to protect her that Banth had his first and only taste of war.

At the time of the War of the Exile, Banth was very young, too young to fight with the Tuathan army, but that had not stopped him from trying. He fashioned a sword from a fallen rowan branch and had actually managed to get all the way to the front line without anyone noticing that there was a wee lad on the battlefield. He did not, however, escape the notice of a particular Fomorian; it was a ferocious Fomorian mercenary named Galar that happened upon Banth and his whittled sword. Galar was one of many soldiers of fortune who had sold his services to the Milesians. The vicious Fomorian seized the boy by the neck, lifting him off the ground until the child was eye to eye with the heartless soldier. Banth pulled at his captor's powerful grip with one hand, while swinging his handmade sword with the other. Galar laughed at the young Tuathan's determination.

"A soldier to the very end," he growled.

"Pity, you may have made a fierce warrior … had you lived."

Galar raised his bloodied skean as he prepared to cleave the brave boy in two.

Banth, seeing the blood-covered sword raised above the Fomorian's head, clamped his eyes shut as he awaited the skean's edge. However, instead of the mercenary's blade, he felt the unyielding earth as he had fallen from Galar's grasp and was lying on the ground, looking up at his former foe. The Fomorian was on his knees in front of the child-warrior and Bhara was standing behind him, holding his cudgel high above his head ready for a second strike at the Fomorian. Bhara brought the war-club down on the back of Galar's head with brute force, dropping the mercenary the balance of the distance to the ground. Whether he was dead or unconscious, Bhara and Banth did not linger to determine. The future king grabbed the boy around the waist and whisked him off to join what members of their clan were left as they prepared to go through the portal that led to E'lore.

Banth could still smell the burning buildings in the village and the stench of the blood-soaked battlefield. He could still hear the screams of the women and children as the Milesians lay waste to their beautiful, tranquil home. His eyes filled with tears at the thought of Bhara. His watery gaze was still fixed upon the empty spot in the quincunx of talismans when the wailing and screaming in his head faded and gave way to the serene quiet of his office. To Banth, the book's absence was nearly as powerful as its presence, the memory of its author even more so.

When the weary myth released his focus, and allowed his eyes to fall back to his desk and its blanket of parchments, he thought of the troubled young faerie that had left him just moments before. Angry or not, Tobas was right about one thing. It would be incredibly risky business, this idea of bringing a nambor to live among them. Nevertheless, it had been foretold, and, therefore, it must be done. There was no changing the fact that what Bhara saw is what was to be. It was not their place to question the prophecy. No, he decided firmly, the only thing to do was to follow Bhara's divination regardless of any apprehension or uncertainty on his part. Banth half-heartedly tidied his disheveled desk, blew out the candles that he had been working by, returned his hat to his head, and made for the door.

He decided that, on his way home, he would stop and pay a visit to Yarn—just in case he had come up with a way out of this.

CHAPTER 5

TOBAS SLOGGED DOWN the path leading away from the center of Aislinn. He had just gained the top of the slope that marked the onset of dwellings on the outskirts of the *baile* proper, when he heard the familiar snap that meant yet another ill-made brog had taken its last walk. The anxious myth stopped and wagged his head, pondering just how many more troubles the world would pile upon him this day. As he hopped from side to side on his left foot, he raised his right and removed the damaged slipper. The newly-split sole flopped to-and-fro as if doing the leprechaun's bidding in one final act of mockery and defiance. Tobas responded by cocking his arm back and hurling the offensive footwear into the dark purple E'lore dusk. This thoughtless act did much to relieve the young myth's frustration, and, with an exasperated sigh, he resumed his trek homeward. With each alternate step, he dragged his newly unshod toes through the soft, dark and wormy ground doing his best to prolong his arrival home. As he passed old Yarn's cottage, he saw that the elder myth was sitting on his front porch, sipping a cup of tea and rocking back and forth in his chair.

Tobas paused at the elder's gate, taking in the detail of the old myth's house. Although the house had looked the same for as long as Tobas could remember, it seemed as if he was gazing upon the old dwelling for the first time. The moss-thatched, tortoise-shell shaped roof teetered in a gravity defying slope of a one hundred and forty-five degree angle to the left. The house itself was actually the rotted out root of an ancient lillyfur tree, which Yarn had claimed at the time of the banishment. Breaches in the hull of the root had been repaired with a mixture of now petrified mud and moss. Portholes had been intentionally cut out systematically around the perimeter to allow for ventilation of the cooking fire inside. Other than the ventilation holes, the structure was solid and without any windows of any kind, unless one counted the small peephole on the front door, which had become fashionable in the last hundred cycles or so.

Yarn's reply when questioned about the lack of windows in his residence was this: "If you want to be inside, go inside. If you want to be outside, go outside. 'Tis too confusing to do both at the same time!"

The only reason it seemed that the fort had not crashed on its side was the generous growth of worm ivy rooted at the base of the lillyfur tree and reaching heavenward up the great trunk and out of sight, pulling the old house upward with it. The front porch, in league with the rest of the dwelling, was also slanted at a precarious angle, which Yarn compensated for by replacing the right side legs of the porch sitting chairs with ones that were a good half a length taller than their left-side counterparts. That and deep grooves worn into the soft planks were all that kept the rocker and its occupant from tumbling off the porch. Tentacles of brilliant white flother flowers entwined themselves around and through any branches and roots that allowed their sprawling growth, the blossoms even playing hide-and-seek with one another in and out of the venting holes. Swarms of danann lotus, crimson kard-pa blossoms, and craigmoss threatened to overtake the myth's humble front porch. In contradiction to the willy-nilly architecture and apparent relinquishment of ownership of the dwelling to the forces of nature, was a small, meticulously painted sign made of a piece of smooth beerchwood reading:

Merrie meet
Merrie part
Merrie meet again

It had been painted by Yarn's wife, Maeve. She had crossed many cycles ago, and on every anniversary of their union, Yarn carefully gave the lettering a fresh brush of pigment as a tribute to his departed love.

"Care for a cuppa?" Yarn hollered when he caught sight of his nephew.

Not really wanting any tea at the moment, Tobas reconsidered when it occurred to him that having a cup of tea could postpone his arrival home until well past dinnertime.

"Love some!" he yelled in reply, and with that he lifted the latch and pushed the gate open. At a somewhat quicker pace than what had brought him this far, he made his way up the front path. A herd of quagga gently grazed in the pasture running alongside the path. As Tobas walked by, one of the females nursing her foal lifted her head lazily as if to acknowledge his presence, then languorously lowered her head and resumed her meal. Tobas continued up the front path. The steps to Yarn's front porch were made of three progressively taller tree stumps wedged into soft earth. Tobas clomped up the stumps and greeted his uncle and neighbor with a nod. The younger myth brought himself to rest in the deep seat of one of the rocking chairs and gratefully accepted a steaming cup of four-petal tea. After a couple of cooling breaths, he raised the cup to his lips for a tentative sip.

"It makes my heart heavy to know that you must face this task," Yarn stated softly as he stared at Tobas' dirty, shoeless foot.

"I do not have the right sort of luck for these things. The others never stood a chance," Tobas replied with a forced smile.

"Well, you have never drawn a long *weeze* in your life! Who else could it have been?" Yarn, too, attempted to break the tension. Their efforts to relieve the anxiety were short-lived. Tobas's concern was not to be abated.

"What am I going to do, Yarn?" Tobas whispered speculatively.

"You are going to go retrieve the nambor, and bring it back here." Yarn replied, deciding to take it as a genuine question.

The fight was all but gone out of Tobas, and resignation was creeping in.

Yarn leaned forward in his chair. "Much time has passed and now our future has come to greet us. We have enjoyed many cycles of peace and regeneration and the time has come to purchase the same for our children. So come now, Tobas, there is nothing to do but to answer the call. Were you not able, you would not have been chosen."

"But I was not chosen, Yarn. 'Tis my bad luck that has put me here."

"Make no mistake, my son, you were chosen. There is no such thing as luck—good or bad. There is only Destiny."

"Then Destiny has made a mistake," Tobas scoffed.

Suppressing a chuckle, Yarn continued to try to comfort the young myth.

"I am afraid that she is not in the habit of doing that, Tobas. Do not think yourself the first myth to consider himself unworthy of Fate's bidding. None have failed before you, and I do not believe you will reverse that course. You were born with the strength. You just have to find the faith."

Yarn had known Tobas's mother, Meaghan, since they were children. They grew up in the same village, played in the same fields, and got into the same mischief together. They were inseparable as children, but as childhood innocence gave way to adult fancies, it was Yarn's brother, Allyn, who stole Meaghan's heart. Meaghan made Allyn promise that not a word of their love, or their intention to marry, would be spoken of until she had first told Yarn. Meaghan fretted and worried herself to tears when it came time to tell her dearest friend that it was not he that she loved, but another. It was just before sunset at the end of a perfect spring day when Meaghan finally worked up the courage to speak to Yarn and confess to him her heart's true desire. She found him in the paddock at the southern-most end of their village. He had just turned the horses out to graze in the emerald green fields, and was fastening the rope latch of the wooden gate when he spotted her standing at the top of the lane.

"There you are!" he shouted, and quickening his pace with securing the latch, he turned and ran up the lane to meet her.

"Where have you been? I have not seen you for days!" Yarn gave her a beaming smile.

When the distance between them was at last closed, Yarn could see from her expression that she was of a serious temperament, and his own disposition quickly changed to match hers.

Placing a hand on each of her shoulders, Yarn had to bend down to look into her downcast eyes.

"Meaghan, what is it? What has happened?" Yarn implored.

The tears had already begun to stream down her face, and she knew that if she were going to tell him, she would have to do it soon before her crying made her words undecipherable.

"'Tis your brother," Meaghan sobbingly began.

Yarn became instantly alarmed.

"Allyn! What? What has happened? Meaghan, speak to me!"

Yarn was in a panic and desperate for his friend to speak. To this end, he gave her shoulders a shake.

"Meaghan, what has happened to Allyn!?" Yarn was frantic.

"I love him! We are to be married in a fortnight!" Meaghan finally blurted out.

Yarn was silent.

"You and Allyn? You *love* Allyn?" Yarn asked slowly.

Meaghan looked up at her best friend with swollen red eyes and a leaking nose and nodded her affirmation.

Yarn's excited demeanor immediately subsided at the sight of his dear lass in such distress. Stretching the sleeve of his shirt well over his hand, he used the dangling cloth firstly to wipe her tears and secondly to wipe her nose.

"And does *he* love you?" Yarn asked softly as he gently held a bit of his sleeve over her nose and instructed her to blow.

"He does," came her muffled answer through the makeshift handkerchief.

"We are to be married," she repeated.

"Ah yes, I remember your mentioning that," Yarn said.

"Can you ever forgive me, Yarn? I feel like I have deceived you so," her confession turned the faucet back on, and tears were again rolling down her cheeks.

"I am sure that *I* can forgive you. The question is can *you* forgive me?"

"Forgive you? You have done nothing to forgive—I am the one who has fallen in love with someone else, not you. You are ... hold on," she paused, "forgive you for what? What have *you* done?"

The tears had finally subsided as Meaghan was slowly realizing that something else was afoot.

"I have not been forthcoming myself, my dear, for you see I, too, have lost my heart to another," Yarn cautiously offered.

Feeling both relieved of her guilt and excited for her friend, Meaghan was beside herself with eagerness.

"Tell me, you beast! Who is it? Would I know her?"

"Yes, I believe that you may have made her acquaintance on an occasion or two." Yarn was mercilessly teasing his anxious friend now.

"Tell me, you great ox, or shall I clobber it out of you?"

After giving his friend a prolonged smile, he said, "'Tis Maeve," Yarn confessed.

"Maeve … *my* Maeve? … my sister, Maeve?" Meaghan was in shock.

"Yes, that Maeve."

"How could you not tell me? How long have …"

Yarn did not let her finish.

"For as long as I can remember. I think from the moment that I knew she existed," he answered.

"So you are not in love with me?"

"You? Make no mistake. I love you with all my heart. We have been together for as long as I can remember. *Love*? Yes. *In* love? … no. You are my very dearest friend, Meaghan. Even I am not foolish enough to ruin that by falling in love with you!" Yarn teased.

"I am so … relieved! I have worried myself sick thinking that I was going to break your heart, when all this time your heart was perfectly safe with my sister!"

The two life-long friends embraced, awash in relief that their friendship was unscathed. Suddenly, Meaghan pulled herself away.

"Maeve … she does not know … does she? She mustn't know, because if *she* knew, then *I* would have known. We keep no secrets from each other. She has no idea, does she, Yarn?"

"As a matter of fact, she does not, and I would like to keep it that way for a while longer, thank you very much …"

This time it was Meaghan who did not let her friend finish.

"I will not hear of it! We are going to tell her this very instant!"

Before Yarn could protest, Meaghan had him by the arm and was pulling him back up the lane and toward the village.

"We could have a double ceremony! Da is going to be most upset, shall cost him dearly …"

Meaghan did not stop talking until they reached her parents' cottage, and even then, Yarn barely got a word in edgewise.

This is where Yarn's dream-like recollection of that day ended and he found himself once again in the present, and on his front porch with Tobas. Yarn's brother, Allyn, had been killed in the The War of the Exile. He and Meaghan had married shortly before the invasion by the Milesians, and Allyn's death ended their life together before it had even begun. She had been strong enough to survive the war, but not the death of her beloved. Meaghan died of a broken heart only two moons after giving birth to Tobas in E'lore.

Yarn instinctively assumed the role of father to the son that his brother did not live to see. He and Maeve had raised him as their own. And though his heart was in anguish that Tobas was about to be placed in this very dangerous circumstance, Yarn feigned a brave front and hid his growing anxiety from his nephew. For Tobas's sake, the less made of the potential danger, the better. Tobas had always looked to Yarn for direction and Yarn had never guided him astray.

Knowing that his uncle's words could be trusted, but still not finding the comfort he sought, Tobas continued, "'Tis insanity, this. This will be our ruin."

"What would you have us do then? Ignore Bhara's prophecy?"

Tobas thought for a moment, trying to align his words so as to be as respectful of their late king as was mythly possible.

"What I mean, *Uncail*, is that perhaps we are putting too much importance on Bhara's foretelling. Perhaps they were merely just … words."

Yarn's back stiffened at the foolish impudence of the young myth's conjecture. After a cleansing breath and a long sip of tea, his apprehension subsided enough to continue.

"No one, Tobas, has ever questioned Bhara's directives. Do you really want to be the first to do so?" Yarn challenged.

"No, I suppose … I mean, no," Tobas, realizing his effrontery, muttered into his tea.

Yarn studied his charge with a patient gaze.

"Well then, nothing to do for it but get it over with. I guess you had better go home and give Sarla the news. She will be so thrilled. It has always been her desire to meet one, you know," Yarn offered.

"Yes, I know … how wonderful for her." Tobas's arrogance had been abruptly replaced with his more commonplace sarcasm. He downed the last of his tea, and with a nod of thanks to his uncle, pulled himself up from the homey clutches of the porch chair. Yarn had done the same and was standing by the young myth's side with a patriarchal hand on Tobas's shoulder.

"The fate of our people may rest on these shoulders, Tobas. You have the strength to do this thing. You only have to find it." Yarn forced a confident front as his faith in Destiny's choice began to wane.

The fate of the clan? On *his* shoulders? Now, the gravity of the situation was really creeping in. With a sigh of forced resolution, Tobas nodded his thanks again to Yarn and stepped heavily down the three stump stairs. The newly realized weight of responsibility drove his feet deep into the ground. At the end of Yarn's front path, Tobas turned gently to his right as if in a daze, his mind adrift in a sea of his own frantic thoughts. As he pondered the distressing reality of the day's events, his feet, apparently functioning independently of his brain, had traversed the distance between Yarn's front gate and the path leading to Tobas's own front door. The anxious myth allowed himself to pause before passing through the turnstile. He scrutinized the dwelling that he shared with his mate and two children as if seeing it for the very first time. The life that he shared with them never seemed as precious as it did now. Unable to be strong for himself, the husband and father in him found the strength to be brave for his family.

With another heavy sigh, he pushed back his shoulders and walked down the path and up the steps to the door. The sweet smell of roasting meat and baking bread greeted him on the front porch as he lifted the latch and gently nudged the door open. His wife, Sarla, had busied herself with preparing the family's eventide meal since she and the children had arrived home from the Ulster Mound. Cooking always gave her comfort. As Tobas entered, she was pouring the tea. Sarla paused long enough to look up and give him a warm smile. Taking in the sight of her, Tobas could feel his resolve fading. As he made his way over to his mate, he was blindsided with a ferocious tackle to his right side.

"No flying in the house, Willa," Sarla disciplined from the kitchen.

However, her chastising fell on deaf ears, as Willa brought her father crashing to the floor.

"Hello, Willa, how was your day?" Tobas managed to get out with what little breath her attack had left him.

"Boring as a stump until we got the news!" she answered.

"What news might that be?" Tobas asked his daughter.

"The nambors are coming, the nambors are coming!" The exciting proclamation was being shouted by Anndra, Sarla and Tobas's son, and Willa's little brother.

"The nambors are coming, the nambors are coming!" he continued to shout as he swooped and whirled his way from room to room.

"No flying in the house goes for you, too, Anndra!" Sarla shouted.

"When are the nambors coming, Da?" Anndra asked, as he swooped in for a perfect, two-point landing on his father's stomach.

"Not nambors, *nambor*. And *it* will arrive shortly after I am told to go and retrieve it."

On the heels of the sound of plates and utensils crashing to the floor, Sarla flew from the kitchen into the front room.

"But I thought there was no flying in the house," Anndra scolded his mother.

"Mind your manners, little one," growled Tobas.

"Sorry, Da."

Sarla ignored them both.

"A nambor coming here? I should have known ... you always draw the short *weeze!* Oh Toby, I am so excited. I have always wanted to see one in the flesh. But to have one here, as our guest, I just, I just cannot believe our good fortune! Oh, there is so much to do to prepare. Do you think the guest room will be enough, or should we build it its own fort? What do you think it will want to eat ...?"

"Our guest?" Tobas exclaimed. "Do not believe everything that you and Yarn read, Sarla. They are clumsy and stupid and smelly. 'Tis not good fortune, 'tis a curse!"

"Oh, Toby, how you exaggerate. They cannot be as bad as you say. They are just as civilized as we are!"

"I doubt that very much!" Tobas said grimacing.

"Will it be coming to market with us, Mam?" Anndra asked.

"I will not be sharing *my* room with it ..." Willa chimed in.

"Can we make it do our chores?" Anndra added wishfully.

"Hold on here. Is no one concerned for me, for my safety? I am the one who has to go and get this thing," Tobas declared, with disbelief at his family's lack of distress over his impending doom.

"Stop being so dramatic," Sarla answered. "You go to Doog four times a cycle to harvest four-petals. Why the fuss now?"

"A nambor is hardly a four-petal, Sarla. What if it bites me?"

"Why would it bite you? Besides, if 'tis the nambor of our Bhara's prophecy, then I am sure 'tis much too developed to resort to such base aggression."

"Since when have you become such an expert?" Tobas teased her.

"I have been studying them for a long time, you know that," she answered with a half-smile.

Ignoring Tobas's sarcasm, Sarla asked, "Do you know what it is?"

"What what is?" Tobas asked.

"The nambor—is it a male or a female?"

"Well male, of course! According to Una, this nambor is brave and strong and smart. I must say that I find the last bit hardest to believe. The chances of any of those qualities existing in a male nambor—very slight, in a *female* nambor—impossible!"

More interested in discussing the nambor than starting another argument about her mate's ignorance and prejudice, Sarla pressed on. "You should not be so opinionated, Tobas, and, besides, you have never even met one."

"I came very close to it last harvest. Remember when we caught that one in the four-petal patch?"

"How could I forget? You talked about it for two moons."

"Well, I was lucky to get out of there in one piece!"

"They cannot *see* us, Toby."

Tobas knew that she was right, as usual. Nambors were generally not able to see myth, especially if the myth did not want to be seen. Nevertheless, he had been so spooked by the near encounter on the last harvest that he had quickly returned to E'lore without regrouping with his fellow petal-gatherers. Tobas realized that Sarla was still speaking to him.

"… Besides, I am sure they are much more developed now. Come up off the floor, then. Supper will be getting cold."

"Come on, little ones. Time for supper," Sarla called to her children.

CHAPTER 6

BANTH'S MIND WAS racing with all the possible scenarios
resulting from the admittance of a nambor to their peaceful world and
none of them were reassuring. His busy and fretful imagination had kept
his thoughts well away from how far he had traveled, and only a well-
timed glance upward alerted him to the fact that he had reached his
destination. He paused with his hand on Yarn's front gate, steeling his
nerves. Questioning his king was something he had never done before
and he was angry with himself for doing it now. It seemed to him that
bringing a nambor to E'lore was an idea fraught with dangerous
possibilities. 'There *must* be another way,' he thought to himself. An
exhausting scrutiny of the parchments had yielded no answers. Taking
comfort in the knowledge that if they found no resolution this night, Yarn
would surely have a generous supply of fermented four-petal tea to dull
the anxiety they were all feeling over obeying Bhara's last decree. He gave
a push on the gate and made his way up his old friend's walk. Yarn,
expecting his fellow myth, was opening the door before Banth had even
navigated the last of the tree stump steps.

"Banth, *fáilte*. Come warm yourself by the fire. You have only just
missed Tobas."

"Tobas was here?" Banth asked.

Secretly grateful that he had been spared more outbursts from the un-
derstandably anxious young myth, he added, "Inquiring about a way out of
his participation in the fulfillment, no doubt."

"You can hardly blame him, Banth. 'Tis a lot to ask of him, to ask of anyone, come to that," Yarn responded.

Banth removed his tattered hat, hung it on a knotted bit of wood protruding from the wall, and rubbing his chilled hands together, turned to walk towards the gently crackling fire to warm himself.

"How in E'lore are we supposed to find this one particular nambor? How many of them must there be by now?" Banth asked, as if the mere question itself was exhausting.

"About four billion, give or take," answered the chair near the hearth.

As Banth stepped closer to the flames, he saw Meeks ensconced in an over-stuffed and lumpy chair. It was one of a pair that Yarn had made for his wife. Textile-covered chairs were considered luxurious and never became popular enough to replace the more commonly used seats carved of cullen and lillyfur wood, but Maeve loved them. She and Yarn would end their day in the chairs together, side by side in front of the fire, evening after evening. When the chairs were new, the fabric was a vibrant emerald green, chosen to pay homage to the land from which they had come. Perhaps fortunately for Yarn, the chairs had long lost their rich color, and with time and use, had faded to a tame sage. The seat and armrests of the chair were threadbare with wear, and the occupant was sometimes subjected to pokes and jabs from the escaping stuffing. When his wife passed, Yarn simply could not bear to look at the empty chair and be reminded that he lived in a world that no longer included his Maeve. Banth took the chair and stored it for his friend so that Yarn would not be subjected to its sorrow-inducing silhouette. It was in the mate to Maeve's chair that Meeks had planted himself, warming his chilled toes and sipping hot tea. Judging from his state of inebriation, he had been there for some time.

"Getting an early start are we, Meeks?"

"And why not? You did not actually believe that the parchments were going to hand us the key out of this situation, did you?"

Yarn shot Banth a look of resignation and with a shrug of his shoulders, handed the director a steaming cup of four-petal tea.

"We have done what we can. We have chosen a seeker of this nambor. There is nothing that we can do but wait," Yarn said to both in general and neither specifically.

"What exactly is it that we are waiting for?" Meeks asked.

"I am not sure, a sign perhaps," Yarn said with as much conviction as he could muster.

"Well, I say 'tis out of our hands … there is nothing to be done for it now. We are in a place from which there is no escape," Meeks added morosely as he mockingly lifted his teacup in a toast.

Banth took a sip from his cup and was not surprised to find that Yarn had given him fermented tea as well. Feeling defeated before the battle had even begun, he succumbed to the calming effect of the tea, and welcomed the promise that by the bottom of the cup, his worries would be significantly reduced, if only for a time.

The three myth sat quietly whilst contemplating their situation, sipping tea before the glow of the fire. After a couple of rounds, they dispensed with manners, dispatched the teacups, and began drinking the fermented tea straight from the large jug in which it had been aged. They sat for some time, slumped in their chairs, staring blankly into the fire. After much staring and slumping, Yarn hoisted the jug he had been cradling in his arm to his lips and took an enormous swig. As he brought the jug back down to rest, Banth stretched over the gap between them and relieved his friend of the pitcher of brew, helping himself to an equally sized gulp. Chuckling to himself, Meeks sank back into his chair, and there the three myth sat in compatriot silence until the entirety of Yarn's reserve of fermented four-petal tea was exhausted.

***

And the light in the glen grew brighter.

CHAPTER 7

ON THE WAY to his office the next morning, Banth thought he should go around to Yarn's cottage and check on how his friend had fared the previous night's over-indulgence. As he came upon the old myth's gate, he heard animated, frantic voices, trying with little success to have a quiet discussion. Banth rested his hand on the gate latch, but did not lift it, taking a moment to decide if he should interrupt the conversation. The director could hear the voices of Yarn and his farmhand well enough but could not make out the words. Banth gently lifted the gate latch, gave it a push and made his way up the cottage's front walk. By the time he was halfway up the path, Banth could understand Yarn's words perfectly, but his companion spoke in incoherent yelps and squawks. The elder myth was talking with Andee, a grogoch, who looked after Yarn's fields and tended his gardens and herds as barter for an old debt. A grogoch, by all accounts looked very much like a faerie, in that they had a head, a torso, two arms and two legs. That's where the similarity ended. Grogoches were covered from head to toe in reddish brown hair that was usually mangled and bedraggled with all manner of dirt and debris. Their large dark eyes, nose, mouth and ears were practically hidden by their bristly and wayward coat of fur. In size, they were almost three times that of an adult faerie. Their rough appearance and sometimes ungracious behavior belied the fact that the grogoch—once attached to a family—was devoutly loyal and protective. Andee had been with Yarn since shortly after the myth's exile from Eire, and the two had managed to work out a way to communicate that only they understood.

Yarn was speaking softly to Andee who, in turn, was gesticulating wildly as he grunted and snorted his end of the conversation. When Yarn caught sight of the director coming up his walk, he ended his exchange with the large, hairy farmer, and with a handshake, sent him on his way. The amiable grogoch gave Banth a toothy smile and a loud, gaseous emission as they passed each other on the path. Banth winced and waved his hand in front of his face in an attempt to disperse the offensive odor. Andee merely gave him a mischievous giggle and then turned and scurried down the path. Before he reached the end, however, he stopped and gave Banth a devilish smirk and another eruption. Practically doubling over with laughter, the rude and smelly creature half climbed and half fell through the rungs of the fence just before the gate. Once he regained his footing, he danced and skipped his way through the surprised quagga before disappearing over the hillside. Dismissing the grogoch's behavior with a shake of his head, Banth turned and continued up the path to the house and walked right up to the elder myth whose gaze was still in the direction of where the woolly farmhand had faded from view.

"What's all that then?" Banth asked.

As Yarn's full, puzzled attention had been focused solely on the re-treating figure of the grogoch, he was startled to find that Banth had completed his walk up the front path and was now standing right next to him. Yarn's head and attention turned abruptly toward the director. "Come, we must waken Meeks and go to see Tobas. 'Tis time."

Looking back to where he had last seen the flatulent grogoch, Yarn added, "I shall put the kettle on, and you wake Meeks, but do it gently, Banth. You know how irritable he can be after a night of ..." Yarn's sentence trailed off.

Banth knew all too well the demeanor to which Yarn was referring, answering him, "Believe me, I am well versed in our friend's post-potted temperament."

Yarn was already frantically stoking the fire for the kettle before Banth had even closed the cottage door behind himself. He could see that Yarn was very excited about something, but decided to let the older myth tell what he had learned when he was ready, which Banth guessed would be as soon as Meeks was awake and aware. Before long, Meeks had been infused with enough regular four-petal tea to help counteract the effects of the fermented tea from the evening before. After putting out the kettle fire and donning their hats and scarves, the three myth were making their way down Yarn's front path.

"What in E'lore is all the rush about?" Meeks complained. "And where are we going anyway?" he added.

"There has been a sign. I think that Andee has seen the sign." Yarn was so excited that he was barely able to articulate his words.

"Are you telling me that you dragged me out of my sleep, force-fed me scalding tea, and practically choked me with my own scarf, because a smelly, gassy grogoch told you that he saw the sign?" Meeks was giving himself a headache with the raised volume of his own voice.

His point, however, stopped Banth in his tracks. It took a little longer for it to hit Yarn, but within a few steps of his mates, he, too, had come to a full stop.

"He is right, Yarn. Maybe we should see for ourselves before we go speak to Tobas," Banth reasoned.

"Yes, yes. Perhaps we are getting ahead of ourselves," Yarn answered.

"'Tis just over the hill, in the meadow with the gooseberry trees is where Andee said he saw it. Perhaps it *would* be prudent to be absolutely sure before we proceed. It would be unforgivable to alarm Tobas and Sarla and the little ones if it, indeed, was nothing more than a figment of a grogoch's imagination. I think that is wise, yes, yes … a look for ourselves," Yarn agreed with himself.

As Banth and Yarn retraced their steps and walked past Meeks, the formerly intoxicated myth simply hung his head and shook it in disbelief.

"Are you coming, Meeks?" Banth called back.

"Who me? Would not miss it for anything," he added with a sarcasm that was wasted on his companions.

"Come along then, look lively," Yarn admonished.

Meeks hung his head and gave it a shake, which immediately reminded him that the side effects of the fermented tea still lingered in his head. He slowly turned to take up the aft position behind his two companions. He followed his comrades back over the distance of the path that they had covered previously. They passed Yarn's front gate, and continued in the opposite direction from the one they had initially taken. To spare their wings from catching on the rails, they each glided over the fence and landed gently in the soft mosses of the meadow that Yarn and Banth had watched Andee skip through some time earlier. Meeks still followed several paces behind, rarely diverting his gaze from the ground below, finding the beautiful Shannon blossoms a welcome distraction from the pain in his still-throbbing head. The three myth walked in silence over the mossy field. Yarn's mind was a jumble of apprehensive reflections, most of them to do with his concern for Tobas should Andee be right about what he saw in the glen. Banth searched desperately for ideas on how to protect the clan from the Fomorians if the attempt to bring back Bhara's nambor should not go as planned. Meeks, who was still soothing his head with blossom gazing, had not noticed when his fellow travelers came to a stop at the crest of the hilly pasture. Unaware that the hike had ended, Meeks crashed fully into the back of Banth. As he extended his bewildered apologies, Meeks realized that Banth was paying him no heed whatsoever; his gaze and attention was fixed towards the glen below.

"What is the problem now? What are you look ... ing at?" Meek's voice faded as he saw what it was that had Banth and Yarn in a trance. There in the glen, between the pair of gooseberry trees was a shimmering, floating ball of light. It was a brilliant blue-green with tentacles waving out from its center. It hovered before a backdrop of ancient standing stones— stones erected prior to the arrival of the myth. The three of them stood on the crest, mesmerized by the sight below.

"Wait ..." a still groggy Meeks whispered as he surveyed the surrounding landscape to get his bearings.

"This is the ... those are the portal trees ... are they not the portal trees?" Meeks asked of neither of his companions specifically. Not waiting for a response, he added, "I do not remember that light being there before."

"That is because the trees have always been there, but the light ... the light is new," Banth responded with childlike awe.

The pair of gooseberry trees marked the passageway used by the myth to gain access to Doog or "the old world" as some of the elders still called it. The four-petals that were so precious to them were only available there, in the old dimension, and the myth used this portal to travel back and harvest the essential leaves. The portal opened four times a cycle. The gooseberry-marked portal was also the aperture through which they had arrived in E'lore, after the War of the Exile.

"What do you think it means, Yarn," Banth asked.

"I have no idea. Did the parchments make any mention of such an occurrence?" he asked hopefully.

"Not that I saw," Banth replied.

"What is your interpretation of this, Meeks?" Yarn earnestly queried his second associate.

"I interpret that those are the portal trees, and before, there was no dancing ball of blue light and now there is. That is my interpretation."

Undaunted by their companion's seemingly endless supply of cynicism, Yarn and Banth ignored his reply and continued their study of the new phenomenon.

Now that the initial astonishment had somewhat subsided, the three myth noticed something that had somehow escaped their attention before. There, among the stones, was Andee. He was lying down between the two widest of the standing stones holding his shaggy paunch, laughing and breathing laboriously. Almost as soon as they noticed his presence, the big, hairy grogoch rolled himself over onto his stomach and scrambled to his feet. Resuming his laughing, he began dancing and skipping around the stones, arms flailing in the air to a melody that only he could hear. The surprised myth watched in wonderment as the woolly creature danced himself into a stupor and fell to the ground again, laughing and panting and rubbing his great hairy belly.

CHAPTER 8

"DA ..." ANNDRA SAID softly, gently shaking his father's shoulder. "Da, wake up," Anndra repeated, not quite so softly, shaking his father not so gently.

"Da, wake up, there is someone here to see you," Anndra implored his sleeping father, in a volume bordering on shouting, while rocking his father back and forth, using both hands.

"What do you want Anndra? Can you not see I am sleeping?" Tobas exclaimed with growing annoyance that his slumber was being disturbed.

"You need to stop sleeping, Da. You need to come to the door now!" Anndra could scarcely contain his excitement.

Just as Tobas was begrudgingly throwing back the moleskin covering their sleeping nest, Sarla appeared in the doorway.

"Tobas, 'tis the director and Meeks and Yarn ... you had better come."

Tobas, forgoing his usual morning ablutions, leapt out of bed, and ignoring the house "no flying" rule, flew into the front room.

"What is it? What has happened?"

"Tobas, 'tis time. We think the time has come!" Banth blurted out.

"Time for what?" Tobas asked.

"Time to retrieve the nambor. We think we know how to find it!" Yarn answered.

"This is so exciting! How do you know? Has there been a sign?" asked Sarla, having walked from the sleeping chamber with Anndra in tow.

Tobas sarcastically acknowledged her enthusiasm with a roll of his eyes, and turned back to their newly-arrived guests.

"Has there? Has there been a sign?" he asked hesitantly.

"We cannot be sure, but what else could it be?" Banth shouted with excitement.

"What else could *what* be?" Tobas, still groggy with sleep, was having a difficult time understanding what they were talking about, much less, why they were so excited about it.

Meeks, not emotionally overcome, but evidently rather thirsty, asked Sarla, "Have you any tea brewed Sarla, I would not say 'no' to a cuppa."

"Yes, of course, forgive me. Director, Yarn, would you care for tea?" she asked.

"If 'tis not too much trouble, yes, please, thank you Sarla," Yarn answered for them both.

As Sarla turned to go to the kitchen, Meeks grabbed Anndra playfully around the shoulders and said, "Come on, let's give your mam a help with the tea."

"I want to stay and hear about Da fighting the nambor," Anndra answered, not moving from his spot.

"Well, I am sure that if your Da does do battle with the nambor, you will be the first one he tells about it. But in the meantime, little one, let's you and I do battle with the tea kettle!" And with this, Meeks snatched Anndra up into the air, and grabbing him by the ankles, flew with him dangling upside-down and squealing with delight into the kitchen where Sarla was starting to brew a company-sized pot of four-petal tea. Meeks might not have suffered adults with much noticeable patience, but the *bairns*—the wee ones—only saw his gentle side.

"Please, come, sit." Tobas offered the remaining two myths a seat, motioning to the chairs by the fire.

"Tell me, what has happened. What sign are you talking about?" Tobas asked with uncharacteristic patience.

Answering for the still overly excited Banth, Yarn told Tobas of the events of the morning, starting with the visit from Andee and ending with the collapse of the giggling grogoch amongst the ancient stones.

Although Yarn's narrative had come to an end, Tobas sat in stunned silence and continued to look at Yarn as if there was more of the story forthcoming.

"Tobas, Tobas, did you hear me?" Yarn asked with concern.

Sarla, Meeks, and Anndra had by now returned with the tea and a tray of sweet heather cakes and scones, and the entire assembled group was staring at Tobas, waiting for some sign of acknowledgment to the news.

"Toby, are you all right?" his wife asked.

Sarla's soothing voice had gently brought Tobas around, and he answered her in a cracked, strained voice. "Fine, I am fine, I just cannot believe that the time is here—Is it really? Are you sure that this is *the* sign? I mean, how can you be sure? What if 'tis something else altogether? I mean, we do not want to do anything hasty here ... or foolish," he added, as his attention shifted from conversing with his guests to his own careening thoughts.

"Well, of course, there is no way to be absolutely sure until we, or rather, you, pass through the trees. We think that the orb is there to guide you to the particular nambor that we seek. If you just went through the portal as usual, it would be practically impossible to find this one specific nambor among ... how many did you say there were now, Meeks?"

"Four billion," Meeks answered soberly.

"'Tis a lot of nambors, Tobas. What else could this light be if not a beacon to set us ... you," he corrected himself again, "on the right path?" Banth suggested.

"I suppose that I would come to the same conclusion if I were you, but I think that you would not be so confident if you were the ones going through the portal yourselves," Tobas answered unreservedly.

The assembled group did not reply, but respected Tobas's misgivings and let him gather his thoughts in peace.

It was Banth who finally broke the silence. "We cannot be sure of how much time we have, Tobas. We do not know when the light came or when it will leave. The fact that it has appeared between the gooseberry trees is the only evidence we have that 'tis meant as a portal itself. We have never seen anything like it in E'lore before. We cannot be sure, but perhaps Bhara himself has conjured it to guide us through his augury and lead us to the nambor of his prophecy."

Yarn, looking tired and distraught, shifted uneasily in his chair as Banth spoke.

Tobas looked at the three older myth, allowing his eyes to rest briefly on one before turning to the next. His gaze shifted to the face of his wife, Sarla, who gave him a brow-furrowed smile. Tobas looked back at the director and not having any words at that moment, simply answered him with a nod.

CHAPTER 9

IN THE CRAMPED director's office, Tobas took in a deep breath as he tightened the leather laces of his vest. With a pronounced exhale, he turned around to face his fellow myth. Forcing a smile for the sake of Sarla, Willa, and Anndra, Tobas did his best to appear calm and unworried about the task that lay before him. He may have fooled the children, but Sarla was not deceived. She knew that her mate was very concerned, not only for himself, but for his family. As he looked at his wife, he wondered if the time that he was spending with them now would be the last. Knowing that these very thoughts were powerful enough to destroy his resolve, he shook his head, shoulders and arms, trying to literally cast them off. Sensing Tobas's mounting dread, Yarn approached his nephew, and thrust a worn hide satchel at him, which Tobas reflexively grabbed. Throwing an arm around the young myth's shoulder and gently guiding him toward the door, the older myth tried to steel his nephew's nerve by briskly dealing with the business at hand.

"You will find two marking stakes just as you have on the harvesting missions. Let that be the first thing you do, as always—mark your portal of return. I have also put two shares of gooseberry root in here," he said sternly as he patted the satchel that Tobas clutched to his chest.

"One share for you and one for the nambor. Do not forget that the larger portion is for the nambor itself. You will not require much to adjust to Doog, this we know. The nambor, however, well 'tis purely speculation as to how much he will require to adjust to E'lore."

"Now," Yarn continued in a lower, more reserved tone. "You will find a double-sized pouch of pooka dust in here as well," he said, giving the bag another pat, while his eyes locked on to those of his nephew. "I know that you understand how to use it, but I caution you, use it *only* if there is no other means available to achieve your goal. We know well of its effect on grogoches, leprechauns, and snallygasters, but nambors … well, let me just say that I personally have never seen it used on a nambor before, so there is more than enough room for doubt here. Now, because we need this nambor as we do, let us use restraint in our methods whenever possible, hmmmm?"

Tobas nodded his understanding, and with that, Yarn gave the young myth a stout rap on the back and gently guided him toward the door.

"Do we have everything now?" he asked the anxious Tobas.

"Yes, yes … 'tis all here," he replied as he shuffled the inventory of his satchel around, taking a mental stock of its contents. His searching hand suddenly found something soft and warm. Pulling it out into the light to give it a closer inspection, he found that Sarla had packed some roasted, wild red deer and brisgein bread. Her loving gesture melted what was left of his resolve, and in that moment he had every intention of resigning from his mission. As he turned to tell as much to Yarn, his astute uncle tightened his grip on Tobas's shoulder and redirected his focus back to his obligation. A distracted Tobas, temporarily unable to sort out his thoughts, followed his uncle in a stupor toward the door. Anndra's foot grazed Tobas's ear as he fluttered and swooshed over the heads of the other myth, his father's pending departure sending him to new heights of unbridled excitement.

"The nambor is this way, Da!" Anndra encouraged him, oblivious to his father's mounting dread. Her husband's bravery brought a lump of pride to Sarla's throat, and she reached around Willa's shoulder, pulling her daughter close to her as she fell in line behind Tobas and Anndra and followed them through the open front door. Banth, Yarn, and Meeks took up the rear. As they left the director's office, Meeks gave a passing glance to the door, which usually took the strength of two to open and close. Deciding to forgo protocol just this once, he left it agape in order to keep his place in the group.

As the procession advanced down the worn path, their numbers increased as other myth from the village joined the parade. The marching crowd spoke in hushed tones punctuated with frequent shouts of encouragement declaring Tobas's bravery and unselfishness. These proclamations shamed Tobas into dropping his gaze as he was propelled by the growing entourage down the path and toward the meadow, which was home to the venerable pair of gooseberry trees. Time raced by as did the thoughts in Tobas's head, and the shock at the sight of the path ending, and the field near Yarn's house beginning, brought the frightened myth to an abrupt halt. Allowing himself to look up for the first time since leaving the town center, he saw the familiar fence encircling his uncle's fields and growing herd of quagga. Encouraged by Yarn's grasp under his elbow, he joined his uncle in flight and the two of them glided over the enclosure in unison, touching down softly amongst the Shannon blossoms and abundant flower-freckled moss. The rest of the procession followed suit, one by one and in pairs, they all fluttered over the rails and continued their trek behind their heroic fellow myth. As Tobas and Yarn arrived at the crest of the hill, which allowed the first glimpse of the glen below and the portal, they saw Andee lying in dance-induced exhaustion at the base of the largest of the stones. Even the sight of the approaching crowd was not enough to will strength into the fatigued limbs of the smelly grogoch, and a barely perceptible lifting of his heavy head was the only acknowledgement that the assembly received from him.

The parade of myth descended the flower-strewn slope and stopped a respectful distance behind Tobas and Yarn, as the two seemed engaged in a private conversation.

"Remember now, Tobas, as soon as you arrive, use the marking stakes. We cannot know what to expect on the other side, and you must be able to find the portal back." Yarn gave a quick glance in the direction of Sarla and the *bairns*, but resumed his conversation with his nephew before Tobas had a chance to do the same.

"Yes?" Yarn asked in a commanding tone in order to keep the young myth focused.

"I will, 'tis the first thing that I will do," Tobas replied, trying fruitlessly to keep his mind focused and clear. His gaze was fixed upon the hovering orb.

"Oh, and another thing," Yarn continued. "'Tis said that they can *smell* fear, so whatever happens, do not appear frightened. It may try to use that to its advantage."

Tobas's surprise at his uncle's choice of last minute counsel was enough to break his concentration as he turned and looked blankly at the older myth.

"'Tis ... good to know, yes ... thank you," was all he could manage to sputter out.

Tobas's choked reply and blank expression clued Yarn to the fact that perhaps that little tidbit of information could have been left out of what might well be their last talk together. A wince and a pat on Tobas's back was Yarn's way of saying that he was sorry. Tobas turned and looked at Willa, Anndra, and Sarla. The apprehensive myth tried to force the lump down his dry throat before taking to the air and flying over to where his little family valiantly stood. He first kissed Willa and then Anndra and lastly Sarla. As he drew his hand down her velvety cheek, he looked intently at her, committing to memory her large, pale brown eyes, her delicate nose that dimpled in on both sides just above her nostrils, and her hair. Sarla's hair smelled perpetually of sweet flowers and fresh dew. As his hand fell down her cheek, he grasped a delicate tendril of her hair and passed it under his nose, closing his eyes as he breathed in deeply his favorite smell. He kissed her again. Tobas gave his wife a wink and a smile, and then turned slowly around to face the hanging, radiating ball of light. From here, the young myth proceeded toward the gooseberry trees alone, leaving his family, clan and home behind on the crest. As he drew ever closer to the ancient gateway, he became overwhelmed with a dreadful sense that not knowing was far worse than knowing.

On the wings of this newfound gleaning, Tobas took to the air, took a deep breath, and without hesitation, flew straight between the trees and into the blue and green orb. As the sphere absorbed Tobas, so did the trees seem to absorb the sphere. As soon as the myth disappeared into the aquamarine globe, it compressed and formed a horizontal line of light reaching from one tree to the other. The string of light stretched, growing thinner and thinner, until it snapped in two. The unfettered illuminations slammed forcefully into each tree and then ascended the gooseberries in an upward, spiraling pattern, emitting a crackling, buzzing sound as they whipped around the trunk and over and under the branches. In seconds, the charged streaks of light reached the peaks of the trees. Without being able to climb higher, they changed course and raced outward, illuminating every branch and twig of the uppermost portions of the ancient timbers. Their course changed, but their speed undiminished, the vivid aquamarine streaks tore through the branches causing some of the smaller limbs to burst into flames and the leaves to launch into the air before falling, smoldering, to the ground. When the light ran out of tree, it crashed into the open air with a deafening bang that shook the ground and sent hundreds of pairs of myth hands flying upward to protect their assaulted ears.

As they became aware that the light was gone, the gathered myth slowly lowered their hands and gazed in disbelief at the singed gooseberry trees. With trepidation, they collectively approached the markers, Banth foremost of the group. He reached out and touched the bark of the tree to his right, pulling his hand back quickly when he felt its blistering heat. The rest of the group stood still, allowing Banth to do the investigating. The snap of an incinerated twig under the weight of Banth's foot was what finally stirred Andee from his slumber.

With agility not usually associated with a creature of his bulk, the grogoch leapt to his feet, and immediately assumed a defensive crouch as he surveyed his surroundings and tried to bring himself up to speed on what had transpired during his unscheduled nap. The crowd stood in anxious silence as Banth gingerly stepped toward the gap between the timbers as still smoldering leaves floated to the ground, leaving fine trails of smoke in their wakes. Banth waved his hands in front of himself, groping the empty air. Finding no obstacles, he continued his slow patrol until he found himself on the other side of the portal. Emboldened by the fact that no harm had yet come to Banth, Andee slowly approached the scorched trees to have a look for himself. However, within feet of the portal, the grogoch let out a shrill yelp and then quickly returned to the safety of the stones, rubbing his ears while emitting a low, sorrowful moan. Turning around to face his fellow myth, who were still following his progress with concern and now eyeing Andee with bewilderment, Banth shook his head from side to side indicating that he saw nothing. He immediately sought out Sarla and found her looking courageously back at him, still clutching Willa to her side, with Anndra hovering quietly over her shoulder.

CHAPTER 10

CLAIRE AWOKE TO the sound of her sister's harried voice.

"Daddy, stop!" were the words the sleepy girl heard as she sat up in bed.

"Come on, Daddy, it's late. Come back inside."

Claire untangled herself from the twisted top sheet and crawled over to the window ledge, which was level with the top of her bed. Brushing back the thin white sheers, she searched the front yard of the old farmhouse looking for her sister. The moon was nearly full, and she could make out the objects in the driveway and front yard: the old Ford pickup, her swing set, the abandoned Craftsman boat the family practically lived in during the summer months before they moved to the farm. Claire could see everything except what she needed to—Colleen. She felt along the sides of the bottom of the window screen until she found the ancient, spring-loaded clasps that held the screen to its frame. She winced as the old aluminum clasps dug into her fingers, resisting her efforts to slide them in their dry, rust-encrusted slots.

The right one gave first, so she used both hands to loosen the left. It met her only halfway, but with a little jostling she was able to lift the screen high enough to allow her to crawl out onto the tin-covered roof, which sheltered the front porch. The palms of her hands and the soles of her feet had grown sweaty in her mounting panic, the beads of moisture acting like glue as she walked to the roof's side, grabbing hold of the corner downspout for support. When she reached the roof's west-facing edge, she stopped and scanned the yard. She could see everything else from this vantage point: the chicken coop, stable, tobacco barn and tractor shed. She could even see part of the "big pond" when the trees swayed just right and the moon peered out from behind the clouds.

That's when she heard it. It took a moment to recognize the sound that, had the sun been in the sky instead of the moon, she would have known instantly. It was the surreal component of the situation that kept her from recognizing *this* noise at *this* time of day. As the odd, but completely familiar noise grew louder, it hit her with a jolt and she knew exactly what was going on. Her father was on another midnight tractor ride and Colleen was trying in vain to stop him. The drone of the tractor's diesel engine completely suffocated Colleen's voice. Her sister had come around from the side of the tractor shed and was now standing in the side yard, shouting and waving her arms at their father as he steered the vintage red machine up the path leading to the driveway. To anyone not knowing better, it looked as if Colleen was cheering her father on in a one-man parade. Judging from the effect of her efforts to stop him, she might as well have been. He toasted Colleen with a half-empty bottle of gin as he took the final turn that led to the straight of the driveway, which in turn led to the fire trail. The fire trail was a seldom maintained, county-owned dirt path that allowed the fire department access to extremely rural areas.

If the tractor took a left, their father would be about an eighth of a mile from a graveled, state-maintained road. However, if he took a right— which he did—he had about eleven miles of moonlit dirt road, which was six miles of road too much for his gas supply and about nine for his gin. As the inebriated driver turned the massive black wheel to the right, he gave out a whoop and hoisted the gin bottle again for good measure.

Claire sat on the roof's edge, tucking her knees under her white cotton pajama gown. She cradled her legs in her arms as she watched her father drive out of sight, her sister, Colleen, standing at the top of the driveway, watching the retreating tractor carry her father into the moonlight.

CHAPTER 11

THE DAY WAS new, yet the temperature had already reached a blistering high, and the sun had started the day's baking of the grass and delicate flowers. The Japanese beetles were delighted with the heat, and crawled contentedly from grape leaf to grape leaf eating everything in their path. The bees were clover hopping, Monarchs were filling up on nectar from the blossoms on the butterfly bushes, and the chickens clucked contentedly as they wandered the yard, snatching up ants and spiders and anything else crawling along too slowly for its own good. The quiet was disturbed by an infrequent moo from a distant cow, and the chirping of crickets both near and far. Otherwise, it was so calm and peaceful that you could hear the metal roof of the old farmhouse searing under the sweltering summer sun.

The house itself had been built in several stages and over several decades. Judging from the absence of any right angles and the undulating walls, it had been constructed by its first inhabitants, farmers, who, no doubt, were more skilled with plows and cows than they were with hammers and nails. When Liam O'Brian saw the old homestead for the first time, he did not see uneven wall joints or lopsided stairs; he saw the perfect place to semi-retire and finish raising his family of five girls. Out here, in the middle of practically nowhere, there was plenty of fresh air, tiring work, and very few of the distractions found in larger towns. The two oldest were already married and starting families of their own, but he still had three to go, and the old farm was the just the place for his dwindling family.

In addition to the main house, the property was speckled with various and sundry buildings, all erected with the same exacting standards as the house itself: uneven and unlevel, but built to last. There was a stable, chicken coop, pigsty, tractor barn and a tobacco barn. According to the locals, it was once a thriving tobacco farm, but a long period of drought twenty years before had forced the owners to abandon their homestead. It had stood vacant ever since, accumulating a debt of back property taxes that greatly diminished its attractiveness to potential buyers.

However, to Liam, the farm was heaven on earth. Striking a deal with the county allowing him to pay off the property's debt for pennies on the dollar, he assumed ownership of the two-hundred-plus acres. A farmer himself at heart, he saw it as a blank canvas with soil well rested and ready to flourish again. Retired from his job as an engineer for a city planning commission up north, he started a small land surveying business in the nearest town. The two men whom he had hired to help him pretty much took care of the day-to-day operations, which left the bulk of his schedule open to indulge in his dream of being a full-time farmer. Since his farming interests were broad and many—ranging from vintage roses to organically-raised cattle—he had trouble deciding on one plan of endeavor. But he was as content to pursue all of his interests seemingly at once and promised himself that he would eventually choose and concentrate on only one of them.

Fifty feet to the north-facing side of the farmhouse, in the reclaimed old fruit orchard, the youngest of Liam's five daughters meandered through the grape arbor with its twisted vines heavy with grapes and leaves. She looked just like her parents and every one of her four sisters. She had her mother's wavy brown hair and good English skin, and her father's hazel green eyes. Being born to a woman who stopped growing at four-feet and nine inches could not be overcome by a six-feet-tall father, and by the age of eleven, Claire was only three inches shy of reaching her eventual adult height.

As the young girl made her way under and around the contorted, knotted vines of the arbor, she thought about her dream from the night before. It was a recurring dream and it invaded her sleep on an average of twice a week. It never deviated from the original script and precisely summoned every vivid detail of that night, from the eyelet stitching on her sister's cotton pajamas, to the feel of the timeworn tin under her feet as she witnessed the surreal moonlit proceedings from her second-story post. She had all but forgotten about that night until the first dream presented itself about six months before, making its debut on the night of Colleen's wedding. It was the first time that she had gone to sleep under a roof that she no longer shared with any of her sisters. At first, the dreams made her anxious, but now she found them oddly comforting.

A raucous moo from one of the neighbor's wayward cows that brought Claire back to her daylight reality and the chore that she had been half-heartedly attending. In the little girl's left hand, she held an open canning jar containing about three inches of water. With her right hand, she was gently brushing mounds of bright-green, leaf-eating Japanese beetles into the glass vessel. Claire felt bad for the beetles, but her father said if she did not shoo them off the grapes and peaches, there would not be any grapes or peaches left for them. Besides, it was a good source of protein for the chickens, which meant better eggs. Still feeling bad for the bugs, but not feeling the need to question her father, she kept flicking the beetles into the jar until the volume of beetles was threatening to exceed the volume of water. Clasping her hand over the mouth of the Mason jar, she gave it a shake to make sure all the beetles had a swim and then made her way out of the orchard, heading for the chicken yard. Seeing the little girl coming, the chickens started collectively making their way toward her, clucking excitedly.

At the front of the pack was Tarzan, the more dominant of their two roosters. Although always first in line, he was usually the last to eat, as he seemed more concerned with keeping the hens close together and accounted for than with nourishment. After one more shake of the Mason jar, Claire cast the beetles in a half-moon pattern in front of the hungry Rhode Island Reds. Being too wet to fly, the beetles lay on the ground, ignorant of their fate as the day's breakfast special. With a keen red eye always on the lookout for strays, Tarzan clucked menacingly, herding the hens as they voraciously gobbled up the writhing wet beetles. Watching the grateful chickens peck up the shiny green delicacies gave Claire another pang of guilt, but trying her best to ignore it, she turned and walked back toward the orchard.

Hearing the rusty squeak of the back screened door, she looked up to see her father coming down the back porch steps, the aroma of his doubly strong cup of instant coffee wafting behind him.

"That a girl," he said, patting her on the head as he walked by.

"We'll have the biggest peaches and the fattest chickens in the county, thanks to you!" he shouted back to her as he made his way to the tractor barn. Claire watched her father until he disappeared behind the shed. That would probably be the last that she saw of him until dinnertime.

She walked over to the back porch and knelt down by the spigot protruding from the side of the house and refilled the now empty jar. With her eyes cast to the ground—as they usually were—she was making her way back to the orchard when she saw one. She bent down and brushed at a clump of clover, one of thousands threatening to overtake the grass in the yard surrounding the house. After carefully parting the cluster, she broke the stem of the one that had caught her attention, bringing it closer to her face for a better look. There, hiding under one of the petals, was a tiny little fourth petal, undetectable to most human eyes, but to Claire, it stood out like a sore thumb. Gazing back down, she saw another, and another. She set the glass jar on the ground, carefully choose an area that contained only the three-leaf variety, and sat in the lush groundcover to look for more. Cathy and Colleen would roll their eyes at their little sister when she came into the house clutching handfuls of four, five, and even the occasional six-leaf clovers because it usually meant that clover picking had taken priority over chores. Claire would carefully splay the clovers out between the pages of the enormous dictionary that was kept on her father's bookshelf along with the *Encyclopedia Britannicas* and the *National Geographics*. She could tell when her sister found her clover stash because her name was shouted suddenly and with great irritation. "Claire!" Colleen would yell as she brushed the shriveled clovers away and tried in vain to read the green-tinted and moisture-warped pages underneath while trying to do her homework.

Wanting any excuse to escape her beetle drowning duties, she settled into the thick clover patch. Hearing the roar of the tractor's engine as it shifted gears and rambled toward the gate leading to the open pastures, she knew that her father wouldn't notice if she took a break from her chores for a little while. Picking the lucky charms with her right hand and collecting them carefully in her left, she thought about her sisters and how much she actually missed having them around. It got very lonely on the farm, especially during the long weeks of summer vacation from school—like now. During the warm months, her father was busier tending to the business of farming than he was to the business of an almost eleven-year-old girl.

However, by nature and necessity, she was resourceful, and had learned to entertain herself. Claire's only outside source of distraction was her weekly riding lesson. Faithfully, every Sunday at noon, Claire's father would take time from his busy agriculture schedule to drive her to Hampden Stables. Situated right on the main road that led to town, the stable itself was an immense A-framed barn fitted with heavy swinging double doors on each end. The east-facing doors would be left agape on lesson days for the admittance of students. The west-facing doors led directly into an enclosed arena, where lessons took place when the weather would not allow outdoor training. It was in this stable that Mr. Linton kept his eight horses on whose backs lifetime love affairs began.

Claire always stood as patiently as possible while her father took a moment to talk to the trainer about nothing in particular. On most Sundays, he would have brought along a dozen or so eggs or tomatoes or peaches or corn, which the New England native would graciously accept on behalf of himself and his wife. The anxious, would-be equestrienne's forced façade of patience was betrayed by her quivering legs, the visible give-away that the smell of sawdust, leather and horse sweat had taken over her very sense of reason. Realizing that their conversation had gone on too long for her to take, her father would excuse himself with a handshake and leave her to her lessons. As she watched him climb into the old Ford pickup, she wondered if he brought her there every week because *she* loved it so much or for the free manure that Mr. Linton would allow Liam to haul away by the truckload whenever he wished. Though she never knew which reason it was, she decided that either was fine with her, as long as he kept bringing her.

Her father had promised her that once she had completed her lessons to Mr. Linton's satisfaction, he would buy her a horse of her own. Claire lived for the fulfillment of this promise and even stayed after class to help muck out stalls, feed, or tack-up for the next class—anything that she could do to help and learn. She kept the stable back on the farm clean and swept and ready, so that no notice would be needed for it to take in an occupant.

When she wasn't able to ride the real thing, she tied ropes around the base of the handlebars on her bike and pretended that they were reins as she "galloped" down the dusty fire trail or through the yard and farm buildings, down the slope toward the pond and across the dam. Her room was home to every conceivable piece of horse-related paraphernalia, and more nights than not, she fell asleep reading *Horse and Rider* or *Horse Fancy*. For Claire, there was no doubt that she was ready.

And so went her days and weeks. With only farm animals and her own imagination for company, she made up her own activities, and when she ran out of ideas, there was always housework to keep her busy.

Her life bore little resemblance to the way it was when they first moved down to the farm four years before. There were five of them then: Daddy, Cathy, Colleen, Claire and Herself. The two eldest sisters, Deirdre and Erin, had already married and started families of their own before the move. "Herself," as the girls came to call her, was their father's second wife. Being a widower, he saw his former secretary as the mother figure that his girls needed. The girls saw her as a money-grubbing imposter with absolutely no maternal instincts whatsoever. She sure was shocked when a year after the honeymoon, their father quit his high paying job, sold their five-bedroom house in an affluent suburb, and moved the family five hundred miles south to a three-bedroom farmhouse built before the Civil War. That was not what Herself had bargained for. Gone were the cocktail parties, the beach house, and the weekly manicures and beauty parlor visits. Now, the nearest town was thirty-some miles away, and it consisted of a gas station, a feed store, and a quick-mart, where you could get all the beef jerky and night crawlers you wanted, but you were out of luck if it was a manicure or perm that you were after.

It was more than Herself could take. One week and one day after moving down to the farm, she packed her bags and headed back north. The girls never saw or heard from her again. When her father sat Claire down to give her the news that her stepmom had left, Claire remembered thinking that she should be sad, but she wasn't. She was glad that Herself was gone and it was just them again. On the inside, she was bursting with gratitude and relief. On the outside, she feigned sadness and even managed to summon a few tears. This, she thought, would be the response that her father was expecting. She didn't want to hurt his feelings by showing him how happy she was. She didn't want him to know what a colossal mistake marrying that shrew had been.

Then it was back to the four of them, but not for long. Cathy finished her last year in the local high school, and then moved back up north to live with their father's sister while she attended university. Colleen met her future husband during her senior year of high school and shortly after graduation, they got married and she moved into an off-campus house where she was attending college. And then there were two, leaving just her and her father, and not much to do.

Like her sisters, Claire was a very smart girl. Unlike her sisters, Claire was not disciplined enough to apply herself to her studies with any consistency. She liked to learn new things, but the rigid environment of the private school that her father had sent her to was stifling. The teachers were, by most accounts, unapproachable, unsympathetic and unyieldingly southern. She did not learn about the Civil War, she learned about the War Between the States; Pocahontas was on the short list for sainthood; boys took shop class, girls took home economics, and if it didn't happen south of the Mason Dixon line, it wasn't worth knowing.

In most every class, while her physical self may have been behind the desk, her thoughts could not be farther away. For Claire, it took a lot more than an automaton in glasses lecturing menacingly in front of a classroom to persuade her mind to bend toward anything that did not have four legs and a mane. She liked art class, and English class was bearable, but the rest of the classes were a struggle for her to pay attention to. The fact that making friends seemed just as difficult for her as math and science only added to her overall disdain for the whole experience. Except for languages and art, Claire just was not interested in school, and on every report card, her teachers made the same observation: "Claire could do so much better if she just applied herself." Except for "As" and "Bs" in English and art, she was a solid "C" and sometimes "D" student. Every time she showed her father her report card, he would ask the same question:

"Are you trying, sweetheart?"

"Yes, Daddy," she would fib.

"As long as you're trying, honey, that's all I ask."

She always felt guilty as her father signed her report card, knowing that she wasn't telling him the truth.

Somewhere between the clover harvesting and daydreaming, the morning slipped by unnoticed, and the sound of their neighbor's tractor lumbering down the dirt road with a load of hay for his cows jostled Claire into action. She had not done anything productive yet, and if her dad came in from the fields and saw that all she had to show for her morning was a handful of clovers, he would be disappointed in her. Her father's disappointment was something that Claire made great effort to avoid. With her left hand full of four and five-leaf clovers, she brushed off her grass-covered knees with her right hand before picking up the Mason jar and heading for the back porch. As she pulled the screen door open, it emitted its signature creaking noise before slamming into the door jam and bouncing into place as she walked into the dark-cooled back porch. Racing across the old plank floor, the sight of the washer and dryer reminded her that she had meant to wash the bed linens that day. Claire stepped through the open door that led from the porch to the kitchen where she carefully laid her bounty of clovers on the counter.

She took the Mason jar to the sink and filled it from the tap. Claire returned to her precious pile of lucky clovers and just as carefully as she placed them on the counter, she picked them up and put them in the water-filled jar. That done, she raced out of the kitchen, through the dining room and then the living room before rounding the corner that led to the front hall and the stairs. She sprinted up the crooked and worn flight of stairs, her legs just long enough now to take the steps two at a time.

The first bedroom at the top of the stairs was her father's room. He slept in a twin bed that was one-half of a matching pair that was in the room before Herself left. Claire remembered her father's bed looking a lot bigger when they first moved down there. That was before Liam ripped the headboard and footboard from the frame, dragged them down the stairs, through the hall and out the front door where he tossed them onto a raging bonfire of logs, saplings, and the other twin bed. So now, the single bed was headless as well as footless. Her father said that he liked it better this way, and that it reminded him of an army cot, and that an old farmhouse was no place for a highbrow headboard anyway.

She yanked the thin, summer-weight bedcover from the foot of the bed where it was pooled and unwanted. She pulled and tugged at the sheets, which, at first, were unwilling to forfeit their hospital-corner anchors. His pillows were flat and hard—stained with gin sweat and cigarettes, their threadbare cases not faring much better. In less than a minute, she had the linens in a pile in the doorway. Claire lifted the bundle and carried it over to the stairs where she tossed them over the railing and watched them glide softy down before landing at the foot of the staircase.

Proceeding to the end of the hall, she opened the door to her room, and stripped her own bed. Bundling the dirty linens into a ball along with clothes from the floor and some socks that had somehow managed to find their way into the clothes hamper, she bunched them in her arms and hand-carried them. Socks could not be trusted to land in a pile once tossed down the stairs. Laying one of the dirty sheets out flat as if getting ready for a picnic, she piled all the laundry into the center and pulling the corners together, making an enormous satchel, she slung the whole lot over her shoulder and carried it to the back porch Santa-style.

Claire loaded the washing machine, poured in the powdered detergent and set the cycle on "normal" wash. Closing the lid with a familiar metallic thud, she could now take care of more important matters. She left the porch and walked through the dining room and into the family room, heading straight for the bookcase. She got up on the arm of her father's favorite chair and reached for the dictionary, which was hanging off the shelf just enough for her to get her hands on it. Claire lowered the heavy book slowly. Keeping the hardcover reference book tightly closed, she carried it to the kitchen. Every page from "A" through "K" was covered in lovingly preserved, dried clovers. Pressing her thumb on the black tab marked "L," she slowly opened the front half of the dictionary. Claire took a pair of scissors from the drawer and pressed each clover face down on the page, snipping off the stem just at the base. The process continued until all the clovers were in between the open pages. She closed the book carefully and carried it back to the family room where she put it back on its shelf.

Since her dad had only had coffee for breakfast, she knew that he would be riding up on the tractor any minute now, famished from a morning's mowing on no more than some caffeine and sugar. Looking through the cupboards for ideas, she decided on pancakes with corn in, bacon and fried eggs. Breakfast was always her favorite dinner. She had plugged in the electric griddle for the bacon, and was cracking eggs into the bowl of pancake mix when she heard the familiar roar of the tractor's engine, chugging its way up the hill from the big pond. Ten minutes later, as she was giving the bacon a flip, she heard the back screen door creak open, then slam shut, and her father's heavy work boots scuffing across the wood floor of the back porch. Seconds later, the door frame between the kitchen and the porch was filled with her dust covered father. "Boy, what a scorcher!" he declared, as he dropped his dirty hat on the floor in the corner and strode over to the sink. He filled a glass from the dish rack with water, drained its contents, and then rested the glass upside down on the lip of the sink.

"What's cookin'?" he asked, in a tone unreflective of his state of physical fatigue.

"Corn fritters, bacon and eggs," Claire replied.

"Excellent choice. Do I have time for a quick shower first?"

"Sure," she answered.

"Make that three eggs for me, I'm starved," he shouted from the family room as he made his way to the stairs.

Their eating habits had changed rather drastically since their move to the farm. Whereas before they would eat a breakfast in the morning, a lunch around noon, and dinner in the evening when her father came home from the office, the schedule was different now. Liam, with few exceptions, skipped breakfast in favor of an enormous cup of coffee, usually finished on the tractor en route to one of the fields. The noon meal, or "dinner" as it was called in the south, was the largest meal of the day, with the evening "supper" usually being more of a snack really.

Claire reached into the old Frigidaire, and took five eggs from a basket. The eggs were from the Rhode Island Red hens that roamed the farm, and they were enormous. The shells varied in shade from dusty rose to deep burnt sienna, but on the inside they were invariably the same: two bright orange-yellow yolks swimming in masses of clear albumen. All the food that came from her father's garden was bigger, darker, and more intensely flavored than anything she remembered eating before. The fruits and vegetables were gigantic and wonderful. Claire remembered when she and her sister, Colleen, would walk up the dirt fire route that led to the farmhouse, looking forward to an after-school snack of tomato sandwiches. Claire always made three sandwiches for them to share because one was not enough and two was too many. Claire missed her sister.

She heard the pipes moan in protest as her father turned on the upstairs shower and thought for a split second about how probably none of the kids in her class were fixing dinner for their dads; they all had moms to do it. Just as quickly as she had this thought, she realized that she wouldn't trade places with any of them if that meant bringing Herself back. Forcing the thoughts out of her head for fear that thinking about it might somehow make it come true, she returned her attention to the griddle of bacon. Hearing the pipes sigh with relief that the shower had been shut off, she cracked the eggs into the sizzling butter dancing on the bottom of the frying pan and went to the back porch to transfer the clean sheets to the dryer—a welcome remnant from their life up north. She transferred the linens, pressed the "start" button, and went back to the kitchen just in time to give the eggs a gentle flip. She had just finished putting the third egg on her father's plate, which was already crowded with pancakes and bacon when her dad came into the kitchen.

"What'll you have to drink?" he asked as he reached into the fridge for the orange juice carton. Without waiting for a response, her father poured two glasses of the bright orange liquid. Liam placed Claire's glass above her plate, and after taking a huge gulp out of his, placed his half-empty glass above his own.

"This looks good," he said as he pulled his chair out from the table.

Claire passed the maple syrup to her dad, and he drenched his stack of cakes with syrup as he devoured his second piece of bacon.

Liam Marwood O'Brian was a private person. Claire loved her father and she was sure that he loved her, but they were not close. They were simply father and daughter—genetically connected, but emotionally detached. Since her mother's death, it seemed to Claire that her father approached their children's rearing more as a sense of duty, and his love was not always a demonstrative one, as she remembered it being before. He had given his daughters everything they needed and sometimes even what they wanted. The giving of material things was sometimes easier for him than the giving of emotional access. Subsequently, Claire and her father did not talk about anything but that which was necessary to discuss. This fact, coupled with her father's ravenous appetite, made for a quiet meal.

Claire finished her dinner at about the same time as her father was dragging his last wedge of corn-laced pancake through the syrup and egg yolk soup pooled on his plate. Leaning back in his chair, he polished off the last of his juice, gave the empty glass an exaggerated thump on the table, and declared that to be the best dinner he had had all day.

"Listen, I promised Old Man Campbell that I'd come by today and have a look at what's ruining his tomatoes. Leave these dishes. I'll do them when I get back."

"I'll get the dishes, Daddy, there aren't that many" she replied.

"I insist. You cooked, I'll clean. I mean it, Claire."

"Okay," she gave in.

Grabbing the hat that he had thrown on the floor when he came in from the barn, he headed for the back porch door, knowing full well that the dishes would be done before he got back.

Claire cleaned up the dinner dishes, put the freshly laundered sheets back on their respective beds and gathered the dirty clothes from her father's room, carrying them to the back porch to be done in the morning. She went back upstairs to her dad's room, lugging the vacuum, a rag and some furniture polish with her. She found that if she spent ten or fifteen minutes in one room a day, she could pretty much keep the house clean without having to do it all at one time, thus cutting in to her time spent outside.

The house was never as clean as it had been when Colleen still lived there, but Claire didn't feel at all guilty about it. When her older sister came over, she usually spent the first few hours of her visit bridging the gap between her idea of clean and Claire's. Claire figured that she would rather receive a couple of looks of disapproval from her big sister when she was there than spend more time cleaning when she wasn't. After emptying her father's ashtray, she tidied up his dresser and gave the wood surfaces a polishing. Claire then chased the Hoover over the carpeting. Tomorrow she would "clean" her room.

By the time her dad came back from Old Man Campbell's farm, Claire had watched a little television, had eaten a peanut butter and jelly sandwich, taken a shower, painted her toenails, finished the last chapter of the book that she was reading, and had just turned the television back on when she heard her dad's pickup kicking up the gravel in the driveway. She pulled back the living room curtain in time to see the last rays of the day's sun bathe the front yard in a serene orangey glow. As usual, it had taken quite a bit of studying—not to mention quite a few cold beers—to figure out what was plaguing their neighbor's tomatoes. Claire was looking out the window to gauge by her father's parking job just how much "studying" they had done.

A few minutes later Claire heard the unmistakable squeak of the back door porch followed by the rhythmic thud of her father's heavy boots on the old plank floor. This was followed by another familiar sound: the clink of ice falling into a highball glass and the spritz of a freshly-opened bottle of seltzer water. With drink in hand, he made his way through the dining room and into the family room to settle into his Lazy Boy and turn on the evening news, which was his customary way of ending the day. The sound of the ice hitting the glass had been her cue to collect her things and head upstairs so that her father could have the room and the TV to himself. As Liam O'Brian entered the family room, his daughter had already uncurled herself off the couch, gathered her book, nail file, polish, and empty soda glass. She was almost to the doorway leading to the dining room when her father entered the room.

"How are Mr. Campbell's tomatoes?" she asked as he was crossing the threshold.

"His what? Oh yeah, his tomatoes. Well, the bugs think they're delicious," he joked as he made his way toward his favorite chair. He attempted to set his highball glass down on the coaster at the edge of the end table. He succeeded on his third try. Claire knew that it was time to leave her father to his television and cocktails, so she politely excused herself.

"You know what, Daddy, I'm really tired. I'm going to turn in." Claire said, politely reciting her well-worn self-dismissal speech.

"Okay, daughter, good-night," was all he said in response, his eyes never leaving the television screen.

She walked into the kitchen, placed her glass into the sink and left, turning the light off behind her. As she walked through the family room on her way to the stairs, she told her father "Good night" and gave him a kiss on his crew-cut exposed, sunburned forehead.

"Good night, daughter. Sleep tight, don't let the bed bugs bite," came his well-worn reply.

Claire walked up the old crooked stairs to her bedroom at the end of the hall.

Hers was the smallest of the three bedrooms in the house. She could have moved into one of the larger rooms vacated by her sisters, but none of them were the same color, and she loved the color of her room—cherry Pez pink. The floor was the original wide, hardwood boards that were used throughout the old house. The curtains on the room's one window were white and sheer, and because they were too long, they pooled in white half-moon-shaped puddles on the floor. The furniture was mismatched: her father's large, square cedar armoire, a brown end table, a cream-colored dresser with gold decorative trim and a white four-poster bed. On the book shelves at the foot of her bed, along with the books about horses, were statues of horses, postcards of horses, and snow globes with tiny horses inside. The only non-equine objects on the shelf were a cheap, dime-store statue of the Virgin Mary—she had no idea how she had come to have it— and a framed three-by-five photograph of her mother and eldest sister, Deirdre, as they boarded the QE1 to join Liam in America. The war had ended and Deirdre was only a few months old when she and their mom left England. Claire's mother cradled her eldest sister in her arms, as the only photo that Claire had of her mother was taken moments before she embarked for the states.

On the ceiling of her room were horse posters with just enough space between to mark where one ended and the next began. The reason that there were horse posters on her ceiling was that she had already used all the available space on her walls. Looking around her room at the hundreds of horses that adorned it gave her a sudden and animated sense of exhilaration. Her birthday was coming up; the day after next, in fact. 'A horse would make a wonderful present for her eleventh birthday, she thought to herself.' She knew that she was ready, but did her father think that she was? That was the question. Claire knew better than to try to plead her case to him. The decision was solely his, and it would be based on Mr. Linton's critique of her capabilities, not her own.

Climbing into bed and sliding herself in between the nice clean sheets, she stared at the horses on her ceiling, and let the images mesmerize her until she could keep her eyes open no longer. So it was with thoughts of riding a horse of her very own around the big pond, over the gate, and through the fields of the big pasture galloping through her mind, that she dozed off to sleep.

Claire woke slowly as the familiar sound of the tractor's diesel engine shoved and bullied its way into her ears. As she forced her sleep-clogged eyes open, she was confused by the darkness that enveloped her. Clumsily untangling herself from the blankets and sheets, she reached for the alarm clock on her nightstand. Leaning over the edge of her bed, she angled the clock's face against the moonlight streaming through her open window and gave her eyes another wipe as she tried to make out the position of the clock's hands. The long hand was almost on the four and the little hand looked to be squarely on the three.

"Dad-dee," she whispered to herself. Claire set the clock back on the small table before crawling back to the edge of her bed where she wrestled the window screen open. She was just in time to see the tractor ramble into view and set its path for the moonlight soaked driveway. When her father started bellowing out the chorus of "The Ziegfried Line," she knew that the gin was driving and her father was merely along for the ride. She pulled the top sheet around her shoulders and sat crossed-legged on the mattress edge. As she watched the tractor slowly churn up the gravel drive, she hummed along to her father's off-key tune.

> "We'll hang out all the washing on the Ziegfried line,
> have you any dirty washing, Mother dear?
> We'll hang out all the washing on the Ziegfried line,
> if the Ziegfried line's still there."

Claire knew from her father's recording of the song that the last line of the chorus was "Cause the washing day is here," but her father preferred his version of it, and frankly so did she. So it was his version of the old war song that she hummed and sang along to as Liam made a much practiced right turn from the driveway and onto the county fire trail. She sang along long after her father's voice had faded and until she could no longer hear the loud diesel engine of the old red tractor.

***

Tarzan's crow had grown loud enough by now so that it had broken through Claire's subconscious and she was being dragged—for the second time in only a few hours—into consciousness. Along with the rooster's crow, she could hear the tractor engine's roar.

'I wonder if he's heading out or just getting back', she thought to herself. Either way, she knew that he would not be in a very good mood until he had downed several cups of strong coffee along with just as many antacids. Claire stretched her arms over her head as she looked out the large window next to her bed. The white curtains lay motionless against the wall and the air had that clammy heaviness to it that told her it was going to be another humid, hot summer day. She sat up, and doubling herself over, reached for the shelf that extended over the foot of her bed. Stretching her fingers as far as she could, she was able to grasp the corner of the cover of the latest copy of *Horse and Rider*, which she had carelessly thrown up there when changing her sheets the day before. She let herself fall back onto the mattress with a plop. As she thumbed through the magazine to the last article she had read, she kicked the sheets off of herself with her feet and decided to read until the sun came up high enough in the window to roast her out of bed.

CHAPTER 12

TOBAS TUMBLED AND somersaulted in the early morning air while frantically rubbing his eyes, eyes too sensitive for the bombardment of blazing light from the mid-summer Doog sun. Becoming dizzy from the twirling and tumbling, he reached blindly into his satchel and fumbled around until his frenzied hand found the stubs of gooseberry root. He plucked and pulled at the binding until at last they were freed. Allowing the cloth ribbon to cascade gracefully to the earth, he shoved one of the roots into his mouth, chewing frantically. After a few nauseatingly lightheaded moments, his equilibrium returned and he was able to right himself. Tobas resisted the urge to remove the bitter-tasting root from his mouth as he knew it would also help his body adjust to the extraordinary effects of Doog's gravitational pull.

Still chewing away, he returned his attention to his eyes, which still stung a bit, but no longer required massaging. Tobas cupped his hands around his eyebrows, creating partial blinders, and scanned his surroundings. As rapid blinking brought the moisture back to his assaulted eyes, he could make out a shape not too far from where he was hovering. Remembering Yarn's words, Tobas knew that the first thing he must do was get his bearings and mark exactly where he entered Doog's dimension, so that there would be no question as to how to leave it. He fumbled through the satchel's contents again, feeling around for the two wooden stakes to be used as guides to indicate his exit. As his eyesight returned, an oddly familiar shape was coming into focus. The clearer it became, the more confused Tobas became. As he was able to open his eyes more and more, the one shape turned into two shapes—two strangely familiar shapes. Becoming impatient with the progress of his ocular adjustment, Tobas winged his way toward the blurry objects, forcing his eyes open as wide as he could. Just a few yards along, he leaned backward and brought his forward flight to a full stop. In disbelief, he fluttered and stared at the now unambiguous objects—not believing what he saw. There, standing in front of him against the brilliant blue Earth sky, were a pair of gooseberry trees, identical to the ones that he had just flown through.

"What is ...? Where are ...?" he muttered to himself as he twisted about, looking left and then right and then left again.

'Am I still in E'lore?' he thought to himself as he dropped his eyes past the trees, searching for the faces of his wife and children. As soon as his survey shifted to the ground, he had his answer. He knew that he could not still be in E'lore, because swaying and brushing against the trunks of the trees like undulating waves was grass, tall, thick blades of lush green grass, glistening in the bright summer sun. There was no grass in E'lore. He immediately thought of his Uncle Yarn, who would occasionally accompany Tobas and the others on their trips to harvest four-petals. Yarn would pick one or two—just for show—and then he was off, breaking away from the rest of the gathering to stroll and flutter through the endless meadows of grass. Yarn told Tobas that in all of Doog, no grass was greener than it was in the land of Eire. Returning his attention to himself, Tobas understood that it did not matter how green the grass was here, what mattered was that there *was* grass. Of course, the blinding brilliance of the sun should have been a dead giveaway, but so desperate was Tobas to be done with this whole business that he was willing to believe anything, even the highly improbable, and even if only for a moment. Looking back at the pair of trees, Tobas was flooded with relief to know that his way home was so clearly and unmistakably labeled.

With his vision adjusted, he turned from the gooseberry trees and surveyed his surroundings. He was in the middle of an enormous field, which was actually composed of two gradually sloping hills joined by a deep ravine through which gurgled a clear, spring-fed stream. Bridging the two uplands to

his left was a long mounded dam, fenced in on the right before the steep
drop to the ravine and bordered on the left by a large pond rimmed with wild
honeysuckle and weeping willow trees. Tobas's balance had fully returned,
and the dizziness in his head and sickness in his stomach were gone. Turning
back around to make sure that the gooseberry trees were still there, he took
the root from his mouth. Realizing that he had lost track of the wrapping that
he had taken it from, he simply shoved the wet, sticky, chewed root and its
dry mate back into his satchel. Securing the bag's flap and giving the strap an
adjustment over his shoulder, he anxiously checked the portal marker again
before slowly and carefully winging his way toward the pond.

As Tobas adjusted to the new properties in the different dimension, he
was reminded of the first item on his *very* short list of things that he liked
about Doog. In E'lore, flying was extraordinarily taxing on the myth physically, so they preferred walking and flew only occasionally, and even then,
for very short distances. In Doog, however, the gravitational pull was significantly different from that in E'lore, and the myth found that they were
able to flit about at such high rates of speed that their movement was virtu-
ally undetectable by nambors. The more adjusted Tobas became, the faster
he could fly and soon he was able to put most of his anxiety at bay, taking
comfort in the fact that nothing in this dimension would be fast enough to
catch him. With his nervousness ebbing away, the myth began to take notice of his surroundings, not only as a means of earmarking the route back
to the portal, but in appreciation of the sheer physical beauty of Doog. The
colors in this dimension were, in most cases, separate and distinct from one
another. The clouds were brilliant-white against the deep-blue of the sky,
which was marked boldly against the bright-green of the grass or the leaves
of the trees atop dark-brown trunks. The colors in E'lore did not contradict
each other as much as they fused and blended into one another. In E'lore,
the sky turned a muted blue-green, where it met the land before segueing
into an emerald-green, which was the perpetual color of the moss that covered the ground. The trees, as well, borrowed the brilliant green of the moss
before the trunks and branches turned a solid sorrel, sepia, ochre or ginger,
depending on their variety. Tobas decided that both were beautiful, but that
ultimately, he would rather never leave E'lore, not for the harvestings and
certainly not for the task that he was set on now.

As Tobas cleared the fence running down the length of the dam, a vast area of stark white began peeking at him through the trees. Picking up his pace even more, he zigzagged his way across the dam and up a slight incline, which was a well-worn path between several barns and sheds. When Tobas cleared the last shed, the vast area of white grew into an enormous farmhouse. He stopped, suspending himself in mid-air with the imperceptible flapping of his wings. The house was nestled benevolently on a lush green lawn surrounded by bushes and beds of flowers so vigorous and abundant that they seemed to be conspiring to take over the old homestead. Tobas thought of how much Sarla would love to study these flowers and plants with their thick, plentiful blossoms of brilliant and varied colors. As soon as he thought of Sarla, he naturally thought of Willa and Anndra, as well. He rubbed his eyes and raked his fingers through his hair before intertwining them and bringing them to rest on the back of his neck. Giving his neck muscles a windershins stretch, he then rocked his head from side to side. Finally, he brought his hands down to his sides with a vigorous shake and thus exorcised his impish desires to head straight back to the pair of gooseberry trees. Seeking a higher altitude, he made a quick lap around the house itself. No nambors. Recognizing a farm when he saw one, it occurred to him that the bigger, stronger males would be out in the fields, plowing or harvesting.

That thought propelled him even higher, above the tree line. At this altitude, the glare of the sun and his diminutive size make him indistinguishable from small birds or large dragonflies. Feeling safe at this height, he made a rigorous survey of the area surrounding the big white farmhouse. Beyond the numerous outbuildings were lush green pastures separated by nature with stretches of woods and spring-fed creeks. The farm itself was practically hemmed in with a thick ringlet of trees, their sprawl stopping short of the left side of the driveway and picking up again on the right side. Had Tobas given them a moment's more of attention, he would have recognized them to be sacred rowan trees. But the myth was in search of nambors, and when he saw no signs of life other than grazing cows, he fluttered his way back to the old house.

"Where in E'lore is everyone?" he muttered to himself as he winged his way over the roof.

Seeking the shadier side of the house, he landed on the limb of an oak tree whose vast, sprawling branches cast a net of shady protection over the entire northeast side of the old dwelling. Tobas sat, rested, and contemplated. Having nothing upon which to formulate a plan, and feeling slightly peckish from all that flying, he half-heartedly pulled his packed lunch from his satchel. As he freed the meal from its bindings, the smell did more to make him homesick than to encourage his hunger. But with nothing else to do but wait, he bit into the fillet of roasted venison, and chasing it with a nibble from the loaf of *brisgein*, pondered pointlessly on how it had come to pass that *he* was sitting in this Doog tree so far from home. Tobas chewed and swallowed and fretted as the rare summer breezes, heavy with the smell of honeysuckle and freshly mown hay, washed over him on his oaken roost.

It was a scratchy, creaking noise followed by a loud bang that pulled Tobas's attention away from his meal and his worries. He sat motionless until he could determine where the noise had come from. On the other side of the house from where he was perched, he saw movement. A nambor. It was small, probably a nambor child, and wore coverings that allowed its legs and arms to stick out. It had white shoes on its small nambor feet. The human creature was walking away from him and toward one of the many buildings surrounding the house; in the crook of its left arm hung a basket. As it made its way across the yard, it suddenly stopped. Tobas held his breath. The nambor crouched down and picked up something from the grass.

'I did not see it drop anything', the myth thought.

As the nambor lifted the object closer to its face, it continued its stroll across the grass. Whatever it was that the nambor had dropped, Tobas saw it place it in the basket before reaching out and pulling on the gate to the fence of a small enclosure, in the back of which was a white shed with a ramp leading up to a latched door. Tobas saw the creature enter the outbuilding and disappear into the darkness within. A few moments later, the door to the shed flew open and out came a gaggle of fowl, some flying, some running, and all very excited to have been freed from the confines of their coop. From behind the curtain of squawking and cackling and flying feathers came the human child. She left the shed door open and walked the length of the chicken yard, the clucking hens following closely at her heels.

She opened the gate and stood to the side as her feathered charges clamored and stumbled over each other in their race to get to the lush green yard and the plethora of crunchy things they would find to eat there. Two roosters brought up the rear, their bright red eyes always on the lookout for danger and wayward hens.

When Tobas saw the front of the nambor for the first time, it confirmed what he had first suspected, and he breathed a sigh of relief. He could tell that she was a young female from her short stature and feminine features. While the little girl was inside the coop, Tobas grabbed his satchel and left the oak branch in favor of a closer look from amongst the blossoms of a butterfly bush growing just outside the back entranceway into the farmhouse. As the nambor came closer, Tobas recognized the brown, flecked, oblong shapes in the basket that was still hanging from her left arm. He watched her as she passed right under him and started up the rugged cement stairs leading to the back door. Just as her sneaker-covered left foot came down on the first step, she stopped. Looking down at the grass to her right, she walked a few paces before crouching down and again pulling something out from between the thick green blades.

'Again?' the puzzled myth asked himself.

Tobas tried to angle his view around the little girl to see what it was that she kept picking up, but before he could see, she had dropped it in the basket with the fat brown eggs and was again approaching the stairs. As her left foot came down on the first step again, she stopped. But this time, she was not looking down at the grass. The little girl instead turned and looked behind her, surveying the side yard to her left and then to her right. Tobas sat perfectly still as a tingle ran down his back, giving him a sudden chill despite the heat from the oppressive Doog sun. But with a puzzled look and a shrug of her shoulders, the girl turned back around. This time she climbed all three steps and entered the back porch, the screened wooden door slamming behind her.

Tobas exhaled and collected his wits. With no clue as to why he had been so unnerved by the girl's behavior, he left the butterfly bush blossom and was making his way back to the oak branch. He had not flown but a few feet when the screen door opened and out came the girl again, this time with an empty glass jar in her hand. As she came bounding down the stairs,

Tobas panicked and dropped down into the green groundcover blanketing the bottom of the flower bed, next to the house. Claire came around to the same flowerbed and reaching between the flox blossoms, turned the spigot knob, holding the Mason jar underneath the rusty faucet. She mopped her brow with the back of her wrist, smearing the perspiration across her forehead. Her hair lay flat against her head while the still dry ends curled and swooped in the humidity. Switching the jar into her other hand, she wiped at a single bead of moisture that was rolling down her forehead and making a beeline for her right eye.

"Why does it have to be so hot?" she mumbled to herself.

With the water level just right, she cranked the spigot closed, but did not remove her hand from the knob. She felt it again, but this time, she didn't look around; she didn't have to. This time, she knew. Someone was there. She was being watched.

Slowly, the little girl pulled her hand back from the spigot. She swirled the water in the jar while holding the glass up to the sun. Claire stalled as she pretended to inspect the humble jar's contents. Although she did not know how she sure that she was not alone, she did know that she was not afraid. What she felt was something that she somehow recognized, but could not quite put her finger on. She wasn't threatened; she was curious. She was excited. She decided to bluff.

"I can see you, you know," she whispered softly.

Claire unmistakably heard the tiniest little gasp of surprise before the diminutive man buried himself deeper into the English ivy that had overtaken the garden bed below the flox blossoms. A contented grin overtook her face as she continued to scrutinize the water in the Mason jar.

"Why are you watching me?" Claire asked softly, hoping to coax the spy out of hiding.

As she spoke, Claire did not move a muscle in the direction of the little creature, worried that any movements—sudden or slow—might frighten it off. At a snail's pace, she lowered herself to the ground and sat in the shaded grass. Claire folded her legs, right over left, and tucked the Mason jar into the ground with a twist.

Extending her left arm, she leaned on her hand and let her right hand casually brush the grass and clover. Undeniably, the presence of this obviously displaced creature was completely out of the realm of "normal" by most definitions. With no evident sense of how or why, Claire knew that the fact that she had perceived, and was talking to this being, was perfectly natural and somehow normal in the definition of the world as it applied to *her*. She sat perfectly still, stroking the blades of grass, hoping to coax whatever it was out of its obvious trepidation. Just as her left hand was falling asleep, her patience was rewarded with a rustle in the ivy and the emergence of the miniature man. Raising her head ever so slightly, she looked right at him and said softly, "Hi."

"Oh!" was all that the little creature managed to say before dropping back into the ivy.

"You can see me?" Tobas asked warily.

"Of course I can see you. Why? Are you supposed to be invisible or something?" she asked jokingly.

Tobas felt ridiculous telling her that "yes," he was supposed to be invisible—to *her*—when he was so obviously not, so he elected not to answer.

"Come on out. I'm not going to hurt you," Claire offered him, sensing his panic.

"I'm not afraid of you, nambor!" he replied from the safety of the thick English ivy, with as much bravado as he could muster, grateful that his fellow myth could not see how anxious a mere female was making him.

"Then why are you hiding—wait ... what did you call me?" Claire queried.

"My name is Claire, not 'nam ...' whatever you said."

"Nambor. 'Tis not your name, 'tis what you are," he answered, slowly peering above a three-pronged leaf.

"Well if I'm a 'nam ...'"

"Nambor," the faerie repeated.

"... A nambor, what are you?" Claire asked.

"A myth, of course."

"A *myth*? Do you have a name?"

"Of course I have a name!" Tobas shouted indignantly.

"There's no need to be rude!" Claire felt a bit frustrated that her efforts to make friends were going unnoticed.

Her response made Tobas chuckle.

"What do you care? As if manners matter to you," he implied.

"Well of course they do! Why would you think such a thing?" Claire protested.

"Settle down there. I am not looking for trouble from you," the myth said as he took a few steps back.

"What *are* you looking for then?" she asked.

"Well, certainly not you!" came the nervous and hasty response.

Claire studied her garden guest more closely. Suddenly she gasped.

"Are those … wings?" she asked breathlessly as she leaned in to get a better look.

"Oh, my gosh, those *are* wings! You're a faerie, aren't you?"

Claire's mounting excitement, coupled with the fact that she was now literally on all fours and crawling toward Tobas was too much for the apprehensive myth, and he took to the air. Judging the uppermost branches of the nearby butterfly bush to be out of her earthbound grasp, he lit on the shrub's topmost blossom.

"You can fly!" Claire was beside herself.

"Of course I can fly, you silly nambor," Tobas rudely responded.

Tobas's blunt retort was wasted on the excited child, as she shielded her eyes from the blazing sun in an effort to keep the winged creature in her sights.

"I really cannot waste any more time on you, little one. Tell me, where are the others?"

"What others?" she asked.

Tobas gave her an exasperated roll of his eyes before responding. "The other nambors! I am looking for the bigger ones! The males, where are *they?*"

"I have no idea what you're talking about," she answered absently as she continued her awed scrutiny of her winged visitor.

Claire was now on her feet, and with eyes still shielded, was circling the butterfly bush, clusters of fragrant purple flowers cascading to the ground as she brushed against the laden branches.

"My mother used to tell me stories about you!"

"About *me?*"

"No," she answered and giggled, "about faeries."

"To tell you the truth, I never actually believed those stories, but she wasn't making it up, was she? There really are faeries. Where did you come from? Are there any more …?"

Tobas cut her off.

"I do not have time for this!" he shouted angrily.

"My mother said that there were four days in the year that you could be sure to see them … if you were in the right place, that is. Otherwise, you just had to get lucky …"

"Look here, I do not want to hear stories about your mother … I need to know where the other …"

"… February 1st, May 1st, August 1st and, of course Halloween were the best," Claire continued, ignoring his admonishment.

Tobas's fear, frustration, and overall anxiety had finally gotten the better of him and his judgment. In a flash, he was off his perch and in Claire's face.

"I said no more stories about your mother's … stories! Where are the others?"

Even though he was a being distinctly different from her, Claire knew aggression when it was inches from her face, and she instinctively went on the defense.

"What are you talking about? What 'others'?"

"Do not play tricks with me, nambor."

Tobas's fear-generated anger and rudeness had hurt Claire's feelings. Supernatural being or not, she was not going to tolerate his disrespect any longer. His behavior had changed him in her eyes from an object of fascination to one of disdain. His offensive behavior overshadowed his very marvel, and whereas before she wanted to get closer to him, she now wanted nothing more than to get as far away as possible.

Sensing now that this creature had perhaps not come in peace, she had no intention of revealing to him her father's whereabouts, even though her disclosure of his location would have to be a vague and general "somewhere around here." Having made this decision, she finally answered him.

"I have no idea what 'others' you are referring to, but there's no one here but me ... and the chickens," she added after Tarzan's timely crow butted into their conversation.

Claire bent over and grabbed the Mason jar.

"I have chores to do. I don't know how you got here, but it's time for you to go."

Giving him a steadfast glare to let him know that she meant business, she brushed the grass off her knees and backside and started making her way toward the orchard.

Things had gone from bad to worse so quickly that Tobas hardly realized what had happened until it had. Intuitively, he reverted to the tactic he used at home when he and his mate were having a row. He fluttered over to the retreating girl, and in a much softer tone, he said, "Surely, you do not live here all by yourself. Where are your parents?" he asked in a cooing voice.

But Claire was having none of his reconciliatory efforts, and in a booming voice that knocked the faerie off balance, she yelled, "Gone! My parents are gone! Now go away!"

Claire's angry outburst had very nearly brought the young girl to tears. She had never accepted the idea that her mother was gone and that Claire would never see her again, but her unexpected choice of words had brought a vision of her father no longer being there, and this frightened her to her very core.

Tobas's attempt at making amends was short-lived, and Claire's response only renewed his sense of urgency to find the nambor of his mission. The myth remembered the dust that Banth had put in his travel satchel, and quickly dug the pouch out of his sack. Taking a moment to muster some nerve, he unbound the pouch and plunged his hand into it. Pulling his hand out with just as much determination as he had used putting it in, he held it up defiantly as some of the tiny particles dripped from his over-stuffed fist and cascaded down to the ground in a pearlescent stream. With his hand still raised high, Tobas fluttered his way back over to Claire. His courage bolstered by his fistful of lethal weapon, he stopped menacingly just inches from the little girl's face.

"You leave me no choice, nambor. I will give you one more chance to tell me of your own free will—or else!" Tobas threatened.

"Or else what, you rude little … thing?" Claire, more angry than threatened, answered.

"Or else this … *deantha na firinne!*" he recited as he threw the nacreous dust into Claire's face.

With a couple of coughs and sputters, Claire waved her hand at the lingering powdered potion.

"I don't believe you! What are you trying to do, poison me?" Claire, whose desire to befriend the faerie was now turning to a desire far from friendly, shouted at him.

"Poison? What? No, 'tis just pooka dust. It will wear off after a bit," he answered softly, forgetting to be menacing.

"Come now, tell …" Tobas caught an earful of his own voice and judging it to be too friendly, he lowered his pitch and attempted to sound more threatening.

"Now tell me," he tried again. "Where are the others? I do not have any more time to waste on a foolish little girl!"

Claire, clearly beyond her capacity for patience, swatted at Tobas as if he were a troublesome pest, and turning about, made her way in the opposite direction, back toward the house. Tobas was flabbergasted. As if to eliminate any possible mistake on his part, he reached into the pouch of dust. This time, he removed a fistful of its contents more gingerly than he had before. He scrutinized the magic powder as wisps of the light-catching beads encircled his hand and began spiraling up his arm.

"Looks like pooka dust," he whispered under his breath.

He slowly raised his hand to his nose where he gave the dust a nervous sniff. "Smells like pooka dust," he whispered again.

Tobas raised his head to watch the retreating figure of the little girl. As he looked back at the glistening particles of his ineffective enchanting dust, he felt it—a tickle in the back of his nose. Before he could turn his head, he let out a rib-straining sneeze that scattered the pooka dust to the four winds and left him with sparkling blue boogies running from his nostrils. Claire heard the myth sneeze as she approached the back stairs. Instead of her customary "bless you," she gave the faerie a "serves you right!" followed by a "humph" before climbing the concrete steps and retreating into the darkness of the back porch.

Tobas was totally unprepared for this turn of events. If the pooka dust had no effect on a small, weak female nambor, what was he going to do when he found the strong, brave, warrior nambor of the prophecy that he was sent to retrieve?

"Moot point that ..." Tobas muttered as he watched the last of his great, invincible dust cascade to the ground.

Exhausted from his confrontation with the little girl, he sought refuge back on his oak perch. As he straddled the limb, he lifted the shoulder strap of his bag and brought it to rest in front of him. With his elbows resting on the bag and his chin resting on his hands, the myth stewed in his own bewilderment. He hadn't a clue on how to proceed.

"What would Sarla do?" he grumbled to himself as the bright-green oak leaves rustled in the breeze around him.

***

Claire, being very annoyed at having been attacked by the little creature and his pesky dust, stomped and sneezed her way across the old wooden floor of the back porch. When she entered the kitchen, she headed straight for the sink. The frustrated little girl slammed the Mason jar down on the counter before she remembered that the bottom of it was covered in grass and dirt. She turned the cold water faucet on full blast. Cupping her hands under the cascade, she caught the cold water and splashed it on her face, giving the surrounding counter and her shirt a good soaking as well. Grabbing the dish towel drying on the back of a chair, she hurriedly dried off.

She was so annoyed at the little faerie's rudeness, that she was focused more on the attack itself than on her attacker. The encounter with the other-worldly creature took a back seat to the insult she felt at having her friendly gestures completely ignored.

Wanting to avoid another encounter at all costs, Claire decided to occupy herself with activities inside. She grabbed the vacuum, Pledge, Windex and some paper towels and headed up the stairs to her room. Lugging the heavy Hoover up the old, unleveled stairs exhausted what was left of an energy reserve used up by the heat and excitement and frustration. The mentally-drained young girl walked the length of the hallway and entered the sanctuary that was her room, where she deposited the Hoover in the corner and put the cleaning supplies on the edge of the dresser. She crawled across her bed on grass-stained knees and pinched the clasps on the window screen, which was still raised from the night before. The screen was having no parts of being closed, and Claire, too exhausted to care, flopped herself onto her rumpled bed. Here, she stared at her ceiling of galloping horses and frolicking colts and thought of how bittersweet it had felt to talk about her mother again. She closed her eyes and let the warm tears stream down her clammy cheeks.

CHAPTER 13

ALTHOUGH TOBAS WAS far less knowledgeable about nambors than Sarla and Yarn, one thing he did know was that the nambor family unit was exactly like the myth family unit. Being a father, himself, he knew that a young female would not be left to fend for herself. She had parents, and Tobas decided to wait, in hiding, for them to return to their young.

"Such despicable creatures," he murmured with disgust as he shimmied backward until his back was resting against the trunk of the old oak tree. Using his satchel as a footrest, he crossed his arms defiantly, leaned his head back and braced himself for a wait. "'Tis a shame I wasted the pooka dust on that little one," he muttered as his mind began to wander. "When the adults return, I will take the father and get back home," he muttered matter-of-factly to himself as he adjusted his position to get more comfortable.

It was that thought that made Tobas bolt upright, almost knocking his bag off the limb in the process. In all their preparations for selecting and sending someone to Doog to find and fetch back the nambor of Bhara's prophecy, no one had bothered to tell Tobas just *how* he was supposed to do that. *How* was he supposed to bring the creature back to E'lore? Was he supposed to inebriate the beast with pooka dust and drag it back through the portal? Was he supposed to charmingly persuade it to simply come with him? Perhaps he was meant to appeal to its sense of duty to save a race of beings that it never even knew existed!

"Impossible, impossible and doubtful," Tobas answered his own questions aloud from his treetop perch.

As they were always want to do, his thoughts drifted effortlessly back to E'lore, Sarla and the children. Tobas missed Sarla and his *bairns* desperately. Thoughts of them flooded his senses and overwhelmed his very reason to the point of extinguishing all common sense. In no time at all, the desperate myth convinced himself that the fulfilling of Bhara's prophecy was an unattainable goal. Even if the nambor they needed *was* here, here is where he would have to stay. Maybe if *all* of the eligibles had been sent instead of just the unluckiest one, then maybe the four of them could have brought the nambor back, but just *one?* 'No, it could not be done with just one,' Tobas decided.

"That is it then," Tobas muttered aloud as he picked himself up off the branch and brushed at the loose bits of bark clinging to his shirt. There was nothing else for him to do but to go back to E'lore, even if it meant going back empty-handed. A windfall of solace revived his spirit and the relieved myth quickly assured himself that his plan was the right course of action. Before any sensible thoughts could invade his determination and change his mind, Tobas snatched up his satchel and took to the air. He had flown over the farmhouse and was hovering just above the tin roof covering the front porch when he realized that he did not have his bearings. He spun around looking for the sheds and barns that he had flown past before. He came to a startled stop when he saw that he was hovering right in front of an open window, on the other side of which was the nambor female, resting in a nest of white linens. His curiosity getting the best of him, he fluttered to the window's ledge and peered inside the human's chamber. The first things that Tobas saw—as was true with anyone who sees Claire's room for the first time—were the dozens of pictures of quagga-like creatures covering the walls. Although quagga were small and striped, these creatures came in all sorts of colors and sizes. Some were running, some standing, some on two legs and some on all four. Not understanding or caring really about the fascination with this Doog animal, Tobas decided that the chamber contained nothing interesting enough to delay his return to E'lore. But, as he turned to make his way back across the tin roof, something caught his eye. There, on a shelf at the foot of the nambor's nest, was a photograph. Tobas recognized it as such because Sarla and Yarn collected them. On four-petal excursions, sometimes the harvesters would come across a likeness of a nambor caught on thin pieces of shiny parchment, which they would bring back to Aislinn for Yarn and Sarla to study. Sometimes they would not so much "find" as "borrow" these likenesses, but they all knew how much interest they held for the elder myth and his fellow nambor aficionado, so effort was always made to bring these souvenirs back to E'lore.

After a careful check to confirm that the nambor was indeed asleep, Tobas silently fluttered his way over to the bookshelf. He adjusted his satchel so that the strap was over his head and the stuffed sack hung down his back. With his hands free and bag secured, he reached out and grabbed the photo with both hands. His first attempt to lift the photo nearly dragged him down on top of it. The scrolled frame weighed almost as much as he did, but he was resigned to taking this memento back to Sarla, perhaps not so much as a gift for her, but in hopes that it would somewhat soften the point that he was returning without the nambor of the prophecy. Readjusting the satchel strap, and with new determination, he grabbed the frame again. This time, he managed to hoist the photo a good half-inch off of the shelf, but not without knocking the Virgin Mary down in the process. The sound of the inexpensive ceramic piece toppling onto the wooden shelf was all that Claire needed to wake her from her half-sleep. Her eyes shot open and, unfortunately for Tobas, they were already staring right at him. An involuntary gasp escaped Tobas's lips. Resolute in his decision that the picture was coming back to E'lore with him, he gave it an adrenalin-infused heave-ho, and to his surprise, it cooperated. Tobas caught a lucky break in that a corner of the frame caught in the strap of his bag. Although this helped to steady his hold on the memento, it did nothing to overcome the sheer weight of it, and Tobas knew that he would be sacrificing the ability to fly very high or with much speed.

His resolve, now equal parts determination and fear, impelled him through the opening left by the stubborn window screen and across the front porch roof. When he reached the roof's edge, he plummeted toward the ground below just as he heard Claire yell after him, "What do you think you're doing? Get back here, you little jerk!"

Flapping his wings doubly fast, he flitted across the yard, his feet and the bottom of the photo frame dragging through the grass. When Tobas saw the tractor barn, his bearings returned to him and he remembered his way back to the portal. It was then that he also heard the now familiar creaking and banging sound of the back porch door and knew, without having to see, that the little girl was coming after him. For a split second, he thought of dropping the picture and thus ensuring his safe escape, but he decided that he was more concerned about Sarla and Yarn's certain wrath than with the nambor-child's irritation.

Tobas pressed on, his muscles burning from the strain of carrying so much weight on his delicate wings. Not able to fly over the gate leading to the field that contained the pond and the dam, he flew through the rungs, dragging the heavy frame with him. As the exhausted myth gained the higher ground of the dam, the gooseberry trees came into sight and bolstered his intention.

Not able to squeeze through the gate rungs like her quarry, Claire lost precious time unlatching the bolt and swinging the heavy turnstile open. When she finally got through, the winged thief was already halfway across the dam. Wishing that, for once, she had ignored her father's rules and left her bike in the yard instead of putting it back in the shed, she thought that she would be on top of him by now if she were on two wheels instead of two legs. But she was not giving up and willed her legs to move faster. An errant Holstein cow drinking from the pond alerted Claire to the fact that the gate to the grazing pasture had been left open.

'I've got you now,' she thought to herself when she realized that there were no more time-consuming obstacles between her and the robber-faerie. As Tobas flew panting and straining against the weight of his treasure through the open pasture gate, Claire was on his heels.

The ancient and twisted pair of gooseberry trees was moments away when Tobas decided to gauge his escape with a quick look over his shoulder. The irate nambor-child was so close she was reaching for him with an open, out-stretched hand.

"Give me back my picture!" she shouted just as the thief winged through the gooseberry tree portal, with Claire immediately behind him.

And then there was silence.

A half-hearted moo from a cud-chewing cow was the only sign of life on the sprawling old homestead.

CHAPTER 14

EVERYTHING HAD GONE black. Claire could not see a thing. The very air around her seemed thick and heavy, and it took effort to move her limbs. She stretched her arms out into the gooey blackness in front of her, groping to the left and right and directly ahead, all the while taking small, shuffling steps forward. Her head was throbbing and she felt sick to her stomach.

She couldn't understand where the light had gone.

She brushed at her face. When her hands came up empty, she resumed reaching out into the concentrated nothingness in front of her, hoping to grab hold of something familiar. Then she stopped. Bending at the knees, she splayed her fingers out and felt for the ground that she was standing on. Her hands had found something that they knew. She grabbed fistfuls of the dirt and brought them up to her nose. It smelled damp and mossy and almost sweet.

"Hey! Wait a minute ... where did you go?" she shouted into the blackness around her.

"Come on ... where are we?" But her questions were not answered.

The throbbing in her head was now excruciating, and the telltale symptoms that were the precursors to fainting were beginning. Claire knew that she needed to sit down, and she did so unceremoniously with a bruising crash-landing on her bum. As she reached her hands up to embrace her pulsating head, she heard them.

Voices.

At first, they seemed far away, and they echoed as if she were hearing them through a long tube. Then suddenly, they sounded as if they were right next to her, and then they faded off and sounded distant again. Louder, then softer, fading in and out, the voices seemed more numerous now. Her head hurt so badly that she wanted to close her eyes, but she was beginning to feel afraid so she forced herself to keep them open. When she tried to focus, nothing came into view, and her eyes felt as if they had shrunk to mere pinholes. Pulling her hands from her head, she rubbed her eyes hard. Opening them again, she looked ahead into the murky darkness, this time not trying to see anything. She simply gazed ahead, focusing on nothing. Forcing her burning, irritated eyes to stay open, she began to make out shapes. They seemed to start as small dots very far away, and appeared to grow larger as they drew nearer, and then seemed to swerve away before getting too close.

Claire's eyes were weary; she could no longer keep them open. She let her tired lids rest and thought of her bed back home and how desperately she wanted to be in it. As she surrendered to the dizziness and confusion, she let herself slide to the ground and brought her aching head to rest on her outstretched arm. She lay there on the sweet, mossy soil. Without the burden of trying to keep all of her senses alert, one voice came through clearly above the others.

"Oh dear, the poor thing! Tobas, did you give her enough gooseberry root to chew on? She doesn't seem to be doing very well."

"Well, not exactly," Tobas responded.

Sarla's agitated look told Tobas to explain.

"There was no time! No, I mean ... I never meant to bring *her* back! 'Twas an accident, that!" Tobas defended himself.

"Who is this then? Is *this* the nambor of the prophecy? But 'tis ... 'tis a female!" Claire could just barely hear the dot that was Meeks.

Too frustrated with her mate and too worried for Claire, Sarla decided to wait for a less urgent time to discuss this with Tobas and turned to Yarn.

"Best to give her the powdered root. She cannot chew if she is not conscious," Sarla reasoned.

"Or dead," Yarn added, directing his response to Tobas.

"I do hope this is in time," Sarla whispered softly as she mixed the pulverized root with a drop of spring water from the nearby brook.

"Yarn, will you see if you can lift ..."

At which point Claire's stomach violently interrupted the conversation by emptying itself on the ground.

"Ah, good! That's what she needed. Give us a help, will you Yarn?" Sarla urged her companion.

It took all of Yarn and Meeks's and Tobas's efforts to lift the helpless little girl's head while Sarla gently opened her mouth, and spread a dab of the root paste under her tongue.

"Tobas, Meeks, help me harness the cart—we cannot have her lying on the cold dirt and moss," Yarn instructed his fellow myth. "Be right back, dear," he whispered to Sarla before the three of them made their way to Yarn's pasture and herd of amiable quagga.

But Claire did not hear anything after the dot said, "Ah, good!"

She was out cold.

CHAPTER 15

CLAIRE WAS WAKING slowly. Her hearing seemed to be coming back as she heard the sound of others milling about, reminding each other to be quiet with frequent "shhhs" and "careful, do not wake hers." When she opened her eyes, the dots were gone. Taking their place were fuzzy figures; talking, out-of-focus, human-like, fuzzy forms. The vague, murky shape closest to her had a soothing, comforting voice and manner. Claire was becoming less frightened and nervous as she came to realize that this one shape was actually trying to help her. The figure's voice was caring, yet it also had an air of authority as it seemed to be telling the other shapes to go and get this thing or that, and they obeyed.

"Nothing to do now but wait, poor thing. I do hope she will recover soon. If we have done anything to harm her, I will never be able to forgive myself, or you, Tobas," Sarla whispered softly.

"Me? How could it be my fault? I did not ask that thing to follow me through the gooseberry trees!" Tobas defended himself.

"You let her come through the portal without the root. You know perfectly well that traversing the portal without countermeasures is highly dangerous. Really Tobas, how could you do such a thing?" she answered, still keeping her voice lowered.

Yarn, who was helping Sarla keep a vigil at their new guest's bedside, interrupted the couple's banter with a whispered, "Did you say gooseberry trees?"

Tobas was too busy with his continued defense to hear his uncle.

"You did not see her, Sarla. She was completely unreasonable! And vicious!" he added for good measure.

Yarn realized from experience that there was no point in trying to talk to Tobas until the young myth had time to calm down. The older myth resigned himself to sitting patiently at the foot of the nambor's makeshift sleeping nest until the opportunity to ask his question again presented itself. As he watched Sarla tend to their unexpected guest, he noticed how quickly "the transformation" was affecting the nambor child. When the myth had come to E'lore, they were much larger than they now were. They had towered over the native creatures and landscape. In less than a moon's cycle, their stature had diminished until their size fell in line with their new environment. The myth were now perfectly proportionate to their habitat. Yarn estimated that their new guest was already half the size she was when they struggled and strained to fit her into Sarla and Tobas's home just last evening. Sarla had witnessed the accelerated change, as well, and was cinching the excess fabric of Claire's shorts with a length of rope in response. In a fleeting thought, Yarn wondered if the human child would also grow wings as they had done.

Tobas had no energy to ration for anything other than his own circumstance, as he continued to vigorously defend his actions in Doog. "You are all so worried about her. No one seems to care that I barely made it back alive!" The overwrought myth's face fell when he realized that his mate was no longer participating in their argument.

"She is taking so long to adjust. What if she does not wake up?" Sarla asked under her breath.

"Well, if that should happen, 'tis not my fault. No one wanted to listen to me, did they? I have said it all along: nambors are weak and stupid. 'Tis that ... that *thing's* fault if she does not come around ... and I will not take the blame for it, know that right now! I was against this from the very beginning. Maybe, just maybe, I was right about these creatures all along!" Tobas ranted.

"Oh, do settle down, dear. We need calm and quiet now. Agitation and panic do not make for a healing environment," Sarla replied serenely on behalf of her semi-conscious patient.

Yarn took the opportunity to ask Tobas his question again when he saw that his nephew had no response to Sarla's declaration.

"Tobas, did you say 'gooseberry trees'?"

The defensive myth looked blankly at Yarn as his attention shifted from his wife to his uncle. "I'm sorry … trees?" he stammered.

"Yes, you said earlier that 'twas not your fault that she had followed you through the gooseberry trees. What did you mean?" Yarn asked, more adamantly now that he finally had Tobas's attention. His query caught Sarla's notice, as well, and she looked up from her patient to hear her mate's response.

Tobas reflected for a moment before he realized what Yarn was referring to and when he did, he answered him straight away, "The gooseberry trees, yes. 'Tis another pair on the other side," was all the response he gave.

Yarn and Sarla stared at Tobas waiting for more, and when no more came, Yarn stuck his neck forward and arched his eyebrows, giving the young myth an unspoken "… and?" expression.

Tobas wasn't sure what more his uncle wanted him to say, but he elaborated as best he could. "When I went through the trees and the blue light, I came out in a different place than we do when we go on harvests. 'Twas not in Eire, I was someplace else altogether … a farm, actually. I chewed the root and I was getting out the stakes to mark the exit when I saw that the exit was already marked."

Again, Tobas stopped short of his uncle's satisfaction, but caught on just short of needing to be encouraged again to continue. "The portal was marked on the other side just like 'tis here, with a pair of gooseberry trees. They were just like ours … for a moment, I was not sure that I had gone through. I actually thought that I was still here … until I saw the grass." Tobas thought to tell them about the rest of his time in Doog, and was about to, until he remembered the photo that he had "borrowed" from Claire's shelf. Instead he blurted out, "That reminds me!"

He hastily flew through the dried skin covering the chamber entrance and returned moments later dragging the framed picture of Claire's mother and eldest sister, Deirdre.

"This is for you, Sarla!" Tobas tried to keep his voice down, but was too excited to do so successfully.

"Shhh, Toby, please," Sarla asked of her enthusiastic mate as she glanced over at the slumbering Claire who seemed undisturbed by the commotion around her.

"This is for you," he repeated in a whisper.

"Where did you find this, dear?" Sarla answered the question for herself: "'Tis not hers, is it, Toby?"

Tobas knew that his answer would not please her even before he gave it, so he gave her a shrug and scrunched his face instead. Realizing that her mate's heart may have been in the right place when he took the photo, she took a deep breath and exhaled before responding.

"'Tis a lovely thought, but if she wants it back, back it will go," she said in a voice and demeanor that respected her patient's rights and gently cradled her husband's feelings at the same time. Yarn, quite certain where his nephew's heart had been when he pinched the framed likeness, was not so gentle in his response.

"Is this intended to smooth over the fact that we are without the nambor of the prophecy?"

Tobas had hoped that since no one had brought up this fact yet, it was going to be overlooked. When he realized that it had not been, he decided to go on the defense, only this time, he actually had a valid argument.

"'Tis not possible without help, *Uncail!* How was I to bring the creature back to E'lore? No one told me *how* to bring the creature back!" Tobas was mentally preparing the next leg of his retort when Yarn raised his hand as a signal to stop.

"Yes, my son, we realized just that moments after you disappeared through the trees, and for that, I take responsibility."

Tobas was surprised by Yarn's admission and at the same time relieved that he no longer had to vindicate himself.

And with that, Sarla decided to clear the chamber. Yarn and Tobas would have to continue their discussion in the front room so that Claire could get some rest. As she herded them out of the chamber she said to Tobas, "Thank you for the gift, dear. 'Twas very sweet of you to think of me in such a trying circumstance."

Turning to Yarn, she added, "I will give a call when she comes about."

Once she had cleared the chamber of onlookers, she returned to Claire's side. Pulling the skins over the girl's shoulders, Sarla tucked them under her chin.

"Pay my husband no mind, his mouth is usually halfway down the path before his brain even knows that it has left the house! You sleep as long as you need. I'll be here when you wake," the gentle faerie whispered to her sleeping patient.

Sarla stroked a stray lock of hair from Claire's face and gently kissed her forehead. Claire was now certain that she could trust at least one of these creatures. Finally feeling safe, she exhaled deeply for the first time since crossing through the portal. Succumbing to the softness of the skins and the warmth of the fire, she fell into a deep, recuperative sleep.

CHAPTER 16

'WHAT A BIZARRE dream,' Claire thought as she stretched her arms over her head and gave out a long sigh, followed by a much-needed yawn. Opening her eyes startled her into the realization that she hadn't been dreaming. She was surrounded by unfamiliar sights, not by the horse-covered pink walls of her bedroom. She was somewhere entirely different. The bed she was in was less like a bed and more like a nest lined with soft animal skins, the same skins that covered her. As she propped herself up and began to look around, she felt that the room she was in was intended for someone much smaller than she. The fireplace, though practically miniature, was functional, with a warming blaze crackling and sputtering away. As she took in her surroundings, the details of her "dream" were coming back to her. She remembered following the annoying little man through the pair of old, twisted trees in the main pasture, and then the darkness. The recollection of the panic and queasiness and talking dots was so vivid that Claire felt a lurch in her stomach. She sat herself upright, anticipating the need to be sick, when the animal skin that covered the entrance to the room folded back in one corner, and Sarla poked her head through. Seeing that Claire was awake, she fluttered in carrying a tray of tea and cakes and a bit of gooseberry root, just in case.

"Good morning, dear. Are we feeling better today?" she asked.

"Um ... yes. I mean good morning, and yes, much better, thank you," Claire answered rather calmly in spite of her astonishment.

"Tobas tells me that you are called Claire, is that right?" Sarla asked softly as she set the tray down on a side table.

Though her vision had not come completely into focus, and images were framed in a soft, feathery glow, she could see well enough to know that this creature was very similar to the aggravating little man that turned up at the house. Only this one was not at all aggravating, just the opposite, in fact. She was calm and kind, caring and gentle.

"You gave us quite a fright, but I had faith that you would come through just fine. How about a cuppa tea?" Sarla asked, but did not wait for a reply as she had already poured and was adding some 010 ferticle sap to the brew before she finished the question.

Not wanting to offend the gracious creature, Claire reached for the cup as slouches of the now excess fabric of her top pooled at her elbows.

She felt as if she were playing with her old tea set as she gingerly took the tiny cup, worrying that she might crush it if she was not careful.

"Mmmm, we will have to work out a better system, I see," Sarla said after realizing how disproportionate the cup was to the girl.

"No, really, it's fine. I'll manage," Claire answered, not wanting to seem unappreciative. She took a sip, which emptied the vessel.

"No worries. We will get this sorted right out soon enough!" Sarla whispered as she refilled her patient's cup.

Claire instantly liked this little creature. Although she obviously was a faerie like the one that stole her mother's picture, to Claire she could not be more different and as the little girl held out her cup for more tea, she wondered how the two were related. In order to keep her hostess from working so hard, she decided to delay having another sip of tea.

"Where am I?" she asked instead.

"Yes, of course, you have many questions, yes? Perhaps you should get a bit more rest before we get into all of them."

"No, please, tell me. Where am I?" Claire asked again.

Realizing that her guest had every right to have her questions answered, Sarla lit upon the red deerskin blanket and with a smile, answered her worried patient.

"My name is Sarla, and you are in E'lore."

"I've never heard of E'lore. Is it far from my house?" Claire asked.

Sarla smiled graciously, delighting in the innocence of the question.

"Yes and no," was the careful answer. "The entrance to our world is not far from your home, but in other ways, 'tis farther away than any stars or the moon that you see at night."

"Your *world?* I don't think I'm following you," Claire responded.

As Sarla smoothed and tucked the soft skin blankets, she had begun to explain when the hide covering to the door pulled back and Tobas's head appeared.

"Sarla, they are here. They would like to see ..." Tobas looked at Claire and nodded his head in her general direction.

"Claire?" Sarla responded, half asking and half reminding her forgetful mate of their guest's name.

"Yes ... her," he answered, again nodding his head at the girl as if there were more than one misplaced female human in the room, and he needed to be clear about which one he was referring to.

When Sarla's mouth curved down at the corners in vexation, Tobas's head popped back out through the curtain, and the moleskin glided back into place.

Sarla playfully rolled her eyes to Claire, shook her head, and smiled.

"That's him! He stole my picture! I was chasing him and then ... then it went all dark ... and I was here ..." Claire tried to recall, but some pieces seemed to have gone missing.

Sarla tried to calm her baffled patient.

"Shhh, now, 'tis expected that you will have trouble remembering everything so soon. You still need a great deal of rest. Not to worry, it will all come back."

"But, who is that? And who are 'they'?" Claire continued despite Sarla's attempt to soothe her troubled guest.

"'That' is Tobas—he is my mate. 'They' are our elders, our leaders, our friends. They just want to have a visit and formally welcome you, but I fear 'tis too soon for visitors. I can ask them to come back later," Sarla answered.

"No ... I ... suppose I could," Claire answered slowly, not being sure of what a "visit" entailed.

"I do not want you to do too much too soon, dear," Sarla cooed to her guest, but Claire's curiosity would not abate.

"Maybe for just a minute?" she offered.

Sarla studied her charge for a moment before relenting.

"Here, let me help you then," she said as she came around to Claire's side and placed a loving hand on the girl's shoulder.

Sarla led Claire into the front room where the assembled myth awaited. Motioning her to a pile of skins bundled on the floor, Claire sat cross-legged as Willa and Anndra draped a large blanket over her shoulders at Sarla's request.

"Her name is Claire," Tobas blurted out unexpectedly.

Having given everyone a start at his sudden and one-sided introduction, all attention had briefly diverted to him. Sarla brought accord back when she excused herself to make tea, taking Willa and Anndra with her. Banth followed her lead and turned the focus back to the situation at hand.

"I am called Banth. This is Meeks," he said, gesturing toward his companions. "And this is Yarn."

With his introduction, Yarn gave the girl a polite bow of his head. Yarn was, and always had been, fascinated with the nambor race. He and Sarla had spent many hours discussing their evolution, and arguable gifts and shortcomings, a fascination that Tobas never understood or tolerated with much patience.

"Hello" was all that Claire could think to say.

The introductions were followed by a silence that lasted a bit too long for anyone's liking or comfort. It was Banth who broke the quiet. "You gave us a bit of a fright, you know. Are you feeling better?"

"Um ... yes, I think so. Could you tell me what's going on here? Am I dreaming? No, wait, if I was dreaming, could you tell me that I'm dreaming? Okay, let's pretend that I'm not ... dreaming, I mean. Where? Who? What's going on?" Claire finally asked.

"Not to worry, we will have you back home in no time, in no time at all," the director answered enthusiastically.

Banth's reply prompted a deep and unusually loud throat-clearing from Yarn, who then motioned to Banth to meet him by the hearth. As the director joined his friend fireside, Sarla returned with the tea tray, which she offered to Claire and Meeks. While the myth blew onto his steaming drink, Willa and Anndra each grabbed a heather cake and returned quickly to their posts at Claire's feet. There they nibbled absently on their treats, never taking their eyes off of the nambor girl who was growing increasingly uncomfortable being the focus of so much attention.

Once Sarla had seen to her guest's needs, she herded her children away from Claire with a handful of cakes each and the promise that if their guest should want for anything, they would be the first to know.

Banth returned and sent Meeks to the hearth to join Yarn. Yarn had shared Tobas's accounting of the duplicate pair of gooseberry trees on the other side of the portal, as well as the fact that the portal did not lead to their usual four-petal harvesting fields, but to a place that most likely was nowhere near Eire. As Yarn shared this news with Meeks, Banth took a seat opposite the little girl and blew cooling breaths onto his tea, trying his best to smile and act as if all was well.

Claire watched the conversation at the hearth and looked at the false smile that Banth wore as he nodded politely and blew on his now cold tea. Trusting her instincts, she blurted out, "What on earth is going on?"

The excitement in her voice startled Banth, who was in mid-slurp. Globs of tea fell from his lips and onto his lap as he struggled for composure. Yarn and Meeks rejoined the group, and Anndra and his sister were halfway across the room before they were intercepted by their mother, who sent them back to their seats with a tilt of her head and a point of her finger.

Sarla had flown to Claire's side and was doing her best to console her when Yarn cleared his voice to speak.

"We were hoping that you could help us find a particular nambor, I'm sorry—human, that we seek, possibly your father." Yarn said softly.

"Or brother, perhaps ..." Banth added when Claire did not immediately reply.

"I don't have a brother. My father?" Claire tried to process what they were saying.

As Yarn and Banth did their best to interrogate their guest with diplomacy, Meeks and Tobas had begun debating among themselves.

"There is no mistake. The portal must lead us to *the* nambor," Meeks argued.

"I am not disagreeing with you. I am saying that it cannot be done alone, it will require several of us to bring the creature back," Tobas countered.

The two myth then fell silent in order to contemplate the other's thoughts and wash them down with tea.

"'Creature'?" Claire whispered to herself as Yarn did his best to regain her attention.

"Tell us about your family, dear," Yarn asked genuinely.

Claire pulled her gaze from Meeks and Tobas, who had now rejoined the group. "My sisters have all moved away, and I don't have any brothers. It's just me and my dad," she answered Yarn.

"Ahh," Banth purred, giving a knowing nod toward the others.

"Tell us about *him*," he encouraged.

"Why would you want to know about my father? What does he have to do with this?"

"Well, you see" … Yarn began.

"The Fomorian are coming, and he is supposed to protect us from them, or help us defeat them or whatever the prophecy says he's supposed to do!" Speaking out of turn, Tobas cut to the chase of the matter.

The party sat in disbelief at Tobas's rudeness, and Yarn's patience had been exhausted.

"That will do, Tobas!" The elder myth scolded.

"The who … what are you rambling on about now?" she responded, the disdain in her voice matching that of Tobas's interjection.

Deciding that any energy spent on Tobas was a waste, Claire turned back to Yarn.

"What are you talking about? My dad doesn't know anything about this, or you," she told him.

"Well, yes, that is most likely true," Meeks answered.

As the three myth looked at each other, none of them sure as how to proceed, Banth was the first to offer an answer: "'Tis a frightfully long story, so to spare you the details …"

"Spare me the details? I have no idea where I am, how I got here, or how to get home, so if it's all the same to you, I think I'd like to hear the details!" Claire interrupted. Even though she wasn't sure what was going on, one thing she was becoming sure of was that she had something they needed, and she decided to dispense with manners and stand her ground. She looked at each of the myth in turn, and her unflinching gaze told them that this was not negotiable. Tobas, Meeks, and Yarn sat silently, knowing that Banth should be the one to speak, and waited for him to begin. As Banth gathered his thoughts, Sarla spoke in defense of Claire.

"She's right, director. She deserves to know."

"Maybe they have magic," Tobas interrupted. "When I used the pooka dust on her, it had no effect, no effect at all!" he exclaimed.

Sarla shook her head at her mate's confession.

"Really, Toby, she is just a child," she admonished.

"Is that true, Tobas?" Yarn asked, his voice tinged with disappointment.

Before Tobas could answer, Claire had started giggling to herself at the suggestion that the sparkling ashes that the annoying little man had thrown in her face were supposed to have magical powers. The only effect they had had on her was to make her sneeze.

"That was supposed to be magic dust? Well, if making you even more annoying than before was a product of magic, then I guess it worked." Claire did not care if her remark embarrassed the impolite myth.

Sarla could not help but smile at Claire, even at the expense of her mate, and went back to the kitchen to refresh the old teapot.

"What effect did you think it would have?" Claire added.

"That was pooka dust, nambor!" Tobas shouted, flying to within inches of Claire's face. "I have seen it stop nambors twice your size in their tracks!" he lied boastfully.

"Stop calling me that!"

Claire had had enough of this particular faerie's rudeness. In answer to his challenge, she stood straight up, banging her head on one of the exposed beams in the ceiling in the process. The loud thud, and the resulting "ouch!" from Claire, brought Sarla flying into the room.

"What is going on in here?" she asked as she came around the corner. Seeing Claire holding her head in pain brought her immediately to the little girl's side.

Sarla cooed softly, "Let me see, dear," as Claire pulled her hands away to allow Sarla to inspect her injury. Sarla gave out a little wince, followed by her diagnosis, "Just a wee bump, nothing too serious. 'Tis hard dear, I know, I am afraid we do not need as much room as you do," she said with a smile. "Have another cake, and I'll be right back with something to keep the swelling down."

As she passed Tobas, she gave him a scornful look.

"What did I do?" he asked innocently.

Claire sat back down and picked up a sweet cake from the tiny platter. She nibbled on the tiny pastry in silence as the four myth stared at her.

Sarla returned quickly carrying a green bouquet as large as she was.

"Here you go, dear. Hold this on your little bump, and it will stop the swelling," she coached.

As Claire took the bouquet from Sarla, she realized that it was a bundle of five-leaf clovers.

"I never thought to use these for bumps on the head before," Claire said smiling at Sarla as she took the bundle. "I'll have to remember this when I get back ...," Claire left her sentence unfinished.

Banth looked at Claire with hesitant surprise and was about to speak when Sarla declared that it was time for Claire to get some more rest. She then motioned to Willa and Anndra to come help their guest back to her chamber. The brother and sister were at Claire's feet in a flash.

"Can you manage?" she asked of her children as they helped the tired little girl to her feet.

"Yes, Mam, yes, Mam," they each answered.

Sarla then looked at Claire, and gave her a nod that she was in good hands. Claire smiled in return.

"I will be right in," she called after the human girl and the myth *bairns* as they made their way carefully to Claire's chamber.

Sarla began clearing away the dishes. Banth, who understood Sarla's protectiveness of her charge, waited for Claire and the children to leave the room before speaking. "Sarla, we really must speak to her. You saw her response to the bundle of five-petals—that must be of some significance. Perhaps her father *does* have magical powers. You, yourself, have told me of how few nambors are able to find four-petals, much less five-petals. If she has seen them before, her father must be one of these rare finders!"

"I think she has had quite enough excitement for now. She needs more rest and fewer of your questions," Sarla replied with authority as she continued cleaning up.

"But, Sarla," Banth continued. However, Sarla had made up her mind. Addressing all of the male myth together, she said, "This lass has been through an ordeal that we ourselves are all too familiar with. Thanks to us, she is in a strange world far from the home she knows. As brave as she may seem, she must be terribly frightened, so for now, we are going to help her. Once we help her regain her strength, we are going to answer her questions—*all* of them. Because unless one of you has figured out just how we are going to return this child to her own world—and is not sharing it with the rest of us—I do not believe that she is going anywhere any time soon, so your questions can and will wait!"

Sarla had silenced the men. They knew that what she had said was entirely true and entirely right. Though they could not be sure of how much time they had, to treat Claire so blatantly as an object for their own use was wrong. Tobas walked the three older myth to the door, where, before taking their leave, they thanked their hostess for her hospitality and asked if they might call on her again the next day. Sarla warmly granted their request and promised that if anything unexpected or unusual arose, she would notify them immediately.

Tobas closed the door behind their departed guests. His hand still gripping the latch, he seemed unable to move from where he stood as if held in place by some unseen force. Sarla turned her gaze back and saw his remorseful face. Understanding that no more stern words were needed, she said to him gently, "Toby, will you please fetch some more wood for the fire? I will need to start cooking soon if I'm to make enough to feed us all."

Tobas, feeling helpless when it came to matters to do with the nambor, gratefully accepted the errand. Grabbing his scarf from the hook next to the door, he answered, "Of course, yes, be right back," and he hurried out of the cottage.

Sarla smiled at the closed door and turned her attention back to her patient. As she approached Claire's chamber, Anndra came swooping through the tanned hide covering with his sister right on his heels. Willa was teasing her brother mercilessly about something, what it was Sarla did not hear over her son's high-pitched squeals of "Stop it, Willa!"

She watched them disappear into Anndra's room before pulling the skin aside and entering the room where Claire lay quietly in her animal hide nest. The weakened little girl's energy did not last long, so something as simple as walking exhausted her quickly. Although the dizziness had almost all but subsided, her vision had not completely returned and she had trouble staying awake for very long periods of time. The meeting with the myth and her confrontation with Tobas had worn her out, and she was glad to be going back to bed. Sarla sat beside her and carefully brushed her hair back to take another look at the bump caused by her collision with the ceiling beam.

"You won't even know 'twas there by mealtime," she said softly.

Giving the skins a motherly tuck under Claire's chin, she stroked the tired girl's cheek. Sarla gazed upon the girl's fair skin and dark hair as she tried to decide whether or not to ask the question that Banth wanted to ask the nambor earlier in the front room. Sarla felt with growing certainty that Banth's question would have been misguided. She had just made up her mind not to when Claire said, "You can ask me."

Sarla was astounded by her guest's acute perception, which made the invitation all the more impossible to resist.

"You have seen that many five-petals before, but your father is not the finder, is he?" she asked, already certain of the answer.

Claire chuckled at the thought of her father seeing anything that close to the ground from his tractor seat.

"I don't think Daddy has ever found a four-leaf clover, much less a five-leaf," Claire answered. "I find them all the time. I see one, then another, and next thing you know, I have handfuls. In fact, that's what I was doing when I stumbled onto your husband," she continued.

"When you met Tobas, you had been picking four-petals?" Sarla asked.

"Well, actually, I hadn't found very many four-leaf. I was only finding five-leaf. Usually I find lots of fours and only a couple of fives, but that day ... yesterday? ... it was just the opposite. Every once in awhile, I'll get really lucky and find a six-leaf or two. Daddy tells me that it's one of the things I do that most reminds him of my mother. He says that she found four-leaf clovers all the time, too, and five-leaf, as well. He said that she saved all of hers, but I don't know where. I've never found them. My father teases me and says that it's the luck of the Irish, or that

I'm half leprechaun and things like that." She let out a subdued giggle and smiled as she envisioned her father telling her these things, but she quickly redirected her thoughts back when she felt herself becoming anxious.

Sarla could feel Claire's growing distress and tried to calm her fears. "Come tomorrow, if you feel up to it, Banth and Yarn will be back, and you can ask them anything you want to. But for now, you need to sleep. I will wake you in a bit for the evening meal. But, until then, please try to get some rest."

Sarla gave Claire a smile, but before she had reached the door, Claire called her back. Sarla gently fluttered over to her. "Yes, dear?" she asked softly.

"I just wanted to say 'thank you' for being so nice to me. You were right out there you know … I'm scared … I want to go home."

Sarla stiffened slightly at the realization that Claire had overheard her talk at the front door. Her regret over this, along with Claire's confession, kindled tears in Sarla's eyes.

After a slight pause, Claire added, "*Can* I go home, Sarla? Am I going to be here forever?"

"I'm afraid I do not have the answer to that, Claire," Sarla answered her candidly. "That is the very question that I wish to ask of Banth and Yarn tomorrow," she continued. "We will ask them together, shall we? In the meantime, I need you to rest. No matter what the answers are tomorrow, you will not be able to do anything with them if you do not have your strength."

Giving the skins one more tuck, she smiled at Claire and then took her leave. Sarla peeled back the sewn skin curtain and walked silently through the opening. Claire was fast asleep before the curtain closed.

***

Tobas was just getting back from retrieving more wood for the fire as Sarla and her brood were entering the kitchen.

"Thank you, dear," she greeted him gently.

Tobas put the stack next to the cooking fire.

"I have brought more. I thought I would leave it outside so as to not take up too much room in here."

After a survey of the meal preparations, he nervously asked, "Can I help?"

Sarla was a bit taken aback by this uncharacteristic display of unsolicited helpfulness. Not wanting to discourage his efforts, she replied, "Well, yes, please, if you and Anndra would find some toadstools for roasting with the vegetables that would be lovely."

"You heard your mother. The men must go hunt down the elusive, myth-eating toadstools," Tobas joked with his son in an effort to return the household to a lighter, happier mood.

"Toadstools do not eat myth. Myth eat toadstools, Da!" Anndra replied with the exaggerated sarcasm that a child likes to use when educating a parent.

"Yes, of course. I always get that backwards somehow." Tobas teased.

As Anndra rolled his eyes at his father, Tobas wrapped a scarf around the boy's neck. Grabbing a basket by the door for collecting the fungi, he nodded goodbye to Willa and gave Sarla a grin before following Anndra out of the house.

CHAPTER 17

TOBAS AND ANNDRA came through the door just as Sarla and Willa were putting the last of the platters on the table.

"Just in time," Sarla said to her husband as he made his way over to her, handing her the basket of unneeded mushrooms.

"Where is she?" he asked in a hushed tone, nodding toward the extra chair that had been placed at the table.

"Just woke her a bit ago. She should be out shortly," Sarla answered.

Looking at Claire's chair, which actually was not a chair at all, it was the table from the front room, he said, "Are you sure that is going to be alright? Is it big enough?" his voice reflected a mix of concern and teasing.

"I think it will do for now, Toby. We will make other arrangements if 'tis not." Sarla could tell that Tobas had taken her words to heart, and she was proud of him for his new effort.

As Claire entered the room, they all noticed a change in her right away. She seemed to be smaller than even just a short while before when the elders had visited. She could now stand in their cottage without her head scraping the beams above. She had also regained color to her cheeks, and her eyes had taken on a brightness that they did not have when she arrived. The first thing that Anndra noticed, however, was her lack of shoes.

"Look, Mam, she has toes just like us!" he announced with a small child's usual dismissal of politeness. His observation earned him a quick "Anndra!" from his mother.

Claire just smiled.

"No, it's okay. Besides he's right," she said, giving Anndra a little wink.

"I am glad to see you making yourself at home, dear," Sarla encouraged her reluctant houseguest.

"Actually it's not that," Claire responded as she gazed down at her pink polished toes. "It's my shoes. They don't seem to fit me anymore. I don't understand it. Nothing seems to fit anymore." She let out a small laugh, trying to disguise her confusion.

Sarla thought that perhaps she needed to tell Claire of the reasons for the change in her size, but decided it should wait for later. "Please sit and fill your plate," she invited her guest.

Sarla and Willa had prepared three times as much food as usual to compensate for their oversized guest, and the table was weighted down with roasted meats, root vegetables, and fresh breads. Sarla had adapted one of her water buckets to be used as a tea cup for the little girl, and she brewed the company-sized teapot just to be able to fill it up once for her. Claire, in appreciation of her hostess's extra effort, gave her a warm smile and a soft "thank you."

Everyone helped with the serving as plates were passed around the table. Tobas carved and served the roasted venison, Willa portioned out the braised root vegetables, Anndra was in charge of bread, Claire spooned sauce-covered toadstools onto the slices of meat, and Sarla poured and sweetened everyone's tea. Table manners were very important in the O'Brian house, and Claire had been taught that no one at the table lifted their fork until their hostess had taken her first bite. A bit to Claire's surprise, the same rule applied in the Kirwan home, as well, where everyone respectfully kept their hands in their laps until Sarla lifted a forkful of vegetables to her mouth. Bringing her clean fork back down was the signal for everyone else to dig in. Sarla resisted the urge to give her mate an "I told you so" look as she could tell that he was sufficiently surprised at the "primitive" nambor's display of advanced etiquette. He simply returned her smile with a nod and a smile of his own as everyone devoured their meal in happy silence.

The quiet was broken only once when Claire said, "Sarla, this is delicious, thank you so much," which solicited another nod from Tobas acknowledging that maybe, just maybe, he had judged nambors unfairly. Once rounds of agreement and praise had been given by everyone else at the table, the meal continued quietly until every plate and platter had been cleaned of second and third helpings.

CHAPTER 18

After words had been forged into language—
words delivered of sounds, which had been conceived from symbols.
Yet before language could give birth to the written word,
allowing events and histories to be recorded—
ancient civilization's legends, facts and half-truths in between,
were handed down
from generation to generation in the form of "Tellings."

FOR THE MYTH, keeping the history of their people alive was a paramount responsibility assigned to only the most dutiful in character and loyal in heart. It was a charge that lasted the "teller's" lifetime. When this chosen one's life was nearing its end, he and he alone would determine the successor to this crucial trust, and the last of the teller's life was spent passing on the long and glorious account of their people to the one who would carry on the tradition. For the myth of E'lore, this responsibility rested capably in the hands and heart of the eldest clansman, Yarn Kirwan, of *An Daingean*.

Every three cycles, the myth would make the pilgrimage to Aislinn from all corners of the realm to hear The Telling, and Claire had arrived in E'lore at the approach of the end of the third cycle. The gathering to hear Yarn chronicle the history of the clan was a time-honored and much antici-pated occasion, an event that was cherished even more since the Tuathan's precious and powerful book had been lost to them. Every time that the occasion for The Telling came around again, the myths' numbers had grown so much from the time before, that it now took as long for the faeries to collect themselves at the appointed gathering place as it did for Yarn to recount their history.

Devotion to this myth custom never failed to draw the entire population of E'lore to the gathering, but *this* Telling had brought them with renewed enthusiasm as word of the "Aislinn nambor" spread like wildfire throughout the realm. Even the leprechauns, who usually had no interest at all in myth traditions, had returned to Aislinn after nightfall to see this nambor for themselves. It was in and around a lily-strewn cove at the western-most shore of Lake Sheelin—a spot furthest from the clamorous waterfalls—that the shoemakers joined the myth of the wood and of the mist, and settled in for an evening of storytelling under a starlit lapis sky. Some of the gathered did not yet know of the nambor or of Bhara's passing and were to learn of it that very evening.

Yarn had seated himself on a large rock protruding from the shallows at the edge of the cove to ensure that the myth of the mist could stay near and in the water and still hear his voice. The low-lying branches of the trees were burgeoning with alighted faeries, perched among the leaves in groups and in pairs, some sipping tea and some huddled together, catching up on old news and discussing recent events.

For Yarn, it had been the whole three cycles since he had seen some of the other clans of E'lore. As he scanned the assembled crowd, his eyes came to rest on a mist myth sitting weightlessly on a wet, craggy outcrop. She was gracefully sipping a cup of tea and was herself peacefully scanning the congregation. Yarn allowed himself to stare at the ethereal creature unabashedly. The myth of the mist were so different from the myth of the wood. Their eyes were as opals set against the palest of blue skin, so pale as to be almost translucent. They were lithe and graceful, and observing them in motion was like watching music walk or poetry dance. The wings of the mist myth were much larger than those of the wood. They were half again the length of their bodies, long and narrow and—like their skin—translucent. Because of their damp domain, their wings were perpetually dotted with drops of dew, which, under the soft glow of the moon, looked like hundreds of tiny pearls caught in a delicate mesh of transparent silk. Intriguing to Yarn, as well, was the fact that the male and female mist myth were distinguishable only by size, the male merely a taller version of the delicate female. Just as Yarn could feel himself becoming inextricably mesmerized by the exquisite mist faerie, his line of sight was broken by the arrival of a wood myth to her craggy retreat which, after exchanging greetings, she proceeded to share with him. Yarn recognized him as Pethbol, Aislinn's best hunter, and one of the eligibles that had been gathered in Banth's office. Pethbol was strong in body, quick in mind, and, as if that were not enough, beautiful to behold, as well, a combination that was intoxicating to the female myth and infuriating to the male. Yarn no longer felt obligated to male competitiveness, and was able to look at the couple and appreciate the sheer majesty of their pairing. The wood myth, in stark contrast to his fair companion, was of flesh-toned skin with wings only a few shades darker than his complexion. The wood myth males were taller, stouter and less ornate than the wood myth females with features and physiques distinctly masculine. In contradiction, the female was unmistakably fairer, curvaceous and graceful. The male's wings were thick and round, whereas the females were almost as long as their bodies, each narrow, elongated wing ending with a delicate, feathery point. Yarn's line of sight was again broken, this time by Sarla as she fluttered over to his perch carrying a tray of tea and cakes to keep him energized through the long evening ahead.

Tobas, Willa, and Anndra had taken their seats right on the cove's lapping shore. For the last two Tellings, Tobas paid acute attention to the nuances of Yarn's descriptions and the inflections of Yarn's voice at key points in the narrative. For it was to him that Tobas was sure Yarn would leave his legacy, the legacy of narrating their magnificent and noble history. Sarla never tired of hearing the tale. She and Yarn were intellectual contemporaries, and they had dissected and discussed every subtlety of the legend in their inexhaustible pursuit of knowledge and understanding. Not only were they intrigued with their own past, but they had burned many a candle to a nub pouring over their collaborative writings on the nambor race, as well. According to Yarn, nambors were and are the most magical of all creatures, but in the process of their advancement, they had separated themselves from their own world. The "civilized" nambors had blanketed their surroundings and themselves in false materials, effectively severing the once powerful spiritual connection they had with their earth. If only they would do away with the trappings of their civilization, Yarn would theorize, the nambors would connect once again with the natural energy of their dimension and would rediscover their inherent magic.

Several of the assembled myth openly voiced their apprehension at the telling of their legend to an outsider, a nambor no less. It had been decided by the director and his counsel, however, that whatever the circumstances surrounding Claire's arrival in E'lore, she should be considered and treated as an honored guest. The potential risk of disclosing their history and, therefore, their true nature had not been lost on the counsel. For lack of a better solution, they decided to deal with that situation when and if it presented itself.

For Willa, this would be the second time that she had heard the story, although the first time she was too young to fully understand. As for Anndra, this was his premier attendance to the gathering, which made him feel very grown up indeed. So great was their excitement that they challenged each other for what they perceived to be the best vantage point. Sensing that a sibling skirmish was about to begin, Sarla made a preemptive strike and taking Willa by her left hand and Anndra by his right, she escorted them to the moleskin laying at Yarn's feet and instructed them both to make themselves comfortable and mind their manners. Each of them content with their mother's solution, they lay themselves on the skin—tummy down—and, with their respective chins resting in their upturned hands, they settled themselves in for an evening of storytelling. Sarla had left Claire with Tobas and the two were soon joined by Banth and Meeks. At Sarla's request, they had moved away from the water's edge and promised to keep an eye on their otherworldly guest, making sure that she kept bundled and dry.

Yarn, himself, was nestled in a soft, billowy mound of moleskins, and sensing that his audience was very near to being settled in, poured a cup of tea from the pot provided him by Sarla, and took a long sip. Still holding his cup with his elbows propped on his crossed knees, he surveyed the eager spectators. As he scanned the anxious faces before him, he collected his thoughts and designed in his mind how he would begin the long telling of the legend. Yarn had never experienced so much trepidation before a Telling, and he had narrated the history of the myth innumerable times before. But this Telling was like no Telling before. Never before had the legend of their people been revealed to an outsider. It was never allowed for fear that the myths' secrets and knowledge would somehow be used against them. Although he himself shared in the apprehension of some of the others, he had not voiced it. Needing more time to collect himself, Yarn slowly brought the cup back down and set it on a level expanse of his rocky roost. Much to the disappointment of his audience, he reached for the pot and just as slowly refilled his cup with more of the clear amber brew. As he lifted the delicate vessel once more to his lips, he scanned the congregation for the faces most familiar to him. He found his friends Banth and Meeks, Tobas, and then Claire. He allowed his gaze to rest on her face, and as he did, it suddenly struck him that she looked perfectly natural sitting there amongst his fellow myth. Other than her slightly larger size, she did not appear the least bit foreign. She looked like *one of them*. Yarn cocked his head to the side as he pondered his observation. His scrutiny also filled him with the sense that there was more to this nambor than she was being given credit for. Yarn then became aware that Claire was looking back at him. Fearing that his exaggerated staring was impolite and making her uncomfortable, he gave their guest a gentle nod and a smile, took another sip of tea and decided to begin.

The Telling was a mixture of poetry and prose, history lesson and bedtime story, and Yarn decided to begin the chronicle in the same way as he had always done.

"For more cycles than I care to recall, the privilege of narrating the legend of our clan has been mine. Most of you have heard our story many times. Some of you have come to the gathering this eventide for the very first time," Yarn paused and gave Anndra a wink.

"For a few, you have made the journey for the Telling every triennial cycle since our very first, very meager assembly all those many, many moons ago. This is the tale of our beginnings, our struggles and triumphs, our traditions, and our secrets. As you know, the Telling is shared between myth and myth alone. Yet this evening, it will be my privilege to share our glorious history with one who is new to our world and our ways."

With these words, Yarn gestured toward Claire as a means of introduction to the gathered inhabitants of E'lore. His subtle presentation of
their guest was met with murmurings and whispers of speculation, which
politely subsided when Yarn lowered his arm.

Yarn gave Claire a wink and a gentle smile as he sipped his tea and allowed his audience to recompose themselves and settle in.

"We," he commenced with a grand sweep of his arms as if embracing
the entire assembled crowd, "are the descendants of the children of the
goddess, Danu, the mother of all the gods. We are the descendants of her
children known as the Tuatha de Danann, and being the children of a goddess, they themselves were gods," here, Yarn always paused to let the
enormity of the status and importance of their ancestors duly impress his
newest listeners. With his preamble concluded, he dared not disappoint
them by taking a prolonged pause. He continued their story, the story that
was their legend and their crest. Each myth, young and old, wore the saga
of their people as proudly as any clan wears a tartan or any realm declares
their standard.

This is the tale he told.

THE TELLING

part one

THE TUATHA DE Danann were beautiful and graceful beings, accomplished in art and poetry and highly skilled in methods of magic. Danu wanted her children to live in a place as divine and magical as they, so she bid them to travel to the land that would come to be known as Eire. She conjured for her *bairns* a boat made of mist so as not to alarm the natives of the isle with their mysterious and unexpected arrival. The ship of clouds landed in the place called Connaught. After three days time, the mist subsided and the children of Danu began to make their way among the people living there, a people known as the Fir Bolg. But it soon was made known that the Tuatha were not welcome. Danu's children tried to soothe the frightened Fir Bolg with enchantments and gifts of magic, but this only proved to frighten the primitive beings even more. Their determination to live in this land, as was their mother's wish, was resolute, and the Tuatha tried to live peacefully among the Fir Bolg, but to no avail. Knowing only violence as a means to resolve differences, the natives of the island engaged the Tuatha in battle. The Fir Bolg's weapons gave meager resistance against the weapons and powers of Danu's children, and their leader, King Nuada. It was sheer will and tenacity on the part of the Fir Bolg that the battle saw the dawning of three suns before it was decided. So impressed were the Tuatha with their rival's valiant defense of their home that after taking victory in what was to be known as the First Battle of Moytura, the children of Danu gave Connaught to the Fir Bolg while they, the Tuatha, took the rest of the land of Eire. In return, the Fir Bolg, who were so awed with the skill and generosity of mercy shown by the Tuatha that they held their conquerors in the highest regard. In this manner, the two races inhabited the isle together and in harmony.

The Tuatha and Fir Bolg lived peacefully on the lush, green island while across the sea to the north in the land known as *Albain*, lived a race as fond of war as the Tuatha were of peace. They were a people as hard and rugged as the land in which they lived. Using the sea and the cloak of night, they raided and looted the neighboring isles, burning entire villages to the ground and slaying civilians. Their lust for wealth and appetite for conquest made them the most feared people of their land. These sea raiders were called Fomorians.

The leader of the Fomorian was a very powerful king by the name of Balor of the Evil Eye. He convinced his people that his powers were far greater than those of any other king, and his powers were indeed formidable. However, what invoked the greatest fear in the hearts of his enemies was the power of his third eye. The legend explains that as a young chieftain, Balor stumbled upon a ceremony of the native *Druwi*, in which the priests were preparing a potion of wisdom. When his forbidden observance was discovered, the *Druwi* punished him by disfiguring Balor with a third eye with which to do his spying. This eye was gruesome and distorted. It wept blood and was said to shoot deadly flames of fire capable of scorching everything unfortunate enough to be the object of its gaze. Balor was quick to seize upon the opportunity to turn this curse to his advantage. It was this hideous third eye that earned him the reputation of being immortal, as no one was able to defend themselves against this cursed weapon. As Fate would have it, Balor's defeat came from the most improbable source—his own daughter.

Balor of the Evil Eye was married to a prophetess named Caithleann. She was a beautiful and gifted seer and sorceress. She, herself, unwittingly reinforced the belief that her husband was immortal by predicting that he could not die save by the hand of his own grandson. Being a man distrustful of everyone around him—even his own blood—he decided to leave nothing to chance and to insure his continued rule, he locked his own daughter in a stone house on a nearby island. The overly suspicious king allowed only his wife, Caithleann, to attend to her. Although a prison, the small isle was lush with vegetation and bountiful with small game and fish. Caithleann was so distressed by her husband's treatment of their daughter, Eithne, that she regularly secreted her out of her stone stockade, and together they rode along the shores on horseback, swam in the warm waters, and picked berries and flowers with which they would make wine and tea for their evening meals.

On one of the women's outings, they happened upon a young man who was fishing in the inlet where Caithleann and Eithne loved to bathe and swim. The young man, begging forgiveness for intruding on their private time, shared his catch with the mother and daughter as a token of his apologies. He introduced himself as Caine of the Clan MacCainte. He explained that he had fished and hunted on this island since he was a small boy and was unaware that anyone else had discovered its charms. After some polite conversation, Caithleann decided to take Eithne home, lest Balor make one of his surprise visits and find her gone. When they returned to the inlet the next day, the young man was there again. Caithleann had never seen her daughter as happy as she was in the company of this young man, and as Caithleann herself thought the young man to be delightful company, she did nothing to discourage him from joining the two of them in their activities on the island. As thrilled as she was for Eithne, she also realized the potential danger this could present to her husband, Balor. The prophetess had decided that the next day she would talk to Eithne and explain to her the possible danger that she was putting her father in and of the prophecy that Eithne herself was ignorant of. The next morning when Caithleann arrived at the stone house, she knew immediately that the foretelling would be realized. There, in front of her daughter's prison, was Caine's horse. As Caithleann dismounted, she heard the voices of her daughter and the young man as they emerged from the house holding hands and talking to each other in soft, gentle voices. At the sight of her mother, Eithne's eyes dropped to the ground, and the young man, finding himself feeling awkward, kissed Eithne lovingly on the cheek, and bowing his head to Caithleann, prepared to mount his waiting steed.

"Wait." The prophetess asked gently, "Do you love my daughter?"

"With all of my heart, My Lady," was the immediate response.

"Then your place is here, with her. Although her father will not allow this union, do not take leave of your love—or your child," she added pensively.

With this, Eithne and Caine embraced, overjoyed with Caithleann's foretelling of a child. As she watched the blissful pair, Caithleann's delight was as zealous as theirs, but her joy quickly subsided as she realized the magnitude of the danger this now placed the young couple in. Balor's wrath was great, and it would take all of the seer's skill and power to protect her daughter and grandchild from her own husband.

Caithleann kept her daughter's secret as Eithne and Caine lived in the stone house until the birth of their son, Lugh. With the help of Caine's parents, Lord and Lady MacCainte, Eithne, Caine and their newborn son were taken from the island and settled in the remote northern-most region of *Albain*. Under the guidance of the Clan MacCainte, Lugh could be safely raised away from the treacherous paranoia and wrath of his grandfather Balor.

Balor's mania for obstructing the fulfillment of his wife's prediction became an obsession. When Balor realized that he had been deceived, he raised an army to hunt down his betraying daughter and the grandson that threatened his immortality. Caithleann made no secret of her involvement in her daughter's defection, which put the two at mortal odds. However, as powerful as Balor was, he was no match for his prophetess wife. Wise enough to realize that going to war with her would only hasten his undoing, he left the home they shared to live in the camps and caves with his army. The two never looked upon each other again. Her husband's actions were all it took to sever the already brittle bond between them. Marital love can seldom rival maternal devotion, and Balor's vengefulness against their only child had destroyed the ardor that Caithleann had once known for her warrior husband. Although bordering on insane, Balor was still clever, and Caithleann reasoned that if she stayed in *Albain*, Balor would deduce that the only reason she had to be there was to be near her daughter. Not wanting to betray Eithne's whereabouts, Caithleann took her leave of their home and on an overcast and dreary morning, one moon before the summer equinox, she left the wild and beautiful land of *Albain*. Widowed in her heart from a husband she no longer knew, and separated from her only child, she set sail in solitude for the land of green lushness, tranquility and enchantment. Under a guiding talisman, her boat made its way undisturbed across the sea to the land of the peaceful and magical Tuatha, and the home of her sister, Sorcha.

***

Ten and five cycles had come to pass and Caithleann delighted in her new life on the verdant isle. Her sister, Sorcha, was the Tuathan sorceress, and, as such, Caithleann was privy to the rites and ceremonies performed by her sister and the native priests. The *Druwi* priests were the keepers of the culture and lore, guardians of the unwritten and ancient laws, and advisers to the king. However, it was their gift to foretell the future that most intrigued Caithleann. Her gift was given to her through heredity, but theirs was not; their powers were derived from the earth itself and their inseparable connection to it. The *Druwi* accepted Caithleann into their fold and she spent days numbering on days with the priests and her sister in the meadows and forests, the lakes and streams, studying the earth and its laws and unlocking its secrets.

Caithleann's new and tranquil life could not suppress her anguish over her separation from Eithne, and the pain in her heart had become unbearable over the years. Bolstered by the belief that they would be safer under the watchful eye of the *Druwi* of Eire, herself and her powerful sorceress sister, Caithleann summoned Eithne, Caine, and Lugh to join her. Now in his fifteenth cycle, Lugh had grown into a kind and peaceful young man, skilled in hunting, tracking and horsemanship. Ever mindful of his hostile beginnings, Caine had also disciplined his son in the ways of the warrior, and Lugh had become proficient with the skean, axe, spear and sling. It was the sling that Lugh was truly passionate about and the weapon with which he practiced the most. Here, in this beautiful and bountiful land, they lived as a family under the peaceful rule of the Tuatha de Danann.

Their happiness, however, was short-lived. Balor had not relented in his search for his daughter, or the grandson who was destined to be his destroyer. In the year of Lugh's twenty-third birthday, Balor's spies informed the cursed king that his estranged family could be found living among the Tuatha. Balor mobilized his entire fleet, loading each ship with every able-bodied soldier in his army and set sail for Eire. The Fomorian landed on the shores of the Emerald Isle, and the Children of Danu were once again at war.

The Second Battle of Moytura was more ferocious and bloody than the first. The Tuatha may have been outnumbered, but even the war-mongering Fomorians were no match for their battle skills. As the war raged on in the lush fields of Eire, it was the fulfillment of a mother's prophecy that sealed the fate of the vengeful Balor.

The Fomorian king fought side by side with his soldiers on the battlefield, slaying a Tuathan for every Fomorian that fell. Because Balor was not able to recognize his alienated grandson, he paid no attention to a flaxen-haired young warrior making his way across the carnage-strewn field. Armed only with a slingshot, the rugged and determined soldier was but a few paces away from Balor when the Fomorian king finally gave him a second look, but it was too late. With a mastery earned from a lifetime of practice, the son of Eithne released the stone from its sling and slew his fiendish grandfather in front of the entire Fomorian army. Balor's soldiers stood in stunned awe at the sight of their invincible king lying motionless and bleeding on the ground. Without a leader, the Fomorians fought no more. The Tuatha de Danann did not believe in the practice of taking prisoners, so those of Balor's army who had survived were free to make their way back to their homeland across the sea. The stunned and aimless soldiers meandered about the blood-soaked field, gathering up abandoned skeans and axes. They shared the burden of carrying their weapons and their dead king to the rocky shore where their boats waited to take them home.

Although the Tuatha de Danann had readily defeated the Fomorian, their victory had come with a price. Among the hundreds of Tuathan slain in battle was King Nuada. Nuada lost his arm in the First Battle of Moytura and his life in the Second. Lugh, the hero of the battle, became king of the Tuatha of Eire.

For two generations, there was peace and the Tuatha lived in undisturbed pursuit of all things artful and magical. The peace endured until the fateful day in a quiet fishing village when a lone waterman spotted foreign sails on the horizon.

part two

*** *The Arrival of the Milesians* ***

IT WAS TENS of hundreds of cycles before the birth of the Christian Saviour. The children of the goddess Danu had ruled the isle with a gentle hand, watching Eire's population grow as the native Fir Bolg and many abandoned Fomorian assimilated themselves into their conqueror's fold. The people were farmers and fishermen and the practice of trade with their neighbors in *Breatunn* was gaining ground and growing their coffers.

It was a fisherman pulling in his first catch of the morning that saw the far-away sails on the muted horizon off the shores of what would become County Kerry.

A party of eleven discreetly armed men was dispatched to await the landing of the foreign vessel. The small, soundly constructed craft was pulled in and its two passengers diplomatically greeted and escorted to the village of *An Daingean*. They were fed and given warm, dry accommodations while they waited the arrival of Lugh, for whom a messenger had been dispatched as soon as word of the sighting reached the village.

The guests were as gracious as their hosts and had brought with them gifts of wine, cured fish and olives from their native land. The elder of the two envoys was equally generous in his expressions of admiration for the land itself, its beauty and bounty, for which he was sure the Tuathans were most grateful. The visitors' seemingly endless and effusive flattery heaped upon Ireland and its people soon sounded less like polite accolades and more like a heap of blarney. The two Tuathan charged with entertaining the new guests were Caine, father of the king, and Yarn, the fisherman who first spotted the visitor's boat. The contingent of eleven armed men had quietly returned to the shore to keep watch in case their guests had not come alone.

The older of the two foreigners did all of the talking while the younger, his aide, ate and drank silently. The talkative one, who had introduced himself as Ith, thanked his hosts for their gracious hospitality before excusing himself to answer the call of nature outdoors. Caine and Yarn gathered close in the back of the thatched dwelling to converse away from the aide.

"Does he think us fools? 'Tis no emissary that we have under our roof, 'tis an advance party." Caine's voice was hushed but he could not suppress his rage.

Yarn agreed but still offered an alternative explanation. "Perhaps he has been cast out and is seeking shelter and a new home," he proposed. Although in his gut, his instincts told him this was not the case. Caine waited for Yarn to exhaust his list of possible explanations for the presence of their visitors, but alas, he had just the one. "Let us see if Lugh arrives at the same conclusion without the forewarning of our perceptions," Yarn said after a brief silence.

"Agreed," replied Caine.

It was the sound of approaching hooves that sent Caine and Yarn outside to retrieve their guest and greet their king.

Caine escorted Ith back into the dwelling as Yarn grabbed the reins of Lugh's steed. The king arrived with an escort of four soldiers and Yarn knew that they embodied Lugh's unexpressed apprehension. He and Yarn merely exchanged nods as the guards secured the horses and took position—two on each side—at the opening to the small cottage. Yarn entered first. Ith, his aide, and Caine were seated as before, near the hearth, with earthen cups replenished with wine. When Yarn entered, the three stood in unison in time for Lugh to make his entrance. Yarn took the liberty of making introductions as Caine was not accustomed to referring to his son in such a formal manner.

"I present Lugh Ri, King of the Tuathan. This is Ith of Espaine." Yarn kept the introduction short and unadorned.

Ith extended his hand in greeting, which Lugh politely accepted. Ith wasted no time in showering the king with unrestrained praise of Lugh's kingdom and its hospitable inhabitants. As Ith expounded his views on the boundless attributes of Eire, it occurred to Lugh that this visitor, as far as he knew, had actually seen very little of the island. In fact, he had only seen the small parcel between the inlet where his boat was pulled ashore and the thatched cottage in which they now gathered. For having seen so little of a place, he certainly was anxious to let it be known how enamored he was of it. After what Lugh hoped to be a courteous amount of patient listening, he asked his garrulous guest questions about *his* homeland—of its people and land and ruler. Ith answered with half-sentences and disconnected adjectives. He revealed to his host that he was from a land known as Espaine, and that he had come here with the blessings of that land's ruler, King Milesius. Ith used many words, but said little of any importance. The envoy was more interested in talking about Ireland. After two unsuccessful attempts to steer the conversation back to Espaine, Lugh excused himself, motioning for his father to follow and for Yarn to stay. Once outside, Lugh said abruptly to his father, "They are planning an invasion. They must think us simple to be taken in by their scout's endless *flummery* and *codswallop*. Perhaps he is to distract us while their boats take position." Lugh and his father stood toe to toe and eye to eye as the young king aired his thoughts to his trusted counselor.

"Yarn and I have come to the same conclusion, my son. We did not want to tell you beforehand, but we felt certain that your opinion would be the same. He has carefully evaded answering questions about his homeland or of the purpose of his visit," Caine added before giving the conversation back to Lugh.

"By not answering our queries, he has given us the truth. We need only to discover when and in what numbers," Lugh replied. He cast a look toward his four guards, who still stood post outside the cottage entrance before adding, "I am confident that we can persuade him to tell us what we want to know."

Resolutely, father and son turned and made their way back to the protected dwelling. Caine pulled aside the heavy deer hide covering the entrance and stepped in, holding the skin aside for Lugh. Ith and his companion rose to greet the returning king, but Lugh motioned with his hands for them to sit again. Lugh picked up the clay cup that held his untouched wine. Ith raised his own cup in a toast before polishing off its fermented contents. When his eyes came back down to meet Lugh's he was unaffected by the king's humorless demeanor until the monarch spoke: "Tell us when the invasion will take place and how many men your king has at his disposal."

The hand in which Ith held his empty beaker began to shake slightly as the emissary tried to steady his nerves and gather his thoughts. "My king," he began before Lugh cut him off with a raised hand. Lugh nodded toward the opening, which prompted Caine to call for the guards. As the four Tuathan soldiers entered the dwelling, Ith's nervousness became more pronounced and he stammered his protestations. "Mi Rey" was all he managed to say again before two of the soldiers escorted him to his feet.

"Tell me quickly or tell me slowly—the choice is yours," Lugh was saying as Ith's traveling companion leapt to his feet. With fleetness and agility that no one had thought to credit him with, the disregarded aide was off of his stool and behind Ith. Seizing his fellow countryman from behind by the shoulder, the assistant reached into his own robes. The flames from the hearth's fire reflected in the blade of the dagger that the aide now held by its jewel-encrusted handle. This flash of light was all that Lugh saw of the weapon before it disappeared into the back of the emissary from Espaine.

Ith's eyes were filled with perplexed wonder until the searing pain of the flesh wound, ripped lung and pierced heart overwhelmed his surprise.

The Tuathan were stunned. Blindsided, they were temporarily immobilized with horrified amazement. As they stood aghast, the assassin-aide scurried under the deer-skin covering and fled into the waning dusk.

"GO!" Lugh shouted to his soldiers, his left arm raised and pointing toward the entrance, his right arm full of the murdered emissary. Caine took Ith's body from his son and laid it back, resting it on the neatly broomed clay floor. The king stumbled rearward a few steps until his aft-waving hand found a bench. He raised himself up and rested on the rough-hewn seat.

So insignificant was the presence of the aide that he had not been introduced or asked his name. This unnoticed and unnamed attendant to the now dead envoy had changed the course of events for the Tuatha de Danann. While Lugh, Caine and Yarn were convinced that the arrival of the two outlanders indicated a prelude to invasion, the murder of one or both of them would be the causation of an invasion for revenge.

Whether the manslayer was found alive or dead seemed to make no matter. Were he alive and finding his way back to Espaine, he was either hired to prevent Ith from betraying the king's intentions or to secure a cause for war, as he would cast the blame for Ith's murder on the Tuathan. Were he dead, it would be two bodies that Lugh would be held responsible for. Either way, Milesius would have just cause for his invasion.

In that portentous moment in a humble cottage in the quiet fishing village of *An Daingean*, the war with the sons of Mil was irrevocably set into motion. As Lugh watched Ith's blood soak into the dried clay that was the cottage floor, his chest tightened from the crushing weight of foreboding, which now burdened his heart. As he began a mental timeline of preparations for the inevitable arrival of the army of Espaine, he could not fend off the foreboding that any counterattack that they could surmount would not be enough. With a leader's wisdom, Lugh new that war had already begun. Although the blood of so many had been shed on Erinne's ground, none would have the impact that the death of this one emissary would have on the future of the land and her inhabitants. The fate of the children of Danu was now on a course that they no longer controlled. The Tuatha de Danann were unknowingly spending their last days on their cherished Emerald Isle. For Ith was no mere envoy, he was the beloved uncle of King Milesius himself. This was the calm before the bloody storm that would be known as the Battle with the Milesians.

In less than the cycle of two moons, the army of Milesius was approaching Eire's shore. Lugh, his father and Yarn had been correct in their presumption that Ith's arrival had been a prelude to invasion, but Milesius had sent his favorite uncle to convince the inhabitants of the green isle to surrender peacefully. The king did not wish to wage a long and costly battle. He merely wished to have the lush, beautiful island for himself. However, shortly before the return of Ith's aide, who had managed to elude Lugh's guards and find his way back to Espaine, King Milesius died. It was his queen, Scota, and their sons who set out to fulfill their king's dying wish of claiming Ireland, as well as exacting revenge for the murder of Ith, for which the aide laid blame squarely at the feet of the Tuatha de Danann.

The Milesians arrived in numbers that the Tuatha could never have fathomed possible. As the Tuathan army prepared, Sorcha and her priests took position on the peaceful shore of *An Daingean*. As the ships approached, she created towering waves which tossed their ships about as if mere wooden toys. Many were cleaved in two and sent to the bottom of the raging sea, but it was not enough. She conjured dense fog and blistering winds, which caused some ships to lose bearing and go adrift, yet still the fleet gained on their destination.

Sorcha did all within her powers to keep the Milesians from finding her beloved Eire, but their numbers were too great for even her unparalleled powers. The invading armada landed on Ireland's shores intent on conquering the isle and all who inhabited her.

The Tuathans fought fiercely. It took only two days of savage battle for the Milesians to all but annihilate the children of Danu. At dawn on the third day—without taking counsel with his father or his trusted friend, Yarn—Lugh rode alone into the Milesian camp to negotiate terms for surrender in hopes of sparing the lives of what few of his clan members remained. When Yarn and Caine awoke and saw the empty bedding of Lugh, they gathered what soldiers they could and set out for the Milesian camp, knowing in their hearts that they would find their king trying to negotiate on behalf of his people. Caine, Yarn and their men rode boldly into the encampment where they indeed found Lugh outside of the main tent conversing with the leader of the Milesian army, Heber. Heber stood between his brother, Heremon, and their mother, Scota, and opposite of Lugh. None were distracted by the approaching enemy party as they were all surrounded by armed Milesian soldiers. Caine and Yarn stopped mere feet from the assembled leaders and could hear the negotiations, which sounded to be somewhat amicable.

"We greatly admire your bravery and sense of duty to your people," Heber was heard to say. "However," he continued, "there is the matter of my father's dead uncle to consider in these talks." Yarn could feel his spine stiffen as he detected a subtle change in Heber's tone. He desperately wanted to reach for his skean, but knew that he was being watched and could not afford such an aggressive gesture. Heber had by now drawn his weapon. As he did, so did Caine, Yarn and the assembled Tuathan soldiers. The Milesian leader scanned the faces of the apprehensive Tuathans and gave his uninvited guests a smile. He brought his gaze back to Lugh, and with smile absent, the son of Milesius looked squarely into the eyes of the Tuathan king and said, "This is what I propose to you, leader of the Tuatha de Danann. We shall split Eire in half. We will take the top half and you can have the bottom half."

With a quick and vicious thrust, Heber ran his sword through Lugh.

Caine let loose a guttural scream as he urged his mount toward his son's killer. Yarn reached out and grabbed the reigns of Caine's horse, wrenching the creature's neck to the side, forcing it to change direction. With a wave of his arm, he signaled the meager assembly of Tuathan soldiers to follow. Several of them had already engaged the Milesian soldiers as they attempted to retrieve the body of their fallen king. They were all mercilessly slain.

part three

*** *Eire is Divided in Two* ***

IN THE COURSE of their exhaustive studies of their physical world, Sorcha and her priests had discovered gateways caused by rips in the very fabric of their world. They learned that these fissures opened and closed in a synchronized pattern, a pattern predicted with unfailing accuracy by the layout of the massive stones in the great henge of southern *Breatunn*. It seemed that their world was not the only one that existed. There were many—how many they were not yet sure—but in their research to that point, they had found and recorded the properties of ten realms other than the one that they inhabited. Four were merely marked by a rupture in the very air surrounding them, but which led nowhere, six of them they were able to enter and explore. One of these six was even more lush and beautiful than their Eire, and it was on this world that Sorcha and her priests focused a great deal of their attention. The sorceress became so enamored of this alternate and secret world that she gave it the name of Aislinn, meaning dream. Sorcha, her sister, Caithleann, and the *Druwi* also learned that these worlds could not be explored without a price, and they quickly determined how much time they could spend in each alternate domain before these tolls were extracted. They explored always in pairs and always for specific spans of time so as not to succumb to the transforming effects, which seemed to be unique to each world.

The gateway to Aislinn was the first that Sorcha and her priests had discovered. The fact that it was priming to open then, on its own, in concert with the Milesian invasion, Sorcha and Caithleann had interpreted as a positive omen. She and her sister had "seen" the outcome of the battle before it had begun and had started their plan of evacuation before the first battle cry was roared or the first skean had been drawn. They knew that the Tuathans would not live in this new world and remain as they were, but at least, they reasoned, they would live.

After the slaying of the Tuathan king, a handful of Milesian soldiers had been dispatched to the unprotected villages to carry out the practice of slaying the innocent and burning the cottages and crofts to the ground. Caithleann, Sorcha, and several *Druwi* priests found those few villagers who had managed to escape the massacre, and led them to the portal to Aislinn, seeing them safely through. The rescuers turned their attention to the battlefield and guided the willing, unwilling, and wounded to safety, as well. It was not until two priests dragged the slain body of Lugh to the entrance of the Tuathan's new world that Sorcha realized that her sister was not near. The sorceress frantically called out to her sibling, but no answer came. She ran to their temple, which was actually a petrified rowan tree, hollow from centuries of lifelessness. There she questioned the priests as they bundled the Tuathan talismans for transport to the portal; none had seen Caithleann. By her order, the *Druwi* priests left with the clan's treasures and headed for the gateway. Sorcha stood alone in her deserted sanctuary looking out over the crimson-stained jade fields of her homeland.

She closed her eyes.

Sorcha set free her mind's eye and sent it soaring above the fields, meadows and forests of Eire in search of her missing sister. It did not have far to go. Tears were streaming down the sorceress's face as her reddened eyes opened and then closed fast again, forcing a fresh flood of tears to spill through her thick, dark lashes. Sorcha made her way out of the ancient topiary temple. As she traversed the field strewn with the victims of the Milesians' insatiable appetite for revenge, she came upon the body of her beloved sister, Caithleann. Unblemished by wounds or outward signs offering a reason for her demise, Sorcha knew what her sister's fate had been. With the news of her grandson's death, Caithleann turned her devastation into a gift. She had given herself as a sacrifice to ensure the safety of the Tuathans who had shown her complete acceptance and given her the most joyous years of her life.

Sorcha knelt by her sister.

The sorceress placed her left hand over Caithleann's eyes and her right hand over her sister's heart. Sorcha closed her eyes and bent her head down until her chin touched her chest. Inhaling deeply, she slowly raised her head up and back until her face was turned heavenward. She opened her eyes. As she did, tendrils of light emanating from her fingertips spiraled around Caithleann's body, lifting it off the ground and enrobing it in blue light from head to toe. Her gaze still focusing skyward, Sorcha brought her hands together, index finger touching index finger, thumb touching thumb. The blue tendrils of light, which had absorbed the body of Caithleann, swirled and flowed upward through the triangle created by Sorcha's converged hands. The tears returned as she watched the gentle Eire winds carry her sister up and away.

Sorcha knelt there, perfectly still, refusing to look away until all signs of Caithleann had dissipated, when a slight flutter in her stomach sent her hands down to her belly. She answered the quiver with a soft caress and abandoned her survey of the sky after whispering a last "I love you" to her sister.

The sorceress wanted to go to the portal to help with the transfer of the surviving Tuathan to their new home before the fissure closed and trapped them in Eire with the revenge-thirsty Milesians. The battlefield was long deserted as the army of Espaine had grown tired of routine killing, and desiring the more gaming pursuit of hunting and plundering had gone off to join their comrades in the villages. Sorcha knew that time was precious and as soon as the soldiers realized that the villages had been abandoned, their search would lead them to the evacuation sight. But first, she needed to go back to her temple.

After a quick inventory to be sure that all four of the Tuathan symbols had been carried off to safety by the *Druwi* priests, Sorcha slipped into a hidden room that held a fifth and most powerful talisman. She emerged, cradling a book. She gently placed the book on a tanned ruby hide that covered one of the two altars in the center of the hollow tree. She passed her hand lovingly over the gold inlaid symbols decorating its cover. She laid her hand on the emblem in the lower right-hand corner, and in a windershins direction, gently caressed each symbol: from the sword to the cauldron, then left and downward over the golden symbols of the spear and the stone before bringing her hand to rest on the center, an embossed replica of the book itself, a golden five-leaf clover gracing its cover. The sorceress spoke to her tome in what might be the last moment that she would have with her life's work for some time. She pulled the book to her chest as she recited a protective incantation over her beloved manuscript. She then raised the book heavenward and asked the goddess, Danu, herself, to protect the fifth talisman of her people and see that no creature of this world, or any other, found a way to use it against her children. Sorcha then took the beautifully embellished book and slipped it into a plain, coarsely woven sack. She pulled the sack to her chest, wrapping her arms tightly around it. After a quick survey of her now empty temple, she hastily took her leave to join the others and enter the new world that she, too, would soon call home.

Sorcha had just reached the carved-out entrance to the hollowed rowan tree when she was met by a *Druwi* priest.

"Mephistis? Why are you not with the others?" she asked breathlessly.

"I have come to retrieve the book, my queen," the errant priest replied.

"I have the book. We must go," she stated as she tried to pass between him and the door's edge.

"Let me take that for you. 'Tis too heavy for you to carry," Mephistis offered calmly.

"I have the book, Mephistis. Let us go join with the others. Now."

The High Sorceress made her intent exceedingly clear.

Mephistis moved from Sorcha's path and took his place behind her, as they ran across the open field before taking cover in a dense copse of trees, which would keep them secreted until they reached the Tuathan village and the opening to Aislinn.

But neither Sorcha or Mephistis or the book made it through the portal.

CHAPTER 19

CLAIRE AWOKE WITH a start. She could not gauge how long she had been asleep except by the color of the sky which was no longer plum but a purplish black. Yarn was still narrating from his rocky dais, Willa and Anndra sound asleep at his feet. Claire had no trouble slipping past the watchful eyes of her three faerie "guards," and went in search of Sarla. She found her a short distance away rinsing teacups and pots in the clear rushing stream that fed the lake. Claire crouched down, and lifted two dirty cups from the tray. She waited patiently for a break in the current of fog and when it came, she immersed the cups in the cold waters of the stream to purge them of their tea remnants. Sarla smiled at Claire and mouthed an appreciative "thank you."

"I'm afraid I fell asleep at some point during the story," Claire whispered sheepishly. "I hope no one noticed."

"Not a soul at the gathering could cast a stone at you for it, dear. 'Tis quite a long tale to get through without a wee nap here and there," Sarla answered her with her customary cheerfulness.

They continued the process of rinsing the dishes in silence for some time until Claire broke the quiet with a barely audible "Sarla."

"Yes, dear," came the gentle reply.

"Will you tell me more about the priests, the *Druwi*?"

"What would you like to know, dear?"

Sarla took the two teacups that Claire was holding from her grasp, and after setting them softly back onto the tray took Claire by the hand and led her to a craig-moss mound a few steps away. Sarla motioned Claire toward the soft rise and she, herself, lit upon a cluster of mistletoe hanging from the branch of a rowan tree. The two were eye to eye and Claire was the first to speak.

"Are they like the people called Druids?"

"They are one and the same. *Druwi* is their ancient name."

"I've never heard anyone talk about them the way Yarn did," Claire said gently. "I don't think that anyone thinks that way about them now," she added with a tinge of discomfort.

Sarla thought of her promise to Claire, her promise that nothing would be held back, and that her questions would be answered honestly and completely. Preparing to do just that, the faerie readjusted her position on the mistletoe cluster and looked the young girl directly in the eye. In Claire, Sarla found all of the qualities of which she believed her species to be capable. She delighted in spending time with the young outlander. Claire was bright and self-assured and seemed perfectly at ease in the company of those who were older than she. Sarla was thankful that she had been there when Claire needed someone to care for her, and allowed herself to imagine her role as Claire's mother were they not able to return the nambor *bairn* to her home. The vision filled Sarla with joy at the possibility, but her elation was brief. She chastised herself for being so selfish; they must do everything in their power and beyond to get the little girl back home and back with her own kind. Sarla had grown very fond of Claire, indeed, and felt the same protectiveness of her that she felt for Willa and Anndra. The realization that soon there might be nothing that they could do to return the little girl to her home filled Sarla with anxiety. Her intuition told her what her heart was not ready to hear; that not finding a way to send her back, and soon, was going to put Claire in harm's way.

"What do you mean, dear? Who does not think of them that way anymore?" the faerie asked.

"My father, for one," Claire answered quickly.

"Ahhh," Sarla replied with a smile.

Claire said nothing and waited for Sarla to continue.

"You remember in the Telling when Yarn explained about how we came to be here—how we left our old home?"

Claire scrunched up her face and shook her head slightly from side to side as an apologetic answer of no.

"Oh my," Sarla said with a soft sigh. "I should have realized that this may be too much for you to stay awake through, dear." Sarla gave her charge a loving and sympathetic gaze. "Well, our world, E'lore, is one of many worlds out there. Your world, Doog, is another. They carry on, side by side, having no idea of the existence of the other. Well, the priests, the *Druwi*," she continued, "knew of these other worlds because of an ancient stone circle in *Breatunn*."

"Are you talking about Stonehenge?" Claire asked, surprised by the course that their conversation was taking.

"I am, dear," Sarla continued undaunted by Claire's astonishment. "The ancient people of *Breatunn* knew of these other worlds too. Although 'tis thought that they may have lacked the ability to understand *what* these other worlds were, one thing they did not lack was the ability to mark *where* they were." Sarla paused for just a moment, then continued. "The Tuathan sorceress was shown the henge by the *Druwi* priests, and soon she had learned not only the signs for when the openings to these other worlds were going to appear naturally, but how to open them *herself*. 'Twas her ability to spot the doorways to these other realms, even before they opened, that saved the Tuathan people. When our clan was all but exterminated by the Milesians, she and the *Druwi* led us to the gateway of E'lore."

Sarla paused again, drawing a deep breath before uttering to the nambor what had never been disclosed to one outside of the Druid sect or the myth clan before. Claire waited patiently.

"The henge is a … well 'tis two things, really.'Tis a map and a key. Not only is it home to several of the portals itself, it shows—if you know how to study it—how to spot the portals elsewhere. According to the priests, the openings to these other worlds are abundant and almost everywhere. Because the stones are the only actual markings of these openings that they are aware of, the *Druwi* gather there, not to practice ancient pagan rituals, but to protect innocents from stumbling through these gateways where they would most likely be lost forever. Some of the guardians are new to the faith, but most are descendents of those from before, from those very priests who helped us to escape the Milesians. They are destined and sworn by bloodline to protect Stonehenge and its true purpose."

"So … why does everyone think that it's some kind of giant, prehistoric calendar? I don't mean just regular people either, but scientists too. Why haven't they figured it out by now?" Claire asked.

"'They' and your father, I suspect, believed what most everyone has been led to believe about the circle, and we cannot fault them for that. The truth be told, Stonehenge is not a 'calendar', dear. It never has been. Although it has been quite a fortunate turn of luck that that is what it appears to be."

Sarla smiled at her companion, and allowing herself to fall from the mistletoe cluster, she fluttered back down to the ground, alighting just at the stream's edge. Lifting a dirty cup from the basket, she resumed the task of washing up the considerable number of dishes and vessels dirtied by the gatherers who had come to hear the Telling. Claire followed her, and as the two of them gently wiped the cups and rinsed them in the clear, crisp stream water, Sarla's explanation continued.

"Long ago, in the time told of in the Telling, nambors were not as they are now. They did not need to have the world explained to them. They simply allowed themselves to believe in what they could see and feel. At the time of the Tuathan's banishment, the portals were revered and accepted. The only reason for protecting their purpose was to protect the myth from their enemies. After the War of the Exile, 'twas fear of the unknown that kept humans away from the stones. The henge held a mystical quality for them, and since they did not understand it, they feared it.

"The *Druwi* used this fear to their advantage, and for a very long time, Stonehenge was allowed to mark time in its peaceful field with little more than the grazing cows for company. As the human race evolved, man's overpowering need to explain the world and everything in it became all consuming. They looked again to the stones and their possible purpose. 'Twas not long though, before the guardians realized that the purpose of the stones would never be discovered by these 'seekers of truth' because the truth was not logical. Humans had long since lost their ability to accept that which simply *was*, and would never embrace an answer that could not be rationally explained. The only concern for the henge that the *Druwi* still had was the fear that someone would persist in looking for a stronger connection between their sect and the stones. Eventually, someone would be clever enough to realize that their relationship—still so strong after so many centuries and so many religions—bore testament to a deeper connection than the one commonly agreed upon.

"To draw attention away from the truth, the priests sought to distract others from researching their association with the ancient stones by changing the public's perception of *them*—the *Druwi*. If the bulk of the world thought them to be practitioners of a fanciful religion, then they would not think of them as anything more than bothersome and leave them to their practices. 'Twas in this way, by compelling disrespect for the very religion that was their reason for being, that they have kept the truth elusive and safe. If the world of scientists and zealots knew the true power of the stones, all would be lost."

Claire was quiet for a moment as she absorbed Sarla's very thorough answer to her question. Doing her best to suppress a rising chuckle, Claire said, "Sarla?"

"Yes?" the faerie answered.

"*You* sound like a scientist," at which point the chuckle escaped and was immediately joined by laughter from Sarla, as well.

The two carried on with the washing up, smiling, and rinsing cups side by side. With only the gurgling of the rushing water and the clashing of clay and porcelain penetrating the tranquil calm, they continued immersing and wiping until all the cups were clean. In the darkness above, the waned moon reminded Claire of the abandoned crescent-shaped cutting tools hanging next to the tobacco scythes in the tractor shed back on the farm. The moon hung low and heavy in the aubergine sky like a cream sickle. It seemed to be so close that Claire was sure she could reach out and hang a cup on its tip. Occasionally, exclamations and laughter from the gathering would remind them that they were not alone, which Claire found strangely comforting in this strange place. When the last cup had been dried and returned to the basket, the two looked at each other and smiled, but neither made any motion to leave.

"Sarla?" Claire whispered.

"Yes, dear?" the faerie whispered back.

"My mother's name was Caithleann."

CHAPTER 20

CLAIRE LAY RESTLESSLY under the moleskin covers. The deep plum glow of the sky outside her window was morphing into a pale grape with edges of lavender; the harbinger of the break from night to day. Sunrise was Claire's favorite time to be outside and when the dawn's colors were this spectacular she needed no other motivation to get out of bed. She stretched and yawned away the night's sleep. With her eyes still fixed on the intense hues beyond the window's ledge, she raised her knees to her chest and then plunged her legs forward, pushing the skins off of her and into a puddle at the bottom of the nest. However, when Claire pulled her knees back to her chest, her pajama bottoms did not make the return trip. There, in the haphazard pile of skins at the foot of her bed, were the bottoms that were now large enough to hold one-and-a-half Claires. The stunned little girl reached down just past her feet to collect the wayward bloomers. Shallow waves of anxiety mixed with confusion slowly lapped through her head, as she scanned the room for something to wear. Her wandering eyes came to rest on some strips of braided fabric that Sarla had fashioned to hold aside the skins covering the windows. She pulled the oversized bottoms back up over her legs, holding onto the top as she slid out of the nest and shuffled over to the window.

The curtain tie-back came off easily and Claire wrapped it around her waist, pulling the excess pant material above the braided belt. She tied it off with a firm knot and then folded the surplus material back down over the waistband. Her top was an easy enough fix as she rolled the shirt sleeves up until they ended once again just above her wrists.

Claire was shrinking.

Knowing that the light show outside was fading away with every passing moment, the girl shifted her attention from her wardrobe troubles to her intent to go outside. She dragged the roughly hewn bench she used as a riser to help her get in and out of the nest over to the window. The bench raised her high enough off the floor so that she was able to swing her right leg over the ledge, which was quickly followed by her left. Pushing the skin cover away and behind her, she sat in the window, legs dangling over the edge as she judged the distance between the ledge and the ground. With her mom's voice in her head saying, "In for a penny, in for a pound," she hoisted herself off and away from the ledge and landed with a soft squishing sound in the lush tendriled growth that encircled Tobas's and Sarla's home. Brushing the overgrowth out of her way, she climbed out of the brush and surveyed her surroundings. Through breaks in the ground-hugging, swirling fog, she made out the outlines of the worn dirt path stretching in two directions across the front of the house. She paused to allow a particularly dense stream of mist to pass and then strode out of the lush thicket and onto the path.

Standing at the path's edge, Claire glanced up and down the trail looking for anything that would make the choice for her as to whether to go left or right. To her immediate right was Tobas's and Sarla's house, and beyond that, another cottage and another. To her left, it appeared to be more of the same. Just as she was saying to herself, 'just choose', she heard it—a sound that she knew as well as she knew her own name, a sound that made her blood rush and her heart pound. She jerked her head to the left from where the noise had come and listened for it again. Hearing it a second time was all the confirmation Claire needed, and she was off like a rocket, running up the trail and toward a fenced enclosure. As she sought the source of the sound, she caught sight of a rather unusual cottage. She eyed the dwelling briefly, making note of its extreme leftward slant and wondered what the inside must look like. She registered a reminder in her head to investigate this cottage some other time as her adrenalin-riddled legs had no intention of slowing down now. It was the rough-hewn railings of Yarn's pasture enclosure that finally brought Claire to a stop. When she reached the fence, she bent down and climbed through the lower-most rungs searching what was obviously a grazing pasture for signs of the source of the exquisite sound. At the same time that she heard the third whinny, she saw it—a quagga. It had grazed its way into view over a moss-covered mound, and when it saw the girl, it picked its head up and made its unhurried way over to her. Unsure whether this creature—definitely equine, but not a horse—was friendly or savage, Claire retraced her steps back to the other side of the railings from where she offered soft cooing noises for encouragement. The quagga walked up to the fence and seemed intent on going through it. It shoved its lovely striped head through the rungs offering it willingly to Claire to cover in pets and scratches. With its smallish dark eyes, mohawk-mane and muted stripes, she recognized it to be more closely related to a wild zebra than a domestic horse. Zebra? Horse? Who cares? It's beautiful and it's here and I bet I can ride it, the little girl reasoned.

Too excited for good judgment, Claire climbed up and over the third rung of the fence and lowered herself carefully and gently onto the clueless quagga. The mohawk-maned beast did not bolt or buck, but instead strained its neck to try to catch a peek at what was mounted on top of it. It curved its neck to the left and the right, striving to have a look for itself. When this failed, the mount resorted to option B: Get the thing off me and then look at it while it's lying on the ground. Toward this end, the quagga positioned itself alongside the fence and leaning on it heavily, took a few steps forward, rubbing its side along a length of the fence.

But this tactic was nothing new to Claire. Mr. Linton had a horse at his stables—Buttons—who would do the same thing. Buttons was much older than the other horses, and she felt that she had paid her dues and was ready to retire. Unfortunately, Mr. Linton had other plans. Due to the fact that Buttons was no longer interested in galloping, rearing or any other activities that involved physical exertion, she made the perfect mount for beginning students. In the first few weeks of Claire's lessons, she was assigned Buttons. Although a bit cranky and cantankerous, Buttons did have a wonderful sense of humor—and timing. The students would make their way around the indoor training ring with Mr. Linton, who, armed with a riding crop, shouted commands from the center. Buttons would wait until her master's back was to her before she would walk right up to the enclosure's metal siding and give her rider a hard, long rub against the corrugated aluminum panels. The first time it happened, Claire was caught completely by surprise, and ended up with a tear in her riding pants and a pretty bad gash in her leg. It only took the one injury for Claire to be able to gauge when Buttons was planning her rider's premature dismount, and the young student became quite adept at slipping her feet from the stirrups and draping the targeted leg over her steed's neck until the threat passed.

Armed with the same sense of humor as her former teaching mount, the quagga lowered his head, nibbled at the moss and Shannon blossoms, and when he thought the timing was precise, rubbed vigorously against the posts and railings of the enclosure, trying nonchalantly to force his unexpected passenger to the ground. Claire's balance was impeccable thanks to her lessons at the stables, and she was able and content to play this game as long as the quagga was willing to. She only hoped that it never occurred to him to drop and roll—that was not as easy to evade.

Soon the unwilling mount became more interested in eating than in Claire, and it meandered away from the fencing, strolling casually toward the open field and the promise of lusher grazing. Claire attempted to steer her ride with gentle prods from her heels and tugs on his mane, but the quagga and Claire did not speak the same language, and her prompts went unheeded. 'No matter,' she thought. Happier and more "at home" than she had felt since she found herself in this strange place, Claire lay backward, rested her head on her mount's rump, and lost herself in the sway and rhythm of the quagga's stride and the sound of his teeth ripping the moss and blossoms from the ground. She kept her eyes open long enough to watch the sky lose its purple splendor in exchange for the soft, muted vanilla tones that marked the daytime in E'lore. Claire could feel herself dozing off when she heard a deep, soft voice.

"His name is Algy," it said.

Claire recognized the timber of the voice immediately and knew whom she would see standing there even before she put herself upright and turned around.

"But if a ride is what you are looking for, then old Algy here is not your best pick. Biggles would be the one you're after."

"Well, actually, he's the one that did the picking," Claire offered shyly.

"So there are others?" she added.

"Oh yes, many," Yarn answered. "Most likely the largest herd of quagga anywhere," he added proudly.

Claire suddenly realized that perhaps she had been too forward in helping herself to the zebra-like creature. As this notion washed over her, she quickly dismounted, apologizing profusely before her feet even touched the ground.

"I'm so sorry. I wasn't thinking that they belonged to anybody ... I was just so excited ... I just didn't ..."

"No, no, you've done nothing wrong, my dear. You are perfectly welcome anytime—anytime at all." Yarn was doing his best to put the embarrassed girl at ease.

"Really? Thank you," she answered.

"Sarla will be coming to wake you soon—mustn't let her find an empty nest, hmmmm?" Yarn teased her as he placed a hand on her shoulder and gently guided her toward the fence.

"Besides, if our timing is right, perhaps I can get myself invited to breakfast," he playfully added.

Claire gave Algy several strokes and a kiss on his soft, bristly nose before following Yarn to the fence, which the faerie gracefully flew over. Claire marveled at his wings and his ability to fly as she climbed through the fence rungs. Once on the other side, they both headed toward the soft, dirt path that led back to Sarla's and Tobas's cottage. As the two walked side by side, Claire casually reached across and took Yarn's swaying hand in hers. The startled myth turned his head toward the young girl, but Claire kept hers down for fear that if she looked at him, she would have to give his hand back. The old myth felt the smile welling up from his chest and did not discourage it from overtaking his whole face. Hand-in-hand and in comfortable silence, they walked the worn path up to his nephew's house. Yarn held the gate open for Claire. They had just made it to the porch when the front door flew open, and they found themselves face-to-face with a frantic and breathless Sarla.

***

The following morning, Claire repeated her exit through her bedroom window and headed straight for the enclosed pasture that she had found the daybreak before. She closed her eyes and breathed in the gauzy lavender sky as she made her hurried way up the dirt path. When she finally reached the rough-hewn railings, she plunged her head and half her torso through the middle and bottom rungs and began making clicking and cooing noises to the unseen herd. When no response came, she moved further down the enclosure and repeated her call—still, no reaction. She climbed up to the middle of the three rungs to have a look around. Not a quagga in sight.

Even though Yarn had told her she was welcome to befriend his herd, she was still apprehensive about helping herself. She hopped down off the railing and was walking down the fence line when her foot brushed against something on the ground. She recognized the object instantly, even in its rugged and unadorned simplicity. It was a bridle. It was bit-less and fashioned of braided strands of soft, still-green reeds. Claire reached down to gather up the double reigns when she saw the coarse sack that was lying on the ground next to the tack. She draped the bridle over the middle fence rail and cautiously picked up the bag. The girl pulled at the cord that cinched the sack closed, but stopped and glanced around as if expecting to find someone watching. When she saw no one, she returned her attention to the bag and carefully opened it. She pulled it to her nose and took a sniff. The scent was subtle and slightly sweet. She folded the opening of the bag down to get a look at what was inside but what was inside was already making its way out. Dark vermilion wisps, now free from their bonds, rose from the inside of the purse as if summoned by a charmer. The crimson curls were laden with a thick sweet perfume reminding Claire of the honeysuckle that grew with unapologetic abandon on the farm. Claire brought her nose down level to the pouch opening and drew in a deep breath. The aroma, having been invited, was all too happy to oblige. The scent propelled itself straight out of the pouch and up both of the unprepared girl's nostrils. Claire immediately dropped the bag and brought her hands up to her nose, pinching the two sides together in an effort to stop the tingling. Just as she did, she felt a hand on her shoulder accompanied by a calm, but amused,

"Too late for that, dear. Besides, you may want to leave that open in case it does not find another way out," Yarn instructed gently as he pointed to her nose.

Claire barely had time to furrow her brow into a wordless "huh?" when his meaning became clear. Escorted by a warm tickling rush, the ruby wisps took their leave through her ears, sending her shoulders scrunching skyward as the resulting goose bumps made her shudder. The mischievous vapors circled her head twice before spiraling up and away into the early morning air.

"What is this?" the bewildered girl asked as she reached down and picked up the pouch once again.

"I really must apologize, my dear," Yarn offered as he reached out and took the bag from her. Claire's attention shifted from him to the pouch and back, all the while rubbing her still tingling ears and itchy nose.

"By the time I had thought better of leaving these for you to discover on your own, 'twas too late. Terribly unfair of me not to have warned you first," he added.

Claire did not repeat her question, but merely gazed at the elder myth in confusion.

"Yes, right!" Yarn exclaimed when he realized he had not answered.

"These are coaxing berries. The quagga are quite fond of them. Thought they might come in handy for finding you a more adequate mount this morning. They should be picking up the scent any time now." Yarn explained.

But Claire was no longer listening to her friend. She heard something far more riveting, and it was getting louder and closer.

Yarn turned his gaze in the same direction as Claire's just in time to see them. First there came ears and bouncing mohawk manes, then heads and necks and finally chests and legs. The coaxing berries had worked their spell and Yarn's entire herd of quagga was now making their excited way toward the myth and the girl, and they were wasting no time in doing so.

"You had better take a handful," he suggested as he offered the open pouch to Claire. "They will be expecting their reward, and all at the same time, I'm afraid!"

When the last of the berries had been as evenly distributed amongst the quagga as their eager pushing and shoving would allow, Yarn excused them all with an authoritative, "That will be enough of that, you greedy beasties. Off you get!"

Claire was impressed that this simple command actually had the desired effect on all of them, save one, that is. The remaining quagga stood his ground firmly and even shoved his thick neck through the fence rungs to nuzzle Claire's hand, ascertaining for himself that there were indeed no berries left.

"Behave now, Biggles," Yarn playfully admonished his pet while giving him a vigorous scratch behind his right ear.

"This is Biggles? This is the one you said that I may be able to ride?" Claire's higher pitched voice gave away her excitement.

"I dare say that he would rather enjoy a good look around, would you not old boy?" Yarn's affection for the stocky, striped creature was impossible for him to hide, and Claire sensed a kindred spirit in the elder myth. Yarn slowly pulled the handmade hackamore off the fence post, all the while rubbing Biggles' nose and cooing to him in soft, deep tones. He slipped the crownpiece over the beast's large fluffy ears. After securing the browband, he carefully pulled the noseband down and over the soft but bristly muzzle. He checked that the cheek pieces were smooth and not tangled before scooping up the reigns. Yarn fluttered his wings and flew the reigns up and over the equine's neck before resting them gently on the animal's withers.

"Are we ready, then?" he asked Claire when he landed back on the ground.

Too excited to speak, she managed only to nod her head "yes."

Biggles, evidently, *was* keen on having a look around. As Yarn and Claire made their way over to the paddock gate, the quagga followed on the other side of the railings and met the two at the turnstile. When Yarn reached for the bolt that held the gate secure, Claire was already sitting on the highest railing, and when Biggles passed by, she grabbed a handful of mane for support and lowered herself onto his waiting back. She laced the double-strand reins between her middle, ring and pinkie fingers and secured her seat by squeezing her thighs against her mount's rib cage.

"All set?" Yarn queried before he swung the unlatched gate open.

Again, a vigorous nod "yes" was all she could manage.

"Off you go," he said as he gave the gate a pull and liberated the steed and rider from the enclosure. Biggles rocked his head up and down and let out a loud and hearty snort. Yarn had barely opened the gate before the anxious equine burst through the meager opening, nearly ripping the delicate handcrafted reins from his passenger's grasp. Claire was flush with exhilaration as her ride lurched forward toward the open dirt path. However, it was not the open and beckoning trail that Biggles had his sights set on. It was a particularly green and lush mound of footlefern growing with tremendous enthusiasm just a few paces before it. Within two strides of the opened gate, the hungry quagga came to an abrupt halt, dropped his head and began gobbling up the sweet, thick blades. His unexpected stop sent Claire lurching forward, and had it not been for her last-second grab of mane, she would have spilled headlong over the beast's head and plunged face-first into the footlefern herself.

Yarn could not conceal his amusement or the grin that came with it as he walked over to the noshing creature and the disappointed little girl. When he saw how deeply despondent Claire was he gave his beloved pet the best false scolding that he could muster while smiling, and offered his new friend a very sincere, "Do forgive him, dear. He is but a slave to his nature and needs."

Claire, although disappointed, loved the humor in her mount's antics.

"Come on then. Accept his apology and give us a smile," the myth encouraged her.

Claire let a moment pass.

"*Did* he apologize?" she asked playfully.

"Well, not yet, perhaps, but I am quite sure that he will as soon as he's done with his nibbles," Yarn answered, delighted to learn of Claire's subtle sense of humor.

The myth turned his attention back to the feasting quagga and continued his jovial admonishing of the oblivious beast.

Claire found herself wondering if Yarn was a father with children of his own. If he weren't, that would be a shame, she thought. He would be a good father.

When Biggles finally had his fill of the sweet green sprouts, he lifted his thick striped head, allowing slobbery wet tendrils of fern to dangle and fall from his mouth.

"Ahh," Yarn sighed, "looks like we're ready to have another go!"

He gathered the slack in the reins and handed them to Claire.

"I do not expect that he'll be willing to go too far, but perhaps you could persuade him to go as far as the marketplace. If so, there is a particularly rumpled and untidy shack that will be the first stall in the market that you come upon, or the last, depending on which way our friend here decides to go." Yarn gave a gentle rub on Biggles' withers for emphasis.

"It will be occupied by some equally rumpled and untidy creatures. Now, I do not want you to be alarmed," he inserted quickly. "They are a bit ... different, shall we say. I hope that you will not be too startled by how ... unfriendly they are. 'Tis not that they *mean* any harm—well perhaps they do ..." Yarn's voice trailed and his gaze shifted downward as he began to think better of where he was advising Claire to go.

Just as Claire was getting ready to ask him what he was speaking of, Yarn jerked his head back up, looked straight at the girl and continued. "They are just a bit ... ill-tempered is all really," he said, "although frightfully gifted to be sure. So, you'll go to the *cordswainer's* and have them fashion some *brogs* for you. We cannot let you continue to go around half *lomnocht*!" he finished in the old language.

Had Yarn not given Claire a soft pat on the top of her left foot as he said "*brogs*," she might not have understood him to mean that she was to go and get some shoes.

The kind and gentle myth grabbed a handful of rein and led the still chomping Biggles to the well-worn pathway.

"Best to keep to the path," Yarn advised.

"Now, do not be shy about letting him know who's in charge," he continued. "Give him a tug when he gets a mind that 'tis him and not you." Yarn gave the reins a stout tug to demonstrate.

Claire was flooded with a sense of déjà vu as her diminutive instructor placed a firm hand on her lower back and pushed her knees forward and tighter around her mount's rib cage. His attentive adjustments mimicked, practically movement for movement, Mr. Linton's final inspection of the rider's form before releasing his equestrian apprentices into the ring. Claire's gaze locked onto the myth's visage and she swallowed hard to squelch a rising lump in her throat as she let her mind fill with images of home.

Biggles had already chosen his direction and set upon the path towards Aislinn when Claire realized that Yarn was waving to her, and the distance between them was growing. She cleared her head just enough to give him a wave in return. When she was sure that it was safe, she released the welling homesickness that she had been trying to suppress and let the warm tears flow with abandon—tears she was glad that Yarn could not see.

Claire was only too happy to leave the navigating to the carefree quagga and he plodded along down the blossom-rimmed trail giving his rider time to collect her thoughts and herself. It was the rhythmic patter of his hooves that finally gave the girl something else to focus on and allowed her to put aside her heavy-hearted daydreams for the time being.

At some point, Biggles had taken the time to replenish his gobful of greens and was chewing nonchalantly on some juicy aubergine blossoms that had the misfortune of being within his reach. Claire reached down and gave her ride a scratch on his neck and let her hand glide over his coarse mane as she leaned back again into her seat. She rubbed him absently on the withers as she took in her surroundings. As breathtaking as the blooms and foliage lining the path were, Claire wanted nothing more than to just ride. She remembered Yarn's words as she took up the slack in the reins and gave Biggles a determined squeeze with her knees and calves. She was somewhat surprised when her command yielded the desired effect, and the quagga adapted his stride accordingly to a trot. Her mount's gate was a bit rougher than she was used to, but it didn't take her long to find his rhythm and post in time with the strike of his hooves. They trotted along just long enough for Claire to feel like herself again and for Biggles to finish his blooms. Then it was time for him to pluck another mouthful from the woods' edge and resume his leisurely walk.

The outline of the path was clean and distinct, leaving Biggles two options: soft, unobstructed loamy trail, or profuse, tangled, impenetrable thicket of blossoms and vines. He lazily chose the first, leaving Claire the freedom to ride and gaze and take in the impossibly beautiful landscape.

She had noticed that the light seemed to have diminished somewhat since she and her new four-legged friend had embarked on the trail, but there was no mystery as to why. The trees that grew along the path's edge were blissfully blighted with all manner of surplus growth from the over-crowded floor of the surrounding woods. The ascending foliage unabash-edly wrapped their shafts around the tree's base as they surged upward to-ward the more abundant light. Once they were securely attached to their hosts, the vines shifted their energy to more ornate pursuits. Small buds of every possible color began erupting with abandon all along the vine's length as it continued its unhindered journey up the trunk and into the tree's very branches. Even the bough's end could not discourage their advance, and they continued their growth into the very air where they were met by like-minded growth from the other side of the trail. The eager blooms wrapped themselves around and around one another in a joyous greeting, weaving an unbreakable knot before each turned back and went in search of another branch to conquer. The tree, for its part, wore the vines and their blooms like coveted jewels.

While the lush greenery framing the path was just as resplendent as the growth in the trees that created a living canopy over the trail, the ground vegetation had one characteristic that the elevated growth did not. The flowers on the ground stood still.

It was the slightest, almost imperceptible, movement at first, but it was enough to catch Claire's attention. Had she just given the overhead vista a casual scan, she would have missed it. If all she invested was a passing glance, then she never would have seen its true nature. Claire brought her knees up and took a kneeling position on the quagga's broad rump. It was from this slightly higher vantage point that she studied the flora with genu-ine curiosity and admiration. And for this, she was rewarded. Prompted by her appreciation, the vines and tendrils that were entwined in the lower branches unraveled themselves and spiraled downward as if *they* wanted a closer look at *her*. The equestrienne held perfectly still as the bud-laden vines swirled and swayed around her head, leaving visible trails of their in-toxicating scent. As the ballet slowed, Claire could focus on the unusual colors displayed by the impending blossoms that studded the vine with reckless profusion. The small burgeoning buds were a blaze of yellow, ringed in what the mesmerized little girl could most closely label as lime-green, which then yielded the very tip to an unrestrained magenta. Claire was assigning these colors in her head, but these were not the colors that she was seeing. She did not have words for the colors that she was seeing. These shades and hues were unlike any that she had beheld before. They were simultaneously color and illumination—radiant pigments that seemed to both consume and reflect light on a whim. Were the task given to her, she thought, she could never in her lifetime find words beautiful enough or generous enough to identify them justly. As Claire took in the otherworldly shades and scents, the outer petals of the infant flowers began to change. The yellow blushed from the base outward to a periwinkle blue, and when it reached the magenta tip, the whole petal peeled back to reveal an emerald-green underside. The buds were blooming right before her eyes. The yellow to blue transformation continued until all but the last two of the innermost petals were pared back. These two remaining bracts flanked a bouquet of sapphire blue stamen, which bobbled wildly to-and-fro in celebration of their newfound liberty. The petals that had peeled back from the stamen formed a cone shape, culminating in a ruffled plume of emerald-green, speckled with periwinkle and tipped in magenta. The last two unfettered petals began fluttering madly as they tripled in size and were drawn back to lay parallel to the cone-shaped body. The sapphire stamen then thrust backward to reveal a tawny, thorn-shaped protrusion. This pointed knob began swelling out from under the blue plume, pulling the inside of the bloom out with it and into the open air. It was not until two cherry-red freckles above the thorny growth blinked open that Claire moved for the first time since the vines descended from the canopy covering the trail. The freckles blinked again before locking their gaze directly onto that of the startled girl. The flower-feathered bird gave Claire a wink and a nod. With a sharp forward thrust of its newly formed head, the bird's glorious sapphire crown spilled over its brow and then settled back in a regal splay across its emerald crown. With a gentle snapping sound, the bird liberated itself from its floral dock and fluttered about Claire's head, dodging in and out play-fully, much like the hummingbirds that blanketed the columbine and coral bells back home. When the blossom flew away, another bud took its place and the whole breathtaking spectacle began again. It was in this astonishing living tunnel, where distinctions between flora and fauna, color and light, could not find residence that Claire and Biggles plodded on toward Aislinn, a trail of blooms and birds waking in their tracks.

Biggles would stop when the ferns and blooms were plentiful and especially delicious, and trot or gallop along when they were not. Claire, for her part, sat patiently atop her untrained mount, completely content to follow his agenda. She wondered how long it had been since she left the pasture and Yarn. She had all but lost any sense of time since she found herself in E'lore. She could not for the life of her figure out what day of the week it was. The myth, it seemed, did not feel the need to mark time's passing in the smaller increments that were all important back home. Here, what mattered was the coming and going of seasons; the time that had passed since *they* had arrived in E'lore and the length of the lives lived by their kinsmen. The hours in a day, the days in a week, the weeks in a year, none of these intervals were even recognized by the myth. The shortest accrual of time marked by the inhabitants of E'lore was the space from one full moon to the next. And so for now, Claire decided, she was not going to recognize time either. With a pronounced sigh, the girl reclined back. With her head resting on Biggles' ample croup and her hands clasped over her stomach, Claire closed her eyes and let out another exaggerated breath. The hypnotic rhythm of the quagga's stride and the slumber inducing scents wafting from the nearby copse of whortleberry trees conspired to keep the little girl from staying awake. And they might have succeeded had it not been for the fact that the whortleberry grove stood just outside the southern-most access to the Aislinn marketplace, and the cacophony and clamor were quickly approaching a decibel that no one or thing could possibly sleep through. The bustle and noise meant nothing to the brave Biggles who plodded on and into the marketplace traffic without a flinch.

Claire had pulled herself upright and was casually rubbing her eyes and stretching her back when she heard, "Mind yourself below!"

She instinctively ducked just in time for a trussed stag to clear her head by inches. The slain animal floated through the air aided by six myth—three at the head and three at the hind legs. Each faerie gripped handfuls of the woven rope that secured the beast as they laboriously winged their way to the *fia's* croft. Whether by intent or fatigue, the faeries and their cargo were losing altitude quickly and Claire watched as several myth, who calculated themselves to be in the direct path of a crash landing, scurried off the main thoroughfare to safety. With the last of the energy in their reserves, the hunter-myth gave one more heave-ho and managed to deliver their bounty to the rear of the croft where it would be hung and prepared. The market-place avenue filled again as the threat of being swatted by a soaring stag passed.

Claire turned herself in her seat to take in anything that she might have missed during the commotion. Yarn had told her that the stall she was seeking would be either the first or the last, depending on which path she took. They had not traveled so far that she could not still see the first cot-tage in the marketplace queue. From her vantage point, it looked lovely—orderly and very colorful—full of what looked like scarves and hats, blan-kets and wraps, all waving softly in the gentle E'lore breeze. Satisfied that she had not already passed it by, she turned herself back to face forward. The bazaar was alive with activity, in the cottages and crofts and in the street. The myth who tended the stalls, were industriously fulfilling the needs of the myth who had come to share in the fruits of their fellow fae-ries' labors, and the lane was teeming with all kinds of transport of goods to-and-fro.

And Biggles ambled on as if he knew exactly where he was headed.

Claire took in all the sights of the lively market, catching bits and pieces of conversations here and there.

"Do you have plenty that I could take one more?"

"Those bracks were lovely with our tea. Any chance you have them again?"

"Just the one joint will do fine, *go raigh maith agat*," a patron thanked the butcher in the ancient tongue.

Claire's attention was bartered back and forth, each new sight and sound bidding for her notice until a rather odd looking cart wobbled into her line of sight and claimed her focus. The precarious buggy was made of woven straw and so full of kindling wood that the driver was perched atop the very sticks he was hauling, rather than waste precious space leaving the seat vacant for himself. The cart rolled on four mismatched wooden wheels. The front left wheel bent inward. The front right wheel, though straight, was not round, but slightly oblong instead. The rear left wheel was round, but half again the size of any of the other three. The rear right wheel had a distinct tendency to lean away. The effect of these peculiar fittings was that the cart bobbed up and down as it lurched backward and then forward and then to the side. Somehow, the cart advanced down the market trail, the boisterous creaking of the overburdened wheels growing louder with each bob and lurch.

The task of pulling the cart was given to a brindled mole, fitted with a tiny harness, the reins of which were held absently by the myth perched atop his cargo of wood. The mole, unaffected by the goings-on, made his way down the path as he had done many times before and would most likely do many times again. As the driver attended his rein holding, a second myth fluttered about the sides and back of the wagon, snatching up kindling that could not help but fall from the wonky, overloaded barrow and onto the path below. The pedestrians, who needed to get by the kindling wagon, gave it a broad berth lest they risk being crowned by a cascading stick. As Claire watched the whimsical cart, she wondered what kept the driver from making the necessary adjustments to the wheels, but the fact that he had not, amused her just as much as the sight of the receding wagon and its attending faerie frantically retrieving the wayward tumbling twigs.

The amused girl was just righting herself forward on her perch when she saw a large, shaggy, sasquatch-looking creature bending over a woodpile as it gathered lengths of the cut timber in the crook of its immense hairy arm. Her natural reaction was one of apprehension, but the woodpile was situated in the middle of the lane, and the myth milling about the adjacent stalls seemed to take little or no notice of the beast. When she realized that no one else seemed to be alarmed by its presence, she relaxed her shoulders and let out a sigh of relief.

The creature, however, did not have the same reaction when it saw Claire. Satisfied that its arms were filled to capacity, the hairy brute stood upright and turned around where the first thing it saw was the shy nambor girl atop the striped quagga. It was immediately overcome. The startled beastie dropped his armful of firewood and scurried screeching and cawing to the shelter of the backside of a nearby tree, which covered merely a fourth of his height and girth. Unconvinced of the tree's ability to conceal him, he spotted a flowering shrub a few paces away and decided to seek camouflage behind it.

Taking a few moments to steel his nerves, Andee took a deep breath before making a break for the bush, screeching and cackling and waving his arms about before falling silent again once he was behind the flower-strewn hedge. Claire watched the creature's antics in wide-eyed wonder while few of the passing myth gave the grogoch's conduct any more attention than a bemused smile or a shake of the head. She waited a moment to see if that was the end of its confounding antics before she decided that perhaps it would be best if she did not wait to find out. She abruptly gathered up the slack reins and turned back around to face forward. In doing so, she realized that Biggles had stopped and had done so in front of the *cordswainer's* cottage, a ramshackle, disheveled dwelling and the last in the row of stalls and cottages that made up the Aislinn marketplace. Although Claire did not have to look any closer to be sure that this was indeed the shop that Yarn told her to find, she hesitated and kept her seat on the quagga's broad back. She gave a quick glance behind to see if there was any more activity from the peculiar, hairy creature, but he was nowhere in sight, so Claire turned back toward the untidy, shabby stall.

A pair of myth were speaking with the decidedly unmyth-like creatures on the other side of the stand's front counter. Claire could not make out what was being said until the male of the myth pair ended the conversation by saying, "Enough of your *flummery* and *footle!* Make the brogs and be quick about it!"

The myth took their leave and left the irritable creatures to mumble and groan amongst themselves. The spectacle made Claire think better of approaching the cottage and its operators. She decided that it would be best to leave before the shoemakers had a chance to notice her. No sooner had she tightened her grip on the reins intending to lead Biggles away, when a soft, gentle voice spoke into her right ear.

"Do not let their rudeness discourage you, Claire."

The girl, whose nerves were already a bit on edge, was visibly startled as she let out a gasp and turned to see who was there.

"Would you like for me to go with you?" came the gentle voice again.

Claire did not answer, but instead looked at the face that belonged to the voice, too startled to speak.

"Forgive me, I have misplaced my manners. I am called Pethbol." At which point the handsome faerie extended his hand.

Fortunately, for Claire, responses such as returning a handshake were automatic and she instinctively extended her hand to meet his, still gazing at the ethereal creature in stupefied awe.

Seeing that the girl needed more time to collect herself, the chivalrous myth continued. "I thought that, this being your first trip to our fair *baile*, you could perhaps use a guide."

Claire thought to ask how he knew that this was her first outing, but decided that probably was not important. Pethbol's genuine and friendly manner was difficult to resist, and Claire quickly regained her composure.

"Yarn," she answered, "has sent me here to get some shoes."

Pethbol's eyebrows arched, displaying his surprise. "That is an impressive undertaking for a maiden voyage," the faerie said, trying to disguise his surprise with humor. "If you will allow me," he continued, "I think that I can be of some service."

Claire gazed back toward the *cordswainer's* cottage where the leprechauns were still grousing and grumbling about their previous customers.

"Yes, please," Claire blurted out without hesitation. Her response made Pethbol smile.

In reply to her acceptance of his help, the graceful creature grasped the reins at the quagga's muzzle and led the agreeable creature toward the shoemaker's stall, where he secured the woven straps to a wooden railing. Before Claire had time to think, Pethbol had winged his way right up to her, grabbed her around the waist and had landed them both gently back to the ground.

"Ready?" he asked as he released her.

"Yes, um … Thank you," she stammered as she looked up at the quagga's back and then back down at Pethbol. Even with all the excitement and distractions, it registered with her that she and the myth were mere inches from being the same height.

"Here we go, then!"

Claire thought to herself that her new chaperone seemed more enthused about this whole ordeal than she was. Because she did not want to disappoint Yarn, she told herself, she would accept the faerie's generous offer of help. By the time she had made this decision, Pethbol was already several paces toward the stall and Claire had to run to catch up to him.

"Hoigh!" he greeted the ill-tempered shoemakers who were still so entangled in their bellyaching and complaining, that they had failed to notice the faerie's presence.

"Hoigh!" Pethbol repeated, this time with an accompanying set of loud thumps on the counter's worn wooden surface.

The leprechauns fell silent in unison and all three turned to their new patron.

Pethbol waited for a greeting in response, but the three disgruntled shopkeepers said nothing; they simply stared mutely at the undeterred faerie.

Pethbol turned to Claire and smiled before turning his attention back to the shoe makers.

"Yes, well then," he began, "we have come about having some *brogs* made."

The leprechauns remained still and silent.

"I said, we have come about some *brogs*," Pethbol reiterated.

This time one of the three *cordswainers* stepped forward, rested an elbow on the counter, and after eyeing Claire up and down, turned to Pethbol and responded, "*That* is a nambor."

Pethbol stared at the uncooperative shoemaker, waiting for him to make his point clear, which he immediately did.

"We dunna have to make brogs for nambors—'tis not the bargain. She may be wee, but I know a nambor when I see a nambor, and I be lookin' at one there," the stubborn leprechaun finished with a slight nod toward Claire.

Pethbol *had* overlooked this point as apparently had Yarn.

But Pethbol did not let the irritable creature keep the upper hand for long.

"Now see here," he stalled as he carefully slipped his right foot from its shoe and aligned it next to Claire's unshod left foot. Claire caught on quickly and was wise enough not to glance down toward her feet.

"I am well aware of the agreement," Pethbol continued to stonewall.

"Can you believe this?" he turned and asked Claire as he feigned disbelief.

The faerie shook his head from side to side as he stole a glance downward at their feet paired up under the counter.

"I am well aware of the agreement," Pethbol repeated emphatically as he returned his gaze to the leprechaun opposite him.

"The shoes are not for her. They are for me, yes?" he finished without batting an eye.

"For you?" the diminutive creature asked. "Are they now?"

"Of course they are," the faerie answered.

"Would there be a problem with the ones you be wearing now?" the leprechaun queried, making no attempt to mask his sarcasm.

Pethbol allowed the faintest smile to come across his face before responding.

"Are you amending the bargain, *leipreachan*? Are you proposing that we are entitled to but one pair of brogs at a time?" Pethbol challenged his adversary.

"'Tis not *you* that be needin' our wares," the ill-natured creature answered peevishly as he cast another scornful look at Claire.

Pethbol did not falter at the shoemaker's accusation. The dauntless faerie leaned over the counter until his face was a hair's breadth from that of the leprechaun.

"Do you doubt me, *cordswainer*?" he asked with authority.

The shoemaker looked back at his two still silent comrades. The only help they offered was a half-hearted shrug of their emerald-green-frocked shoulders. He turned back and rested his resentful gaze squarely on Pethbol's smiling face.

"Just make them … pretty," the amused faerie added as he turned to Claire and gave her a wink.

The duped leprechaun looked back and forth between Pethbol and Claire. Since a centuries-old oath bound him, he could not refuse the clever faerie's request.

After a short, boisterous fit of what Claire could easily assume was leprechaun cursing, accompanied by loads of very destructive rummaging about underneath the counter's surface, the bamboozled shoemaker finally resurfaced and thumped a small, well-worn box down on the work surface.

"Let's have it then!" he thundered at Pethbol.

"Have what?"

"Your foot! What do ye think?" he bellowed back, his face turning crimson from exasperation.

"Ah, of course," Pethbol teased him.

"You had only to ask," he tormented the agitated creature further.

Pethbol fluttered up to the ledge and rested his still uncovered right foot on the counter.

The shoemaker pulled a length of soft reed from the small box, and while holding one end to Pethbol's heel, he pulled the reed up the length of the faerie's foot to the top of the big toe. Satisfied that this was a good measure, he unceremoniously pinched off the surplus with his gnarled fingers and passed the reed backward where one of his compatriots took it from him. He then took another length from the same box and wrapped it around the faerie's foot at the widest point below the toes and snapped the soft twig where it met its own beginning. This, too, he passed blindly backward.

"Would you like the other one as well?" Pethbol goaded the leprechaun as he offered up his left foot to be measured, also. "You never know. They may not be a match." The entertained faerie could no longer help himself.

"And that will be your problem if they be not," the unamused leprechaun growled back.

"If 'tis a brog to fit the other foot you be after, then you'll have to bring the other foot back another time! We've work to do before the *oiche* comes, you'll know."

"We shall leave you to your labors then," Pethbol said with a nod, releasing the vexed leprechaun from his torment. He hopped off the counter and rejoined Claire. As they turned to leave, the other two leprechauns, who had until then been practically bereft of speech or movement, suddenly sprang into action. With their arms flailing and their tongues wagging, they joined their agitated companion and together the trio lamented anew their pitiful existence and that ancient, cursed oath.

Pethbol gave Claire a leg up and handed her the reins once he had freed them from the wooden railing.

"Will you be heading back, then?" he asked as she took the woven straps from him.

"Yes, I probably should," she answered.

"I have a few errands to run, but I can join you after if you would like—I will not be long."

Claire was already self-conscious about having taken so much of the faerie's time. She felt the influence of her British mother distinctly when it came to matters of accepting help and being a burden on other people's charity.

"We'll find our way, I'm sure. Just stay on the path, right?" she asked.

To which Pethbol replied with an unenthusiastic nod.

And thank you for all your help, really," she added, carefully turning down his offer to be of further assistance.

"Of course," was his slightly dejected response, his gaze lingering a bit longer than he intended.

"I do hope we wear the same size," he blurted with a smile.

Claire thought that she detected the slightest bit of awkwardness in the faerie's tone, but she quickly changed her mind.

"Well, thank you again," she answered for lack of a better reply.

Pethbol said nothing, but gently led Biggles onto the path and headed him north, a direction that would complete the circular path and take Claire right back to where she started—at Yarn's pasture.

Claire gave the faerie a smile and the quagga a soft squeeze with her heels. It was the second time on their journey that the striped mount heeded her request. A few paces down the trail leading away from the market, Claire turned around and was surprised to see that Pethbol was still standing there. She gave him a wave and another smile, both of which he returned. When she turned back to face forward, she was still smiling. She gave Biggles a scratch and a rub on his thick neck.

"Let's go home," she whispered to her four-legged friend. The implication of her words was lost under a cloud of contentment.

As Biggles and Claire left the bustle and din of the marketplace behind them, they found themselves once again in a beautiful wood. The ever-ravenous equine was thrilled to be surrounded by the sumptuous delicacies that blanketed the forest's edge, and Claire, for her part, was just happy to be seated atop her mount with the woods and her thoughts to herself. She laid the reins across the quagga's withers and rested her hands on her thighs as she scanned the surrounding trees for more of the morphing bird-flowers. And in this way they ambled on, Biggles' tireless jaw crushing bloom after countless bloom and Claire swaying happily in rhythm with the quagga's unsophisticated gate.

Claire was pondering how Pethbol had known that she was going into Aislinn and why he had been so nice to her. She thought of the grouchy shoemakers and the odd behavior of the equally odd beast at the woodpile. Claire was happily preoccupied with her thoughts as she reached out her hand and let her fingers comb through the soft tendril-like leaves of a low-hanging branch. That is when she felt it: a frigid breeze that came up behind them suddenly, causing her spine to stiffen and goose bumps to crop up on her arms and legs. She twisted in her seat to look for the source, which she had no trouble finding since it was roaring toward her like a stampede. Thick, cyclonic rivers of fog hurling down the path like earth-bound tornadoes. It was then that Biggles sensed the impending threat and reared on his hind legs in protest. The equestrienne instinctively grabbed for an anchor as she felt herself sliding back and losing her seat. Fortunately, her hand found the quagga's thick sturdy black mane and she filled her right hand with the dense bristles. The speeding, icy mist was already spiraling around her mount's fetlocks, working its way up his hindquarters before his front hooves came crashing back to the ground. Biggles needed no instruction to understand what to do next. Run! Claire felt his weight shift as he prepared to lunge ahead. She pulled herself forward until her legs were just behind the quagga's front shoulder blades as she reached up with her left hand and

clenched a matching fistful of mane. She lowered her torso, bringing her
body perpendicular to the equine's neck and shoulders. Claire clenched her
thighs against his barrel and tucked her head. Biggles took off, his hooves
gouging clods of dirt out of the trail, his nostrils flaring. The fog raced past
the galloping quagga and his rider as it crisscrossed the path in front of
them, the powerful updraft blowing back the vegetation at the wood's edge,
sometimes ripping it from the ground as it rampaged down the earthen trail.
Claire raised her head just enough to survey the path ahead. The violent
streams of fog were intertwining with one another, then doubling back as
they brushed against Biggles' legs before looping again and soaring forward
once more. Biggles was not easily dissuaded and forged ahead. As the cou-
rageous quagga thundered down the path, Claire saw an anomaly in the tree
line ahead, a distinct cluster of trees that were unlike any of the others. They
were dark, almost black from what she could see through the occasional
ruptures in the cloud squall. Claire was not the only one to notice the unusual woods, so had Biggles, and they were racing toward it. Though unwilling to temper his gate, he did let his displeasure be known with a series of
agitated snorts and grunts. As they got closer to the odd-looking parcel of
woods, Claire realized that the timbers had been burned. It was as if the one
particular cluster of trees had been set ablaze, yet its immediate neighbors
had been left untouched. The surrounding forest, bush, and vegetation were
green, lush and unscathed, while this very specific grouping was black as
soot. But it was not until the rushing, swirling cloud streams met the blackened forest that Claire became truly frightened. When the tempests of fog
met the scorched timbers, they let out an anguished, mournful, human-like
sigh as they crashed against the singed trunks like waves of water against a
rock, sending the already spooked quagga into a full-fledged panic. The
clouds lapped against the trees and surged up the burned stems before
folding back on themselves and ebbing away and back down the trail. The
fog could not enter the black wood. Claire watched as the defeated mist,
plundered of its rage, withdrew humbly back down the path and into the
surrounding forest. As the trail ahead cleared, Claire saw that it took a distinct bend to the right. She reached up and grabbed the right rein, giving it a
pull in hopes that she could persuade Biggles to notice the curve as well. He
did, and without diminishing his pace the snorting quagga veered and

carried the two of them away from the wailing, lamenting fog and the black forest.

As Biggles' sense of doom diminished, so did his pace, and before long, his gallop turned into a trot and his trot to a walk. The exhausted quagga's breathing was labored and his muscled chest was covered in a foamy sweat. Claire swung her right leg over her mount's neck and slid down his side and off his back, her legs quivering from the strain of holding onto her bareback seat. She looped her arm through the dangling reins and walked by Biggles' side as they both tried to get their breathing and their beating hearts to return to normal.

The two had walked peacefully and with no further interruption for some time when they came upon a clearing. Through a gap in the trees lining the path, Claire could see a lovely meadow and welcomed the chance to get out the relative darkness of the tree-canopied trail. Biggles needed no prompting and his walk burst into an excited trot when he saw the moss and blossom-covered pasture. Claire let him jog ahead as she followed him through the break in the trees and over a fog stream into the open field. While the quagga sniffed around to determine which blossoms he would eat first, Claire dropped to her knees and let out a long-held sigh. The moss was warm and inviting and the weary girl stretched herself out, her hands clasped behind her head, her ankles crossed. She breathed in the gently scented air and gazed up at the soft vanilla sky. A whinny from Biggles brought her back upright as she surveyed the hillside to see that he was all right. He indeed was, more so than he had been since they left the market at Aislinn.

Sitting amongst the moss and delicate flowers covering the hillside, Claire was immediately reminded of home and wondered if the old farm was still her home, or if, in fact, *this* was her home now. As she sat amongst the blossoms, with Biggles steady and relentless munching the only sound she could hear, she thought of Yarn, Sarla, the marketplace, and the strange fog on the trail. She had trouble focusing her thoughts as they vacillated between memories of her father and sisters and the bond that she was beginning to feel with the inhabitants of this incredible and strange world.

As she reached out to pick a particularly fragrant and beautiful blossom, a sense of déjà vu flooded her brain and tensed her muscles. She was not alone. Unlike before, in the yard next to the house, this time she was afraid—she felt vulnerable and threatened. Claire had only the time it took to turn her head around to see what was there before he was on top of her. His enormous fur-covered hand stifled the scream in her throat as he clamped it over her mouth. She wrapped her two hands over the back of his massive paw, trying to pry it off her face, but his strong arm made no notice of her efforts. It was in this way, with his hand over her mouth and her hands locked onto his, that the grogoch who had behaved so oddly in the marketplace, dragged Claire off the hillside and into the fog stream just a few yards away. A still grazing Biggles was the last thing she saw before the thick roaring mist whitewashed everything from sight. The dense moisture was frigid, and as the cold pierced her skin, the little girl became even more frantic. Still pulling at the hand that was holding her prisoner, her muffled cries and frenzied kicking did not slow the grogoch's pace as he crawled along the fog bed dragging Claire like a rag doll over the rough terrain. Although she could feel her skin being scraped and bruised from the assault of the rock and stick-strewn sediment of the fog streambed, her focus was on extricating herself from the smelly creature's grasp.

Then, just as quickly as her assailant had seized her, he stopped. Claire, too, stopped kicking and screaming as she tried to see what had prompted him to halt. The terrified girl saw nothing but the dense haze passing over her head and heard nothing as the sound of the rushing fog filled her ears. Claire forced deep breaths through her nose in an effort to calm herself. She closed her eyes and breathed deeply for several moments until a sudden change in temperature brought the panic back. She opened her eyes to see that the cloud-haze was thinner and she could feel herself being lifted. Once the mist fell away, she could see that Andee had indeed climbed out of the fog flow and was again dragging her behind him as he crawled very slowly up an embankment. The great hairy beast lay perfectly still, his hand deadlocked over Claire's face. Her writhing and wiggling had bought her just enough space between her face and his hand so that she could open her mouth. Instinctively, she dug her nails deep into his thumb and bit down hard on the hairy flesh between the first and second joints. His gnarled skin was too thick for her bite to cause him any pain, but it did surprise him, and in response, he pulled her up the slope until her face was inches from his.

With his left hand still clamped over her mouth, he placed his right fore-finger over his mouth forming a vertical line from his nose to his chin as he pursed his leathery lips and made a "shuuush" noise. Claire was startled and confused, but as he made the same motion a second time, he relaxed his grip and slowly removed his hand from her mouth. Taking the same finger that he had used to ask for her silence, he extended his arm and used it to point at something over the crest of the embankment.

Claire allowed herself to follow his stare, and grabbing hold of a root exposed by the force of the speeding fog, she pulled herself further up the slope. Once her line of sight was unobscured by the embankment, she could see the meadow below and far beyond. She recognized the hillock where she had been sitting before Andee grabbed her, and realized that if she had picked a spot just a few more feet to the right of where she was, she would have seen from there what she was looking at now. But it was the meadow, or rather what was *in* the meadow that had Andee's attention, and now hers. Sprawling over the meadow of crushed Shannon blossoms and moss was a camp.

A tent, unlike any dwellings that were in Aislinn, had been erected in a chaotic fashion punctuated by random piles of wood and mounds of dis-carded trash and debris. The material of the makeshift lodging was torn and gouged, with soot marks streaking up the sides and flowing down from its peaks. As Claire studied the unexpected sight, a thin line of smoke streamed forth from the front of the tent. Suddenly, the entrance to the shelter flew open and a figure emerged, trailed by dark billows of smoke that rose quickly on the updrafts in the breezy meadow. Coughing and hacking, the figure unsuccessfully brushed at the smoke engulfing his face, but he de-rived no relief from the sooty fumes until he had walked several paces from the tent opening. Still coughing and seeking fresh air, he brushed at his garments, stirring up even more residue and inflaming his cough. As his choking subsided, his gaze shifted upward and he began visually scanning the surroundings of the encampment. As soon as the sooty figure looked up, Andee's hand found the top of Claire's head and pushed it down, caus-ing her to lose her footing and backslide down the slope that was conceal-ing them from view. As Claire groped for a root or branch to stop her de-scent, she felt a strong hairy hand grab her right oxter and draw her back up. Once she had regained the lost ground, she hooked her left arm over the exposed root that had aided her before, securing her position.

Andee again placed his woolly paw on top of her head, this time without the overwhelming force he had unintentionally used before. As he held Claire's head down, he slowly and cautiously raised his own to again peer over the crest of the slope and at the scene below. He slowly took his hand away from Claire's head, and reaching under her arm again, he gently lifted her so that she too could again see the meadow below.

The grit-covered figure ceased his survey of the hillside and was seen by Andee and Claire reentering the smoke-filled tent. Once he was inside, Andee quickly rolled over onto his back and slid down the embankment landing gracefully on his feet before leaping over the fogbed and taking off in a lumbering gate toward the cleared path. Claire, still hanging on to the tree root, and having no clue as to what was going on, simply watched— mouth agape—the retreating figure of the woolly grogoch. Suddenly, he stopped. Turning back in the direction from whence he had just come, he lumbered back toward the astonished girl, through the fog stream and back up the embankment. Unhooking her arm from her root anchor, he lifted her effortlessly to her feet. Claire stood, stunned, as Andee wrapped his strong shaggy arm around her waist and hoisted her up. Pinning her against his right side, he proceeded back down the slope and resumed his course toward the path, toting Claire under his arm like a sack of potatoes.

CHAPTER 21

YARN HAD JUST filled the kettle with water and was placing it over the glowing fire when he heard his front gate slam closed. About the same time, he made out the strange series of grunts, groans, and squeals that comprised the language of the grogoch. The grunts and groans were getting louder and the squeals were turning to shrieks as Yarn set the kettle down and dried his hands. The myth opened his door and saw Andee coming up his front path, his left arm flailing wildly and his right arm carrying a parcel wedged tightly to his side. Ignoring the steps, Andee leapt from the path to the porch in a graceful, effortless motion belying his stature and bulk. When the excited grogoch saw Yarn standing in the open door, he instantly dropped his parcel so as to include his right arm in his eccentric gesticulations. The "oof," which came from the parcel when it impacted the hard planks of the myth's front porch, distracted Yarn from his hairy friend's discourse. Recognizing the scratched and bruised bundle as Claire, he immediately went to her side and helped her to her feet. Yarn divided his attention between the dirty and disheveled nambor and the excited grogoch who was still motioning and yelling frantically. As he helped Claire brush away the dirt and moss imbedded in her clothes, he implored Andee to calm down. The agitated creature ignored Yarn's frequent interruptions of: "Slow down, slow down ... breathe ... 'ten steeple?' What? I cannot understand you."

When Andee abruptly stopped his narration, he placed his furry hands on his furry knees as he panted and gasped to catch his breath. Yarn, uncertain whether this signaled the end of the story or merely a need for air, took the opportunity to finally look at Claire and assess her condition.

"Are you badly hurt, my dear? What in E'lore happened?"

Claire had no idea what Andee was saying, but, unlike Yarn, she was sure that she knew what he was talking about. As she pulled twigs from her mangled, knotted hair, she shot the winded grogoch a dirty look before answering.

"I guess I'm okay—no thanks to *that*," she replied, as she looked over at the hyperventilating creature.

When she and Yarn finished looking over her wounds to determine if any were in need of immediate attention, he asked her again, "What happened?"

"I don't know. I was just sitting on a hill. I was just sitting and Biggles was eating when, all of the sudden, there he was! He grabbed me over my mouth and dragged me away!"

Yarn gave Andee a glare of his own, only his was not based in anger, but in confusion. Grogoches may be many things—most all of them unpleasant and smelly—but violent was not one of them. Once a grogoch attached itself to a family or clan, its loyalty was unflinching, and it would serve and protect that clan until its last breath, if necessary. No, Andee was not trying to harm Claire; he was trying to protect her. *Were* he trying to harm her, she would not be standing on the front porch now—that was certain. But protect her from what? He turned to Claire again.

"And he brought you here?" Yarn asked her.

"Not at first," she answered. "First he dragged me up the fog bed and then up a bank above a meadow."

Now that Claire had the benefit of being able to relive her experience without fearing for her life, it was slowly occurring to her, as well, that Andee's intentions were not as they had first seemed. She was just beginning to continue when Yarn asked, "Why? What was on the bank? What does he mean by 'ten steeples'?"

"No, there was nothing on the bank. We were hiding, I think. There weren't any steeples. Are you sure that's what he said?"

"I am not sure about any of it—he is far too excited and talking too quickly for me to understand most of what he is saying." Yarn suddenly realized what Claire had said.

"Hiding? Hiding from what?" he asked.

It was in that moment that Claire figured out the faulty grogoch translation.

"I think he means 'tent people.' He was hiding us from the people in the tent."

Her answer startled Yarn, but he let her relay, uninterrupted, what she and Andee had seen in the meadow below the bank of the fog stream. By the time she had finished, Andee had regained his breath and was brushing at Claire's hair with his calloused paw as if just realizing that her transport under his hairy arm might not have been very comfortable for her. Claire accepted his gesture as an apology, as she now understood that he had never meant to hurt her.

Yarn raced to the porch's edge as he yelled back frantically to Claire, "Where? Which way? Did you come across a field? Through the woods?"

Claire met the myth at the end of the porch. The view from Andee's armpit had been of the ground and not much else. "No, no fields or trees, all I saw was the path," she answered the anxious Yarn.

"The path? He brought you down the path? Well it must have been from that direction," he gestured with his arm raised. "Aislinn is that way," he again gestured, but in the opposite direction. "So he must have come from the east." The old myth continued to look up and down the path and across the field, for what, even he did not know. Claire turned to look at the woolly farmhand who was now sitting on the threshold of the porch, legs dangling and swaying over the side.

Claire thought to do the same, but as soon as her backside touched down on the worn porch planks, she thought better of it, and stood back up, opting for leaning against the cottage instead. As she watched Andee and his hairy, swinging legs, she realized that he was the woolly creature trying to hide from her in the town center.

"I saw you!" she exclaimed, taking a step toward Andee.

"I saw him ... in the market. He was getting wood ... when he saw *me*, he went crazy! He started waving his arms all over and making weird noises." Claire studied the grogoch for a moment before turning her gaze toward Yarn.

"Why did he do that? I didn't do anything or say anything to him. Does he always do that?" she asked the worried myth.

Yarn turned his attention from the path and looked at Claire. "Odd, that," he replied as he shook his head and looked intently as his hirsute friend. He knew that he should say something—give her an answer of some sort—but he could not, mainly because he did not have an explanation for the bristly beast's reaction to the little girl. But his non-committal response belied a real concern. He had never known Andee to respond to anyone or anything in this way, and not knowing what made Claire so different troubled him very much.

"Let us come back to that later, if that is all right. Tell me where you went and what you saw, dear." Yarn did his best to calm his voice, hoping in turn to calm the anxious girl.

As Claire recounted her trip to Aislinn for Yarn, she felt a bit awkward when she got to the part where Pethbol joined her at the *cordswainer's* cottage. She wasn't sure why. "And then Biggles and I headed back on the path leading out of the marketplace," she summed up.

Yarn did not respond as he was too busy staring at Claire. Even with everything that Claire had just told him, he had allowed her simple question about Andee's initial reaction to her to overtake his thoughts. His woolly friend's behavior had him stymied. Yarn fixated on the girl's face as if it held an answer, as if the key to what was happening lay hidden in her visage. When he realized that Claire was staring back, he rattled his head from side to side and excused himself.

"Do forgive me ... how rudely I am behaving ... what were you saying? Where did you go after the *cordswainer's?*"

Had Claire not returned in the manner that she had, Yarn would have asked how her dealings with the leprechauns went, but that seemed a moot point now. She was a bit puzzled by the normally unflappable myth's behavior, but she resisted the urge to ask what he was thinking and chose to finish recounting the events of her trip.

"So how did you come to be on the hillside, dear?" Yarn's wits were slowly returning as he tried to focus only on the details of Claire's return journey and not on Andee's stranger than usual behavior.

"We left the shoe shop and just took the path that led away from the market, and everything was fine until ... until the fog came." Claire paused. She had almost forgotten about the strange trees and the angry fog since her episode with Andee.

"Fog? What about the fog?" Yarn encouraged her to continue.

"Um, it came up behind us, out of nowhere. It wasn't like it is here," she added, pointing to the benevolent mists that swirled and flowed their way across the fields and meadows on their way to the lake. Claire stumbled through her recollection as her mind raced ahead to the black forest.

"And then, we were headed toward the trees." She looked up at Yarn as she continued. She wanted to see his face when she told him of the peculiar wood and the peculiar effect that they had on the cloud storm. He did not disappoint her.

"Trees?" he asked in a choked voice. He diverted his eyes from the girl.

"Black ... burned ... but still alive," Claire recalled. "The branches were full of leaves—black leaves—but they didn't move."

Yarn listened intently although he focused his gaze on Andee and not Claire.

"Move?" he replied.

"Everything around us was swaying and breaking, the trees were bending in half, the flowers along the path were ripped out of the ground. It was like a tornado. But the black trees did not move. They stood perfectly still even while the fog was trying to get past them. The storm was trying to get into those trees, but it couldn't. The black trees wouldn't let it in." Claire dropped her eyes. "It made them sad," she added when she recalled the fog's sorrowful moans as it retreated back down the path.

Her observation made Yarn look at her for the first time since she began her recollection of the raven wood. He could not put his finger on what it was. They were *missing* something about this nambor—they were *all* missing something. The myth moved his gaze back to the woolly beastie sitting on the porch's edge. Andee knew what it was. Andee knew what it was the first time her saw her.

Yarn forced his eyes down to the planks of the worn old porch. He thought about acknowledging her last comment with a lighthearted dismissal so as to keep her from fretting too much. But in that moment, Yarn realized that Claire did not need any more protection from her own thoughts and observations. Yarn and the others had dismissed her as an insignificant consequence of a failed endeavor. Perhaps, he thought, that collective conclusion had been the mistake.

Neither said another word until Claire remembered her lost mount.

"Oh no!" she exclaimed.

Yarn intuitively knew what had sent the girl into a fresh state of panic and tried to reassure her, "Ah, not to worry, dear. He knows his way home."

As if on cue, Biggles came trotting down the path, reigns swaying back and forth in rhythm with his gate. The quagga made his way straight for the pasture turnstile where he let out a single whinny to announce his arrival.

"Excuse me please, Claire," Yarn said softly. He hopped down the trunk stairs and walked toward the gentle beast. When the myth got up to his beloved pet, he removed the handmade bridle and gave the beast a scratch behind the ear and a tug on his mohawk mane before opening the gate, which Biggles galloped through, eager to rejoin the herd.

When Yarn returned, Andee had moved closer to Claire, intrigued by her gesturing and pointing.

Attending to his quagga had given Yarn time to pull his thoughts together. "Now then," he began as he climbed the stump stairs. "After the black wood, you found the meadow?"

"Yes," Claire answered simply, detecting a subtle change in Yarn's demeanor, not angry so much as more in focus than it had been before he tended to Biggles.

"Yes, I think I know this place," Yarn stated as his gaze fell to the porch planks.

However, instead of his comment encouraging Claire to continue, as he had hoped it would, her thoughts were in another place altogether.

"What was in those woods? Why wouldn't it allow the fog to come in?" she asked of an unprepared Yarn.

As he shared Sarla's belief that all Claire's questions needed to be answered honestly, he answered her honestly and without hesitation.

"A power ... an energy that we have not encountered anywhere else in E'lore. We do not believe it to be evil, nor can we say that 'tis benevolent with any certainty. We know that they are rowans and therefore sacred, but have no idea what lay beyond them. We have accepted this and give the black wood its due respect."

"Has anyone ever gone in there?" Claire continued her line of inquiry.

"No! And please have no thoughts of being the first. I should think that finding yourself *here*, in this strange place should be all the excitement and adventure that one girl could ever possibly need," he answered, his fatherly disposition quickly reinstated.

"Now," Yarn carried on. "What happened after you came upon the meadow? 'Tis where Andee found you?"

"Yes."

It was at this point that Andee reasoned out what it was that Claire and Yarn were conversing about. Andee alternated between thumping himself on his chest and pointed toward the east-leading path. After several moments of pointing and grunting and reenacting his abduction of the girl, including his toting her up to Yarn's front porch, the grogoch finally settled back down and looked triumphantly at Yarn as he panted and tried to catch his breath. As a reward, Yarn gave Andee a hardy pat on the shoulder, sending up a cloud of dirt and debris and dislodging twigs and leaves from the creature's tangled and knotted hide.

"Well done, my old friend," he said to the smelly beastie, which pleased Andee to no end. The myth turned his attention back to Claire.

"Come, we must get you next door to Sarla. You, my dear, have several rather nasty scratches, which had best be tended to straight away," he offered in a protective tone.

Claire allowed herself to be led to the stairs, and when they had reached the dirt path leading to the front gate, she turned to Yarn.

"Who were those people we saw in the meadow? Do you know them?" she asked as Yarn reached out and pushed the front gate open for her.

Instead of answering, he turned to Andee and signaled to him to stay right there and that he would be right back. The grogoch merely nodded his understanding and reclaimed his perch on the porch's edge, swinging and swaying his feet in the cool E'lore air.

***

Claire let out a wince as Sarla washed the back of her legs and badly scratched bum. Yarn had excused himself from Claire's company almost immediately after leaving her in Sarla's very capable hands. As Sarla tended to Claire, Yarn joined Banth, Meeks, and Tobas who had been gathered around the fire drinking tea for the better part of the day.

"What happened to *her?*" Tobas asked as he peered around Yarn to get a better view of the fuss being made around Claire.

"She will be fine, just a few scrapes and scratches—Andee dragged her over a fog bed," Yarn responded, unconcerned that his answer made little sense to them.

"Why would Andee drag her across a fog bed?" Banth asked, wanting for more details.

Yarn did not answer him directly, but replied with, "It seems that we have company, my friends."

Banth, Meeks, and Tobas asked no more questions. Instead, they waited for Yarn to tell them of his news. When Yarn had finished and his fellow myth were current on the recent events, they agreed to meet again that evening at Yarn's cottage.

CHAPTER 22

AS WAS HIS intention since the affairs of earlier in the day, Tobas took an early leave of the dinner table, telling Sarla that he was going next door to have evening tea with Yarn. Since his story had the advantage of being the truth, although not the detailed version of it, Tobas was able to say it convincingly and without alarming her. After thanking her for a delicious meal, he kissed his *bairns* and his wife, and gave Claire a nod before he took his leave. When he reached his uncle's front door, he knocked softly as he pushed the door open and let himself in. They were all gathered in the sitting room: Yarn, Banth, Meeks, and to Tobas's surprise, Andee. He, too, was enjoying a hot cup of four-petal tea before the crackling fire. The beast met Tobas's perplexed gaze, and in lieu of a greeting, let out a thundering eruption followed by an unapologetic grin before he resumed drinking his warm brew.

"Ah, very good, we are all here then," Yarn stated as Tobas entered the warm, cozy cottage. He gestured to Tobas to take a seat at the large, central table before reaching in the cupboard for a clean cup to give the latest member of the gathering. Needing refuge from the noxious creature, Banth and Meeks were all too happy to vacate their comfy chairs by the fire, and took up seats at the large main table, as well. They were soon joined by Yarn, who had brought the tea tray and a fresh kettle of boiling water.

Tobas thanked Yarn as his uncle poured hot water onto the dried petals that covered the bottom of the young myth's cup. Reasonably sure that
deliberations as to how to proceed had started without him, he asked of the
assembled elders, "So, do we have a plan?"

"We will be heading out there as soon as you finish that cuppa,"
Meeks could not resist answering, since he was quite sure of the effect that
this response would have on the younger myth. As usual, he was right.

"What? Going out where, exactly?" Tobas asked, having abandoned
efforts to cool his scalding tea.

"Andee is here to take us to the meadow where he and Claire saw the
tent," Yarn answered calmly.

"Without knowing who they are? Does no one else think that to be ...
dangerous?" Tobas questioned, unable to mask his anxiety.

All three of the older faeries turned their heads simultaneously to regard the youngest.

Naturally, it was Meeks who could not resist replying, "And how then
do you propose that we find out who they are?"

"I well ... I suppose, but ..." Tobas tried to answer.

"According to Andee," Banth assured Tobas, "we can observe from a
perfectly secure vantage point. As far as risks go, 'tis a lot safer than not
knowing who has taken up residence in E'lore without our knowledge."

Yarn nodded to Tobas as confirmation of the wisdom of Banth's
words. Meeks had no response other than draining his beaker of tea, which
he continued to cup in his hands as he waited for the others. Nothing else
was said as the rest of the group finished their drinks, and one by one, the
empty teacups were brought to rest on the ancient wooden table. Banth
thumped both of his palms against the worn boards as a rallying call and
stood up.

"Let's not delay any further. We need to head out," he addressed his
fellow myth.

Without response, the gathered comrades rose from the table and
started for the front door. By this time, Andee, for whom the warm fire,
warm tea, and comfortable chair had proved a sleep-inducing combination,
had to be stirred back to consciousness with a firm pat on the shoulder
from Yarn. Once awake, he was full of exuberant energy and was out the

door and on the front porch before the rest of them had even reached the threshold.

The drawn-out tea break had served its purpose as the *baile* was now cloaked in a protective blanket of darkness. Yarn and Banth had thought it best to wait for nightfall to investigate their unannounced visitors. There was no point in alarming the rest of the village until they had reason. The party proceeded through Yarn's gate and headed east up the path between his cottage and enclosed pasture. The secret assembly disappeared up the trail as they followed the grogoch into the E'lore night.

It was as the caucus approached the onset of the wood that their progress was halted. Andee had come to a full stop, just steps from a gently gurgling stream. The hairy grogoch cocked his head upward, taking in huge gulps of air through his flaring nostrils, grunting and groaning as he interpreted the scents. Here Andee kept his companions waiting until Meeks grew tired of the delay and resumed the trek in the direction that they were headed before Andee's interruption. All followed his lead save the grogoch, who, on seeing that the rest of the group was forging ahead, began flailing his arms and squawking frantically at them until they once again stopped.

"What does he want?" Banth turned to Yarn and asked.

"I have trouble understanding him when he gets excited like this. We just need to stop and give him a moment to calm down," he answered.

"We do not have time for this foolishness," Meeks grumbled as he turned from the spectacle of the beast's behavior and resumed their course.

Andee's frustration mounted as it became clear that he was not being understood, so he decided to choose a tactic that would be understood. In two bounding steps, he seized upon Yarn. Andee lifted the stunned myth by the arm, twirled him in the air and set him upright and forward-facing on his broad, hairy left shoulder. Yarn clenched a fistful of his mount's dirty mane and beat his wings to steady himself on his precarious perch. With a gnarled and hairy fist latched to his left ankle, Yarn had little choice but to go along for the ride. The old myth folded his wings tightly against his back to save them from tearing on protruding limbs or brush. Satisfied that his hostage was secure, the grogoch leapt across the babbling stream and made for the wood, the rest of the group having no recourse but to follow.

After covering the rough terrain on the other side of the stream, and after traversing the tangled underbrush of the subsequent wood, the myth were too tired to protest Andee's actions anymore, and merely followed behind him as he toted Yarn through the unyielding thicket blanketing the forest. The myth were too focused on their tiring legs to hear the rush of the fog as it spiraled and snaked its way through the scrub in search of the fog stream river that led to the falls. Andee had not only led the anxious group to the exact spot where he and Claire had first seen the foreign encampment, but had done so while avoiding the conspicuous, ambush-inviting path. Andee hopped across the fogbed and climbed up the embankment. The hairy guide pulled Yarn off his shoulder and as effortlessly as hanging an old hat on a familiar catch, Andee hooked Yarn gently on the same protruding branch that had been Claire's vantage point before. Yarn and Andee were joined one by one by the rest of their group as the tired myth caught up to them and scrambled up the earthen barricade. After drawing a collective deep breath, the twilight delegation peered over the embankment at the camp in the meadow below.

"I've not seen a tent like that before," Tobas was the first to offer an observation, his voice quivering.

"Nor I," responded Meeks, when he had recovered his breath sufficiently to speak.

They both turned to Yarn, who had turned away from the sight below and now lay against the loamy bank of the fog stream, his gaze cast downward, his hands clasped together.

"Yarn?" Banth, his voice as steady as he could make it, invited the older myth to share his thoughts.

Yarn recognized the dwellings, although the last time he saw them he was a young man in Eire and he and his clansmen were preparing for the Second Battle of Moytura. It took him a moment to steel his nerves before answering.

"Fomorian. That is the tent of Fomorian soldiers." Yarn's words rode the crest of his heavy and distressed exhale.

"'The Fomorian come'." Banth reverently repeated the words spoken by their king moments before his crossing.

Unlike Banth and Yarn, Meeks needed no more time to ingest this information. He turned to Yarn and ordered, "Tell Andee to return to the village and warn the others. We must evacuate Aislinn!"

Banth looked at Meeks incredulously.

"I beg your pardon," he stated somberly. "Am *I* not the director of this clan?" he asked his agitated colleague.

Yarn held his tongue and tried feverishly to collect his turbulent thoughts.

"We have no time for protocol! That is a Fomorian army down there! Do you think that they have gone to the trouble of finding E'lore to stop in for a cuppa tea? Where are your senses, Banth?" Meeks was beside himself with distress.

"My senses are precisely where they need to be! Events are unfolding exactly as Bhara predicted. I do not believe that we have achieved all that we have to turn tail and run like a startled *shoal* of *bradan!* And I do not believe for an instant that I am going to tell my clansmen to pack up and lope off in the middle of the night!"

The agitated debate was cast aside when the previously peaceful encampment came to life with raucous and bawdy noise. The four myth repositioned themselves so as to see the goings on, temporarily putting aside their dissenting views to assess the changing conditions below.

The opening in the front of the large Fomorian shelter had swung open, disgorging its occupants onto the littered, garbage-strewn meadow. The first three figures to exit the tent disappeared purposefully into the darkness, while the rest of the entourage swaggered and swayed behind them. Several of the soldiers stumbled and fell to the ground. Their comrades, being in no position themselves to lend a hand, simply left the fallen mercenaries on the debris-saturated ground and wandered off, zigging and zagging their way into the darkness behind the others.

The group atop the embankment watched the curious scene below with open-mouthed wonder.

"Why they're completely *sotted!*" Tobas observed with surprise.

"Yes, drinking is their second most honed skill," Yarn offered dryly.

"War being their first," Banth whispered as an answer to Tobas's questioning look at Yarn. Banth grabbed hold of a protruding root and began scrambling up the dirt barrier.

"What are you doing?" Meeks asked him, his hand on his arm.

"I mean to go down there as soon as you let go of me," came his determined response.

Meeks was gob-smacked.

"He's right," Yarn interjected. "The opportunity is now. We shall not be given one like it again, I can promise you that."

"I cannot believe what I am hearing! You have both taken complete leave of your senses." Meeks was wide-eyed and shaking his head in disbelief.

"Now *is* the time—while they're sleeping it off in the field. Believe me, none of the Fomorian you just saw will be back before dawn's light," Yarn insisted.

"But we have no weapons! We are unarmed!" Meek's concern would not abate.

"We do not mean to engage them, Meeks. We need to know why they are here and *how* they are here. A chance like this one presents itself only once, and we are taking it!" Banth finished.

Knowing that his companions were determined in their resolve, Meeks still hesitated, but loyalty to his clan won out.

"Fine … tell our smelly friend to take watch here, and I will come ahead with you."

And with that, Banth reached his hand toward his hesitant friend and helped him up the fog stream bank.

CHAPTER 23

BANTH, MEEKS, AND TOBAS crouched on the crest of the hillock while Yarn explained to Andee that he was not to follow them, but stay behind as a lookout, and warn them if need be. Though reluctant—and feeling that he deserved a more interesting part of the action—he acquiesced and took up his post behind a rocky protrusion halfway down the steep hill. The remaining four sized up the best approach and determined the most inconspicuous place from which to enter the main tent. Nodding in agreement that it was time to proceed, the faeries took to the air, hovering just inches above the mossy meadow. Had their flight been witnessed, they could easily have been mistaken for a cloud casting a gauzy shadow as it passed before the waxing moon. In no time, they found themselves at the rear of the large tent from whence they had seen the Fomorians stumble into the night. Taking shelter in the deep folds of the surplus tarp puddle on the ground around the support stakes, they waited for any signs that they had been seen. Certain that they had made it this far undetected, Banth took the lead and slipped through a tear in the dirt-encrusted fabric. After a few moments, his head popped back out and he motioned for the rest to follow. Noiselessly, the three myth followed their director into the unknown.

Yarn went first. Keeping to the shadows on the fringe of the tent's interior, he quickly found Banth, who had established a hiding place behind a sack of root vegetables thrown carelessly to the dirt floor. They were soon joined by Meeks and finally Tobas. The spies crouched in the shadows, again waiting to be sure that they had gone unnoticed. Once convinced that they had, they sought a higher vantage point and found one in the roughly hewn rafters of the shelter from which the Fomorian had hung slabs of skinned meat and whole game birds to dry.

From there, peering through the swaying slabs of dried and decaying flesh, they could make out a rudimentary table that was more a bundle of logs strapped together with crude ropes than an actual table. Long-burning candles had secured themselves to the surface in hardened pools of their own wax. Against the far wall were dozens of skeans, claymores, and celts thrown carelessly into a pile. The tent, however, had not been completely abandoned. A *cocaire* was preparing root vegetables and toadstools gathered from the nearby forest and tossing them into a crude pot hanging above a slow fire. Across from the cook, sitting serenely on a makeshift chair fashioned from a chiseled stump, was a figure covered in a thick black cloak. He would have gone unrecognized as anything more than a heap of murky cloth had it not been for the hands protruding from his sleeves. The fingers of the hands were impossibly long, bony and gnarled, and white as snow. The inconceivably long fingers finally succumbed to their nails, which were long and black, and curled under at the tips like those of a raven.

Neither of them seemed to take notice when the tent's enormous front flap flew open allowing the entrance of three large, dirt-encrusted figures. The largest of the three Fomorians to enter the tent was carrying a coarse brown sack, which he unceremoniously slammed down onto the table. The large, angry warrior then turned and began pacing back and forth in front of the fire. The cook kept peeling, but refrained from throwing the vegetables into the pot for fear that he would pelt the large, dirty soldier in the shins with chunks of pared tubers. After a few minutes of pacing the Fomorian walked around to the far side of the table and placed his hands on opposite sides of the sack. He leaned heavily on the makeshift table and stared imperiously at the black-robed figure. After leisurely pulling the hood from his head with his terrifying talons, the raven-clawed creature folded his hands in his lap and waited for the Fomorian leader to speak.

"I suppose that it brings you no small satisfaction to learn that you were correct, wizard," the leader growled.

The wizard wisely offered no response.

"This book cannot be opened, Mephistis," the frustrated Fomorian snarled before resuming his pacing by the fire.

Yarn's spine stiffened at the utterance of the ancient wizard's name.

With the general's back turned, one of the two guards who had followed the leader into the tent, sidled up to the primitive table. With a child's curiosity, the guard pried open the loosely tied strap at the mouth of the dirty sack and peered inside. His comrade backed himself against the tent wall and stared straight ahead, shaking his head violently back and forth, occasionally glancing over at the goings-on on the makeshift table. The curious Fomorian guard cocked his head to the left and then the right before slowly reaching his hand into the rough satchel. His cautious companion resumed his head shaking with greater fervor as he watched the witless guard pull his hand from the bag only to find it cloaked in a fiery orange-yellow light that wrapped itself around his intrusive fingers, palm and wrist, and was working its way up the soldier's arm.

The second soldier backed himself even further into the tent's folds, his shock and fear leaving him practically paralyzed. The whips of light had by now circumnavigated the foolishly curious Fomorian's head, shoulders, and torso and were spiraling downward to his feet before the unsuspecting creature had time to fathom his predicament. When the inflamed illumination hit the floor, it reversed course and doubled back up the guard's body before ending in a single flame suspended over the brute's head. Here the unattached flicker hovered just long enough for the poor Fomorian to gaze up at it. Once he looked at the solitary blaze, it turned bright blue and the curious creature dissolved into soot, the ashen outline of his former self suspended in place briefly before cascading to the floor in a pile of indigo ash.

Once the wizard was sure that the displeased leader had calmed down somewhat, he spoke in a composed voice. "The book will only open when it is time for it to do so, Galar."

These words did nothing to sooth the angry Fomorian. In fact, if anything, they angered him even more. In a single stride, he had pulled his sword from its scabbard and was hovering over the cloaked figure, the point of the skean resting menacingly under the conjurer's chin.

"I can see that for myself, old sorcerer. If you can be of no more service in this situation, why, pray tell, do I need to suffer your company any longer?"

Mephistis kept his posture, staring unflinchingly into the face of the enraged Fomorian. The wizard may have known little about how to open the Book of Sorcha, but he knew plenty about the fiery Fomorian race.

Again, after a cautionary pause, he answered, "Because, my Lord, I am the only one who can read the words of the Tuatha. As I told you, their language was banished with them by the Milesians. They and I are the only ones left who understand it," Mephistis lied calmly.

"Do you dare speak to me as you would to a child? You think me in need of tutoring in the events of the past?" was the outraged response.

The wizard did not answer immediately.

After a weighted pause, he added the decisive answer to the Fomorian's question. "I know the secret of how to pass from our world to this one ... and back again." He whispered the sentence's end, playing his trump card.

Angered by the wizard's response, but understanding that he could not do without the sorcerer—not yet at least—Galar slowly lowered his sword, his eyes still locked with those of Mephistis.

"Mind your tongue, old wizard, or I will wear it on my belt as a luck charm," Galar snarled as he backed away from the scolded sorcerer and returned his skean to its scabbard.

Still staring malevolently at the now silent wizard, the angry commander continued his tirade. "You lead me to this land of the Tuatha, yet I see no Tuathans. You lure me here with the promise that this book," he gestured indignantly at the object on the table, "will show me the future, yet the book has shown me nothing."

The leader of the Fomorian then turned his attention back to the coarse brown sack. As he approached the table, his brow furrowed at the sight of his now lone guard shaking in his very boots against the tent wall. Galar looked around the enclosure for the second soldier. When he could not see him, the leader walked around to the other side of the rudimentary table and scanned the flooring. Seeing the pile of blue cinders sent his eyes to the back of his head as he let out a frustrated grunt and a scowl in the

direction of the less curious of his two attendants. Shaking his head back
and forth, he picked up the bundle with greater care than he had set it
down. The general peeled the covering down, revealing the upper half of its
contents, taking mindful care not to touch the bag's occupant. Galar walked
slowly toward the hearth as he rotated the sack and its cargo in his hands.
Turning back toward the table brought the object in his hands into full view
of the concealed myth. What he held in his hands was a book. As he passed
it back and forth from his left hand to his right, bits and flakes of the cover
fell away from the friction of the rough, dirt-hardened sack. As the book
rotated to face the flames of the cooking fire, the reflection from the blaze
illuminated a sliver of gold on the book's cover. The light from that illumination bounced around the tent from one reflective surface to another like
a ricocheting star. The radiance ended its journey in the flames of the
cook's fire where it burst into green-gold sparks that singed and flashed in
the ashes accumulating in the unswept hearth. This time, he set the book
down on the makeshift table carefully and with both hands.

"I should be more agreeable to do battle with these descendants of
Danu if I were privy to the outcome," the leader muttered under his breath.

The Fomorian leader's mercurial temperament shifted without warn-
ing or apparent motive, and he picked the book back up and then slammed
it down with such force that large sections of the cover and binding sheared
off from the impact. Reeling himself around, he reached out and grabbed a
stein of mead left on the hearth's mantle, and in one gulp drank its contents
minus what streamed down his face and soaked into his tunic. Galar then
hurled the empty vessel into the roaring fire, causing the flames to hiss and
the *cocaire* to gather his remaining toadstools and scurry off to the relative
safety of the far side of the tent.

Finding no relief for his mounting frustration, the leader motioned his
remaining guard outside. After a menacing pause in front of the quiet wizard, the Fomorian, shaking his fists toward the roof of the tent, let out an
angry roar before following his guard through the shelter's entrance and
into the E'lore darkness.

The myth took this as their cue to leave. The cook had deemed it safe
to return to his duties before the fire and did so. The wizard had drawn his
long black hood back over his face and resumed his motionless posture by

the fire's side. Slowly, one by one, the myth retraced their steps until they found themselves back in the concealing folds just outside the tent's rear-most section. Yarn peeked up from their hiding place, and somewhat to his surprise, found Andee still awake and completely attentive. The grogoch scanned the meadow carefully before giving the signal that the coast was clear. First, Yarn and Meeks flew up the steep hill. Banth and Tobas fol-lowed. Soon they were all once again on the other side of the embankment from where they had first observed the Fomorian camp. In moments, Andee joined them, flinging himself over the crest, nearly crushing Meeks when he landed. The momentum from the clumsy beast's misgauged leap sent him sliding down the length of the downgrade on his backside. When his great hairy self finally stopped, he stretched his stick and straw-encrusted arms behind his head, bringing his oversized noggin to rest in his cupped hands. Determining that his retreat had been a complete and glori-ous success, he crossed his ankles and rested at the base of the slope, smil-ing and snorting at the growing moon above.

CHAPTER 24

CLAIRE INSISTED ON helping Sarla clean up from dinner. Willa and Anndra had been excused on the condition that they go to their rooms to work on their studies. Sarla washed while Claire dried the glazed clay plates, saucers and teacups. The two worked in comfortable silence until the last of the dishes had been cleaned and dried and placed neatly in the cupboard. As Claire laid the dish linens across the backs of the dining table chairs to dry, Sarla had refreshed the tea leaves in the company-sized teapot and filled it with boiling water from the kettle over the fire. She walked into the front room with the fresh pot of tea, two clean cups and several sweet cakes that had somehow managed not to be eaten by her children, and with a nod of her head, motioned to Claire to follow her.

"I'll be mother," Claire said as she poured some of the dark fragrant brew into the cups. She gave each a generous dollop of thick, sweet fernticle sap and stirred the steaming elixir until it had dissolved. Sarla nibbled on a heather cake, her legs curled under her, her relaxed wings unfolded and swaying gently to and fro with contentment. She watched with delight as her charge prepared their tea.

When Claire saw the faerie staring at her, she giggled and offered an explanation.

"Oh, sorry, that's what my mom used to say. Whoever fixes tea for everyone calls herself 'Mother'," she explained.

"'Tis lovely, I think" Sarla said gently.

Claire sipped her tea and bit into a sweet cake as she tucked her legs under and scooched back into the chair giving only a passing thought now as to how the chairs were not too small for her anymore. As she sipped her perfectly sweetened tea, she looked around the room over the rim of her cup, appreciating the way in which Sarla made her family's house a home. The walls had been stained a tranquil sage-green, which was a perfect background for the flother flowers and kard-pa blossoms that had somehow managed to find their way into the dwelling. Once inside, they grew with abandon, winding their way up the walls and along the floors. In creative and odd contradiction to the natural growth, there were old shoes wedged behind the vines that covered the walls. Broken slippers and *brogs* of all shapes and sizes arranged haphazardly along the wall following no apparent pattern other than that taken by the vine's chaotic growth. Claire smiled at Sarla's sense of humor and admired the colorful, free-natured mural that she had created. When the little girl looked closer, she saw that there was something inside each of the shoes. She unfolded her legs and got up to take a closer look. She did not have to get very close to recognize the objects. They were photographs. Some quite small, some rather large, all were wedged lovingly into each abandoned shoe. A few of the photos were so old that they were not on paper but on tin.

"You've been collecting these for a long time," Claire remarked as she made her way down the wall.

"Yes, the harvesters bring them back for me. Yarn has quite a collection himself," Sarla answered.

"So that is why …"

"'Twas a gift," Sarla answered, knowing that Claire was referring to the black and white photograph of Claire's mother and sister.

Sarla had placed the framed photo next to Claire's nest in her chamber. It was one pilfered gift that would not find a place on the shoe wall.

Sarla motioned for Claire to come back and sit, and as she was settling back into the chair Sarla said, "Tell me about her."

She looked at her hostess in puzzlement.

"I'm sorry?"

"Tell me about your mother," Sarla answered patiently.

"Oh." Claire's spirits seemed to sink a bit at the thought of talking about her mom. Sarla noticed the change but did not retract her request.

"There's not a whole lot to tell. I mean … she died … a few years ago," the girl answered.

With this, Sarla's heart sank, and she could feel tears beginning to well up in her eyes. She had known that the little girl had lost her mother when Claire referred to her in the past tense by the brook, on the night of The Telling. 'So cruel', she thought, 'for a child to lose her mother.' Sarla did not want Claire to focus on her mother's death, so she encouraged her in the opposite direction.

"Tell me about her from the time when she *was* with you."

"Well, let's see," Claire started, shifting in her seat and pushing her folded legs to the side.

"She wasn't born here, I mean there, I mean not in America. She was from England. My father met her during the war."

"That would be the second world war, yes?" Sarla asked, judging that Claire's father would be about the right age to have served then.

"That's the one," Claire replied. Since she knew of Sarla's and Yarn's interest in humans and their history, she was not at all surprised that Sarla would know this, and so she continued. "He was stationed near where she lived with her family in Salisbury."

Sarla paused at mid-sip, but regained her wits without Claire taking any notice.

"There's a huge cathedral there," the nambor girl continued. "Even though my dad is not religious, he would meet her at this church on Sundays. Her whole family would go: her parents and all her sisters and her brother. My mom's father wouldn't let my dad sit anywhere near her. It would be my grandparents, then my mom, then my four aunts and uncle, then my dad. It was the same when he went to her house for dinner. My grandfather sat them as far apart as he could. Dad said it was a wonder that he even recognized my mom at the altar when they finally got married. He said he figured that he'd just wait for a girl to show up in a white dress and he'd grab her by the hand and say 'I do' before anyone could object. My dad's always joking like that." Claire paused and tried to wash away the rising lump in her throat with a healthy sip of tea. She noticed that, unlike when she first arrived, she could now take several gulps of tea before the cup was empty. She looked again at how much extra room she now had in the chair and almost changed the subject before Sarla's impeccable timing lured her back to the conversation at hand.

"Do go on, dear," she said softly.

Claire looked up to see that the faerie was holding up the cake platter to offer Claire another sweet. Claire accepted and said "thank you" as she gathered her thoughts.

Sarla merely smiled over her teacup and Claire continued.

"The house where my mom grew up was not far from Stonehenge.She and my aunts and uncle used to play on the stones when they were little, they would take a picnic and make a day of it. They played Marco Polo or pretended that they were Druid priests and hold trials and sentence each other to be sacrificed. Mom was always so happy when she talked about playing on the stones. She would talk about them like they were people— like her friends. I think she really missed *them* more than anything else. Anyway, she told me people think that the priests—the Druids—built Stonehenge. My mom said that they were wrong. The priests were not the builders of the henge, but the 'keepers' of it. I never knew exactly what she meant by that—until you explained it to me when we were washing the cups in the stream. She went back after my sister Colleen was born, but by then, so many people had chiseled out bits and pieces of the stones, or written on them, that they had to rope it off and put guards all around. When she tried to go under the ropes to eat her lunch, they made her leave—they wouldn't let her near them. She was so upset. I don't think she was ever quite the same after that." Here Claire paused and Sarla sat quietly, giving her time to reflect on the memories of her mother.

"Is that why you were asking me about the priests on the night of The Telling?" Sarla asked by way of encouraging the conversation. She already knew the answer.

Claire nodded.

"Whenever she told me about her trip back, she seemed to get upset all over again. My dad said that it was the Druid's fault that no one could go near Stonehenge anymore. He said that if they would stop running out to the stones and lighting fires and pretending to make sacrifices every time the seasons changed, they wouldn't have to keep everyone else away. He said that it was probably built by a bunch of cavemen and that everybody should stop making such a big deal about it. My mother never went back to visit again. After a while, I couldn't even get her to tell me about the stones anymore. I would ask her, but she would just go quiet and say, 'some other time, maybe.'"

Claire had not noticed, but by then, Sarla was leaning forward in her chair, and her wings were folded tightly behind her back.

"Claire, dear," she started with her customary gentleness, "What was your grandmother's name?"

"Claire." Claire answered. "My mom named me after her."

Sarla's pause was unmistakable, but she collected herself as quickly as she could.

"And what about *her* mother? What was her name?" Sarla continued.

"Caithleann. Why do you ask?"

Not ready to answer her just yet, she pressed on.

"Do you, by any chance, know what your great-grandmother's mother's name was? I realize, of course, that you could not have met her, but would your mam have told you her name?"

Claire, having no way of knowing where the line of questioning was leading, had no reason to be alarmed by it, so she answered her.

"Actually, I can tell you until pretty far back. It's kind of strange, really. All of my grandmothers were the fifth girl in their families and they all had the same name—well the same two names, I should say."

Seeing that Sarla was not going to ask what she meant, but instead was waiting patiently for her to continue, she did.

"My great grandmother's name was Caithleann, *her* mother's name was Claire, *her* mother's name was Caithleann and *her* mother's name was Claire, and so on and so on. A little weird, huh?" Claire paused and set her teacup down. "Actually, that's not entirely true," she suddenly added. "Mom said that at some point the two names were Caithleann and Sorka? ... Sorsha? ... anyway, something too hard to pronounce. It was a really old Gaelic name and it translated to English as 'Claire' so they started using Claire instead."

Claire half-expected Sarla to laugh at the strangeness of her family's naming practices, but was not at all surprised when she did not.

"Oh boy, I think I've had too much tea," Claire moaned, her hands on the lower half of her tummy. "Excuse me for a minute?" she asked as she unfolded herself and got up from the chair.

"Of course, dear," came the faerie's reply.

As the nambor child made for the water closet, Sarla tucked herself back into the chair, her wings once again extended and fluttering, gently fanning the smile that now stretched from ear to pointed ear.

***

With Andee's guidance, the group found their way back through the thick wood and on to the path leading back toward Aislinn. The journey to this point had been made in complete silence, each of the four myth distracted by their own thoughts and theories. Once the forest and the Fomorian camp were behind them, the myth felt it was safe to speak.

"He has the book," Banth and Meeks stated in unison, their declaration directed toward Yarn.

"So it would seem," was his understated, preoccupied reply.

A slightly puzzled Tobas joined in. "That was *the* book? The book that's missing from our talismans?"

"Yes," the three older myth replied at the same time, their gazes never leaving the ground.

"I thought that the book had been lost in the battle, how can that wizard have it?" the younger myth asked.

No one answered his question.

"Mephistis has sold himself. He has betrayed the order … and us," Yarn's tone was cold and outraged. "I did not know that creature until that filthy Fomorian called him by name, but that was him, doing Galar's bidding and leading our enemy to *us*." Yarn answered angrily.

Banth, the *bairn* in him terrified by the name of the mercenary Fomorian who intended to kill him back in Eire, cleared his throat and found his voice. "Yarn, what can they do with the book? What could be their purpose in bringing it here?"

"I should think that they mean to open it, to know of its powers. Allowing the assumption that they have spent tens of hundreds of cycles in pursuit of the book's secrets, proves that they are no closer to knowing how to open it now than they were when they stole it from us at the entrance to E'lore."

"What?" Tobas's asked with surprise. "'Twas not lost?"

"Come, we had better get home," Yarn responded with a firm grip on the back of the young myth's arm.

Yarn and Tobas walked down the loamy trail together. The older myth's thoughts were a jumble of unanswered questions, not the least of which was why Mephistis lied to the Fomorian general about the book. The writings inside were not in the language of the Tuathan—Sorcha was not of Tuathan descent. Her language was the language of the native people of Eire. Mephistis could not possibly speak Tuathan as they only spoke in their mother tongue amongst themselves, privately. Uncle and nephew plodded on toward Aislinn with the director and Meeks following behind. Andee was all too happy this time to bring up the rear.

CHAPTER 25

SARLA WAS SO deep in thought that she had not taken notice when Claire returned. The young nambor had time to reclaim her chair, refill her tea cup, and choose a heather cake from the still full platter. It was not until she said, "I think these are my favorite," that Sarla's attention was jostled back to her guest ensconced in her cozy little chair nibbling sweets and drinking tea.

"Oh, there you are," the beautiful faerie said as she regrouped her composure, which was not at all accustomed to going astray.

"I'm so sorry, dear. I've missed what you said," she whispered.

"I think these are my favorite," Claire repeated. "Will you teach me how to make them?" she added.

Sarla's heart rejoiced at the request. She had been waiting for Willa to show interest in such things, but as yet, she had not. Sarla was thrilled to be presented with an opportunity to share one of her passions. Yet, in spite of her excitement, she answered with a simple "yes."

"Only if you tell me more about your mother," she added playfully.

Claire's response, however, was not as lighthearted. She really did not like talking about her mother, but insulting Sarla would be even more painful to her than reliving memories of her mom, so she acquiesced.

"There's not much more to tell, really," the little girl started. "My oldest sister, Erin, was born in England. The war had ended, and while Daddy was being discharged, Mom and Erin went ahead to the states and moved

into a little white house right next to my grandparents—my dad's parents,"
she clarified. "Dad came home and soon there was also Deirdre, Catherine,
Colleen, and me. Everything was great. Daddy had just gotten another
promotion and he and Mom were actually looking for a larger house since
there were so many of us by then. I remember sitting on the couch with
Colleen and they were on their way out to meet the real estate agent when
the phone rang. I couldn't hear what my mom was saying. I just remember
her taking her coat off and handing it to my dad. She was standing in the
kitchen doorway on the phone. I think she was crying. My dad told me and
Colleen to get our coats on and find the others because we were going out
for ice cream.

"When my mom saw us, she put her hand over the phone and said,
'You girls go ahead, have fun. Bring me some strawberry, okay?' She was
trying to sound like everything was fine, but we could tell that it wasn't.
When we got back, her suitcases were packed and she was sitting at the
dining room table, waiting for us."

Claire's narrative had stopped and Sarla encouraged her gently.

"What was wrong? Who had she been speaking to?" she asked.

"It was my aunt. My grandmother, Claire, was sick," was all she offered at first.

Sarla gave Claire the choice to continue or not by sitting quietly, ready
to listen should the little girl want to go on. After a few silent moments, she
did.

"They didn't know how much longer my grandma had, so my mom
had made plans to go back to England right away. She said she was sorry
that this had happened so quickly, but that she would be back before we
knew it. We gave her hugs and kisses and my older sisters were crying, but I
don't think that I really understood what was going on exactly."

Here Claire paused again.

"That was the last time I ever saw her. She never came home," Claire
finished softly.

Sarla rested her empty tea cup on its saucer and put the duo on the table. She then extended her wings and fluttered over to Claire, took her
empty cup from her hands and placed it on the table, as well. Landing on
the chair's arm, the faerie took Claire's left hand in both of hers. When the

tears had finally stopped their silent streaming down the heartsick girl's cheeks, Sarla pressed her one more time.

"What happened to your mam, dear?"

"They said that she never made it. They said her plane crashed into the ocean. She never made it to England."

Claire's tears were flowing freely once more. Sarla's eyes, too, were filling quickly with hot, salty tears as she motioned to the weeping child to scooch over. With her wings tucked tightly behind her, Sarla took up the new space beside Claire. She placed her right arm around the sobbing girl's shoulder and took the nambor's left hand in hers. Here, the two sat side by side, no more questions to ask or answers to give.

CHAPTER 26

THE HOUR WAS late. Willow and Anndra had long been sleeping, and Claire, exhausted from her talk with Sarla, had retired some time before the four myth returned from their reconnoitering.

"Move forward? How can we move forward?" Meek's anxious and spirited voice carried across the main room of Tobas's and Sarla's home, where the members of the expedition to the encampment had gathered. At some point in their trek back to Aislinn, Andee had left the group and taken his own path, to where, none of them could be sure.

"We must delay. We need time to return to Doog and find *the* nambor of the prophecy!" Meeks continued. He was annoyed and highly agitated, not a state that his colleagues were accustomed to observing. *Annoying* yes, but not overwrought, not like this. Yarn kept a concerned eye on his friend.

When Sarla heard the men return, she closed her book and went to the kitchen to make preparations for a late tea. As she came around the corner with the burgeoning tray, she saw her Anndra sitting on the floor at the opening to Claire's room. She quietly laid the tray on the dining table and walked softly over to him. As she pulled away the moleskin that concealed the chamber's opening as well as half of her son, he made no movement to acknowledge her presence.

Sarla kneeled down so as to be heard only by him and said, "What's going on here then, Anndra?"

"Just looking at it," he answered.

"Not 'it' dear, her," Sarla corrected him.

"Just looking at her," he offered. "Will it … her … she be staying, Mam?" he asked, looking up at his mother as he did.

"I do not have an answer for that yet, dear. Would you like for her to stay?" Sarla asked with her customary gentleness.

"I would, I think," Anndra replied, having returned his gaze back to the moleskin nest and its slumbering occupant.

After a contemplative pause, he added, "She's a bit lovely, isn't she, Mam?"

"Do you think so?" Sarla answered, trying her best to subdue a smile.

"Yes, I think she is," he replied. "Rather like a whole pile of heather cakes that you have all to yourself and do not have to share with your sister. Lovely like that," he volunteered.

Sarla, somewhat dazzled by her boy's analogy, let free a broad grin. Knowing her son as she did, she also appreciated how much of a compliment it indeed was.

"I agree, dear," she whispered to him. "Perhaps you could tell her so when she wakes in the morning."

His mother's suggestion turned the child-faerie's face three shades of crimson and caused him to scramble to his feet. The embarrassed little myth half ran and half flew back to his own chamber, leaving the swaying skin over the doorway as the only proof that Sarla had not been alone just moments before.

She felt a subtle twinge in her mother's heart at the realization that her youngest, at only five cycles old, was becoming aware of decidedly mature concepts as his simple world expanded and changed with each cycle that passed. But for now—for a little longer, she hoped—he was still her sweet *aingeal* and her smile refused to leave as she returned to the dining table and took up the task of taking tea to her guests.

Sarla entered the room carrying the tray that overflowed with cakes and breads and set it down on the small table by the fire. In the middle was a steaming pot of tea surrounded by empty cups. One cup, however, was not empty. It was this cup that Sarla removed from the tray and carried to Yarn. As the tired and grateful myth accepted the refreshing brew, she slipped a folded piece of parchment onto the lip of the saucer. A puzzled Yarn looked up to ask of its meaning, but his hostess had since fluttered away and gone back to the kitchen. Yarn held the saucer in his right hand, and as he half-heartedly blew at the steam rising from the cup, he deftly unfolded the piece of parchment with his left. Scrawled hastily on the crinkled paper in Sarla's penmanship were the words:

"We must speak."

Amongst the other assembled myth, Meek's ire had not abated.

"Bhara stated very clearly that there was a nambor, 'a brave warrior,' a nambor that we are to seek out and bring back to E'lore. Obviously, in light of our new circumstances, we can safely assume that the army of Fomorian in the neighboring meadow is the very reason that we need this soldier-nambor. Only we do not have *that* nambor. We have a mistake that tripped through the portal and landed squarely in the middle of a situation that *it* can be of no help with whatsoever!"

Yarn winced at Meek's rude referral to Claire as an "it," but fought the urge to call him out on his effrontery, instead asking that he lower his voice with a firm "shssssh."

Knowing full well that Meek's last comment was directed at him, Tobas dropped his head into his hands, clutching at his hair before lifting his head again.

"I have told you … I did not mean for the girl to come through the portal. There were no others there … no soldiers … no warriors … only her." Tobas dropped his head again. "'Tis my fault," he added.

"No, of course 'tis not your fault," Banth tried to comfort the young myth. "No one blames you," he added.

"'Tis his fault!" Meeks criticized. "I am not going to busy myself with pleasantries here! He was sent on a mission and he failed! Keep with your manners and soothing words as you will, but that is the certainty of our situation. The Fomorians have held up their end of Bhara's prophecy, while we have made a complete codswallop of ours!"

"That will do, Meeks!" It was now Banth's turn to lose his temper. "What is done is done! Casting stones will do nothing for our cause now. We must be as united as we have always been. *Together* is the only way that we have ever come through adversity. This time will be no different. We are

a clan. What one has done, we all have done. We will get through this together or not at all. No more laying blame. That is an order!"

Banth had not uttered that phrase once during his entire administration. He hoped that fact would add an oppressive weight to the phrase now.
It did. Meeks folded his wings inward and walked to the tea tray. He filled a
cup and after a short hesitation, filled another. He sweetened one and carried them both over to where Tobas sat heavily in his chair. Meeks extended the sweetened cup to the dejected myth who accepted it with a
barely perceptible "thanks." The older myth placed his non tea-cupped
hand on the young faerie's burdened shoulder. Tobas chose not to look up,
but kept his eyes focused on the curls of steam rising from his drink. After
a pause, Meeks gave his shoulder a squeeze and a stout pat before making
his way over to the hearth and taking up his post deep within the worn seat
of the fireside chair.

"Now then," Banth cut the silence, "all heads together. What are we to
do?"

Yarn started things off by pointing out that that not only was there no
longer an illuminated portal marking the path to this *chosen* nambor, but
they had not ascertained how or when the Fomorian planned to attack. Did
they even have time to try to find and retrieve the augured nambor?

"Without a clearly marked, direct pathway, most likely not," Banth
answered.

Meeks had quieted down after Banth's scolding. A few lip-burning sips
of tea, however, seemed to have re-directed his thoughts. "We are no match
for them. We have changed since coming here. We are a fraction of our size
since the banishment. We have wings, but in an atmosphere that does not let
us fly any great distance or with any great speed. I had not minded that so
much until now," he said into his tea cup as he took another scalding drink.

"They, on the other hand," Yarn offered, "are just as I remember
them except for Mephistis. I really would not have known him had he not
been called by name. He bears no resemblance to the young priest that I
knew in Eire."

"Yet, he and the book are together. What could this mean?" Banth
muttered softly. "Is *that* the question? I mean, do you suppose that this is
about the book and not about another war … with us?"

Yarn picked his head up from his cup, and answered, "No, I think Mephistis means to have both."

In the wake of his response came silence, while brows were furled and tea was sipped.

Tobas shattered the quiet when his half-empty cup came crashing down to meet its saucer.

"He said to the sorcerer that his confidence would be helped by knowing the outcome," the young myth exclaimed. His statement was met with silent stares.

"Do you not see? *We* have the advantage! The Fomorian told the wizard that he has come here to find us, but he will not find us, will he? Galar is unaware of how we have changed since the exile. If he knew, he would not need to know the outcome beforehand," the animated myth finished.

"How does being a fragment of their size and without weapons give us an advantage, exactly?" Meeks was doing his best to phrase his question in a non-insulting way.

"We have the benefit of surprise! They are expecting us to be the same. When they see that we are not, we use that time to our advantage!" Tobas excitedly blurted out.

"Are you referring to the time when they are doubled over with laughter?" Meeks's sarcasm had returned with full force.

"He means when they are confused and caught off guard," Banth sympathetically offered.

"Oh, *that* time," Meeks's cynicism ceasefire had lasted about as long as his cup of tea.

"Perhaps they think that we will open the book for them. Apparently, *they* are not able to, judging from what happened to that guard," Banth thought out loud.

"Yes, I found that to be most interesting," Yarn responded.

"How do you mean? Besides the obviously interesting bit, that is?" Meeks asked.

"I have seen the book touched and carried by many, both *Druwi* and Tuathan, when we were in Eire, but now it seems to have developed its own ... security measures." Yarn's voiced trailed off as he finished his thought.

"Even Galar would not touch the book directly. Perhaps that *is* their reason for coming here," Banth contributed.

"And naturally, they are assuming that a battle is inevitable. However, if he engages us and wins, then he runs the risk of the book remaining closed forever. And if he engages us and loses …" Banth reasoned.

"'Tis quite a quandary that Galar has himself in. No wonder his nerves are filed down to the quick," Meeks added.

"Exactly!" Banth exclaimed. "So you see Tobas may be on to something. The Fomorians are assuming that we are as we *were*."

"I still do not see how that is an advantage," Meeks replied.

"Because they will not be looking for *us*, which will serve us very well when we return and steal back the book!" Banth exclaimed.

Meeks looked blankly at the excited director.

"And who do you suggest be the first to try to open it?" he asked him dryly.

"Do not look at me!" Tobas called out without lifting his head.

"Yarn, what do you think?" Banth asked, as he turned about to seek out his old friend's face. But during their rousing exchange, none of the three myth had noticed that Yarn had left his chair and gone into the kitchen.

CHAPTER 27

REALIZING THAT THE nature of their conversation would not allow it to be had in hushed tones, Banth adjourned the meeting and moved the assembly to Yarn's cottage. Tobas was filling the empty kettle and unpacking the basket of cakes that Sarla had sent along. Banth and Meeks stood silently before the hearth. As Tobas put the kettle over the fire, Yarn walked through the door and hung his scarf before seating himself in his favorite chair. The discussion picked up where it had left off at Tobas's house.

"Something does not quite fit," Banth murmured as he added kindling to the growing fire.

"What is that?" Meeks asked.

"I said something does not quite fit," the director repeated.

"I heard you. I mean what does not fit?" he asked again.

"You mean why did they wait so long?" Tobas interjected innocently amid his cake-arranging before Banth could answer.

His comrades gazed at him in wonderment.

"Yes, exactly ... why did they wait so long?" Banth repeated Tobas's observation. "What could they have been waiting for? An immediate invasion would have made more sense from a military standpoint. Why such a long wait?" Banth thought that his question was a rhetorical one, but it was not.

"They could not follow us through the portal. No one could," Yarn's voice rang through the room and clutched everyone's attention.

"Sit down, all of you. There is something you need to hear," Yarn ordered. The eldest myth did not wait for his comrades to find a seat before he spoke again.

"In all of Sorcha's studies of the many other worlds that existed beyond our own, she shared her knowledge with only three others, her sister, and her two most gifted priests. One of those priests was that creature that you saw in the tent, Mephistis. The other priest was Bhara."

The room fell silent.

"Bhara was a priest?" Banth managed to get the words to form while the others still could not.

Because Yarn was the eldest among them, he was privy to more of the events surrounding the battle with the Milesians and their escape to E'lore. He was the last of the myth to know this of their departed king; all the others had taken the knowledge to their graves.

"Why have you not told us of this before now, Yarn?" Meeks asked somberly.

"'Twas Bhara's wish," he answered truthfully. "He was not of Tuathan descent, nor was he of King Lugh's bloodline. He worried that this would make a difference," he finished respectfully.

His audience struggled to make sense of this, mostly since there was not enough there to make sense of.

"A difference, how?" Tobas asked.

"A difference in how he would be accepted as our leader. The *Druwi* had been our aids, our advisors, and our counsel in Eire. They were part of our society, but not one of us. When we came to E'lore, we were a clan in the weakest sense of the word. Families were shattered. We were missing fathers, mothers, sons, daughters. We were nothing but a mangled, crippled cluster of misplaced souls. We had no will to fight even for our own survival. But he," Yarn gently swayed his head from side to side as he remembered, "he would not quit. He refused to relinquish hope … or life. We had lost our king on the battlefield. With no leader, we had no direction. Bhara gave us direction. Where we saw hopelessness, he saw a new beginning. Bhara *willed* us back from extinction. Who more deserved to be our new king?" Yarn asked of none of them. Yarn did not like to talk of that day in Eire. His memories were as fresh as if they had happened just that morning.

"And Bhara? Did he lose his family in the battle?" Tobas pressed him further.

Yarn looked at his nephew's fine-featured countenance and allowed the surging pride to fill him with a welcome, albeit brief, peace. Tobas reminded Yarn more of his beloved brother, Allyn, with each passing cycle. And it was at times like this that Yarn could see the fine myth that his nephew was becoming.

"Yes, Tobas, he did. Bhara's loss was as great and excruciating as any Tuathan's."

"'Twas the *Druwi* who introduced our Sorcha to the henge in *Breatunn*," Yarn continued. "It did not take her long to learn its secrets and to master them as well. But, she could not do it alone."

"Bhara and Mephistis were Sorcha's constant companions. In the beginning, they made countless trips to the henge itself. A fortnight alone across Eire, then the voyage across the waters to the shores of *Breatunn*, then another fortnight to the stones themselves. There they would stay, from moon to moon to moon. Had they not had *Druwi* friends at the henge to give them food and shelter, they may very well have worked themselves to death practicing traversing the portals and working on spells that opened them and then closed them again. We were forever sending envoys out with fresh supplies and requests for their return to Eire so they could rest. Eventually they would return, and as soon as they were whole and strong, they were off again. Even the other *Druwi* began to worry that their interest had turned into an obsession, but there was nothing to be done for it. And then, after one terribly long expedition, Sorcha returned with her priests and never left Eire again."

Yarn stopped for a sip of tea. His eyebrows raised in an expression of enlightenment as the reason for Sorcha's permanent return to Eire suddenly occurred to him. It also occurred to him that perhaps he was he was giving too much time to the to the tale he was sharing with his clansmen, given that they had other pressing matters at hand, but the *bard* in him knew no other way to tell a story. Given the nature of the other pressing matters, he thought, a few myth besides himself should know what he was the last to know, now that Bhara had passed. He continued.

"It came to be that Sorcha's skill surpassed the science and became an art, and she began practicing opening portals in our village in Eire. She, Bhara and Mephistis would disappear for days on end, traveling back and forth between this world and that one and the other."

Yarn thought of what a heady time this had been for his friend Bhara, and how happy the future king had been, even in the throes of his ceaseless and exhausting research. He returned to the story before his audience had noticed his pause.

"As you can imagine, keeping order to such a body of work became nearly impossible after a time, so Sorcha asked for help. Her entreaty was answered by Danu herself. Our mother presented her with a gift, a book. It had been made by Danu's very own *sagarts*. 'Twas of the finest vellum, and was bound together with golden thread. On the cover were carved our talisman: the sword, spear, stone and cauldron. In the center was etched a likeness of the book itself with a five-leaf clover adorning the cover. Encircling the clover was an eternal, unbroken knotted design, representing our past with no beginning and our future with no end. 'Twas into this book that Sorcha set down in writing all of their acquired knowledge of the henge and the secrets of the portals."

Yarn pressed on.

"In addition, she kept careful records of her teachings from the *Druwi*: incantations, spells, herbal potions, everything they had passed on to her. Formulas, equations and diagrams filled every margin. She had, by then, become a very powerful sorceress, indeed. And it came to be, after a time, that the book took on a life of its own. It had become a living companion and resource to the very person who had poured so much of herself and *her* life into it. It sensed when she wanted to consult its pages and would open for her as she entered the room. When she wished to record a new finding, it would open to a fresh, clean surface, even though she had long ago written on every page that the book had in its bindings. She had, in fact, recorded enough information to fill a book ten times its size. The first time that she witnessed the book open of its own will, in response to her mere presence, Sorcha realized another truth. In the face of this enlightenment, she returned to the tome's very first page, which by all accounts should not be, and recorded her epiphany:

"That which you seek is causing you to seek it."

"This book," Yarn continued, "possesses the knowledge and power of a people born of a goddess, and whose author was, without question, the most powerful sorceress any world has ever known. Should the Fomorian and that traitor priest discover how to open it, not only will we be undone, but countless other races could be, as well."

"And the parchments then, who wrote *them?*" Tobas asked.

"Bhara and I," Yarn replied. "Of course, as the clan's *bard*, I knew our history by heart. Our laws, what few there were, were a simple enough task, but Bhara could remember nothing of Sorcha's teachings. Their studies of the henge and its portals were lost to him. He would have faint glimmers of a word or phrase, and the harder he tried to grasp them, the more readily they fell away. He likened it to trying to control a handful of sand. Nothing he could do would keep the memories from cascading away." Yarn paused, the sadness in his voice apparent to all.

"What was he trying to remember, *Uncail?*" Tobas asked.

"Sorcha had taught him the spells that would open the portals at will," Yarn answered the profound question simply.

"So how is it that the portal opens for the four-petal harvests? 'Twas not Bhara who opened them?" Tobas asked innocently.

"No, son," his uncle answered.

"Hold on," Meeks was struggling to understand the implications of Yarn's revelation. "If not Bhara, who then?"

"I ... do ... not ... know," Yarn answered slowly as if the words were fighting him—the truth not wanting to be released from his keeping.

The clansmen sat in silence as they each struggled to understand.

"Those spells are in the book?" Banth asked aloud, his voice cracking as it broke the quiet in the room.

"Those spells are in the book," Yarn answered.

"So if the portal spells are in a book that cannot be opened, and Bhara did not open the portals, who did?" Meeks asked again as if Yarn merely needed more time to find an answer. The elder myth did not answer. He simply shook his head.

"What about the light in the glen?" Again, it was Tobas's uncluttered view of recent events that produced the most significant insights. "How did it get here? Could that be how the Fomorian found E'lore?"

"I must confess, 'tis an even greater mystery to me, that ball of light appearing as it did. I do not believe the Fomorian came through the light in the glen. Had they, they would have found us straight away, 'tis just on the other side of the pasture," Yarn answered his nephew.

"So how did they find their way into E'lore, then? Who is creating the openings? Who sent that ball of light?" Banth asked into his tea, well aware that none of his clansmen could answer.

"So that is why you said no one could follow us through the portal," Tobas suddenly exclaimed, remembering what his uncle had said when they began their meeting. "If Bhara knew the spells and then lost them, that means that if Mephistis also knew the spells, he would have lost them, as well. Bhara could not remember so that he could not get out; and Mephistis could not remember so that he could not get in! Sorcha would give her life before she would give the secret to the portals," the young myth concluded triumphantly.

"'Tis the same conclusion that Bhara and myself came to, son," Yarn replied.

"'Tis a fine theory, that, except for the minor detail that Mephistis has indeed opened and come through some portal, somewhere, has he not?" Meeks's observation left Tobas crestfallen.

"Maybe and maybe no," a newly optimistic Yarn replied. If Mephistis had the knowledge of the portals still, he would have come through long before now. No ... I believe that our disloyal priest has been handed what *he* thinks is a bit of luck, but *I* think 'tis something else all together. I believe that we, my friends are not focusing on the most important thing that has come through that portal with Mephistis and his filthy friends.

"The book," Tobas said confidently.

Yarn merely nodded his head in reply.

"But Mephistis was a *Druwi* priest, a confidant to Sorcha herself ... what happened? Why would he betray her ... and us?" Meeks asked.

"Because he was in love with Sorcha," Yarn answered.

"Do let me guess," Meeks said with a sarcastic roll of his eyes, "she was *not* in love with him."

"No, *she* was in love with Bhara." Yarn's reply left his fellow myth stunned.

"Why did she not come with us to E'lore, then. Why would she not come through the portal with Bhara?" Tobas asked.

"She was meant to, but she was taken by the Fomorian—right at the entrance to E'lore, no less. She was bringing the book. 'Twas in her hands and she was passing it to Bhara when they took her. And now we know 'twas that festering pile of filth, Mephistis, that helped them. Before the Fomorian were able to take Sorcha away, Bhara saw her cast a spell. That spell must have been what took away Bhara's memories of the studies of the portals. Mephistis's as well, I'm sure. She was protecting us." Yarn finished.

"Perhaps that was not the only spell our sorceress conjured," Banth added. "Something has kept anyone else from opening that book."

"If Sorcha is gone and Bhara is gone and Mephistis cannot remember, who is opening the bloody portal!" Meeks was unable to focus on anything else.

No one in Yarn's cottage could offer a plausible answer.

It was Banth who carried on. "We will have to put that aside for the present and focus on what is practically at our door—the Fomorians. No matter how they got here, they are in possession of the book, and we know that we *must* get the book back. Even if we are no more successful than they in opening it, at least there will no longer be the danger of their working it out and having a look at what is inside. And besides, it belongs to *us*." His reverence for his clan and their history pressed heavily upon the last word. "Now then, we must list our assets and vulnerabilities," he stated as he began pacing back and forth before the hearth.

"'Assets'? Yes, do begin with 'assets.' Get the shortest bit out of the way first, shall we?" Meeks, exhausted from the evening's affairs, was even more tart than usual.

Banth ignored him. "Assets," he continued without as much as a glance to his peevish comrade.

"We have King Nuada's *claiomh*," Tobas offered enthusiastically.

"An aged sword that none here are able to lift much less wield," Meeks declared.

"And the *slea*, of course," Banth added.

"Ah yes, the spear, 'tis bound to be much lighter than the sword. If we're going to press the old talismans back into service, how about we just drop the Stone of Destiny on their collective heads, and take them all out with one blow?" Meeks grumbled.

"We do seem to be wanting for weapons," Banth confessed to the crackling flames as he paced before the open hearth. "What else? We must have something," he muttered as he resumed his pacing.

"We can fly," Tobas again was the first to speak up.

"Not very fast and not for very long," Meeks no longer bothered to raise his head and directly address his fellow myth when he spoke.

"There is still the ..." But Tobas fell silent when Meeks began laughing cynically from his chair by the fire.

"If you have a contribution to make, Meeks, make it," Banth admonished his friend.

"Otherwise ..." the director raised his hands upward and cocked his head to the side as he tried to make his point.

"Is it time for the 'vulnerabilities' now?" Meeks answered, determined to retain his antagonism.

"Meeks, that will be enough! Why do you insist on making a difficult situation even more so?" Yarn had lost his tolerance of Meeks's cynical observations.

"Because, my friend, this is not a 'difficult' situation. This is a hopelessly insurmountable situation! We have no weapons, we have no defenses. We are lambs surrounded by gigantic, barbaric, revenge-seeking wolves! We have been caught unaware and unprepared and I can no longer listen to all of you prattle on about what we do and do not have, what we can and cannot do. We are finished. 'Tis over! I, for one, would rather spend my energy enjoying my last days, not pining for a solution that will never come! Bhara gave us a chance to save ourselves and that chance has been wasted!" Meeks's words hung heavy in the room.

Meeks allowed the frustration to drain from his face, before addressing Yarn specifically. "Destiny does not always lavish grace, my friend. Her back must be upon some in order for her to smile upon others."

Yarn was the only one able to push aside the oppressive anguish and speak. "Go on then. Get to enjoying. You are not helping matters here."

Meeks gathered his shoes and scarf and padded his way to the front door.

"I am ... sorry ... my friends. Were there a solution ..." Meeks understood that his words were not wanted, so he covered his head and wrapped his neck before slipping quietly through the door and into the night, alone.

After the door closed with a soft snap, Tobas asked of his remaining clansman, "Is he right?"

Neither spoke immediately.

Finally, Yarn answered his brother's son. "Perhaps. No. I can no longer say without doubt."

The three myth welcomed the consequent silence.

It was Banth who climbed above the despondent peace and spoke, "I still say that, if we can do nothing else, we retrieve our book."

Yarn appreciated what Banth was trying to do, but could offer him little encouragement. "I think we all agree, but how? We are no match physically for the Fomorian. Even if we armed every able-bodied myth in the realm, it would be done from the onset. It would be a futile attempt," an uncharacteristically dejected Yarn responded.

"We wait for them to fall asleep, and then we take it," Tobas innocently offered, refusing to relinquish his idea from earlier.

"Were it not for the wizard, I should think it would be as easy as doing just that. But I can promise you that he keeps it near him at all times, and I would wager that his circumstance has made him a very light sleeper," Yarn replied.

As Banth and Tobas half-conversed and half-argued out a plan to return to the encampment, Yarn reflected on Sarla's note from before and their subsequent secretive conversation in her kitchen. Although Yarn knew that Sarla had grown very fond of the nambor girl and at first thought her suggestion may have been born of this fondness, her proffered "evidence" seemed to support her argument. He had to admit that Sarla's theory about Claire *was* plausible. After all, at the time of their passage into E'lore, Sorcha had been with child.

CHAPTER 28

THE THREE EXHAUSTED myth left Yarn's cottage and took their meeting back to Sarla's and Tobas's home, where the tea and food were more plentiful. None were surprised to find that Sarla's kitchen was as far as Meeks had managed to wander. At Yarn's request, Sarla had brought Claire to the front room where she sat before the fire, bundled up in skins and sipping hot tea. Yarn and Banth were speaking to one another in the back of the room, Banth repeatedly glanced over his shoulder at Claire as Yarn spoke. When Banth left Yarn's company and walked to the fireplace, his head lowered in contemplation, Meeks walked up to the elder myth took over the spot vacated by Banth. After standing by him for a moment, he nonchalantly turned himself about so that his back was to the rest of the room, his left shoulder to Yarn's left shoulder, his mouth inches from Yarn's ear.

"What in E'lore do you have in mind, old friend?" Meeks started. "You cannot be thinking of taking on the Fomorian without first fulfilling the king's foretelling."

"I thought that you had better pursuits for the remainder of your precious time here in E'lore?" Yarn rightfully chastised his comrade.

Meeks said nothing, but lowered his eyes and shook his head. Yarn recognized the gesture as an apology and decided, as he had done many times before, to let the matter go.

Meeks kept a hushed tone so as not to involve the others, but Yarn, it seemed, saw no reason *not* to involve the others. Yarn motioned to the director to join him again. Banth ambled his way back to where Yarn stood and tugged on Tobas's sleeve as he passed the younger myth—a wordless invitation to follow him. Meeks sheepishly nodded his apology to the director and to Tobas. Yarn looked at each of his clansmen directly before letting his gaze lock on the nambor girl sipping tea before the fire. The more the old myth thought about Sarla's theory the more it made sense. Claire was the fifth daughter of a fifth daughter as all of the Claires and Caithleanns in her ancestors had been. She was a finder—not only of four-petals, but of the sacred and powerful five-petals, as well. She had adjusted to E'lore at an accelerated rate, as if she had been here before—or her blood had been here before—because she was, if Sarla was correct, a direct descendant of Sorcha and Bhara. She was also, in Yarn's eyes, a very brave warrior, indeed. It had taken the myth all this time to see what Andee had seen the very first time that he saw Claire.

"What if *she* is the nambor of the prophecy?" the patriarchal myth finally declared for all to hear.

At his pronouncement, Tobas stared at his uncle in disbelief.

Meeks's gaze volleyed back and forth between Yarn and Claire, before he shared his unchecked opinion with the intimate gathering.

"But … Bhara spoke of a brave warrior." Again he looked at Claire before stumbling on, "a brave *warrior*, not a …" Meeks refrained from finishing when he saw Yarn's defensive expression, but true to his nature, he could not hold his tongue for long. "Come now, this is no time for foolish conjecture! The nambor of the prophecy is strong and brave—obviously a male—Bhara could not possibly have been speaking of her! Her being here is a *mistake*." Meeks made his position abundantly clear.

"Destiny does not make mistakes," Banth and Yarn responded in unison, both of them were now looking unabashedly at Claire. Their single-minded and single-voiced rebuttal left the outspoken clansman in stunned silence.

"I think that she is meant to go with us." Yarn was the first to break the quiet.

Meeks looked disbelievingly from Yarn to Banth and back to Yarn again.

"And then what? What do you think a small nambor girl is going to do against an army of Fomorians?" his ire rekindled, he asked angrily.

"I have no idea," Yarn answered calmly, a slight smile spreading across his face.

"You have no idea! Well that *is* a relief; here I thought that you had no plan!" Meeks's anxiety and fear now controlled his temper.

Banth slowly approached the nambor girl. The director's mind fleetingly registered how much smaller the nambor was than when she first arrived in E'lore. Her stature had diminished to the point where they could now look at each other eye to eye.

"Will you help us, Claire?" he asked gently.

Banth's kind and sensitive presence brushed away her apprehension. Claire looked at Sarla, who gave her a gentle nod in answer to her unasked question before the little girl brought her gaze back to the director. Claire had no clue as to why she had been awakened and brought to the front room, or what she had to offer that could be of benefit, but answered the benign myth with a smile from behind the rim of her teacup with a soft, "Of course."

***

The group filed down Tobas's and Sarla's front walk and turned after the gate toward Yarn's cottage. Yarn, Banth, and Claire walked out front with Meeks and Andee taking up the rear. Tobas was still on his front porch talking to his wife.

"Tobas, keep all of your focus on Claire. Watch out for her as if she were Willa."

"I do not like leaving you and the *bairns* alone. Please, Sarla, I ask you again, make the preparations, I want us to be ready … I have a dark feeling about all of this."

Tobas was desperate and pleading to his wife's sense of duty to her children. Instead of agreeing with her husband, she merely smiled her patient smile, and cupping his face in her hands, gave him the response that she knew he did not want.

"Our fate has already been decided, my love. We have but to greet it—no matter what it may be. Do not lose your faith now, Tobas. You need it the most now."

Sarla's simple logic had always run circles around Tobas's frantic speculations. He bowed his head and brought his forehead to rest on that of his mate's. The myth pair held this simple contact for some time. Finally, Sarla stiffened her neck and began to pull away. As she did, Tobas caught her lips with his and held them in a gentle kiss.

"*Is tu' mo ghra'*," Tobas whispered to his wife.

"*Is tu' mo ghra'*," she answered him as she gently caressed his face.

"I love you" were the last words that Sarla and Tobas spoke to each other before the fate of E'lore was finally revealed.

CHAPTER 29

"LISTEN TO YOURSELF, Meeks!" Banth tried not to raise his voice.

"You're beginning to sound like ... like a nambor. Banth shot a swift gaze in Claire's direction. Have you no faith in anything?" Banth remanded his fellow myth. Fortunately, Claire was still watching the drunken soldiers lying motionless in the field and took no notice of the director's reference.

Banth, after taking a deep breath, continued, "When did *we* begin to judge others by what they are not?" Banth gave Meeks's shoulder a gentle pat before hoisting himself over the embankment and onto the slope that led to the meadow and the enemy tent below. Banth was followed over the ridge by Tobas and then Yarn. Before Yarn disappeared from view, Andee had already hoisted Claire onto his shoulder and was preparing to go next when he hesitated and looked back at Meeks. The great hairy beast stretched out his left fur-covered hand, offering it to the remaining myth as an aid up the steep rim. Meeks looked at the woolly paw and then at Claire.

"I hope they know what they be doing," he said before letting out a heavy sigh.

Claire said nothing as the distraught myth took Andee's paw and scrambled up the steep grade behind them.

The myth retraced their steps to mimic precisely the path they had taken before, this time with Claire and Andee in tow. They went from the safety of the hillock to the concealing darkness of the tent folds to the cover of the root vegetable sacks inside the smoke-laden shelter. Banth silently gestured to the others that Yarn and Meeks would ascend to the tent's rafters first. It would take the strength of two to hoist Claire to that height, which Banth and Tobas would do as soon as the two elder myth were in position. Andee was to keep a concealed watch on the ground. Within a few moments the four myth found themselves once again hiding among the swaying slabs of meat in the support beams of the Fomorian's dirty, debris-strewn tent. Banth and Tobas squatted on either side of Claire, each keeping a supportive clasp on the girl's arms. Confident that their movements had gone undetected by the Fomorians, they turned their cautious attention to the goings on below.

Mephistis had sensed their presence since they snuck in under the tent folds.

They had arrived at mealtime and the soldiers were gathered at the table drunkenly and boisterously devouring their roasted meat and fire-charred bread. Galar, who dined at the table's head, suddenly raised his soiled fist and then brought it back down to the table's edge with such force that plates and steins jumped in unison, some landing back where they were, some tumbling to the ground. This apparently was an unspoken order, as half of the infantry rose at once and scrambled from the tent.

No sooner had the last soldier gone out and the tent flap had settled back into place when it was thrust open again. The soldiers were returning in pairs, each team carrying a cask as they argued and ordered one another around. The casks were thrown haphazardly into the tent's southern-most corner, and after much shoving and jostling, each of the dirty and disheveled soldiers had his stein of spirits and the cursing and quarreling ceased.

With an authoritative jerk of his head toward the tent opening, Galar ordered two of the guards to take a post. They resentfully did so only after draining their dirt-encrusted steins and wiping their mead-soaked faces with the filthy sleeves of their shirts, which now hung several inches past the tips of their fingers. As the Fomorians took positions on each side of the tent flap, they were joined by two other guards who had just entered the shelter, the smell of the night air still fresh on their cloaks. The Fomorian guards were sufficiently numb from the well fermented libations, and vexed enough that they had been chosen to stand watch, that they simply shuffled aside and made room for the newcomers. The drunken soldier-guards ig-nored the fact that they did not actually recognize these two new guards as members of the camp. They ignored the fact that neither of them looked even remotely Fomorian. Since the presence of the two cloaked figures had not caught the attention of Galar or the others, the besotted soldiers turned their heads forward, and with a shrug, gave their inattention back to the room.

As the rest of the troops settled in for an evening of drink, Galar rose from the table and made his way over to the fire. The Fomorian com-mander stretched his arms over his head to allow the surplus material of his tunic sleeves to slide back and out of the way. He gave the fact that his clothing no longer fit as it did when he arrived in E'lore only a passing thought and brought his hands to rest on the mantelpiece on either side of the coarse and worn sack that held the book. Dropping his head down be-tween his arms, he closed his eyes and breathed in the smoke and fumes of the fire, taking advantage of the break in the din to calm his thoughts.

It was in this newborn quiet that there came a noise of a different kind altogether. A long, low rumbling that the soldiers recognized instantly as they pushed and pointed at one another, making lowbrow comments and accusations. The wizard, however, knew the source of the sound and was looking squarely at the root vegetable sacks that concealed Andee as the drunken Fomorians mockingly waved their hands under their noses and pushed and shoved each other in sophomoric chaffing.

The wizard's gaze slowly left the flatulent grogoch and shifted upward to lock on the half-hidden spies. Mephistis clapped his hands, which caused the soldier to his immediate right to stumble to attention. The sorcerer pointed in the direction of the intruders and the soldier followed his di-rective. It was the wizard's movement that caught Galar's attention.

And then Mephistis saw Claire. Claire looked directly at the wizard and the wizard at her. The ancient conjurer's countenance briefly softened, which did not go unnoticed by Banth or Yarn. Ignoring the others, the wiz-ard looked determinedly at the nambor girl. He had by now risen from his seat by the hearth and was walking slowly toward the five uninvited guests.

Mephistis raised his arms to allow the cloak to slide down his skeletal arms to unencumber his hands as he made his way toward Claire.

Claire instinctively tried to retreat from the approaching wizard, but could not due to the white-knuckled grips that Banth and Tobas had on her arms. The soldier that Mephistis had summoned to attention was quietly approaching the myth from behind. In his hand he held a half-chewed bone he had found tossed to the floor. His eyes were locked on Claire.

The myth looked around frantically for an escape route. Yarn immediately sought out Andee for help, but the loyal grogoch had already pounced upon the bone-wielding soldier and was gnawing viciously on one of the Fomorian's ears. While his fellow soldiers struggled to pull Andee off, another picked up the bone and succeeded in giving Claire a forceful shove in the back.

"No!" Tobas shouted.

The force of the jab sent her flying off her perch and into the emaciated arms of the Fomorian wizard. He caught her by the fleshy part of her upper arms, stopping her fall in midair. With his double-handed grasp, he pulled her closer to him until she was inches from his face. She strained her neck back to keep her face out of his, which made him pull her all the closer. Claire scrutinized his visage through squinted eyes, for it was far too hideous to look at with eyes wide open. His cheeks were cavernous with deep folds of unneeded flesh. His nose was sharp and pointed, like a beak more suited to a bird of prey than a creature resembling a human. His opened mouth revealed jagged brown and yellow spikes, which she could only assume had once been teeth. She winced as his breath caught in her nostrils, filling them with the stench of rotted meat and fermented eggs. The sockets of his eyes were deeply recessed in keeping with his cheeks, but they housed eyes of a brilliant jade green, large and somehow incompatible with the rest of his countenance. To look only at the wizard's eyes would be to look at a creature youthful and full of life. To look at the wizard as a whole was to look at a creature depriving death of its just due. As Claire's eyes met those of the wizard, she thought she saw his expression shift slightly. She did not have time to dwell on this, as the wizard relinquished his grip of her left arm and the leader of the Fomorians took possession of her limb with a painful jolt. The Fomorian soldiers had made quick work of taking Andee and the myth into custody, as well.

Mephistis recognized Yarn despite his diminished size, as the elder myth and his companions were led to the other side of the table. When Galar stared at Mephistis with inpatient bewilderment, the wizard answered his unasked question with an introduction.

"My Lord, I present to you the Tuatha de Danann."

Galar could not conceal his relief, and started chuckling as his gaze volleyed from his miniature prisoners to his sorcerer. Mephistis's emerald eyes were fixed on Yarn as the outraged myth struggled pointlessly against the grip of the Fomorian guard. Yarn did not give the former Druid priest his attention. Instead, the restrained myth focused on the captured Claire.

"This is how you plan to defend your kingdom, with a farting grogoch and a wee girl?" Galar growled with amusement.

Andee, although three times the height of the myth, was half as tall as the Fomorians. The grogoch wrestled against his restrainer, but to no avail. The tent full of soldiers let out a collective, raucous laugh at this, which Galar brought to an abrupt end with the raise of his hand.

"So, this is what is left of the mighty Tuatha de Danann? What a pity that your sorceress did not choose for you the dimension that she chose for us. Perhaps you would be in a better position now. No matter, I will soon finish what I started in Eire. But this one, he said turning to Claire, this one is not one of you, is she? Why is *she* here?" he asked as he scanned the faces of the distressed myth.

"What possible reason could you have for bringing such a useless creature with you?" Again, the gallery of soldiers chuckled, but this time Galar did not stop them.

"Wizard, what is this thing?" he asked, twisting Claire about so she faced Mephistis.

The sorcerer hesitated slightly before answering his master.

"Most likely a mutation of some sort," he muttered. "I am sure that she is of no concern to us," he finished as he reached for her left arm in an attempt to take her from the Fomorian. But Galar did not relinquish his grip.

Mephistis glanced at Yarn, but then retracted his gaze when he saw that Yarn was looking squarely at him. The faerie's temperament had shifted from angry to unsettled. 'Mephistis seems to know perfectly well what she is. Why was the wizard hiding the truth from his master?' Yarn thought to himself.

"If that is the case, then we will start with her," Galar growled, much to the delight of his inebriated army, who began cheering and chanting as their leader proceeded to carry the small girl toward the table on the opposite side of which the faeries and Andee were being held. It took merely a nod of the Fomorian's head and two of the soldiers swept the table clear, the sound of crashing plates and steins temporarily muffling the raucous cheers. Another nod to Mephistis was a wordless order to retrieve the book from the relative safety of the mantelpiece, but the wizard hesitated. Galar growled at the wavering sorcerer, to which Mephistis reluctantly responded by releasing Claire's badly bruised arm and walking unhurriedly over to the hearth. The conjurer carried the sack to the table and allowed is contents to spill untouched onto the rough-hewn and mead-soaked surface.

Galar glared despotically at the slow moving wizard, and continued his commanding gaze even after Mephistis had returned to Claire's side and again had taken possession of her right arm.

Claire once again had Galar to her left and Mephistis to her right, both gripping her with more force than would ever be required for one her size. The girl hung in the air like a rag doll between her two captors. She thought that her arms were going to be ripped out of their sockets such was the force she was straining against.

As the warlord and the wizard approached the table with their prisoner in tow, Galar caught Banth's gaze fixed on the ancient tome occupying the table's center.

"Had a mind to take the book for yourself, did you?" he snarled.

Banth's attention was immediately refocused onto the wrathful Fomorian.

Galar cocked his head to the left, staring at Banth. Banth tried to control his panic as he thought perhaps the merciless Fomorian recognized him as the wee lad he had tried to cleave in two all those cycles ago in Eire. Galar did not.

"Do any of you know how to open the book?" he asked menacingly, "Do you know the spell?"

The breathless clansmen could do nothing but look at Galar in bewilderment.

"WELL DO YOU?" he bellowed when no one came forward with an answer.

"No … no, we do not," Banth answered.

"Of course not," Galar hissed. "In fact, I will wager that we know more about this book than you do," he continued.

"Would *you* like to know what *we* know about this book?" he asked in a disdainful and superior tone. "It is a rather short list, actually. The list of what we have learned," the soulless Fomorian confessed as he and Mephistis continued to walk toward the table with Claire.

"You should think that we would know all that there was to know about it when you consider that we have had it in our possession for more lifetimes than I can recall. Would you not, Wizard … think that we would know all there was to know?" Galar snarled his blameful remark in Mephistis's direction. When no response came, Galar let out a disgusted snort and turned back to his prisoners.

"We know that it was written by a great Tuathan sorceress," Galar continued pompously. "We know that it contains not only secrets to ancient magic, but prophesies for the future as well. We know that only a Tuathan can touch it. Without a genuine descendant of Danu herself to unfasten it, both its knowledge and its foretellings are … LOCKED … INSIDE … FOREVER!" he screamed as bits of undigested meat and bread suspended in drools of saliva sprayed from his mouth.

Yarn counted that as another lie Mephistis had told the Fomorian.

Mephistis and Galar stood before the table with Claire hanging from their grasps. The sheer force of the Fomorian's grip was cutting off her circulation and her fingers were starting to turn numb. What the wizard lacked for physical strength, he made up for in his razor sharp talons, which had dug deeply into Claire's soft upper arm, drawing blood. Unbeknownst to her, it was flowing down to her wrists.

As the guards were dividing their attention equally between their prisoners and their ale, and were greatly distracted by the events unfolding in front of them, Andee was able to slip out of their grasp. Before his guard could regain a hold on the infuriated grogoch, Andee was bounding across the table and, in an instant, had pounced upon Galar, knocking him to the ground, his teeth buried into the surprised Fomorian's neck. As the soldiers came to the leader's aid, Mephistis released Claire, setting her down in a heap on the table's surface. The wizard stepped backward to avoid the fracas as the guards tried to recapture Andee. Claire lay still resting her head on her badly injured right arm.

Andee had relinquished his toothy hold on the now bleeding and enraged Fomorian leader and had scaled the tent's center support post. The grogoch was now swinging from beam to beam, taunting and tormenting the soldiers with his elusiveness.

Surrounded by clamor and turmoil, Galar did not hear when the Fomorian guarding Yarn called out.

"General!" the sentry shouted. His call went unanswered.

"General, General!" he tried again.

Finally, the guard had Galar's attention and the attention of everyone else, as well. The Fomorian soldiers stopped their collective pursuit of Andee in unison, and were staring in amazement at what was going on behind them.

It was the book.

The coveted talisman had started to glow, and what's more, it was no longer resting on the table. It was hovering weightlessly above it. The radiance was gradually giving way to flames originating from within the book itself and shooting out through the pages, scorching a path down the length of the table and upward to the crown of the tent. What had the gathered crowd seized with amazement, however, was that the ancient, gilded tome was opening.

Claire looked up at the flame-enveloped book now hovering in the air mere inches in front of her. She looked past the book at Yarn, Tobas, Banth and Meeks, who were watching her from across the table. They were cut and bruised, eyes wide with fear. Meeks stared in awe at the book, Yarn and Banth met Claire's gaze steadily while Tobas was shaking his head "no." Anguished tears welled up in his eyes.

Galar had, by then, returned to the table and the spectacle that had everyone in the smoked-filled tent mesmerized. His gnarled hand had once again found Claire's soft and badly bruised upper arm. Giving it a violent

jerk, he screamed, "WHAT DID YOU DO?" His astonished gaze was vac-
illating between the little girl and the silent wizard. "WHAT HAS
HAPPENED? WHAT DID SHE DO?" he bellowed in the face of
Mephistis, who refused to answer.

Claire's muscles were burning from the strain of resisting the overpowering strength of the cruel Fomorian leader. She cast one more look
toward the myth. With tears streaming down her face, she fought back the
waves of nausea and light-headedness that were the usual prelude to fainting. She could feel the flames licking her fingers as Galar forced her hand
toward the book. Unable to contain himself, Tobas yelled "No!" and attempted to wrest himself away from the guards. Instead of the guards grabbing Tobas back, the young myth was shocked to see that it was Yarn and
Banth restraining him. And when Claire's gaze met theirs, it was not answered with the fear that filled Tobas's eyes, but something entirely different. They were not afraid for her at all. In fact, Yarn's face was succumbing
to the broadest of smiles. But Claire's focus upon Yarn was interrupted by a
resounding gasp from the crowd. When she followed their collective stare,
her eyes came to rest on her own hand, which was now fully engulfed in the
flames spewing forth from the pages of the book. Galar had relinquished
his grasp and taken several steps back from her. The only thing holding
Claire's hand in the fire was Claire. But at the exact moment that she realized this, she realized something else. There was no pain. Instead of the
flames being hot, they were actually cool. As if in response to this realization, the flames changed, from fiery yellow to cool aquamarine. The crowd
was frozen in stunned surprise, all save for Yarn and Banth. Claire, herself,
gave out a gasp of disbelief, followed immediately by a jerk of her head up
to look back at the two beaming myth. Yarn's smile stretched ear-to-ear.
But he quickly dropped the smile and with a blank expression nodded toward the book. Her brows furrowed, asking "What?" Yarn again motioned
with an exaggerated nod of his head toward the sacred book. Claire subtly
shook her head "no" to which Yarn carefully nodded "yes."

Frightened and confused, Claire continued to stare at Yarn. This time
the elder myth said boldly, for all to hear "'Tis yours to take, Claire."

The terrified and bleeding nambor girl had no idea what was happening, but what she did have was trust in the kind old myth. Nodding her

head in return, she squeezed her eyes shut and brought her other hand up to the floating book. With a hand now on either side of the flame-engulfed tome, she brought her hands together. As she did so, the book began shrinking, becoming smaller as if her hands were squeezing the talisman into a fraction of the size it was when Mephistis released it from the coarse bag and let it spill onto the table. The tent full of bewildered Fomorians gasped in unison and held their collective breaths as Claire's hands finally found the book and took hold of it gently. On contact with her hands, the flames became a soft glow before fading and disappearing into the volume's pages as the book closed softly and slid willingly into Claire's grasp, welcoming her possession. When Claire felt the weight of the book in her hands, she opened her eyes to see the four faeries smiling back at her in awe, while the rapidly sobering Fomorians—gobs open wide in disbelief—still stared at the girl, waiting for the small creature to turn into a pile of blue ash.

Claire was relieved to see that she did not have to figure out what to do next, because Banth, Meeks, and Yarn, having easily escaped their stupefied guards, were by then halfway across the table, with a slow-reacting Tobas a few steps behind. Banth and Meeks grabbed Claire on the fly, and the three hit the soot-covered, debris-strewn floor, running. Tobas and Yarn were but a few steps behind them when Andee came gliding past. Having dismounted his perch in the tent's rafters just as flames from the book's fiery rebirth began to engulf the support beams, his big hairy feet landed a few paces ahead of the fleeing myth.

Claire was losing ground as she tried to propel herself and the book forward. Banth and Meeks reached back to take her arms and help her, but they were too late. Andee had circled around and was right behind her. The two myth barely had time to get out of his path before the lumbering grogoch scooped Claire up. With her tucked under his hairy arm, he raced toward the entrance of the tent. Andee seemed not at all surprised that the tent flaps were held open for him by the two late-arriving guards—the unrecognized guards who had been ignored by the pair of drunken Fomorian sentries ordered by Galar to stand post at the tent's entrance. The two unobservant Fomorian guards had long since abandoned their responsibilities in favor of observing the drama surrounding the intruders.

The fleeing myth did not question their good fortune that these two unlikely supporters had chosen to help them when they desperately needed an ally. As they approached the unobstructed opening, Yarn became awash with a sense of familiarity. He took his last moment before reaching the tent's aperture to steal a look at the "guard" to the left only to find that the "guard" was already looking at him. He held the covering aside and gave Yarn a reverent nod of his head before releasing his hold on the tent flap and allowing it to fall back in place behind the departing myth, closing off the structure as the six escapees rushed into the crisp, clean E'lore twilight.

Galar's rage approached delirium as he stared in disbelief at the traitors who had assisted in the myth's escape. The Fomorian leader drew his skean from its sheath and raised it over his head as he roared the order to attack. Mephistis, however, recognized the two myth confederates. Before they had removed their rough, dirty Fomorian cloaks to reveal pristine, raven robes; before they drew their swords and stood ready for battle, the betraying wizard knew them to be Druid priests. Mephistis also knew that being captured by his former brethren would certainly mean his own end. As the treacherous wizard looked about for an escape, he saw Galar coming towards him with skean raised and eyes aflame with wrath. The sorcerer stood his ground, preferring to die at the hand of the Fomorian than his Druid brothers. Galar, however, had no intention of wasting precious time on the lying wizard and instead turned and proceeded to the rear of the tent where he paused long enough to grab a bow and a handful of arrows from a basket in the hastily made arsenal put in place when the Fomorians set up camp. He sloppily dipped the arrow tips into a pail of aromatic oil before raising them over his head to ignite the oil with the flames engulfing his camp's shelter. The Fomorian then made his own exit into the side of the tent's fabric wall with the help of his razor-sharp skean. Without even a glance backward at his men or the wizard, Galar slipped through the opening and disappeared into the night. Mephistis followed the overlord through the gash in the fabric and fled into the darkness as well—in the opposite direction of his former master.

The Fomorian soldiers—unaware that their leader had abandoned them—pressed on with the attack on the two black-cloaked intruders. As flames took hold of the fabric that was the tent's roof, the stitching that bound the shelter's walls to its cap singed away and the smouldering fabric cascaded to the ground. The Fomorians halted their advance and were instead standing in mute awe at the sight that the burned-away tent now revealed. Approaching from three sides of their position was a legion of black-cloaked Druid warriors; their weapons drawn. They were closing in quickly on the bewildered, but sobered Fomorian army. The two Druid "guards," who had aided the myth in their escape, took off in search of Galar and the betraying Mephistis.

***

The cool night air was bracing and invigorated the myth as they glided away from the tent and headed for the embankment. The grogoch was already several paces ahead of them and was just at the base of the hillock when the faeries floated silently by. It was not until the fleeing myth passed Andee and Claire that they became aware of the battle cries and the sounds of metal upon metal coming from the meadow behind them. Yarn and Banth turned about to steal a look. What they saw stopped them in midair. The canvas of the Fomorian tent was lying in burning piles at the base of what was left of the shelter's framework. Flames and sparks illuminated the night sky as the support columns succumbed to the fire and crashed to the ground. The frightened and uncommanded Fomorian army had scattered to the four winds in an attempt to escape the resolute and seemingly infinite number of Druid soldiers. A legion of black-cloaked, sword-wielding figures carpeted the encampment as the last of Galar's soldiers fell and the meadow was given back its peace.

Although the sight in the meadow had given Banth and Yarn some measure of relief, it did not diminish their desire to be far away from the former Fomorian campsite as quickly as they could manage. Yarn reached out and took Banth by the arm, redirecting him toward their goal, when the dark sky around them filled with light as flaming arrows created a canopy of illumination over the hill leading up and out of the meadow. Enflamed missiles launched from the dark quiet behind them seemingly aimed at nothing and everything at once.

As Galar's arrows lost momentum and began their descent, they fell like fiery rain all around the retreating myth and grogoch. One of the plummeting arrows found its way deep into the flesh and muscle of Claire's right leg. She let out a scream which not only alerted the myth to her distress, but also gave Galar her exact location. Moments later Claire was sent flying through the air herself. Projected forward, out of the cradle of Andee's hirsute hold, she landed forcibly head first onto the ground, the Book of Sorcha offering little cushion to break her fall. The four faeries had already turned around and were coming to her aid when they heard her cry out from the arrow. When she fell to the ground they were already at her side. They immediately removed the arrow, the excruciating pain of which sent Claire out of consciousness. The myth looked back to see what had caused Claire to be separated from Andee. They scanned the hillside, searching for the grogoch. When they found him, they found their answer. For just a few yards back, the hairy beast lay face down in the meadow, the gold-inlaid handle of a Fomorian skean protruding from his back. Yarn leapt to his feet and headed for their downed ally, but was stopped by Meeks's hand clenched firmly on his arm. Before he had a chance to question the younger myth, he saw the reason. Standing behind Andee was Galar. Raising his left leg, the Fomorian placed his foot on the fallen grogoch's back. Clenching the handle of his skean so tightly that his knuckles went white, he locked eyes with Yarn. Without taking his gaze off that of the stunned myth, he drove the sword downward, deep into the woolly creature's back. Yarn let out a guttural scream as he lurched toward the Fomorian leader. The elder myth did not have the strength to fight against the hold of both Meeks and Banth who had quickly grabbed Yarn's other arm once he saw Galar standing behind the fallen grogoch.

The sight of Galar renewed the urgency of their escape. The myth scrambled to get hold of Claire. With Tobas cradling her waist and head and Meeks cradling her waist and legs, the two were able to overcome the handicap of her added weight and took to the air. The burdened myth fluttered frantically, with pure adrenaline propelling them higher and further away from the ruthless Fomorian leader. Banth and Yarn were right behind them, Sorcha's book cradled tightly against Banth's chest.

Yarn struggled and twisted to check behind them for a look at Andee, hoping that somehow he had not seen what he had seen. Banth's unbreakable grasp of the elder myth's arm kept him moving forward and away from his fallen friend. Tears rolled down the heartbroken myth's worn face as he and Banth flew toward the peak of the hill. Their gain of the top of the hillock coincided with a thunderous and ground-shaking crash and they dove to the ground to seek cover in the safety of the woods crowning the meadow's crest. They barely had time to crouch behind the trunk of a young lillyfur tree before shrapnel from the large main support column of the Fomorian tent came speeding past them. Fragments of still flaming pieces of beam and broken ale casks landed violently in the soft, lush ground cover of the forest floor. When the hail of debris stopped, the faeries raised their heads and cautiously came out from behind their lillyfur shield.

The meadow had fallen silent.

Meeks and Tobas tried to tend to Claire, but the E'lore moonlight was not bright enough to allow them to assess the severity of her wounds. Yarn and Banth, in the meantime, stole a glance over the embankment.

Galar had taken only a few steps past the fallen Andee before the Druid priest's sword found revenge for the grogoch. As the warrior-priest looked upon the body of the Fomorian leader, he was joined by his comrade, the other "guard" who aided the myth in their flight from the Fomorian tent. He was shaking his head to signify that they had not succeeded in finding the wizard. In unison, the two Druids looked up in the direction of the hillock over which the four myth and one nambor had made their escape.

"The *Druwi* ... but how did ...?" Yarn asked as he turned toward Banth, the old myth's confusion worn plainly on his smoke-streaked and tear-stained face. Banth shook his head at his friend and placed a firm hand on his arm.

"Yarn, we *must* go."

Yarn scrambled to his feet, stealing one last look over the embankment as he did. He saw Andee lying at the feet of the Druid priests. He could not stop the tears from welling freely in his eyes. Knowing that they would see to his hairy companion did little to relieve Yarn of the guilt that he felt in leaving his old friend behind. Andee had protected the clan to his last breath and Yarn knew that he would never know a more loyal creature again.

Banth grabbed Yarn gently under his arm and helped his elder myth down the embankment and across the fog bed. Once they had cleared the overgrown woods, the four myth took to the air and winged their way through the purple E'lore sky toward Aislinn, their book and the badly wounded Claire in tow.

***

The chaos and combat of the encampment had been replaced with silence and stillness. The bodies of Fomorian soldiers were strewn across the Shannon blossom-filled meadow. The only sounds remaining were those of crackling fires consuming the last of the Fomorian tent.

Once the Druid priests were sure that the myth were no longer in danger, they turned their attention back to the bloodstained and now deathly silent gathering that had been the Fomorian encampment. The priest who had gone in search of Mephistis turned and walked down the hill toward the meadow to give counsel to his fellow priests on purging the meadow of all that Galar had brought with him to E'lore. The priest who had slain Galar pulled the limp and lifeless body of the remorseless leader back to the burned-away camp and placed his body alongside one of his equally lifeless soldiers. Returning to the grogoch, the priest extracted the golden skean that Galar had neither the time nor opportunity to remove himself and skewered it through the scabbard beneath his long black robe. The warrior-priest then gently lifted Andee, and as carefully as he could manage, carried the woolly beast back to the encampment and hoisted him into an empty cart formerly owned by the Fomorian *cocaire*. He was once again joined by his comrade. Taking a look back, they surveyed the camp one last time before taking their leave. Each grabbed a handle of the cart and disappeared into the darkness pulling the grogoch-ladened barrow behind them.

CHAPTER 30

CLAIRE TRIED TO open her eyes. The musky, soft hairs of the moleskin bedding felt good against her cheek, but before she could savor it, the wound in her right leg wailed its presence. The pain's cry alerted all the other bloody and aching injuries, and she felt her surroundings begin to spin. Confusion, exhaustion, and the throbbing pain that danced and skipped through her entire body all succumbed to the spinning in her head. Before the complete darkness of unconsciousness overtook her once more, she thought of her sisters and her father for what she was sure was the last time. And then she thought of Sarla. Her last awareness was of being surrounded by anxious and distressed voices. "What have we done," she heard a woeful male tone.

"Is she alive?" came another.

"I cannot tell. Is she breathing?" asked yet another.

"Claire, Claire … can you hear me?" was the last thing the weak and wounded girl heard.

And then the darkness came.

***

When Yarn and Meeks entered the chamber, Sarla did not lift her head or even acknowledge their presence. She had been by Claire's side for two days, leaving her only to brew more tea and look in on Willa and Anndra, who for the most part, were fending for themselves. For the first time since Yarn had known her, Sarla looked exhausted and helpless. When Yarn put a comforting hand on her back, he could feel that she was trembling. He knelt down by her side and looked into a face that he had never seen her wear before. Her eyes were red and swollen, tears streaming gently down her ethereal face, the saltiness of them leaving discolored tracks on her soft, creamy cheeks.

"Am I watching her die?" she asked Yarn through her sobs.

Knowing the answer, but deciding it was best not spoken aloud, he gently cradled her frail hand in his and gave it a soft press. As Yarn looked down at the sleeping girl, he himself was moved to tears. Sarla had cleaned and dressed her numerous wounds, the most severe of which was the deep gash in her right thigh left by Galar's arrow, which still bled through the woven white bandages. With infinite patience, Sarla tended to Claire's injuries, applying poultices of hops ground with willow bark oil on the gashes that were less severe. Not understanding fully the nambor physiology, she was hesitant to apply anything but spring water and clean gauze to the most serious of the girl's wounds. The young nambor's face was flushed and far too warm, which Sarla understood to mean that some of her wounds were life-threatening. Banth had entered noiselessly through the sewn skin flap covering the entrance and had made his way to Claire's bedside.

"Any progress?" he asked somberly.

Yarn shook his head, trying to save Sarla from having to answer.

No one turned to look when the flap was pulled aside again, this time it was Tobas. Following behind him was a female myth unfamiliar to the group gathered around the frail nambor. The visitor paused at the entranceway, and as Tobas held the skin flap back for her, he coaxed her in.

"Really, 'tis quite all right, come in," he gently encouraged her.

"There is quite a gathering outside," Tobas explained in a whisper. "I thought, perhaps, one by one maybe … they just want to … see her," he stumbled for words.

Yarn gently nodded his approval.

The visitor had seated herself at Claire's bedside. Sarla looked up with a start, but the face of their new guest put her immediately at ease.

"*Fáilte*," Sarla whispered over Claire's feverish, battle-torn body.

The newcomer gave Sarla a warm smile and nod in return.

Sarla, who had barely taken her eyes off Claire since Tobas and Meeks brought her back from the Fomorian camp, could now not take her eyes off the newly arrived stranger. The myth's head was draped with an ornate, emerald shawl of a material that Sarla had never seen in the marketplace in Aislinn. Her hair seemed to be woven of gold, and it spilled out of the shawl in unruly tendrils, framing her face before it cascaded down the front of her tunic. Against the emerald of her wrap and flaxen gold hair, the faerie's skin seemed to change from opaque to pearlescent and misty, like the fog clouds that billow and race across E'lore's mossy landscape. Once Sarla had locked her eyes onto those of her guest, she was entranced. The myth's eyes were dark grey with sunbursts of black and white radiating out from the pupils. Sarla had never seen a myth that looked like this one.

Sensing that her hostess was perhaps becoming lost, the grey-eyed visitor spoke: "If you will, I have brought some mistletoe, to ease her fear ... may I?" the myth asked the lady of the house as she slowly reached for Claire's hand.

"Forgive me, of course, yes," Sarla stuttered as she broke eye contact with the stranger and gently shook her head as if shaking off a befuddling dream. The grey-eyed myth tenderly took Claire's left hand in hers, and after placing the bouquet of mistletoe in her palm, just as gently closed the little girl's fingers around the bundled stems. The myth kept her hand on Claire's and looked back up at Sarla.

"So brave, yet so frail," she offered Sarla in a motherly, praising tone.

Sarla smiled and nodded in agreement.

"Her wounds are fatal," the grey-eyed myth stated softly and matter-of-factly.

These four words turned Sarla's gently flowing tears into body-shaking sobs.

The stranger gazed tenderly at her anguished hostess before continuing with carefully chosen words. "As brave and strong as she is, nothing is more frightening or *dangerous*," she added with emphasis, "than being so terribly ill and so far from home."

The last four words repeated throughout the room.

So far from home, so far from home, so far from home ...

Like incense, they formed ghostly wisps that whirled around the chamber, echoing themselves in soft, haunting whispers:

So far from home, so far from home, so far from home …

The phrase wrapped itself around the myth assembled over the dying nambor and forced its way in to very consciousness of Yarn and Banth and Tobas.

"We cannot let her die here … so far from home," Tobas's voice strained as he repeated the words of the visiting stranger.

It was then Banth who restated the words.

"So far from home."

"So far from home," he said again, the second time louder than the first.

"So far from home." This time it was Yarn who repeated the mantra, and he was on his feet by the time he got to "… home."

"Tobas, go get the cart … get, get it harnessed up! Banth, Meeks grab those skins!" Yarn was shouting out orders.

Tobas was already out of the house by the time Meeks asked, "Yarn, what is going on? What are you doing?"

Taking only a second to pause in his preparations, Yarn looked up at his fellow myth and stated matter-of-factly, "We are taking her home."

"But how do you propose to do that, Yarn?" Meeks asked. "The portal is gone, remember?" Meeks had barely finished his sentence when a frantic Tobas came flying back into the room.

"*Uncail!*" the younger myth tried his best not to shout, "You must come! 'Tis back! … I do not understand how … quickly, you must come and look!" he exclaimed as quietly as his excitement would allow.

Tobas did not wait for his uncle and flew out of the room with as much haste as he had entered. A puzzled Yarn, flanked by Banth and Meeks, followed the agitated myth through the cottage and out of the front door.

Sarla kept her post by Claire's side, looking up at her mysterious guest and offering the faintest of smiles in lieu of the explanation that she did not have. Her guest, however, seemed to not even have noticed the agitated Tobas or the ensuing commotion. The grey-eyed myth sat peacefully, staring intently and lovingly at the wounded girl in the moleskin bed. Moments later, the four myth came bursting back through the opening to Claire's chamber.

"The cart is ready. 'Tis right out front!" Tobas stated excitedly.

"You have not thought this through, Yarn!" Meeks protested as Yarn, Banth and Tobas resumed their preparations. "If she is found ... changed as she has ... they ... the nambors ... they will ask questions. They will find us out! We cannot send her back!"

"That is the chance we will have to take," Yarn answered.

Meeks approached Yarn, and grabbing his friend by both arms, asked him solemnly, "For *all* of us, Yarn? You are willing to take that chance for *all* of us?" Yarn did not answer because he had no answer to give. Understanding that his lack of response was proof of his conviction, Meeks relinquished his grip on the older myth and stepped back in silence. Banth made his support for Yarn's decision known to Meeks.

"He is right. She deserves nothing less than everything we can do for her. And this ..." he continued, gesturing towards the front door of the cottage, just outside of which they had all seen the newly formed portal for themselves, "this can only be an omen," he finished, a touch of awe in his voice.

"And *there* is the other thing! Does nobody but myself care to know *how* these portals are coming about? And just as we are in need of one, no less? When are we going to worry ourselves about the portals, Banth? When?" The director's attention was no longer on his distraught clansman, but solely on the preparations for taking Claire to the newly arrived gateway.

Between Banth's comment to Meeks and Meeks's subsequent one-sided argument with Banth, Sarla deduced correctly that Tobas had indeed stumbled upon a portal.

"Yarn, are you sure this is safe ... for her?" Sarla's voice, strained from crying, could barely be heard above the commotion in the room.

Having too much respect and love for her not to tell her the truth, he replied sincerely, "Sarla, I cannot say. All I *do* know is that we can be of no help to her here. Our only ... *her* only chance is to be back with her own kind. They will know better what to do."

"We cannot risk moving her, Yarn. She is so weak ... and she is not even conscious," Sarla pleaded, taking Yarn's hand into her own, freshly made tears streaming down her cheeks.

Kneeling down next to her, Yarn covered their clasped hands and looked straight into her crying eyes. He replied gently but somberly, "We either carry her alive back to her home in Doog, or we carry her dead to her grave here, in E'lore. What is *your* wish for her?"

Sarla's sobs shook her tiny frame. Terrified for Claire, but trusting in Yarn's wisdom, she nodded her head in silent agreement. As Yarn returned to the preparations for their departure, Sarla turned her attention back to her patient. With a forced resolution, she asked of her guest, "Help me, will you please? We must get her dressed. Her clothes, they are over ..." she started saying to the stranger, but when Sarla looked up, the grey-eyed myth was gone.

CHAPTER 31

THE FAMILIAR SMELL of overgrown pasture slowly brought Claire out of her slumber. She opened her eyes to the brightness of a mid-summer sun and forced them closed again as a gentle gust of wind cooled her face and brushed the hair from her forehead. The sun-warmed grass and honeysuckle-ladened breezes cradled Claire like a newborn and the exhausted girl put up no resistance when sleep overtook her again.

***

Waking for the second time a few hours later, a tickle from a wayward hair made Claire give her nose a rub. She rolled onto her back and stretched her arms over her head, a tiny sprig of mistletoe tumbling from her hand as she did. Something was ... different. 'The sun is so bright,' she thought as she sat up and shielded her eyes from the glare. Claire gasped as her view was filled with a very familiar sight. There, right in front of her, stood the venerable pair of gooseberry trees. The gnarled trunks and twisted branches looked surreal against the brilliant blue sky and swollen, snow-white clouds. Lapping against the knotted old trunks was the unmistakable marker that told Claire exactly where she was.

Grass.

Claire's senses were bombarded with the physical details of her world. Reaching both arms out to the side, she wrapped her hands around the thick green blades. Claire pulled her hands forward, the organic sound of the shredding turf pierced her memory like shards of broken glass, opening the flood gates of her memories of home.

Home.

She was home.

Images of E'lore immediately entwined themselves with the thoughts of her father and sisters. Mental snapshots raced through her head at breakneck speed: Sarla, Yarn, the wizard, the book, Biggles. Hand in hand with these mental memories came physical ones as well. She could feel again the sorcerer's talons cutting into her arm, the arrow piercing her leg. Realizing how severe her wounds must be, she hesitated before trying to get up. Bracing herself to be overwhelmed with pain, she gingerly raised up onto her knees, but the pain did not come. Moving less cautiously now, she stood upright and began surveying her battle wounds, only they were not there. What had been deep gashes were now mere scratches, none were bleeding, and most seemed to be completely mended.

As she tried to figure out how her wounds could be practically healed, she was distracted by a flash of color revealed by the swaying grasses at the base of one of the gooseberry trees. She forged her way through the over-grown pasture, the grasses lashing against her body like incoming surf. Kneeling at the base of the twisted, ancient timber, she laid her hands on a bundle of clothes. This is what she was wearing the day she chased Tobas through the trees. They were clean and folded in a neat pile. Seeing the stack of clothes prompted her to gaze down at herself to see what she was wearing now. She recognized the purple tunic as the one that Sarla and Willa had made for her, only there was something different about it now. It no longer fit. The overshirt was split down the sides and was barely long enough to cover her bottom. As she further surveyed the damage to her garment, she heard a tearing sound. Now it was splitting down the back! Either it was shrinking, or she was—growing!

Her celebration of being home temporarily delayed, in a panic she snatched up the bundle of clothes and started making her way down the slope towards the creek. Running down the lush green hill, something else in the grass caught her eye. Stopping abruptly, she bent down to pick it up. It was a four leaf clover. She thought of stopping to look for more which reminded her of the countless pots of tea she had shared with Sarla, but another ripping noise grabbed back her attention, and a sudden breeze told her that that noise had been the last of the threads losing the battle to hold her tunic together. Putting the plucked clover between her teeth, she sprinted down the hill and toward the creek. Kneeling at the water's edge between a dogwood tree and a young willow, she pulled off what was left of the tunic and bunched it together before plunging it into the cold creek water. She washed her face with the too-small shirt suddenly wishing that she had checked the area for poison ivy first. Realizing that a little red rash would be the least of her problems if her dad found her like this, she continued bathing in the cold water until she felt alert and completely awake.

As quickly as her thoughts were racing, they could not keep up with her hands. She needed to get to the house. Her father must be looking for her everywhere. He had probably called the police. And her sisters! She sorted through the clean and folded pile of clothes and quickly pulled on her underwear, socks, shorts, T-shirt and tennis shoes. Everything was a bit loose, but at least she was covered. She picked up the wet piece of purple cloth that had been the entirety of her wardrobe just moments before, grabbed the excess material at the top of her shorts and started back up the hill and toward the paddock gate. Finally, Claire gained the top of the slope, and though her legs were burning with fatigue, she gladly forced them to move faster—to run. Once the grade of the field leveled off, the little girl shifted her legs into high gear. The closer she got to the paddock gate, the more excited she became.

She was home.

Not soon enough for her, she finally reached the gate separating the pasture from the field surrounding the big pond. She threw the latch up and ran through the gate without taking the time to close it behind her.

She had no idea what to tell her father.

She kept running, up the small bank and down the length of the dam that kept the pond from overflowing into the main pasture. She ran down the dam bank and willed herself the energy to make it up the hill leading past the stable's paddock. As she reached for the gate latch, she realized that she no longer needed to hold up her shorts. She paused to catch her breath and her thoughts.

'What was she going to tell her father? The truth?'

'Who was she kidding?' Claire thought to herself. 'He would never believe the truth. Heck, even *she* wouldn't believe the truth.'

The sum of her lying experience was what she practiced every time she came home with a report card. Now she needed a whopper and fast. Her brain kicked into overdrive as she tried to piece together something that would explain her absence. Where could she have possibly been all this time that even remotely resembled anything *close* to sounding possible?

'Maybe I was kidnapped,' she thought to herself.

'No, I missed the bus ... I had to walk home from school ... I got lost!'

"School's out," she impatiently reminded herself.

There was no plan "B," which only left the truth.

She lifted her head and pulled the latch open just in time to see her father strolling towards her down the path from the driveway. Catching sight of his daughter, he exclaimed, "There you are. I was just coming to look for you," he yelled over the distance between them.

"Daddy, I can explain," she began lying. "I'm so sorry to have worried you ... I had no idea I would be gone for so long ..." Claire stammered as she tried to work out an excuse.

"No, daughter, I'm the one who needs to apologize. I was afraid that if I told you where I was going, it would spoil the surprise. I should have at least come and found you to tell you that I was leaving, but I figured I'd be back before you even knew I was gone."

Claire recognized her father's demeanor. It was remorseful. Claire knew that her father's occasional feelings of guilt usually resulted in thoughtfulness toward her above and beyond her regular ration. But still, what was he talking about? She had been gone for ... how long *had* she been gone? Had it been days? Weeks? Months? She had no idea. Her father was acting as if she had never left. He didn't even know that she had been gone. He hadn't been worried about her. How was that possible?

Her father didn't give her time to think about it for long.

"Well?" her father asked.

"Well, what, Daddy?" she answered. Not having pulled together an excuse yet, she wasn't offering any information until she absolutely had to. Besides, she was really confused.

"Do you want to see your surprise or not?" he asked excitedly.

"Uh, sure, I mean yes … What surprise?"

"Your birthday present! I know your birthday isn't until tomorrow, but I think this is one present you won't mind getting early!" Her father was displaying enthusiasm usually reserved for cattle purchases or tomato plant yields.

"Come on!" he urged.

'Tomorrow? Her birthday was still tomorrow?'

As the two walked up the path toward the driveway, Claire came out of her bewilderment long enough to notice the trailer attached to her father's pickup truck. It was no ordinary trailer. This one was a horse trailer. Her growing excitement put her confusion at bay.

"Where did you get those scratches? I don't remember seeing those yesterday," her father asked in concern. "Were you playing with those barn kittens again?"

"Uh, yeah," she mumbled as she inspected her battle wounds. They weren't even red anymore. Even the more serious ones had scabbed over and looked as if she'd had them for weeks.

As Claire and her father rounded the side of the long white trailer, her senses were assaulted by the smells and sounds of the carrier's lone passenger. The salty-musky smell brought tears to Claire's eyes before she even caught sight of the broad chestnut croup and quarters and swishing coarse black tail of the most beautiful horse's rump that she had ever seen.

"Old Man Sturges couldn't come up for the money for a survey job that we did for him last month, so I traded him the job and that beat-up boat for this little lady."

Her father was doing his best to make amends for his unfatherly late-night tractor rides and overindulging of late. A quick glance toward the open-faced shed next to the chicken yard confirmed that the outboard motor boat—one of the last tangible vestiges of their life up north—was indeed gone. Claire wasted no more time on anything or any thoughts that did not concern her living, breathing birthday present. Without waiting for her father's help, she threw open the latch on the doubled-gated closure, and, after pulling the ramp from its slip and locking it into place, she stepped into the trailer, walking slowly between the horse and the enclosure's left wall. Her father could hear his little girl's soft cooing voice, which was soon interrupted by the clip-clop of the horse's shod hooves taking tentative steps backward out of the trailer. A few hastened steps and a whinny later, Claire's horse was liberated from her transport and standing in all of her thirteen-hand glory in the side yard, head already down nibbling the tender grass and clover. Mr. Sturges had thrown in an old halter along with the trailer.

"She's going to need some new tack," Claire informed her father.

Liam O'Brian smiled at his daughter knowing that if it weren't for him standing there, she would be bursting out of her skin with excitement.

"Mr. Linton is going to go with you to Southern States tomorrow. The two of you can pick up what she needs," he stated as matter-of-factly as he could.

"Mr. Linton knows about her? Has he seen her?" Claire's exhilaration was beginning to escape her control.

"I wouldn't have gotten her unless he approved. He said she was 'perfect.'"

Claire paused her stroking of the horse's thick neck and turned to look at her father. Closing the several paces between them, she wrapped her arms around his waist and squeezed. Through welling tears and a nose starting to stuff, she whispered, "Thank you, Daddy. You don't have to get me anything else ever again."

"Oh, daughter, if only that were true," he joked with his girl as he tried to keep the mood from becoming anything but joyous.

Claire appreciated her father's joke and returned it with a smile and a nod.

"Go on now, I'm sure you have more interesting things to do than stand around here with your old man," he encouraged her.

And right there, that was the thing about Claire's father. When he was bad, he was really bad, but when he was good, they didn't come any better.

"Happy birthday, honey," he said to her before stuffing his hands in the pockets of his worn work trousers and making his way toward the house and the first of many cocktails.

Claire let their talking end there and watched her father climb the concrete steps and disappear into the cool darkness of the back porch. She was
still staring at the closed screen door as her mind came to terms not only
with the fact that she was home, but her father had not even known that
she was gone—no need for implausible explanations. 'How could that be?'
As her thoughts switched to her last conscious memories of E'lore, the
mare lifted her broad head and nuzzled it against the girl, knocking her back
a few steps. Claire turned her full, undivided attention back to the best gift
that she had ever, or would ever, receive. Claire merely giggled and grabbed
the frayed halter, using it to lead the chestnut over to the wide oak stump
that had been a remnant in the side yard for longer than Claire had been
alive. Using the stump to shorten their difference in height, Claire grabbed a
handful of black mane and swung her right leg over the tranquil steed's
back. She paused a moment to scratch at the healed wound given to her by
Galar. She shook her head subtly, not even knowing where to start in understanding what had happened. Instead of heading down the path toward
the waiting pastures, the two stood there perfectly still and quiet, neither in
a hurry to do anything. Claire stretched her torso across her mount's thick
black mane, and gently stroked the mare's muscled neck.

"Your name, we have to decide on your name," she whispered to her
patient friend as warm tears broke free from the wells of her eyes and
flowed unabashedly down her cheeks.

"Sarla," Claire gasped as the name caught in her throat. The tears now
flowed freely as she repeated, "Sarla."

Claire gently squeezed with her knees, which was all the prompting
that her companion needed. As gently as a lazy summer breeze, Claire and
Sarla headed down the worn path between the barns and sheds and made
for the wide-open opportunities of the green, spacious fields.

CHAPTER 32

THE SUN HAD barely settled in the morning sky when Sarla, wearing a sleek new bridle acquired during Claire's outing to Southern States with Mr. Linton, came bounding out of the paddock toward the dam, Claire sitting proudly on her naked back. The girl gave Sarla a smooth but firm pull with her right rein. Responding on a dime, Sarla changed course and glided down the slope of the dam, never breaking stride as she galloped on in a clockwise direction around the pond. Once Claire and Sarla had covered the ground that was the circumference of the big pond, they turned around in order to run around it in a windershins direction. This would give Sarla a running start at the gate to the main pasture. This time, Claire was not going through it—she was going over it. As they approached the fence, and with no prompting from Claire necessary, Sarla changed her lead leg from left to right and in one weightless and breathtaking moment, the two left their earthly bounds and sailed effortlessly over the gate leading to the big field. They landed as smoothly as if the gate had been four inches tall instead of four feet. Which of the two was having more fun was impossible to discern. Claire was filled with the relief of being home, safe, and in surroundings that she knew and understood. Sarla, with the heart of a thoroughbred, her nostrils full of fresh air and nothing but open fields as far as she could see, was in equine heaven. The two, who were now one, ran for all they were worth until the wind from Sarla's speed caused tears to streak across Claire's cheeks and Sarla began to sweat and lather formed on her chest. As they slowed their pace, Claire realized they had lapped the pasture and were now approaching the pair of gooseberry trees at the top of the hill near the gate. Claire slowed Sarla to a trot and then a walk as the portal drew nearer. The two came to a full stop, and Claire drew her right leg back and across Sarla's rump. Still holding the reins in her left hand, she slid down Sarla's left side and landed in the grass. Sarla stood patiently by nibbling the thick, sweet blades as Claire approached the gap between the trees, being careful to stop short of going through. As she thought of what had happened, she wondered what had taken place after she returned home. Was everyone okay? She wished that there were some way to find out without actually going back. Although she desperately missed Sarla, she was still too shaken up to undertake the whole ordeal again. Would they try to contact her? Were they even *able* to contact her? What if they weren't okay? She half-heartedly resigned herself to the probability that she would never know what happened after she left E'lore. She could only hope and pray that the myth were safe and that their world was righting itself even now. As she turned and gathered up Sarla's reins again, she tripped and almost tumbled headlong into the grass. Pulling on the reins anchored by Sarla's strong neck and 1800-pound body, Claire was able to keep from falling. Turning to look for what she tripped over, she saw a softball-sized rock lying in the mashed-down grass.

"Better me than you, girl," she said to her gentle, brown friend.

Claire picked up the rock and cocked her arm back, preparing to throw it out of their path when she suddenly stopped. Looking down at the rock, she pondered it for a second. She then turned and faced the aged pair of trees. After a slight hesitation, the girl hurled the rock threw through the gap. The stone orb sailed through the ancient timbers and landed with a thud six-feet on the other side. Claire's face could not hide her obvious dis-appointment. Maybe, she had thought, if the rock had disappeared and not come out the other side, there might be some way of getting in touch with them—without having to go through the portal herself. As disappointed as she was, she was not willing to test the portal any further. Looking into Sarla's big, soft, brown eyes, Claire realized that she belonged on this side of the gooseberry trees and had no desire to leave again anytime soon.

Petting her mare's soft brown-pink nose with its prickly whiskers, she said: "Come on, girl, you need a walk, and a drink."

Claire reached down to grab the slack reins when a flash of light caught her eye. Something was reflecting the sun's rays at the base of one of the trees. She let go of Sarla's reins and walked cautiously toward the shiny object. Claire smiled as she recognized what it was—her picture. It was the picture of her mother and oldest sister that Tobas had "borrowed" to take back to E'lore. She looked around in the trees and surrounding grass to see if the returner was still there. Holding the priceless photograph to her chest, she turned back toward Sarla and took her place to the left of the mare's big brown head. The happy girl looped the reins through her right arm and cradled her photograph in her left. Side by side, Claire and Sarla walked down the gentle green slope toward the waiting brook.

EPILOGUE

THE TWO DRUID priests walked in tandem down the earthen path in complete silence. Having prevented the Fomorian from attacking Aislinn and assuring that the myth were in possession of their book, the warrior-priests had one final duty before leaving E'lore. In unison, the two abruptly turned off the path and walked into the blackened rowan tree forest—the same blackened parcel of woods that spurned the rushing fog that had terrorized Claire and Biggles. Once past the sooted façade, although dark, the forest was again lush, its floor thick with worm ivy and craigmoss. Had there been a witness to the priest's quest, it would seem that they had vanished into thin air upon entering the parcel, so perfectly matched were their cloaks to the blackness in the thick wood. It was in this complete darkness that the two walked swiftly and noiselessly, without crushing a single blossom or snapping a single twig. As if guided by a sense far more accurate than sight, they maneuvered with preternatural precision through the increasingly impenetrable undergrowth, until finally, the darkness yielded to light and the treacherous and tangled thicket gave way once again to light-loving kard-pa blossoms and flother flowers. The rowan tree forest ended as brusquely as it had started, and the two priests now found themselves traversing a mossy meadow freckled with mint, meadowsweet, and vervain. As they crested a steep circular barrow, the purpose of their journey came into view. In the deep meadow beyond a third circular barrow was an exquisite fortress built in, on, and around an enormous rowan tree. Unlike the wooden cottages of Aislinn, this structure was built of stone; a stone not found in E'lore, but a stone known only to exist in the Preseli Hills in the land called Wales, a place that existed only in the dimension of Doog. The priests knew much about this stone and much about how it came to be *here* in this meadow. But it was neither the enormous tree nor the unique stone that stopped the Druid priests in their tracks for the first time since beginning their journey on the other side of the black wood. It was the light emanating from the portals of the intricate and finely carved castle, a blue-green light with aquamarine tendrils that poked through the fortress' windows and transoms, licking the external walls with light and nudging the kard-pa blossoms entwining themselves up the bluestone parapets. Understanding the urgency of their mission, they allowed themselves only a brief pause to admire the beauty of the unusual light before setting upon the path that led to the citadel. Uncompelled by an announcement, the thick inlaid wooden doors opened slowly inward as if anticipating their progress up the curved stone steps. Once inside, the journeymen were blind to the ornately carved walls, the floors meticulously inlaid with an intricate and unending shield knot design, the hand-blown and stained-glass windows covering the far side of the fortress, depicting in thick leaded crystal the tales of battles lost and won, of defeat and resurrection, of death and life, the history of an entire race of people in brilliant and uncompromising color. These things the priests did not see, for there against the breathtaking backdrop of tainted, iridescent glass was a throne—a throne embracing a queen.

Her seat was a beautiful, young hawthorn tree, its graceful branches swaying gently in a breeze that was not blowing. The tree was festooned with clusters of mistletoe and bouquets of heather and mint bound with luminous strands of gold. Under this canopy, the petite, flaxen haired ruler received her guests, her grey eyes sparkling against her opalescent cheeks and brow.

The two priests made their way hastily to the platform from which the hawthorn tree grew.

At the first of the three steps leading to the top of the platform, the two dropped to their knees. The first priest prostrated himself before the queen, his hands open and turned facing flatly downward. The second did the same, but in his open and *upturned* hands, he held the golden skean that had belonged to Galar, the leader of the Fomorian invasion in E'lore. When she saw the bloodied weapon, the Queen inhaled deeply and closed her eyes. After slowly exhaling, she just as slowly opened her eyes before gently asking the sword-bearing priest, "And the girl?"

As he had been spoken to directly, the priest raised his head and answered, "Your Majesty, the myth have returned the girl to Doog using the portal that you evoked; her condition at present is not known. They have possession of the book and it is now in Aislinn."

The priest, having finished his response, again bowed his head.

Lowering her gaze, she clenched her hands together and squeezed them tightly, allowing herself a moment of reflection. When she rose from her throne, her emerald shawl cascaded from her shoulders in soft, luminous folds before coming to rest in the crooks of her bent arms. She descended the stairs and stood before the kneeling priests.

"Rise, please, both of you. You have done well, my faithful friends, and all of E'lore owes you a debt of gratitude—again."

The Druid priests rose to their feet and the queen stroked the face and kissed the forehead of the first and of the second before taking the proof of Galar's death from his hands. Cupping his smoke-streaked face in her right hand, she gently kissed him again.

"Thank you," she whispered to him and then to his companion.

"If it pleases Her Highness, I will go to see Claire and report back to you as to her condition," the second Druid offered.

The queen silenced the cloaked warrior with an ethereal finger placed gently over his lips.

"No, my loyal priest, I will not ask this of you, you have done enough—you have all done enough. I will see to … my daughter … myself. Go home to your families before they worry beyond bearing. The *Druwi* are once again our saviors and owners of our undying gratitude. Go home. We shall be seeing each other again very soon.

"Go 'neiri an bothar leat," she wished them in the old language.

"And you as well, my Queen," the priests responded in unison.

Their well wishes and farewells complete, the priests took their leave of the Faerie Queen. As they descended the fortress steps, the heavy doors closed behind them, leaving Caithleann to her castle and her throne and the golden skean of her clan's ancient enemy.

Words not often used in Doog:

aislinn: dream, vision

Anndra: Gaelic for Andrew

aran: Gaelic for bread

baile: township

bellwether: a leader

bhara: bear

bradan: salmon

Breatunn: old Irish for Britain

brisgein: a root vegetable known as "silver weed" used to make a dense and
   hearty bread

celt: most common weapon used amongst the ancient inhabitants of
   Ireland; a form of axe made of bronze

chimeric: unreal, fanciful, unrealistic

cocaire: Gaelic for cook

codswallop: nonsense, rubbish

cullen tree: holly tree

cycle: Doog equivalent of approximately one year

Eire: Irish for Ireland

fernticle: Gaelic for freckle

fia: Gaelic for deer

flother: Gaelic for snowflake

footle: to talk or act foolishly, to waste time

galar: Gaelic meaning disease

"Go neiri and bother leat": Irish meaning "have a safe journey"

grogoch: creature resembling an elderly man, though covered in coarse, dense reddish hair; fond of indenturing themselves to individuals or families as farmhands; grogoch are not known for their personal hygiene

kard-pa: from old Greek, root word for heart

kerfluffle: disorder, flurry, agitation

leipreachan: from the old Irish "luchorphan" meaning small (lu) body(corp)

mephistis: old Irish for stench, foul smell

moon: Doog equivalent of approximately one month

nacreous: pearly, iridescent, like Mother-of-pearl

ola: Proto-Indo-European word for cloth

oxter: armpit

pelf: riches or wealth, especially if acquired by shameful means

pethbol: brave, loyal

pratha: proto-Indo-European word broadly meaning food

quagga: a zebra-like animal of southern Africa, extinct since 1870

quincunx: five objects arranged in a certain pattern—like on a domino

sheelin: Gaelic, meaning "lake of the faeries"

skean: double edged dagger used in ancient Ireland and Scotland

snallygaster: an unscrupulous but shrewd person

snickersnee: a large knife

Sorcha: Gaelic for Claire

tara: assembly place, named for goddess Tara; the Hill of Tara was the seat of the High King of Ireland

tea bracks: aka Irish freckle bread; close-grained tea/breakfast bread with fruits and nuts

uncail: Gaelic/Irish for uncle

weeze: the whiskers of the quagga that roam the meadows of E'lore

windershins: counterclockwise or contrary direction

About the Author

Melissa Helm lives in a small town just north of the farm where she grew up feeding beetles to chickens and finding four-leaf clovers. *The Kingdom of the Good People—The Book of Sorcha* is her first novel.

Visit the author website at:
http://www.thekingdomofthegoodpeople.com

www.ingramcontent.com/pod-product-compliance
Lightning Source LLC
Chambersburg PA
CBHW032211190626
46810CB00019B/2438